SWORD
OF SHAME

SWORD OF SHAME

A Historical Mystery

By

The Medieval Murderers

Bernard Knight
Ian Morson
Michael Jecks
Susanna Gregory
Philip Gooden

POCKET
BOOKS

First published in Great Britain by Simon & Schuster UK Ltd, 2006
This edition first published by Pocket Books, 2007
An imprint of Simon & Schuster UK
A CBS COMPANY

1 3 5 7 9 10 8 6 4 2

Simon & Schuster UK Ltd
1st Floor
222 Gray's Inn Road
London WC1X 8HB

www.simonandschuster.co.uk

Simon & Schuster Australia
Sydney

A CIP catalogue record for this book is available from the British Library

ISBN: 978-1-84983-454-4

Typeset in New Baskerville by Palimpsest Book Production Limited,
Grangemouth, Stirlingshire
Printed and bound in Great Britain by
CPI Cox & Wyman, Reading, RG1 8EX

'The Medieval Murderers'

A small group of historical mystery writers, all members of the Crime Writers' Association, who promote their work by giving informal talks and discussions at libraries, bookshops and literary festivals.

Michael Jecks was a computer salesman before turning to writing. His immensely popular Templar series, set during the confusion and terror of the reign of Edward II, is translated into most continental languages, and is published in America. The most recent novels in the series are *The Death Ship of Dartmouth* and *The Malice of Unnatural Death*. Michael was chairman of the Crime Writers' Association in 2004-5.

Bernard Knight is a former Home Office pathologist and professor of forensic medicine who has been publishing novels, non-fiction, radio and television drama and documentaries for more than forty years. He currently writes the highly-regarded Crowner John series of historical mysteries, based on the first coroner for Devon in the twelfth century; the eleventh of which, *The Noble Outlaw*, has recently been published by Simon & Schuster.

Ian Morson is the author of an acclaimed series of historical mysteries featuring the thirteenth-century Oxford-based detective, William Falconer.

Susanna Gregory is the author of the Matthew Bartholomew series of mystery novels, set in fourteenth-century Cambridge, and a brand-new series featuring Thomas Chaloner, a reluctant spy in Restoration London, the second of which, *Blood on the Strand,* has recently been published. She also writes historical mysteries under the name of 'Simon Beaufort'.

Philip Gooden is the author of the Nick Revil series, a sequence of historical mysteries set in Elizabethan and Jacobean London, during the time of Shakespeare's Globe theatre. The latest titles in the series are *Mask of the Night* and *An Honourable Murder*. He also produces reference books on language, most recently *Faux Pas* and *Name Dropping*.

Medieval Murderers

The Programme

Prologue – In which Michael Jecks tells of the creation of the sword and its first shameful use.

Act One – In which Bernard Knight's Crowner John buys his officer a new sword, but soon regrets his generosity.

Act Two – In which Ian Morson relates Nick Zuliani's deadly involvement in election fraud and murder in Venice in 1262.

Act Three – In which Michael Jecks' Keeper Sir Baldwin and Bailiff Puttock learn how the sword could have been used in a martyrdom.

Act Four – In which Susanna Gregory's Matthew Bartholomew and Brother Michael are sent to the remote Cambridgeshire village of Ickleton to investigate why the manor is behind with its rent. They discover passions and tempers running high.

Act Five – In which Philip Gooden's player Nick Revill arrives at a snow-bound house to discover that, even after several hundred years, the Sword of Shame can still wreak havoc and murder.

Epilogue – In which Ian Morson comes up to modern times.

PROLOGUE

'May I see it?'

Sir Ralph de la Pomeroy eyed his guest for a moment, then wandered to the chest that stood at the wall, its lock gleaming in the flickering light from the fire. 'It's a beautiful piece of work,' he said.

It was still in its original, slightly scratched, leather scabbard, a simple enough sheath with bronze at the point and mouth. From it protruded an unadorned hilt with a simple disc pommel and cross-hilt fashioned to look like two dogs' heads, mouths gaping. He took it up, hefting it in his hand again. Even with the scabbard covering the blade, it had a natural balance about it – almost a *life*. It felt as though it held a strange energy all of its own. His fingers tingled merely to grasp the hilt.

Sir Ralph passed it to the priest and stood away, still dubious about this man.

Bartholomew of Holsworthy was English, and Sir Ralph was not entirely sure where the man's loyalties lay. He appeared always to be content with the change of government, but so many folk were still living out in the woods beyond the reach of the law that no one could be fully trusted. This man had lived here before the Norman adventure, and must have known and liked many who'd been executed.

The priest's breath caught in his throat as he drew

1

the blade from the plain sheath with its ox-hide covering. He traced the fine engraving and felt the thickening in his throat at the thought of the two brothers; he was forced to blink to conceal the tears.

'I know this sword.'

The blade had been long in the making. Bran the smith had started work on this, his greatest undertaking, twenty years before the invasion.

Blond, heavy-set, with eyes the colour of cornflowers on a summer's afternoon, Bran showed his parentage. His mother had been raped by Viking invaders during the worst of the reign of Hardacnut, the son of Cnut, who treated this kingdom like his personal purse. He was determined to rival the navies of the Vikings, and set about building many ships, and when the people complained bitterly at his sudden imposition of taxes, Hardacnut came marching with his men. One of them was Bran's father.

His mother had enough love remaining in her for Bran, but after what the Vikings did to her family, wiping out all the menfolk, she had nothing but revulsion for those responsible, and the man who raped her beside the body of her murdered father was the focus of all the spite and bile in her damaged soul.

It was because of his conception that he had chosen to become a smith. Working in the fields with those who taunted him about his bastardy was impossible. In preference he chose the solitary work of a bladesmith.

Not that it had been a bad life. He was married to his darling Gytha, a dark-haired, slender, lonely woman who cared nothing for his birth, but only that he was a kind, gentle father to their children. Not many men were as lucky as Bran, he reckoned. A beautiful wife, two sons: one fair like Hardacnut's men, the other more dark like Gytha's folk. Curious how in his family the boys had taken on the appearance of their fore-bears.

Enough wool-gathering! The iron and steel had been heated, and now his eyes told him that they were at the perfect temperature. He began the long process of beating them together until the heat and the hammering welded them into one coherent strip. Then he hammered them again, reheated the resulting bar, and beat yet another strip of red-glowing metal to it.

After that he deliberately left it alone for several days. It was like a good cider, he always said – cider tasted better for being left to mature, and his blades strength-ened with age. You couldn't hurry a good blade.

It was almost two weeks before Bran returned to it. He took it in his hands and studied it critically. Wiping it on a corner of the great leather skin he used as an apron, he looked at it carefully before deciding how to proceed, and then set it back in his forge. First he rounded off the end which would become the point, and then he reheated it and beat it until the bar grew longer and flatter. The next day he began to give it shape, and he hammered the heated metal into a diamond section.

There were many more stages in the creation of the sword, each of them undertaken with the maximum of care, the swordsmith roaring and cursing when the coals flamed too hotly and the metal began to glow too furiously; taking the utmost caution to make sure that the metal was at the correct temperature at all times, never too hot, never too cold for the task at hand, and then the quenching, to give the metal its flexibility and strength.

The blade was finished. He had taken a week and a half just to smooth the rough metal with his big circular stone. While Dudda, his older son, cranked the handle, the smith ran the blade gently over the rotating sandstone, slowly removing burrs and imperfections. Then they went to the second, finer wheel, and began the smoothing and polishing process, the old smith frowning as he gazed at the metal while it changed from blackened, dull grey to a shining white steel. Still scratched, he set the blade on his workbench and began to polish it with his fine stones, while Brada, the fair-haired second son, sat in the corner of the room and played with off-cuts of metal.

And when all was done, he sat on a stool with a mug of ale in his fist and stared at the blade with pride, saying to his sons, 'When a man holds this blade in his hand, he shall be invincible. No invader shall succeed against it. The man who wields it defending our country shall always overcome!'

When the invasion came, Bran was long dead.

On the ship, Rollo saw a great, thunderous, foaming immensity slamming down on the heads of the men before him. He had time, just, to grab at the mast as the grey/green flood poured towards him, drenching him in an instant.

Rollo fitzRollo, Breton staller to King Edward, set his jaw as he stared ahead between the men bent at the oars. He could show no weakness, not here on the ship with all his men about him. If they saw him worry they would panic. Even now he could see some eyeing him covertly as they strained against the waves.

Hunching his shoulders, he felt the full weight of his mail. It had been smeared with oil before leaving the port, as had his sword and his daggers, but the long byrnie felt as though it was more of an encumbrance than protection. He hated water. Water was the natural enemy of any warrior; how could a man fight when his mail coat and weapons were rusted? And a knight always feared the depths aboard ship, with twenty pounds of steel at shoulders and breast, drowning was inevitable. No, no warrior liked water, he told himself disconsolately, rubbing absent-mindedly at a patch of rust.

A man had to risk all to win renown: that was the thought uppermost in his lord's mind, he knew. Casting a look at the ship ahead of them, he squinted at the man who stood staring fixedly ahead, his back to Rollo. This venture would result in their deaths, or utter glory. To thieve the goods from a merchant at the roadside, that was one thing; this – stealing a kingdom – this was another entirely.

Spray jetted over the prow, and he blinked away the salt. If he were to die, Edith would be safe. He didn't want to think of the dangers to his woman of being widowed with a young child to support. At least he had done his best for her. Edith was at William's castle, and she should be safe enough there. As safe as anywhere else. She wouldn't be able to return home to Britain if Rollo and his men failed.

Water! Another wave burst upwards at the prow, and he ducked in a vain attempt to avoid it as foam swamped the crew. Rollo wiped his eyes, swearing under his breath. If he survived, he would never again go to sea. At least his sword would be safe in its new sheath. The lining of sheep's fleece should protect it from this foul weather.

He was miserable. Every breeze made him shiver, as though he was clad in ice, even his fine linen shirt was drenched. The flesh of his face was taut, like old leather that had dried too quickly in front of a fire, he thought, and then he caught sight of his reflection in a facet of a burnished steel shield-boss, and he grinned sourly at the sight.

The distorted reflection showed a powerful man of three-and-thirty, tall, swarthy, dark-eyed, with a square jaw that was closely shaven – there was no telling when he'd see a barber once they'd landed. His shoulders' breadth was almost the same as those of Mad Swein, the axe-wielding mercenary, and his thighs were as thick as a bull's neck. He was the picture of an experienced warrior, yet his eyes were scared.

Now, glancing about him at the men at their oars, forty of them, bent and grunting with the effort as they came closer to land, he told himself again that this was right. This was what King Edward would have wanted. Yet the doubts remained, and that was why he had the appearance of a haunted man.

When he had learned his swordsmanship, he had always been told to watch the eyes: the eyes would always give away his enemy's intentions. A sudden narrowing was all a man needed to warn of impending attack. After all, it took time to swing a two pound sword. If a man was forewarned, he could protect himself.

Always, when he looked into another man's eyes, he assessed the character of the man. If he had to gauge his own quality in the reflection, he would think himself weakly, mortally fearful. It was no more than the truth, he confessed, forcing his gaze from the mirror.

Only a short while ago he had been a resolute and confident figure. As King Edward's Breton staller, he was used to having the ear of his king at all times. The staller was the king's own representative in the lands he commanded over the water. While King Edward lived, he had no more devoted man in his service. But now the king was dead; Rollo had been forced to seek a new lord, and he had found his man in William the Bastard of Normandy.

The clouds parted. Ahead there was a clear view as a yellow sun pierced the mists. Until now the seas had been grey and a mistiness had lain over the ships. It gave the men a feeling of enclosure, as though God had taken them into His care and was leading them to a landing He had chosen. Rollo sincerely hoped it was the landing which the Abbot of Fécamp had recommended. My lord Abbot had owned lands about here, around a place called Steyning, and he had given William and his ship masters descriptions of the best landing places and the type of country they could expect inland.

Now they could see the land ahead of them, and the men all paused, as though they realized that this green, lush view would hold either their fortunes, or their graves.

Through the gap in the clouds Rollo felt a sudden warmth, and glanced over his shoulder. The sun was beaming down at him, and he was gladdened to think that perhaps this meant God was smiling on him and this whole venture. He knew that Harold had a great number of men he could call on. If he called up the *fyrd*, he would have a much larger force than this, and yet if God was with William, even Harold must fail. And die.

Rollo straightened his back and bared his teeth. This was a good day, a good day to fight.

A good day to die.

Yes. Bran was long dead by then.

Although he had made more blades, he was convinced that he had poured his finest craftsmanship into the one. The effort involved with others seemed pointless. They would not respond in the way that this would; it was perfection. He would sit up late at night with a jug of ale and stare at it, occasionally picking it up and testing the balance, longing to see it with hilt and sheath, but reluctant to sell it on because it would feel as though a part of him was sold with it.

Eventually the decision was taken from him. After six years Bran died. Brada had trapped a wily old wild cat, and Bran was scratched while trying to help his son kill it. The wound soured, and he died one night in early winter, listening to the sobbing of his family all round him. The last words he heard were Dudda's hissed accusation to Brada: 'This is all your fault! You killed father!'

Even when the young priest, Bartholomew, buried the smith's body, watching him placed kneeling in the grave, Dudda was not talking to Brada. It hurt their mother terribly, with so much already to mourn.

Later, Bartholomew was present when the blade was sold in Exeter. It had been bought by a tranter who carried it with three and twenty others in a wrapped bundle, and the vicar, as Bartholomew now was, saw it on a bench at the fair. He saw the mark of Bran stamped into the hilt, and touched it gently, remembering the kindly smith he had buried all those years before.

A short while later, it was a trader from London who saw the blades and wandered over to look at them. Bartholomew greeted him reservedly. He was suspicious of 'foreigners'.

'I am Paul from London. I may be interested in some blades – what have you here?'

'Fine blades, master,' said the tranter.

'So you say,' the merchant said drily.

Bartholomew felt urged to respond in Bran's defence. 'These were made by a great smith locally. They're his best work.'

'Aye? I've heard that line before,' Paul said cynically.

'It is said, "He who lives in falsehood slays his soul; he who lies, his honour",' Bartholomew said sententiously. 'I do not lie – these blades are marvels of his craft. I would be proud to wear a blade like this.'

'You buy it, then!'

The vicar smiled sadly. 'I wish I could afford it.'

'Come on, then. Let's see them,' Paul said to the tranter.

He was a sharp-eyed man, Paul. Brown hair worn long under his old leather cap, and his belly showed his wealth. He had a belt strong enough to take the weight of his gut as he walked about the market, his thumbs hooked in it near the buckle. He was always smiling, and his thin lips were pursed in a whistle as he passed the stall, but then his square face took on a more serious, speculative expression.

It took his notice as soon as he caught sight of it. The workmanship was exquisite compared to the others. As he picked it up and held it at arm's length, he could feel the life in it. Surprised, for a sword blade would usually only appeal to him once it had been dressed with hilt and guard, he eyed it more closely. It was uniform, with a noticeable taper and sharp point. Over thirty inches long, he guessed. The polishing had smoothed the blade to a gleaming silver, and as he looked at it, there were no indications of pitting, just a perfect mirror-finish.

'Where did you say you found this, friend?'

'In an old widow's place. She died a while ago, and this was under her bed, if you'll believe me, master,' the tranter smiled. 'Her man was a smith – might have made this for himself, eh? One of a kind, I'd reckon.'

Yes. One of a kind, Paul thought. He bought the lot, giving his farewells to the priest and the tranter. Once back at his workshop in London, he set it on a bench and studied it. There were six other blades he was working on, two new, and four older ones which needed new hilts. As he worked at these, every so often his attention would wander over to the new blade sitting on his workbench, and he took to touching it, glancing about his room as he wondered which style of hilt would best suit this sword.

The cross was easy. He had seen a sword made by another man some little while before, who had taken a bar of steel and created a piece of art by hammering the two ends over and cutting them until they resembled a pair of dog's heads, one at either side. He would do that for this too, he told himself. And the grip would be good lime wood, with wire and leather wrapped well about it. Above would be a plain steel pommel. There was no need to over-decorate this weapon.

It would be a sword any man could desire. A sword of honour, dignity, and purpose.

The landing was not as bad as Rollo had feared. Their enemy was not yet warned, although Rollo was sure that he had seen flames in the distance, as though a great signal fire had been lit.

His ship raced on and on, until the beach seemed impossibly close, and then, at the last minute, the oars were raised safely away at the shipmaster's bellow, and there was a moment's dread silence.

All over the boat men braced themselves. They knew little what they might meet, but they were only too aware of the reputation of their enemy, a wonderfully resourceful, cunning warrior who had beaten all. He was there, somewhere, and his rage at learning of their invasion would be uncontrollable. Many of them would soon be dead. Swein the axeman flexed his arms and smiled widely as he caught sight of Rollo's set expression, and Rollo grinned in return.

Then they were thrown to the deck. There was an awful grating, and the ship shuddered and jerked, before toppling gently to rest at an angle.

At Rollo's feet, two men collided, their heads slamming together. He shouted to the men at the prow and immediately they began to leap into the waves and thrust themselves through the water, standing on the beach with axes, swords and spears in their hands, waiting to see if any would contest their landing. As the bridgehead grew, some ran forward to a small hill from where they could view the surrounding land while the others disembarked and began unloading stores.

On board, Rollo pushed and bellowed at the remaining men. As he prepared to jump himself, he realized a man still stood by him: one of the two who had knocked heads. This man wore a steel and leather cap, while the other had been bareheaded. The cap's metal edge had smashed through the thin bone of the temple, shattering his eye-socket, and blood smeared the planks beside him. Two sailors glanced at the body, then dropped it into the sea.

Rollo was about to shout when he realized that the man was weeping.

'*He was my brother.*'

'You'll join him if you don't get off the ship and help,' Rollo grated, and swung over the ship's side.

Paul was a master of his craft, but when the sword was dressed, a large pommel of steel balancing the weight nicely, the cross with dogs' heads to protect the hand, a plain black leather grip bound with silver wire, he felt that there was still something missing. Struck with a thought, he took it to a friend, a jeweller.

'Ulric, take a look at this!' Paul said, taking the waxed leather wrapping from it as he entered the little shop.

'A lovely piece,' Ulric said. He was a heavy-set man with a thick greying beard and narrowed brown eyes that scowled all too easily, the legacy of long years working gems and gold into intricate patterns.

'Could you carve me an inscription?' Paul asked.

Ulric shrugged. Paul had often come for fine work.

'What do you want?' he asked as he picked up a burin and eyed it speculatively.

On the beach, as the knights calmed frightened horses and saddled them before riding out and ensuring the host was safe from attack, the carpenters were already at work bringing the heavy sections of pre-built castle from the ships and heaving them over to the chosen site. The hammering and shouting continued from first light through that long day, and in all that time Rollo had no break, just snatched bites of bread and a hunk of cheese washed down with brackish water from a skin. By the end of the day he was exhausted, and he dropped onto his blanket with relief. He didn't even recall closing his eyes, but fell immediately into a deep sleep.

The next morning was chill, and Rollo had to crouch at a fire to warm himself, idly thinking again of his wife and their child. He had been fortunate, Edith was a woman with intelligence and beauty. Before he wed he had been a member of Edward's bodyguard, but it was his attachment to Edith that had established him in authority. Edith was the daughter of King Edward's cousin, and as soon as Rollo married her, he found he had more money and influence.

And then Edward died, and Rollo found himself abroad as the new king was elected. Harold had taken charge, of course. He was the strongest contender – there was no doubt of that. The Godwinson was revered for his victories over the Welsh; he was the country's best general. But Harold had never trusted Rollo. There was nothing for him under Harold's reign. Better to try to win the kingdom for another man, and take what he could.

William claimed his right because Harold was his vassal.

Two years before Harold had been shipwrecked and captured by Count Guy of Ponthieu at Beaurian who had hoped to ransom him. William forced the Count to release Harold to his protection, and while Harold was in his care, he made his captive swear an oath of support. An oath sworn under duress holds no legal standing, but William was confident. He had bullied and slaughtered his way to maturity, killing all those who plotted against him. Power for him was something to be used, not harnessed or jealously hoarded.

Edith and their child needed a secure future, and the best manner of winning it was here at Pevensey, fighting for William.

Bran's son Dudda had never married. After his father died, all the fault of that fool Brada for catching a wild cat, the family had been thrown into poverty. Dudda had stayed with his mother to support her, but Brada had soon left. Dudda heard he'd gone to the coast, seeking a ship in his shame.

It was no more than he deserved. Meantime, while he assuaged his guilt with exile, Dudda was left to look after the homestead. He was by no means a master of the craft of smithing, though, and soon his mother had succeeded in persuading him to join the household of a local thegn. As she said, at least he would be guaranteed his bread and ale each day.

The king himself saw Dudda fight one day, and rewarded him with coins and a promotion. Now he was in charge of his own small host in Sussex. Courageous to a fault, he would always throw himself at an enemy with reckless abandon, and never more so than when attacking the blond warriors from the northern seas. He hated the Norsemen with a passion.

The memory of their treatment of Bran's mother still poisoned all his thoughts of Vikings. He refused to admit that he had any trace of Viking blood in him, and lived only to kill them. It was this which infuriated him when the new king took the host north to protect his new kingdom from Harold Hardrada's invasion. Dudda should have been there too. It was little consolation to hear that King Harold Godwinson wanted him here to protect the coast against the forces of William the Bastard of Normandy.

Dudda wanted to be fighting Vikings, not some Norman bastard.

Cerdic the sheathmaker was an older man than Paul, with hair as black as a raven's wing. His language was strangely accented, because he came from the barbaric far north of the country originally, but his abilities with wood and leather had brought him here to London, where his marvellous sheaths won praise from all who saw them.

Short and thickset, he had a cast in one eye that made it difficult to tell where he was looking as he spoke. A long scar that rose from his wrist up to his elbow was the remaining evidence of his youth when he had last fought in the fyrd.

Today he took the sword with a low whistle of appreciation. 'This is the best you've made in a while. What does this say?'

Paul smiled and ran his finger down the inscription that had been engraved in the fuller. '"*Qui falsitate vivit, animam occidit. Falsus in ore, caret honore*" – that is, "He who lives in falsehood slays his soul. He who lies, his honour,"' he translated loosely.

'Well, with a moral like that, your sword will need something to set it off,' Cerdic said. He was quiet a moment, holding the sword in his hands and considering. Taking it up in his hand, he felt the balance and swung it about him at breast height. 'Bloody good!'

'I'll leave it with you, then.'

Cerdic scarcely acknowledged his departure as his friend left his workshop. He was still feeling the weight of the sword, testing it for its centre, setting his head on one side as he looked down its length, and then nodding to himself. Finally, he sat on a stool and looked at the hilt.

The basic form of the sheath was already prepared – he stored many blanks of wood. Shaped, lined with fresh sheepskin, glued together and wrapped in good leather, with carving on the hide itself, many were long enough to suit this blade. He'd want some good decoration for the sheath, too. Some good bronze. He had some which would be adequate for workaday blades, but nothing for this. With a slate and block of chalk, he made a rough outline of the sort of pieces he wanted, and paid a lad to take it to his favourite supplier. The he began to rummage through his stock of wooden blanks.

It was late in the afternoon when he began to hack into the hard wood he had selected. The adze was sharp as a chisel, and it took little time to shave off the inner surface with a sweeping, careful stroke, the blank resting on the floor and held in place by straps. He had already marked out the dimensions of the sword in chalk, and now he cut out the form of the blade, pausing every so often to rest the sword in the space to ensure it fitted. The precise size didn't matter too much. It was a case of making the hole large enough for the blade, together with its protective sheepskin case, to fit.

His workshop was a small lean-to near the London Bridge gate, and from his open doorway he had a good view of the travellers coming and going along that great roadway. Usually he would win good custom from the people who came up this way because he was on the route to the street of armourers, and many men had need of the smiths. There were always swords to be rehoned, sharpened or replaced. With the ever-present threat of war, men looked to their arms, and even if the sword was good and strong, all too often the sheath was beyond repair. One sword could have six or seven sheaths in a man's lifetime if he was regularly off on journeys.

Today a pair of men arrived. One, a vicar, looked exhausted. Priests tended to be bad customers, they rarely had to wear their swords on their hips when they travelled, but left them safe while others defended them from attack. This man wore nothing. However his companion was interesting – he looked wealthier than Cerdic's usual customer. He had dark hair braided in two long plaits, and his clothing was worn and faded, the russet cloth of his cloak was thinning and stitched together to mend the many tears. A youthful face, but sad: a man who'd seen much of life already. His sword was all but hanging out from a broken sheath. 'My horse. It stood on the thing last night,' he said bitterly.

'Master,' Cerdic said with a grave nod. Warriors deserved respect. 'Let me have a look. Ach! It is stuck in here. The sheath is ruined, but I fear the sword may be too. I'll have to cut the sheath away to see how the blade has suffered.'

'I am called to go with the fyrd . . . That sword. Let me try it.'

Cerdic nodded and passed it across to the man, trying not to grin. As soon as he'd entered the room, the traveller's eyes had gone to the sword on Cerdic's table. And no surprise – it was the most beautiful piece of work in the room. It all but glowed, and the covetous eye of the warrior had fixed on it in a moment. Anyone who lived by the strength of his arm must be attracted to a weapon that had clearly had so much time lavished upon it.

'Master, this is beautiful! It reminds me . . .' the man said, holding it out before him. He turned his wrist, and the metal flashed backwards, wickedly, before coming to rest pointing at the doorway. He span on his heel and raised it to an imaginary enemy, then let it slash down, continuing the movement up and behind him, bringing it around to his breast and pausing, studying it closely again.

'My old sword is damaged; I need a new one. I can't count on a sword that is liable to shatter.'

'Ah, that's not mine to sell.'

'I am a thegn: Dudda son of Bran,' Dudda said with quiet menace. 'I will have this sword, no matter what it costs.'

Cerdic nodded. 'Then you'd best speak to Paul. I can introduce you.'

'Paul . . .' the priest said, running a finger over the insciption on the blade and frowning as he recognized the quotation. 'I wonder . . .'

Rollo was glad to have Swein at his side as he mounted his horse. The great beast was comforting, a good, biddable brute, but if it came to charging a shield wall with lances pointing at them, Rollo would be happier knowing that Swein was near.

Swein was one of those northmen who inspired terror in his enemies and commanded respect from his comrades. Rollo had seen him in battle, and he felt that the Norse blood flowed vigorously in his veins. With an axe in his fist he was the picture of a berserker, worth more than twenty ordinary members of the fyrd.

For all that, he was sure that Swein was not from Scandinavia. The man's accent was more Saxon than anything else. Rollo reckoned he was the son of a minor thegn who had embarrassed his master and been forced to flee. Perhaps he had killed a man and couldn't afford to pay the fine? Whatever the reason, Rollo was simply glad that he was here with him in William of Normandy's host with the other mercenaries. They'd have need of men like Swein if they were going to break the Saxon shield-wall.

He had served in the fyrd himself. Standing in the shield-wall with farmers and peasants, linking shields and grasping their swords or lances. So long as they worked in unison, the enemy would break on them like the tide on an unforgiving shore. And when the moment was right, the shield-wall would begin to shove forward, swords rising and falling to hack at any within range. The line of warriors would stamp forwards, trampling dead and wounded alike, while men behind would stab and slash at the bodies in case a man was feigning death and intended to rise up among the men of the fyrd to cause mayhem.

Yes, the fyrd was strong, and provided that their commander had time to run them through their paces, giving them their commands for even a half day, there was little which could be done to overwhelm them.

That was Rollo's fear: that the fyrd might arrive prepared. The men under Harold were strong and determined, as they should be for they were fighting for their kingdom. But the Normans under William were determined too. They had the sea at their backs, and if they failed, they would die.

Bartholomew was exhausted. He was in London with Bishop Leofric, and had been sent to acquire provisions for the household. Many were congregating on London, desperate to hear how the battle had gone in the north where good King Harold was protecting the realm from the devils from over the sea.

The thought that the Norsemen could be ravaging the lands was terrifying. Down in Wessex, the folk had grown used to peace. The Danes tried to land and ransack towns and churches when they could, and while their attacks had grown rarer, no one could forget the tales of men hacked to death, women raped and discarded to lie beside their dead husbands and children, farms laid waste, priests cut down before their altars . . . Bartholomew was terrified that all this could come to pass again. Well, if the land was invaded, he would go with the host to protect his land, his people. He wouldn't wait to be slaughtered.

He wanted a sword too. He walked with Dudda to Paul's shop, a pleasant house in West Ceape, the busy road that held so many stalls and shops. Inside there were weapons of all descriptions, all serviceable, and some beautifully made.

'I have met you,' Bartholomew said when he saw Paul. 'You bought blades from Exeter.'

'I seem to recall your face,' Paul admitted cautiously. A merchant should always be wary of those who claimed to remember him – it could be this priest remembered a bargain that went sour.

'You picked up a marvellous blade there. We saw one like it earlier today,' Bartholomew murmured. 'One that had a lovely inscription on it.'

'Oh, of course. Yes, I remember now. That is a magnificent sword, isn't it? It took time and skill to have it mounted.'

Bartholomew studied the swords about the room while the other men argued about the price of the sword. It would be a source of pride to Bran, he felt, were the old smith to know that the sword would be bought and used by his own son.

It was as he haggled over another, cheaper but serviceable sword, that the cry was heard in the streets.

'The Normans! The Normans have landed!'

*   *   *

Two days later, Rollo took a force of thirty men to engage any small groups nearby. They must harry any attempted muster, and send messengers if they found a large force.

It was a cold morning, with a mist lying heavily on the ground ahead of them. At the beach, in the security of their stronghold, Rollo had been easy in his mind, but now, leaving the sturdy fortress behind, he felt the first stirrings of anxiety. Ahead of him somewhere there were men watching him. Perhaps practising their manoeuvres.

He had trained with them: he knew how they'd fight. They'd ride to a muster-point, leaving their horses with boys, and run to a ridge or hillock, forming a line six to ten men deep. At the command all would thrust their shields forward, overlapping each with their neighbour, each of them depending upon his neighbour for protection. On the order they could unlink shields, lift them overhead, turn, and reform with a new wall protecting their rear. When directed, they could begin pacing slowly down the hillside, all the while shouting their battle cries and stabbing forward with spears.

Each of them would feel the courage that came from conviction: they knew that Harold had never failed in battle. He was a tough fighter, and he would die rather than lose his kingdom. Each man would be ready, his shield a reassuring weight on his arm, the sword in his fist heartening. Many of the blades that Rollo would encounter would be ancient. Most of them had been used in other battles, older fights. They had been a father's or grandfather's weapon, used against Vikings or neighbours over decades, and now brought here to Pevensey to slaughter these latest invaders.

Rollo had served Edward in many a line. His strong right arm had battered and slashed at enough men, and his sword showed its age. It had been his uncle's sword. His father's had gone to his brother, of course, his older brother. That one was twice as old even as this battered lump of metal. Rollo had been forced to have this one re-sheathed three times, and it had been given a new hilt a short while before they embarked for this coast.

A thump at his thigh brought him back to the present. Like the others, he wore a massive kite-shaped shield over his shoulder, so that after an attack, as he wheeled and hared off, his back would be protected. It was essential, but by God's heaven, it was clumsy.

Harnesses squeaked and jingled. At any other time, on another day, the noise would have eased his spirits. The musical sound of thousands of small rings tinkling together from the men's byrnies and mail neck-covers, sounded like ten thousand tiny bells.

A horse snorted. Another shook his head, and there was a curse as his rider dropped his spear. They were leaving the plain before the fortress where the mist lay spread like a blanket. Before them were thick woods, and Rollo, fearing ambush, spurred his mount into a canter to pass through the dangerous area. It was still and quiet even as he rode in among the trees, and he kept a careful eye open to possible danger, but saw nothing until he heard the scream behind him. He had an urge to crouch low and gallop away, but he restrained himself and glanced over his shoulder. And his bowels turned to ice.

On either side archers had launched missiles at the men behind him. Now, as he watched, three of his men toppled and were leapt upon by the enemy, scramasax blades flashing, and he saw a flurry of blood like red snow erupt from a man's throat. He and his men couldn't ride down the attackers, not in among the trees; they must perish. Better that the survivors should be saved. He roared at his men, drew his sword, and spurred his horse on, ignoring the jeers of the enemy. The wind started to rush in his ears as he pelted along the track, and, when they were almost out of the woods, he looked back and saw that the majority of his force was safe.

There was a flash of light, and the sun breached the clouds. He lifted his reins to lash his horse's flanks again, and then hesitated, feeling a chilly sweat wash over him.

Before him stood a line of byrnie-clad men, at least fifty, all capped with steel and leather, all clutching great round shields, all with the long hair and beards of grown men used to fighting, and all grasping long spears. Even as he set his horse at them, they deployed, and over the howling wind in his ears, the rattle of harnesses and grunts from his hastening steel, he heard the gutteral roar bellowed by the commander. The shields were pushed out, edge on to Rollo, then snapped round so that a row of overlapping circles faced him. Another shout, and he saw the shafts of the spears disappear as they were lowered to point at him, and all he could see now was the deceptively pretty sight of the sun glittering on the spear-points.

There was only a matter of yards to go. He could see no escape: the line blocked his men's path. The only option they had was to fight their way through this small host. He raised his sword and shrieked his defiance, then lowered his head and flung himself and his horse at the shields.

The crash was shocking. Wooden shields shivered with the appalling collision, and he saw grim faces recoil as his horse rammed into them. A man fell back, then down as hooves rose and battered at him. Men stared at opponents, and slashed and stabbed and hacked and thrust, determined to kill before dying. A tall, dark man was in front of him now, a man whose cap came down over his features and left only his eyes shining at either side of his nose-guard. Fleetingly Rollo caught sight of his great sword, sparkling like a diamond in the sun, but then his mount sprang aside, and he lost sight of him.

He saw Swein at his side, the huge man wielding his axe with broad strokes. The huge axe-head clove through caps and skulls, and about him there was already a mess of limbs and sprawled men, but still the shield-wall held, and then Rollo saw a lance thrust forward and pierce Swein's horse's breast. There was already a stub of lance jutting from the beast's flank, and now he seemed to realize that he was dying. He reared, throwing his hooves in all directions, and tossed his mane, but his eyes were wild not with the rage of battle, but with the terror of encroaching death.

Even as he grew conscious of Swein's mount, Rollo realized that his own was floundering. There was less energy in his movements, and Rollo knew that a spear must have reached his vitals. He waved his sword and roared at the top of his voice to call his men to retreat, to pull back so that they might win space to charge again, but as he shouted, there was a high whistling noise, a fluttering whine that ended in a wet slap, and he saw one of his men fall, grabbing frantically for the arrow's fletching that protruded from his back, rolling on the ground and screaming until his own horse, stamping about the field, crushed his head.

The archers were back – there was no escape that way. Rollo knew his horse was soon to die. He kicked his feet from the stirrups, and managed to leap from the saddle just before the brute collapsed, crushing a section of the wall as he fell.

It was the opening he had needed. Hoarsely bellowing to his men, Rollo gripped his sword in both hands and sprang forward. He felt, rather than saw, Swein run to his side, and he knew that two more of his men were behind him. Forming a compact group, they met shoulder to shoulder, heavy shields protecting their flanks as they stamped their way in among their enemies. The enemy withdrew, and suddenly Rollo knew that the decisive moment had arrived. He saw a glint, and into his mind flashed the memory of the man in the midst of the line, the warrior with the dark hair under his Saxon helm. With a weapon like his, he must be the leader.

'With me!' he shouted, and threw aside his shield. Instead he grabbed a small, circular wooden shield that lay on the ground near its dead owner. The shield was covered in fresh skin which had dried on the wood, forming a solid, strong, but light protection. There was a bronze boss in the centre, and now he used that to ram at the men who stood in his path. A lance came near, and he knocked it away, running his blade down the length of the shaft. He saw fingers fly off, a shriek, and the pole dropped, the man falling back among the press. Another man thrust at him from his side, but Rollo blocked the stab and slammed the boss into his face, feeling bones crunch; he punched his sword into the man's belly and ripped it aside. He shoved another from his path, swept his sword across, the point lifted. The blade ripped through the man's throat; there was a gush of blood, bubbles, horror in the man's eyes, and then . . . then he was before the commander.

It took no thought. The man appeared, and Rollo instantly crossed to meet him. The others were with him, he knew that. From the corner of his eye he saw Swein's axe part an arm from a torso, saw a second man approach, and saw the axe whirl into his stomach. It sliced through his cheap shirt of mail, and his entrails were spilled.

Then Rollo was on him.

*   *   *

Dudda had been shocked by the sudden appearance of the cavalry force. He and his men had only arrived last night, tired and footsore from the march, and he had counted on drilling them before a fight. These madmen had arrived before he'd been able to put them through their most basic paces, and now his men were pressed hard. Bartholomew was somewhere near. He only hoped his friend wasn't dead.

The captain was plain enough, sitting up there on his horse. Terrifying in his metal clothing, so high above everyone else. None of the men, including Dudda, had seen men riding horses into battle. Men rode *to* war, yes, but they left their mounts safe behind the battle lines. These men pelted towards their enemy like demons on their chargers.

Dudda raised his sword, the blade tapping the front of his helmet, and he closed his eyes, uttering a short prayer on the cross for victory. His sword's blade gleamed, and he was reminded of that day, many years ago, when he had sat with his father and helped sharpen and polish a blade which his father said was the best he had ever made. He had said, what? 'When a man holds this blade in his hand, he shall be invincible!'

It was enough to make him smile to himself. This sword made him *feel* invincible. Bartholomew said he was sure it was that same sword, his father's best creation. It felt it, certainly. Today, here, he would test it.

Dudda saw the mad captain of his enemies approaching, and lowered his sword, hefting his shield. He was thegn, and no foreign murderers would take these lands from his people again. No more rapes, no more slaughters.

'To me! *To me!*'

The invaders must perish!

*   *   *

Seeing the man smile under his cap, Rollo snarled and lifted his own worn, chipped blade. Circling, he bent, left shoulder to the man, peering over the rim of the shield, waiting for an opportunity. The man's eyes remained fixed on his, and Rollo knew he had an opponent worthy of the name. This was no poor brutish peasant who'd been called to the fyrd at the last moment to try to stem the tide of Norman warriors, but a leader of warriors.

There was a flash in the man's eyes: he'd caught sight of Swein. The axeman was approaching from Rollo's right. While the man was distracted, Rollo bared his teeth and leapt forward. His blade caught on the other man's, he felt the clash of steel, heard the ringing of tempered metal, then the slam as his blade bit into the man's shield, and the two whirled away from each other, circling again.

Rollo grinned, then bounded forward again, his sword hanging low, only to jab upwards at the man's legs, but he had already moved away; Rollo tried a slash at his hamstrings, but he blocked the blow with a casual backwards hack of his sword, followed by a sweeping blow towards Rollo's shoulder. It was a pathetic attempt, and Rollo moved his shield to prevent it, and then realized that the man's sword wasn't where it should have been. A flick of his wrist had brought the blade almost to Rollo's gut. He had to join shield and sword together, pressing down as he sucked in his belly and bent his back away. It was only just in time, and he felt the snag as the steel caught on his byrnie.

His relief was short-lived. He stumbled on a discarded limb and instantly started to tumble. The man's attack was immediate. Rollo could only throw himself sideways, falling painfully on one arm. There he swung up with his sword, and the clang of steel striking was a shivering impact deep in his bones. His shoulder seemed to reverberate with the clamour.

Scrambling to his feet, he saw the sword swing, blocked it, but this time there was a subtle difference in the clash of weapons. A niggle of doubt assailed him. There had been a strange thrill in his blade.

He knew his sword all too well. This blade had been his since his uncle had died, nearly twenty years ago. He'd worn it ever since; had killed fifteen men with it, slaking the steel's thirst for human blood, and never had he felt that odd little twitch.

Another smashing blow, and he felt it give. There was a weakness! The hilt had come loose, or the blade was cracked. It could not continue to take such a hammering from this man. He moved away, retreating, trying to keep his eyes from betraying his sudden concern, but the fellow started to set about him more seriously. The sword flashed and sparkled redly in the sun's glare, and then the commander was harrying him hard, the bloody blade whirling about him, and suddenly Rollo knew he must die.

His hilt was broken, and the leather-covered wooden grip moved in his hand. The blade was no longer fixed to it, and the blade turned without his wanting it to. Now there was no let up, and he could do little but block the attacks. It was pointless to return to the assault, for the blade would turn and not hit true. It was all but useless. There was a shivering in the blade, and he saw it fall in two, his fingers stinging, and saw the fierce delight in the other man's face.

Suddenly there was a roar, and Swein launched himself at the man from his side. Rollo saw the commander's eyes narrow as he turned to face the new threat.

Dudda's blood sang in his ears. He felt as though the spirits of his ancestors were with him. He could not be harmed, not while he wielded this sword, his father's sword. It was a guarantee of victory, and soon he would conquer this rabble of murderers and cut-throats, ready for the real battle when King Harold returned and put the Norman Bastard's host to the sword.

But as he was about to end this man's life, another man came roaring at him, approaching from his left front, running at him with that axe like a Viking from the sagas. Dudda tested his sword in his hand, swinging it up in a wide arc, feeling the way that it came alive. Then he saw Bartholomew run at the new enemy, his cheap sword smeared with gore, his shield, broken and splintered, still on his arm.

Bartholomew lifted his sword, but the huge Norseman swept his axe aside, clashing with the sword, and with a flick of his wrist, sent it flying away. The axehead swept back towards the priest's head, and Bartholomew ducked. His feet were entangled with a set of reins from a dead horse, and he tumbled to the ground.

'No!' Dudda started forward, convinced he was already too late. He reached the Norseman as the axe began to descend, and slammed into the man, slashing at his hamstrings. The man collapsed screaming in agony, the giant tendons snapping with a sound like bones breaking, and Dudda hefted his sword, ready to stab, and then thrust down with all his strength.

He roared with savage delight, and went to Bartholomew. The priest was all right, and he turned back to finish off the axeman . . . and then hesitated, staring. Horror washed over him, and the sword fell from his nerveless fingers.

'Brada? *Brada?*'

Rollo saw his chance. His own sword was useless, but the other was near. He sprang up and launched himself forward. Without breaking his run, he snatched up the

Saxon's sword, and let his momentum carry him on. His thrust passed through the man's bicep near his elbow, and carried on into his flank.

Dudda gave a bestial roar of rage and agony, and tried to release his sword arm, but Rollo was on him. He shoved the blade deeper and deeper, feeling the warm wash of blood over his hands. Even as Dudda toppled backwards, Rollo kicked his body, held the sword aloft and screamed:

'Victory! Victory!'

There was a pause, and then a collective moan seemed to come from the enemy as they saw their leader shivering on the ground, and while they watched, Rollo kicked at his helmet, sending it spinning. He found himself looking down at a man who was younger than him, dark, square-jawed, grey-eyed. There was no time to consider. The man closed his eyes, and Rollo leaned down casually, resting the sword's point on his throat. He lifted it a short distance, ready to plunge it down, and . . .

. . . There was a slamming buffet at his side. He felt the air explode from his lungs. There was a blankness in his mind, and he shook his head with confusion, glancing about him. When he looked down, he saw that a great axehead was buried in his ribs, and he gazed at it with astonishment. It was Swein's.

He lifted his arm to stab with his new sword – but his arm was gone. It lay twitching on the ground beside him, and he had just enough energy left in him to pick up the sword in his left hand and try to turn to repay his executioner, when he felt the axehead move.

Bartholomew wept as he jerked at the axe-haft, sobbing with exhaustion and despair. Setting his foot on Rollo's body, he pushed with all his might, and the axe came free.

As he stood there, gazing dully at the bodies lying on the ground, he saw Dudda slowly crawl to the great Norseman, whose fair hair was red with gore where it lay on the sodden earth. Dudda was weeping with the effort, but the priest heard his quiet voice:

'Brada! My brother! I am sorry! Forgive me!'

Rollo felt a shiver run through him. He tried to remove his helmet, but his hand wouldn't respond, and he remembered it had been cut off. His left hand was too weak to do anything but lie on the ground.

'Brother! My brother! *No!*'

They were the last words Rollo heard spoken. He was suddenly exhausted, and he felt himself slipping into unconsciousness as Dudda, Bran's son, sobbed beside his brother on his knees, and then slowly sank forward to slump, dead, over him.

Some hours later, a party of cavalry was sent to find out what had happened to the raiding force.

They found the tracks easily enough, and in the middle of woods, a man trotted back to the leader. 'There are arrows all over the place. They must have been ambushed.'

Sir Ralph de la Pomeroy nodded and saddles creaked as men felt for their weapons. There was a heightened tension among them all as they continued. Soon they were out of the trees, and found the battlefield.

'Dear Lord God,' a man sighed.

It was a slaughterhouse. Limbs and bloody torsos lay about the grass, which was red with gore.

'Kill any still living,' the knight said dispassionately. They had no facilities for prisoners. His horse began to pick his way through the mess while he glanced about him. He had no feeling for the tatty mercenaries lying dead. None were from his homeland. 'Any we should take back?' he demanded.

'Rollo fitzRollo, the leader. He's here.'

'Bring him, then.'

The horseman nodded and went with another to fetch the body. They threw it onto a horse and bound it carefully with rope about the remaining wrist and ankles to hold it in place, and looked about them cautiously as they worked.

'Do you think we'll win this?' asked a man-at-arms from Bordeaux called Odo.

'I hope so. If not, we're shafted. There's no escape for us.'

'If they can do this . . .'

'A lucky ambush, that's all,' a man muttered from his horse nearby.

'Lucky? They got Swein.'

'Him?' Odo asked.

'The mad axeman. He was right close to Rollo – just here.'

It was sobering to see him lying there, a gaping sword wound in his breast. Many had thought him invincible.

A cough from another man made them both reach for their knives, and they stepped forward cautiously. A wounded mercenary lay nearby, hidden by a horse's corpse. Seeing he was an ally, the two released the grip on their weapons as he choked, blood trickling from his mouth. Odo went to his side as the other wandered off to a Saxon's body, tugging at a ring on a dead forefinger.

Odo patted the man's hand and helped him to a sip or two of water while his companion grunted, pulling at the ring, then shrugged and took out his knife. Soon the ring was in his purse, the finger discarded, and he strolled back to Swein. Then he hesitated, frowned, and leaned down. He pushed Swein's body aside. 'Odo: look at this!'

Hearing the cry, Sir Ralph glanced in their direction.

He spurred his horse forward. As Swein was pulled away they saw he had been lying on top of a sword – a marvellous sword with a great disc pommel and curving cross. 'Give that to me!'

'I found it!'

The knight glanced at him. A miserable cur from the wharves of Le Havre or somewhere, he guessed. 'And I have taken it,' he said with deliberation. He picked it up, and saw the inscription. '"Who lives in falsehood kills his soul . . . ?" was that you, then, axeman? Anyway, come to my quarters when we're back at the fort, and I'll pay you for finding this,' he said to the scowling man-at-arms.

As he passed his sergeant, he murmured. 'If that scruffy churl appears, give him a kicking for his nerve and tell him the sword's worth nothing to him. It's mine.'

'Sir.'

Later that day, Sir Ralph smiled to himself as he picked up the sword again.

It was a perfectly balanced weapon, beautiful and strong. There were only a couple of little nicks in the sharp steel, very little after a vicious battle like today's. It was a marvellous weapon, this. Astonishingly good for a mere local thegn in a quiet district like this. He would have it engraved with his name. Yes, a shield to show it was owned by a nobleman, and de la Pomeroy engraved underneath it, the letters filled with silver, so that all who saw it would know it was Sir Ralph's weapon.

He whirled it over his head and smiled to himself.

Shameful, of course, that it hadn't protected the thegn or his land. Because it hadn't. Its owner was dead, and Sir Ralph was perfectly confident that this country would soon be his Duke's. God was on the side of the Normans.

*　　*　　*

'You know it?' Sir Ralph asked again.

Bartholomew recalled those hideous days, running from the beaches, finding King Harold's host hurrying down from London, joining them in the hope that they would hurl the invaders back into the sea and destroy them all, and then the despair, the total, overwhelming despair, as Harold died, run down by a Norman knight's lance

It had taken weeks to make his way back to the cathedral. His wounds were not extensive, and he had been well nursed with the prayers of his companions. Later, the Normans had arrived, laying siege to the city, hanging and torturing those they caught until the city surrendered. Then came the new rule: houses were torn down to make space for the castle, the symbol of King William the Bastard's power. And when men like Sir Ralph de la Pomeroy arrived to take control, they viewed simple dissent as an excuse for murder.

Bartholomew had seen so many deaths now. So many. And many had been killed by Sir Ralph using this very sword. He shook his head and set the sword back in the scabbard. His fingers were revolted by its very feel. He could not wait until he had returned to the little chapel in Exeter where he had been made chaplain. Perhaps by the time he died he would have grown to comprehend this appalling catastrophe. He doubted it.

Too many good people had died, and brother had killed brother. Dudda and Brada among others. Yes, he had heard Dudda's last words to his brother: 'Brother, I love you . . . forgive me!'

This shameful sword, their father's greatest creation, had killed his line. His fingers touched the silver engraving. 'De la Pomeroy,' he read, and felt sickened.

Sir Ralph was welcome to it.

ACT ONE

Exeter, April 1195

There was a thunderous crash as the roof fell in and a fountain of sparks erupted into the night sky. The air became filled with specks of black ash and fragments of burning straw floated from the flaming thatch of the cottage. With a crackling roar, Gwyn's home of twelve years was destroyed in as many minutes.

The big Cornishman stood impotently in the road outside, watching the destruction in company with his neighbours, who although sympathetic to his loss, were more concerned over the threat to their own roofs by the flying sparks. They had carried leather buckets of turbid water from the well, but there was nothing they could do to save the little building, made of wood-framed wattle plastered with cob – a mixture of clay, straw and dung.

The villagers of St Sidwell, a hamlet just outside Exeter's city walls, had helped Gwyn of Polruan to save what he could of the family's possessions, few that they were, but most of what was in the single-room had gone up in flames. In the plot behind, the hut that his wife Agnes used for her cooking was emptied before it also fell prey to the flying embers – and their three goats, the fowls and a pair of pigs were also taken to safety in a nearby croft.

'How did it start, Gwyn?' asked the man from next

door, a mournful fellow who always stank, as he worked in the tannery.

'That bloody roof again! A chunk of withies and straw as big as my head fell down into the firepit. By the time the smoke woke me up, it was too late!'

The thatch had been laid on woven hazel withies supported by the rafters, always a hazard in dwellings where the fire was in the centre of the floor beneath.

'Thank God that Agnes and the boys weren't here,' said the tanner, relishing the drama that was enlivening the humdrum life of the village.

'Nothing but damned trouble, this week,' grunted Gwyn. 'Both lads are sickening for something, so she took them down to stay with her sister in Milk Lane. She's good with herbs and potions and suchlike.'

As they spoke, the front wall fell in with a crash and fresh streamers of fire spewed up into the night sky.

'What's our landlord going to say about losing his house?' asked another neighbour with ill-concealed satisfaction. He rented his own dwelling from the same man, the owner of several fulling-mills on the river, which processed raw wool for the spinners and weavers of the city.

'Sod him, the tight-fisted bastard!' growled Gwyn. 'If he won't mend a rotten roof, he has to put up with the consequences.'

The tanner nudged him. 'Talk of the devil! Here he is.'

The fire made the midnight scene as bright as day and in its glare, they saw a dark-haired man hurrying towards them, his whole demeanour suggesting pent-up anger.

'What have you done to my house, you Cornish savage?' he yelled as he came close. 'This is all your fault!'

Though Gwyn, like many large men, was normally

of a placid nature, this unjust accusation coming so soon after the loss of his home, made him lose his temper.

'Don't give me that, Walter Tyrell!' he boomed. 'Your lousy roof collapsed on to my fire. God knows I've asked you often enough to get it mended!'

A shouting match soon developed, each man vociferously denying the claims of the other. Surrounded by a circle of neighbours, whose sympathies were totally with Gwyn, the pair squared up to each other, as red-faced as the fire behind them. The two antagonists were as unlike as could be imagined. Gwyn of Polruan was a huge, ginger-haired giant, with long moustaches of the same hue hanging down each side of his chin. Walter Tyrell was of average height, but looked small alongside the coroner's officer. About forty years old, he was coarsely handsome, with dark wavy hair and a rim of black beard around his face. Where Gwyn wore a shabby leather jerkin over his serge breeches, hastily pulled on before he escaped from the burning house, the fuller had a long tunic of blue linen with expensive embroidery around the neck and an ornate belt of embossed leather.

'You'll pay for this, you drunken oaf!' yelled Tyrell, his anger fuelled by Gwyn's refusal to defer to what he considered a social superior. 'No doubt you were too full of ale to bank down your fire before you fell unconscious with drink!'

This was totally unjust, for though Gwyn was as fond of ale as the next man, he had a prodigious capacity and had never been seen to be obviously drunk. In addition, though he often stayed in Rougemont Castle overnight, drinking and playing dice with his soldier friends, this particular evening he had come home before the city gates closed at curfew, to feed his animals and worry about the sickness that was afflicting his two young sons.

'Pay for it?' he snarled at his insolent landlord. 'I've been paying for this pox-ridden slum for a dozen years! At four pence a week, I could have built a mansion in that time!'

As the average wage was only two pence a day, this was an appreciable sum, but Tyrell's unreasonable wrath was now in full flow.

'You'll pay me five pounds towards the cost of rebuilding – or I'll take you to the sheriff's court for judgment. And he's a good friend of mine!'

Gwyn's blue eyes goggled at the thought of such a huge sum.

'You're bloody mad, Tyrell! Where would I get five pounds? And as for your friendship with the sheriff, well, he's a bigger crook than you are!'

Incensed at this slur on both his honesty and that of his high-born friend, the fuller made the mistake of punching the Cornishman in the chest. He might as well have struck the city wall, for all the effect it had.

Gwyn gave a roar of annoyance and with a hand the size of a ham, pushed Walter in the face, so that he staggered back into the circle of villagers, for whom the prospect of a fight outweighed even a house fire in entertainment value.

But now things turned nasty, as sobbing with rage, the swarthy fuller reached to the back of his belt and drew out a wicked-looking dagger. As he brandished this, the crowd fell back, with a communal murmur of disapproval at this unsporting escalation of the quarrel.

'Put that away, you silly fool!' growled Gwyn, but Tyrell came forward and lunged at him with the blade. Gwyn stepped back and automatically felt for his sword – but his hand failed to find the familiar hilt hanging on his belt. He had left it in the cottage and even while confronted by an angry man waving a knife, he fleetingly realized that his most treasured possession was by now probably ruined beyond repair.

A dagger attack was no novelty to Gwyn after two decades of fighting across Europe and the Holy Land, but even he was surprised by the ferocity of Tyrell's assault. Dodging the first wild slash, he tried to grab the man's wrist, but the fuller made a back-handed swing which caught Gwyn on the forearm. The sharp blade sliced through the leather of his sleeve and drew blood from a long cut below his elbow. It was not serious, but the Cornishman gave a bellow, more from indignation at being wounded by such an amateur, than from pain.

'When I get a sword, I'll cut your bloody head off!' he yelled, to the delight of the circle of onlookers. Deciding that this had gone far enough, Gwyn made a feint with his injured arm and in the split second that Walter's eyes flicked towards it, he gave him a resounding blow on the side of the head with his other fist. As the fuller staggered with his teeth still rattling, Gwyn grabbed his knife arm and twisted the blade from his fingers, then pushed him violently so that he staggered and fell flat on his back on the dusty road.

'Clear off, Tyrell! You can have your bloody house back again, what's left of it. I'll rent one further down the street that's got a decent roof!'

The red-headed giant threw the knife down alongside Walter, who clambered to his feet, still gibbering with rage, uttering threats and promises of dire retribution.

'The sheriff will hear of this first thing in the morning, damn you!' he snarled, as he tried to dust down his soiled tunic. 'You threatened to kill me! I'll attain you for assault at the next Shire Court!'

Gwyn, his temper already cooled, grinned at the fuming Walter. 'Will you choose trial by combat, then?'

he said mockingly. 'I'll gladly challenge you with dagger or sword!'

There were jeers from the circle of spectators and his neighbour joined in the row.

'You should sue him, Gwyn! He struck you first – and he's wounded you!'

Landlords being about as popular as tax-collectors, the men of St Sidwell began to scowl and look threateningly at Tyrell, who took the hint and still muttering, loped off towards the East Gate, which though it was well after curfew, had been opened by the porters to let him through because of the nearby fire.

With that particular drama over, the men turned their attention back to the burning cottage, but already the collapse of the walls had partly blanketed the fallen thatch and instead of a roaring inferno, the fire was settling into a steady bonfire.

'There's nothing you can do until morning, Gwyn,' said the tanner.

'Best come home and bed down with us for the rest of the night. My wife can bind up that arm of yours.'

As he moved away reluctantly, Gwyn took a last look at the remains of his home.

'As soon as it cools, I'll see if I can find my old sword,' he growled. 'But I doubt it'll be much use after being in there!'

'Twenty years I've had this – and now look at it!'

The huge man looked mournfully at the weapon that lay across his knees, as he sat on a stool in the guardroom of Exeter's Rougemont Castle.

'I won it in a game of dice in Wexford,' he continued nostalgically. 'It's been with me in campaigns from Ireland to Palestine and saved my life a dozen times!'

A thin, leathery old soldier, the sergeant of the garrison's men-at-arms, looked down critically at the sword, as he passed behind the coroner's officer to refill his ale-pot from a jug on a shelf. The leather scabbard had burnt away, as had the wooden hilt and the remaining metal was bent and discoloured. 'It's come to the end of the road now, Gwyn,' said Gabriel.

'Why did it get so bent, just being in a fire?' asked the other occupant of the chamber, which was set at the side of the entrance arch of the gatehouse. He was a fresh-faced young soldier, who had never yet seen any weapon lifted in combat.

'The ridge timber of the roof fell across it when it collapsed,' Gwyn explained glumly. 'But even without that, the heat will have ruined the temper of the steel.'

'So what are you going to do about it?' asked Gabriel. 'You can't be a law officer without a sword.'

Gwyn dropped the useless weapon to the floor with a clang. 'I can't afford to buy a new one, my wife's expecting another babe. There'll be clothes for that – and we'll need to replace things that were lost in the fire.'

'You'll just have to win another game of dice, lad,' suggested Gabriel. 'Or find a war somewhere, to collect a bit of loot.'

The already gloomy chamber darkened as someone blocked the morning light coming through the low doorway and a deep voice joined in their conversation.

'Your purse empty again, Gwyn? Is it ale or gaming this time?'

The young soldier jumped to his feet and saluted, as Gwyn hauled himself up from his stool to greet the newcomer.

'Morning, Crowner! Just having a grumble about my ruined sword.' He picked up the offending weapon and showed it to his master, who examined it with professional interest. While Gwyn related the unhappy events of the previous night, the young soldier looked at Sir John de Wolfe with some awe. He was a legendary figure in the barracks – a knight, a former Crusader and now the king's coroner for the county of Devon. Almost as tall as the burly Gwyn, he was lean with a slight stoop, his long face and beaked nose giving him a hawkish appearance. The black hair curling to his collar and the dark stubble on his cheeks, as well as his liking for sombre clothing, explained why he had been known as 'Black John' by the troops of a dozen wars over the years.

'This old piece of iron has seen some action, Gwyn!' he said with feeling. 'It's saved my life a few times, that's for sure.'

'As yours did for me, Crowner,' replied the Cornishman, his ruddy face breaking into a grin, the bright blue eyes twinkling. Then he became serious again, as he took back the ruined sword. 'How am I going to watch your back now? I suppose I'll have to rely on that old ball-mace.'

De Wolfe did not reply, but jerked his head towards a doorway on the inner side of the guard-room, where a narrow stone staircase spiralled up in the thickness of the wall. This gatehouse had been the first thing that the Conqueror had built in Devon, after he had ruthlessly squashed the Saxon rebellion less than two years after the battle at Hastings. At the top of the tall, narrow building, a bleak chamber had been allotted to the coroner – deliberately chosen by the sheriff, John's brother-in-law, as the most inhospitable room in the castle.

The two men climbed laboriously up the steep treads to the second floor and pushed through a crude curtain of sacking which attempted to reduce the draughts. Two narrow window openings allowed the wind to whistle in from above the streets far below, as Rougemont was built at the top corner of the sloping city, in the northern angle of the old Roman walls.

As they entered, a skinny young man, dressed in a threadbare black cassock, got to his feet from a stool at the table and made a jerky bow to his master. He had a narrow, peaky face, with a receding chin and a long thin nose which always seemed to have a dew-drop on the end. Before him on the table were rolls of parchment, a pot of ink and some quill pens.

'God be with you, sir,' he squeaked, crossing himself quickly in an almost automatic gesture. 'I was just copying yesterday's inquests for the next visitation of the Justices.'

John de Wolfe grunted, his favourite form of reply, and went to sit on the only other item of furniture, a bench on the opposite side of the trestle table. Gwyn parked his vast backside on a window-ledge, his usual resting place, where he stared again at his useless sword with morose concentration, until his master spoke to him.

'How long have you been my squire and companion, Gwyn?' he snapped.

The Cornishman frowned in concentration as he tried to work it out. He tugged at the ends of his ginger moustache that hung down almost to the collar of his scuffed leather jerkin, which had a pointed hood hanging down the back.

'In 'seventy-four, it was, Crowner!' he decided eventually. 'The year we first went to Ireland to fight for Richard Strongbow.'

'Twenty-one years, eh?' mused de Wolfe, leaning his elbows on the table. 'I think that deserves some mark of recognition.'

'What d'you mean?' grunted Gwyn, rather suspiciously.

'It means I'll buy you a new sword, you hairy oaf!

Meet me at the armourer's yard in Curre Street, straight after dinner.'

At noon, the coroner went home to his house in Martin's Lane, a narrow alley that joined High Street to the cathedral Close. He sat in his gloomy hall, his wife at the other end of the long table, while their cook-maid Mary served them. Boiled salt-fish and a grilled fowl appeared, with beans, onions and cabbage. These were speared or shovelled with a small eating-knife and a horn spoon from pewter bowls on to trenchers, slabs of yesterday's coarse bread which acted as plates.

Matilda de Wolfe, a stocky, pugnacious woman of forty-four, was in a bad mood and uttered not a single word during the whole meal. Mary winked at John as she passed behind her mistress with the wine-jug and grimaced to indicate that Matilda was in a touchy state of mind. He took the hint and held his tongue, knowing from bitter experience that anything he said would be turned against him, even if it was only an observation about the good spring weather.

As soon as the dessert of honeyed, boiled rice and dried apricots from southern France was finished, he muttered some excuse about attending a suspicious death and made his way out of the hall into the vestibule. This was a small area behind the street door, where cloaks and boots were kept. As he sat on a bench to take off his house shoes, Mary came around the corner of the covered passage that led to her kitchen hut, which shared the backyard with a wash-house, a privy and a pig-sty.

'What's her problem today?' he asked quietly, with a jerk of his head towards the hall door.

Mary, a handsome dark girl in her twenties, rolled her eyes. 'That maid of hers, Lucille, she trod on the hem of the mistress's best gown and ripped open a seam, just as she was going to St Olave's to pray! I've never heard such language from a lady!'

De Wolfe grinned and gave Mary a quick kiss as he opened the front door. They had been sporadic lovers in the past, but Matilda's suspicions had become too acute for it to continue.

'I'm off to buy Gwyn a new sword,' he explained. 'But don't let her know, she can't stand the sight of him.'

Curre Street was only a short distance away, a lane on the opposite side of High Street that ran towards the north wall of the city. It had a mixture of houses and shops, the buildings being mostly of wood, though some were now being replaced by stone. Exeter was thriving on its trade in wool, cloth and tin, which were exported not only over all England, but as far away as Flanders and the Rhine. Halfway along Curre Street, there was a substantial timber house with a roof of stone tiles, which had a yard at the side, from which came the sound of hammer on anvil.

Gwyn was there already, with their clerk Thomas de Peyne also in attendance. Though an unfrocked priest, the little man had an insatiable curiosity for all sorts of things and wanted to see where swords were bought and sold.

'Are you sure you want to do this, Crowner?' Gwyn asked uneasily. 'A good sword is expensive these days.' A gruff, independent character, the Cornishman did not want to be obligated to his master.

De Wolfe clapped his officer on his shoulder, a sensation similar to slapping a stone wall. 'How are you going to save my life next time, without a good blade?' he replied with rare jocularity, for the coroner was not renowned for his sense of humour.

They passed through a gate into the yard and skirting

the forge where two men were sweating over a furnace and anvil, went to a hut where the owner displayed his wares. Roger Trudogge, himself an old soldier, sat at a bench, carefully sewing an ornate leather sheath for a dagger, but put it aside as soon as he saw Sir John. They had known each other for years and soon they were picking over his stock, laid out on trestles at the sides of the hut. Thomas followed them around, his eyes wide at the sight of all these instruments of injury and death – chain-mail hauberks, shields, lances, daggers, maces, axes and swords.

It was soon obvious which weapon had caught Gwyn's critical eye. He kept returning to a sword with a handsome scabbard, that lay at the end of the display. Pulling the blade out, he hefted it to test the weight and balance, looked closely at the metal work of the hilt and pommel, then put it back. De Wolfe watched him with half-concealed amusement, as the big red-head made a show of looking at other swords, before drifting back yet again to his favourite. This time he drew it out and made some slashing motions in the air, both single-handed and with both of his great fists. Then with a sigh, he put it back into its sheath and laid it back on the table.

'That looks like the one you favour,' observed the coroner. 'It's even got hounds' heads on the hilt.' His officer had a marked affection for dogs, with whom he seemed to possess a strange empathy.

'It's a beautiful piece of work, right enough,' Gwyn answered longingly. 'And no doubt the most expensive of the lot.'

Trudogge, a burly man with a severe hare-lip, shook his head. 'Strange to say, it's not! One of the best blades I've ever had in my shop, but people are not keen on its history, so I'm selling it for less than it's worth.'

'What's wrong with it, then?' demanded Gwyn, suspiciously.

'Nothing wrong with the sword! It's who it belonged to, that puts folk off.'

The armourer explained that he had recently bought the weapon from the eldest son of the late Sir Henry de la Pomeroy, who wanted to get rid of everything that reminded him of his father. The coroner and his assistants immediately realized what the problem was, as they had been partly responsible for bringing it about.

'That was that bastard from Berry Pomeroy Castle,' exclaimed Gwyn. 'The traitor who turned against our king as soon as his back was turned!' When Richard the Lionheart had been captured by Leopold of Austria on his way home from the third Crusade, his younger brother Prince John had tried to seize the throne while Richard had been imprisoned in Germany for well over a year. Many of the barons and senior clerics had sided with John, including the Bishop of Exeter and Henry de la Pomeroy. However, as soon as the dramatic message *The devil is loose* had reached England just before Richard was released, many of the rebels panicked, suddenly regretting their dalliance with treason.

Thomas de Peyne, a most literate and knowledgeable fellow, knew all the details. 'Our king sent a herald down to Berry Pomeroy as soon as he came home, to tell Sir Henry that his guilt was known,' he recalled. 'But Pomeroy stabbed the messenger to death, then ran off to St Michael's Mount, where the castellan had already dropped dead of fright when he heard that the Lionheart was home!'

'I didn't know that bit of the story,' said Roger. 'What happened to him?'

'I know this, for Cornwall is my land!' broke in Gwyn, still grasping the sword. 'He made his surgeon open the veins in his wrist, so that he bled to death, to avoid the vengeance of the king!'

John de Wolfe nodded his agreement. 'Let's hope the son has more sense – and loyalty!' he grunted. 'Walter, do we know where Pomeroy got this weapon?'

The armourer took the sword from Gwyn, who seemed reluctant to let it go. He drew the blade from the scabbard again and held it so that they could see its quality. 'It's far older than his generation. His son said it was handed down through the family and there was a tradition that it was used at Hastings when William the Bastard defeated Harold Godwinson.'

'There's an inscription on the blade,' observed Thomas. He was the only one of the four who could read.

'What's it say?' demanded de Wolfe.

Thomas squinted at the Latin words engraved down the length of the weapon and gave a rough translation in English. 'It says that he who lives with falsehood, kills his own soul – and if he lies, he loses his honour.'

Gwyn shrugged. 'Seems common sense to me,' he growled.

After the coroner had taken the armourer aside for some haggling, they left Curre Street with Gwyn the proud possessor of a knight's sword. His thanks to his master were brief, but heartfelt. John de Wolfe knew that after more than twenty years' friendship, any effusive gratitude would have been misplaced.

When they returned to Rougemont, the Cornishman sought out Sergeant Gabriel and together they had an hour's sword-play in the castle's inner ward, so that he could get used to the feel of the hilt and the balance of the blade.

In the early evening, Gwyn made his way down to Milk Lane. Though almost in the centre of the city, its name was appropriate, as each of the dwellings had cows and goats on their plots, supplying milk to most of the townsfolk. His wife's elder sister was Helen, a buxom widow who made a living from her five cows and four nanny-goats. Her two sons tended the animals, carrying in hay and grass for fodder, and hawked milk and cheese around the streets, while Helen did the milking and made the cheese in the dairy shed behind the cottage.

This evening, Gwyn ambled to their temporary home, eager to tell his wife of the coroner's generosity, but Helen met him at the door with a worried expression.

'Agnes is unwell, Gwyn. All this trouble with the fire and the boys has done her no good at all. The wise woman from Rock Street is with her now, but I'm afraid it looks as if she's going to miscarry again.'

Next day was Tuesday, a hanging day. An unusually subdued Gwyn went with the coroner and his clerk to the gallows outside the city, along Magdalen Street. The coroner was required to record the event and to confiscate for the King's Treasury any property that the felon left behind.

Today was a lean harvest, as two of the four being executed were captured outlaws, with not a penny between them. Another was an old woman who had poisoned her neighbour by mistake, intending only to kill her house-cow out of spite. She had no property other than a few sticks of furniture, hardly worth the trouble of selling for the Crown. The last was a boy of fourteen, convicted of stealing a goblet worth twenty pence from a shop in North Street.

Once the ox-cart had rumbled from under the cross-beam, leaving the victims dangling and kicking – and when the screams and sobs of the relatives had faded after they had ceased pulling down on the legs to hasten death, the coroner's team walked back towards the city. Gwyn had told his master earlier about his sick children and his ailing wife.

'I'm sorry to hear of your troubles, Gwyn.' The deep voice of the coroner was sincere, though he rarely ventured into personal matters.

Thomas nodded in agreement, always a sympathetic soul. 'You have had more than your share of worries this past day or so,' he squeaked. 'May Christ and the Virgin spare you any more problems!' He crossed himself jerkily in his almost obsessional manner.

'Troubles always come in threes,' he grunted. 'Let's hope this is the end of them.'

'What's wrong with the lads?' asked Thomas, solicitously.

'Brother Saulf, the infirmarian from St John's Priory said they have the jaundice,' grunted Gwyn. 'I noticed as soon as I got up today, that their faces and eyes seemed yellow. He said there's nothing to be done, it seems that there are other cases in St Sidwell's. The monk suspects it's because the midden heap got washed into the well, when we had that flood a few weeks back.'

'I'll pray for them, but I expect they'll soon recover,' said Thomas reassuringly. 'And may the Holy Spirit protect your good wife, too.'

'She's miscarried twice before – and we've lost three babes before they were a month old,' said Gwyn sadly. 'Let's hope the two little lads will survive this.' Though the frailty of young life was accepted philosophically as God's will, John felt deeply for his henchman, as he knew how much he loved his family. To cover up the risk of showing any emotion, de Wolfe cleared his throat and marched on more briskly.

'Must get on! The noon bell has rung, my dinner will be on the table.'

After he had turned off into Martin's Lane, Gwyn

and the clerk continued up to the castle. Here Thomas went to pray for his friend in the little garrison chapel of St Mary, while Gwyn continued to the keep, a squat tower on the far side of the inner ward. He intended eating in the hall with his soldier friends, but on climbing the wooden stairs to the entrance, he was confronted with a familiar but unwelcome figure.

'There you are, you reckless savage!' snapped Walter Tyrell, almost hopping with angry impatience. 'Come with me, the sheriff is waiting.'

He grabbed Gwyn's arm, trying to pull him towards a door at the side of the large hall, noisy and bustling with the everyday business of Devon's administration. The coroner's officer stood like a rock, becoming irritated by his former landlord's persistence. 'What the hell do you want, Tyrell?' he growled.

Today the fuller wore a long yellow tunic under a dark blue mantle – which matched the colour of a large bruise on his left temple, where Gwyn had hit him the previous night.

'I'm indicting you for both the loss of the house I leased you and for assault!' he snapped. 'The sheriff is going to attach you and demand sureties for your appearance at the next County Court!'

'Don't be so bloody silly, man!' boomed the Cornishman, angrily shaking off Tyrell's arm.

'I've got witnesses, some of that rabble that was in St Sidwell's last night.'

'The same witnesses that will prove I asked you many times to fix the roof – and will say that you drew a knife on me!'

'They'll change their tune for the offer of a handful of silver pence!' jeered Walter.

Gwyn was just about to offer to give the man a matching bruise on the other side of his head, when the door of the sheriff's chamber jerked open. The man-at-arms on guard thumped the butt of his pike on the floor in salute as a slight figure stalked out, even more dandified in his appearance than his friend the fuller. Sir Richard de Revelle wore his favourite green, the tunic edged in gold tracery around the hem and neck. A light surcoat of crimson silk carried his family device of a blackbird on a green ground, embroidered on his shoulder. His light brown hair was brushed back from his narrow face, made even more saturnine by the pointed beard below his thin-lipped mouth.

Advancing on the pair near the main door, he brandished a piece of parchment and thrust it at Tyrell. 'Here, Walter, this is what you requested!'

Scowling at the coroner's officer, whom he knew and despised as a loyal servant of his brother-in-law, he added 'My clerk has prepared the writ you desired, so I'll see this fellow in front of me in the next Shire Court.'

With that he turned and marched away before Gwyn could get out a word of protest. The fuller leered at him. 'I've heard you're fond of games of chance – are you willing to wager what the verdict will be before the sheriff next week?'

Though Exeter now had over four thousand souls living within its walls, the portreeves and burgesses who ran the city council still employed only two constables to keep the peace. One was Osric, a tall skinny Saxon, the other an older, fatter man called Theobald. Their headquarters was a tiny hut behind the Guildhall in High Street, left behind by the masons who had recently rebuilt the hall in stone.

The two men, carrying the heavy staves which were their only means of keeping order in the city, left together on patrol an hour before midnight and headed down Waterbeer Street. This was a lane parallel to the main street, which held a mixture of dwelling-houses, shops, taverns, two apothecaries and several brothels. One of their prime duties was to enforce the curfew, keeping an eye out for uncovered fires which might pose a threat to the still largely timber-built city, though dealing with unruly drunks staggering out of ale-houses was their other main concern.

Tonight, neither of these tasks occupied them as they walked down Waterbeer Street. Theobald discovered a corpse by the simple process of tripping over it in the gloom, as its feet were protruding from a narrow alley alongside a leather-worker's shop. Osric held up his horn lantern, which contained a single candle, to shed its feeble light on the body and saw blood oozing from a terrible wound in the neck.

'Someone's down the alley!' bleated Theobald in his squeaky voice and with surprising agility for one with such a prominent ale-belly, started off in pursuit of the rapid footsteps that they had both heard.

The Saxon knelt by the victim, but having seen many corpses during his time as a constable, he knew straight away that he was beyond help. The blood was no longer pumping, but merely oozing from the jagged tear that extended from below the left ear to just above the breastbone, indicating that his heart had already stopped. Osric opened the little door of yellow cow-horn on his lantern to get a better light and held it up above the face of the dead man.

'God's whiskers, it's Walter Tyrell!' he muttered to himself. The constables knew virtually every prominent citizen by sight, especially burgesses like the fuller. As he rose to his feet, Theobald came trotting back, puffing after his unaccustomed exertion.

'Lost him in those back alleys!' he gasped. 'Not a sign of anyone in that rabbit-warren.'

Osric, who was senior both by length of service and

superior brain-power, started to give orders. 'You must raise the hue and cry at once. Knock up the four nearest households – in fact, make it six! Get the men from each to search all the lanes and streets around, seeking anyone abroad at this hour, especially anyone with blood on their garments or shoes. Then go around each of the gates and make sure they let no one out tonight.'

The corpulent officer looked slightly rebellious at this, especially after his recent gallop down the alley and back. 'So what are you going to do?'

'The coroner will want to deal with this from the start, so I'm away to rouse Sir John from his bed.'

As he hurried away, he only hoped that de Wolfe was in his own bed and not that of his mistress, down at the Bush Inn.

'A bloody great slash, Gwyn!' observed the coroner, with professional detachment. 'Right down to the bones of his neck.'

He rose from a crouch and stared down at the cadaver, from which a wide pool of blood had now seeped into the packed earth of the alley. 'It could be from a large knife, a sickle, a hedging hook or a meat cleaver.'

'Or a sword, Crowner?'

Something in Gwyn's voice made John stare at him from under his beetling black brows. 'Yes, it could well be a sword. Why do you ask?'

His officer grunted mirthlessly. 'Because only last night, I offered to take off his head with my sword!'

He gave his master a detailed account of his altercation with Tyrell and the fact that only today, the fuller had got the sheriff to issue a writ for assault.

'But that's nothing, all you did was punch his head in self-defence against him drawing a blade on you! You've witnesses to prove it.'

'And he boasted that he had already bribed others to say differently!' Gwyn pointed to the body on the ground, visible in the flickering light of pitch brands held by a couple of residents of Waterbeer Street. They were part of a small crowd who had been roused from their beds by the constables and were now gawking at the drama, after unsuccessfully racing around the streets looking for the killer.

'Those were just idle words of yours, spoken in the heat of the moment!' snapped de Wolfe. 'You can easily prove you had nothing to do with this.'

'How can I do that?' growled Gwyn. 'I was not at home with my wife, because there is no room at her sister's. I was walking back from Milk Street to Rougemont when this must have happened, as I'm bedding down in the soldier's quarters there.'

The coroner gestured impatiently. 'Nothing will come of this, Gwyn, it's all in your imagination. Who on earth is going to accuse my officer of murder, eh?'

As the words left his mouth, he realized that one person would be delighted to do so. Gwyn, watching his face, knew that the thought had entered John's mind.

'Exactly, Crowner! And with the endless bad luck I've been having these past days, the sheriff's very likely to try it on. Especially since this man Tyrell is one of his cronies and has already brought the assault to his notice.'

De Wolfe pondered for moment, the scowl deepening on his bony face. 'Look, just to be on the safe side, you had better not become involved as my officer in this case. Though I'm sure no one will accuse you, it is wiser for you to keep out of it, to avoid any accusations of partiality.'

'But how can you hold an inquest without my help?' objected Gwyn.

'I can get Thomas to do what's necessary, just this once. If anyone notices, we can say that your family troubles are the reason. In fact, I think you should be with them at this difficult time.'

Grudgingly, the Cornishman agreed and stood aside as the constables arranged for the corpse to be taken away. Though a disused cart-shed in the castle was the usual depository for casual deaths, it was considered too degrading for a prominent merchant like Walter Tyrell. Instead, a mortuary shed in the churchyard of nearby St Pancras was thought more appropriate and soon the mortal remains of the fuller were carried away by four locals, using a detached door as a bier.

The hue and cry having failed to achieve anything, there was nothing for the coroner to do until morning, so he made his way back home, after trying to reassure his officer that all would be well. Gwyn was unconvinced, as he trudged back up the hill to Rougemont. He felt his new sword slapping against his leg as he walked and put a hand on the beautifully-crafted hilt to steady it.

'You've not brought me much luck so far,' he muttered. 'Let's hope you do better from now on!'

John de Wolfe arrived at the castle gatehouse an hour after dawn next morning, to be greeted by Sergeant Gabriel with a message from the sheriff, demanding his attendance upon him forthwith. The coroner delayed for another hour, to show his independence from Richard de Revelle and spent it up in his barren chamber with Thomas, giving him instructions about the inquest on the fuller. Eventually he loped across the inner ward to the keep and with a perfunctory nod to the man-at-arms outside, marched into the sheriff's room without knocking. His brother-in-law was seated behind his parchment-strewn table and looked up in annoyance at John's lack of deference.

'You took your time, I sent for you long ago!' he snapped.

'I'm the *king's* coroner, not the sheriff's!' retorted de Wolfe. 'I'm not at your beck and call. I have other things to do, like arranging the inquest on this fuller.' The sheriff laid down a quill pen and regarded John with a smug expression, which held a hint of triumph. 'Indeed, your petty inquest! I fear that very soon, that matter will be presented to a far more important court.'

John glowered suspiciously at his brother-in-law. 'What do you mean by that?'

Richard stood up, carefully smoothing the creases from his cream linen tunic. 'I think I shall attend this inquest of yours, John,' he said smoothly. 'Where and when is it to be held?'

Guessing what was in de Revelle's mind, John answered grudgingly. 'An hour before noon, in the churchyard of St Pancras.'

The sheriff's neat head nodded curtly. 'I shall be there. Walter Tyrell was a good friend of mine, it is only right that I should pay my respects to his memory.' With an insolent wave of dismissal, he walked to the inner door of his chamber and vanished into his living quarters, shutting the door behind him with a bang.

Fuming with frustration and not a little worried at the way things were moving, de Wolfe stamped back to the gatehouse and sat drumming his fingers on his table. Thomas sensed his master's ill-temper and wisely made himself scarce, claiming that he was off to round up a jury for the inquest.

'You'd better call in at Milk Lane and tell Gwyn that he should keep away,' ordered the coroner, as the little clerk reached the doorway. 'There's no point in exposing him to the spite of the sheriff, for I've a good idea of what de Revelle is trying to do.'

This only succeeded in transferring some of John's anxieties to his clerk and with a worried frown, Thomas pattered off into the busy city streets. An insignificant figure in his threadbare cassock, he pushed his way through the morning crowds of wives doing their shopping, stall-holders and hawkers yelling the merits of their goods, porters pushing barrows and others humping great bales of wool. Calling in at the constable's hut, he confirmed that Osric and his colleague were collecting all those who had been present at the scene in Waterbeer Street and making sure they would be at the inquest. From previous experience, the constables were well aware of the coroner's wrath if the arrangements failed to run smoothly and Thomas was confident that the jury would be assembled on time.

Then he set off again to reach Carfoix, the central crossing of the main roads from each of the four gates, the street plan not having altered since Roman times. Crossing to South Gate Street, he averted his head from the daily scene in the Shambles, where cattle and sheep were being slaughtered in the street, blood and offal clogging the central gutter. He hurried on and turned through several lanes to reach Milk Street, to find Gwyn in the large plot behind his sister-in-law's cottage. He was milking a large red cow, who was munching away unconcernedly from a bag of hay hung from her tethering post. A small calf stood nearby, looking indignantly at this large red-headed man who was pouring half her dinner into a wooden bucket.

Thomas delivered his message about the inquest and Gwyn nodded resignedly. 'I thought this would happen, the bloody sheriff won't miss a chance like this.' He pulled his head away from the cow's flank and called across to Helen, who was sitting on a stool near the back door, plucking a chicken, several more dead fowls lay at her feet.

'I'll finish milking the other two beasts, then I'll kill that goose for you,' he shouted, before putting his hands back to the udder.

'How is your wife?' asked Thomas solicitously.

'Agnes is just the same, thank you,' said Gwyn. 'She's not lost the babe so far, though she is still bleeding a little. The good-wife who attends her says that she must lie still for some days, if she is to keep it.'

'And the boys?'

'They're no worse, but are listless and can't stand daylight in their eyes. Neither have any appetite, which proves they are unwell, as they are usually as hungry as dogs!'

Thomas, a kindly man who always sympathized with the misfortunes of others, did his best to cheer his friend from his obvious gloom. 'I can do little for you but pray, Gwyn, but if there is anything else . . .'

'Thank you, Thomas! I seem to be cursed with ill luck these past few days. If what I fear will happen, I'll need all the prayers you can muster, so keep in practise!'

'Oyez, oyez, all those who have anything to do before the King's coroner for the County of Devon, draw near and give your attendance.'

Opening the inquest, Thomas's reedy voice contrasted markedly with the stentorian bellow that Gwyn used when he officiated, but it was sufficient to quieten the score of men who were shuffling into a half-circle before the small shed that acted as the mortuary. Behind them, a small crowd of onlookers, some of them women, craned their necks to follow the proceedings. They were all in the dusty yard behind St

Pancras's Church in the middle of the city, but most of the jury wished they were elsewhere, as they had other business to attend to.

The door on which Walter Tyrell's body had been carried was now resting on two small barrels outside the shed and the corpse itself was decorously covered with a grubby blanket. Alongside it stood Sir John de Wolfe, a ferocious scowl on his face, his usual expression for such legal events. He wore a grey tunic down to his calves, clinched by a thick leather belt, which carried a dagger, but no sword. The spring morning was chill, so he had a mottled wolfskin cloak slung over his shoulders.

After piping his opening chant, Thomas went to sit on a smaller barrel, a board across his knees carrying a parchment roll and pen and ink, on which to record the proceedings. The coroner stepped forward, his fists on his hips, to glare around the assembled jury and the spectators crowded behind them.

'This is to enquire as to where, when and by what means this man came to his death.' He waved a hand at the still shape under the sheet.

'He was identified to me earlier this morning by his brother and his widow as Walter Tyrell, a fuller of East Gate Street. Now the First Finder will step forward!'

At this command, the older constable Theobald moved to stand before the coroner and doffed his woollen cap, revealing his bald patch. He related how late last night he and Osric had come across the cadaver at the entrance to the alley. 'We heard footsteps running away and I gave chase, but was too late to catch anyone,' he said virtuously.

He went on to say how they had raised the hue and cry, rousing all the householders from the nearby dwellings. Failure to have done this would have resulted in a stiff fine, but the town constables knew their business in this respect. Several other witnesses from Waterbeer Street were called, but all they could add was confirmation of what Theobald and Osric had already described. No one had seen the person running away down the alley nor had they seen Tyrell in the street that night.

De Wolfe then called the widow, who was helped forward by her brother-in-law, a partner in Walter Tyrell's fulling-mill business. Christina, a handsome blonde much younger than her late husband, wore a grey kirtle as a sign of mourning, but was quite composed and seemed in no need of her escort's support.

The coroner softened his manner slightly in deference to her bereaved state. 'What was your husband doing in the streets that late at night?'

The woman shrugged. 'He often went out, either to do business or to meet some friends in a tavern. The New Inn and the Plough were his favourite places. I think he was going to pay some merchant for a consignment of fleeces, but I'm not sure.'

'Can you think of any reason why someone might have slain your husband?' John asked bluntly. 'Did he have any enemies that you were aware of?'

Christina shook her head. 'He never spoke much of his business affairs, sir. I can only think that he was set upon by thieves, intent on robbing him.'

John looked across at Osric. 'Did he have money upon him when he was found?'

'No, Crowner, he had no purse nor scrip on his belt.'

De Wolfe grunted, as at least one motive – robbery – was a possibility, especially if he had much coin upon him to pay a business debt.

Christina had nothing more to contribute and she stepped back, but John motioned to her brother-in-law to remain and demanded his name.

'Serlo Tyrell, sir. I was the dead man's brother – and his partner in the business we run on Exe Island.'

'Do you know of any enemies he might have had, who might wish him ill?'

Serlo, a tall man with curly black hair, was at least a decade younger than his dead brother. He shuffled his feet uncomfortably. 'Well, only the quarrel he had with that Cornishman of yours, begging your pardon,' he muttered.

A murmur ran around the jury and heads turned and nodded. It seemed that the squabble in St Sidwell had become common knowledge in the city.

'That was a petty matter!' snapped de Wolfe, irritably. 'I mean do you know of any reason why someone should want to murder your brother?'

'Well, that big ginger fellow said he'd cut off Walter's head!' retorted Serlo, stubbornly.

As the coroner impatiently waved the man back into the crowd, he caught sight of Richard de Revelle standing at the back of the yard, near the gate. He had a supercilious leer on his face, but rather to John's surprise, made no effort to intervene in the proceedings. No one else had anything to contribute to the sparse evidence, so John addressed the jury-men, three of whom were lads barely fourteen years old.

'The law demands that you now inspect the body and come to a verdict. I can tell you that in this case there is still much to be done to discover who might be the perpetrator, so the inquest cannot yet be completed.'

He glared around, as if daring anyone to contradict him. 'However, the corpse needs to be returned to the family for decent burial as soon as possible.'

He beckoned to Thomas, and reluctantly, the little clerk left his parchments and came across to do Gwyn's job. Turning his head aside, he pulled back the sheet from the dead body, so that the jury could file past while the coroner gave a running commentary.

'You will see the deceased has suffered a massive wound in the neck, which has cut through his skin and flesh down to the bones.'

Some of the jury were old soldiers or had worked on farms where blood and mangled flesh was no novelty, but others became deathly pale and several covered up their eyes, looking through slits between their fingers, as if this would reduce the horror. Curiously, the widow Christina stared stoically across the yard at her husband's corpse, ignoring Serlo's comforting arm around her shoulders.

'The skin shows jagged edges, where the blade of some weapon has been dragged across the neck,' went on de Wolfe remorselessly.

The oldest juror, who John recognized as a former man-at-arms from Rougemont, asked him a question after they had all filed past. 'What weapon did that, Crowner? It must have been sharp and heavy.'

De Wolfe nodded. 'A long knife or a cleaver – or maybe a hedging hook.' He deliberately avoided mentioning a sword, but the old soldier foiled him.

'Could have been a sword, I reckon. Gone deep into the neck.'

'It could have been,' agreed the coroner, but he added evasively, 'But who carries a sword within the city walls?'

There seemed little else to discuss and after going into a huddle for a moment, the jury reached their verdict. The old soldier spoke up for them.

'We agree that he was slain, but we can't tell who did it,' he announced, rather truculently. De Wolfe nodded and put his informal decision more officially.

'Then I proclaim that Walter Tyrell was found dead in Waterbeer Street on the eighth day of April in the year of Our Lord 1195 and that he was murdered against the King's Peace by a person or persons unknown.'

The proceedings over, the jury thankfully melted away and the corpse was transferred to a handcart to take it back to the house. As he watched the widow escorted away by the dead man's brother, John wondered if Serlo would take over more of Walter's duties than just running the fulling mill. Still, it was none of his business and he turned to Thomas, who was gathering up his writing materials.

'That didn't get us very far,' he grumbled. 'I doubt we'll ever find who killed the fellow.'

'Try a little nearer home, John!' came a voice behind him and turning sharply, he saw it was the sheriff, who must have walked around the edge of the yard to come upon him unawares.

'And just what do you mean by that, Richard?'

De Revelle, richly attired against the cool day in a cloak lined with ermine, gave his brother-in-law a sardonic smile.

'You know well enough what I mean. That great lump of a Cornishman that you employ is at the bottom of this – and I mean to bring him to justice, for it's clear that you'll do nothing.'

'Gwyn? Don't talk such nonsense, why should he be involved in this?'

De Revelle leered at John. 'He struck Walter Tyrell, then threatened to cut his head off – by the looks of that wound, he almost succeeded!'

'My officer had nothing to do with this! You're just intent on making trouble.'

The sheriff pirouetted on one of his fashionably long-toed shoes. 'So why wasn't he here doing his usual duties? You are keeping him out of sight, perhaps?'

The gibe was too near the truth for comfort, but

John retaliated. 'The man has family troubles – both his wife and his children are sick.'

'Don't try to evade the issue, John. I have two witnesses who will swear to hearing his threats. Tyrell had quite rightly appealed this ruffian, both for assault and for restitution of the house that was destroyed through your man's negligence.'

Impatiently, de Wolfe swung away from his brother-in-law. 'I've got better things to do that listen to your vindictive nonsense, Richard.' He gestured angrily at his clerk. 'Come on, Thomas, we've work to do back at Rougemont!' He strode away, but the sheriff's voice followed him.

'I'm having him arrested, John – for assault and suspicion of murder!'

That afternoon, a group of worried people gathered in the Bush Inn in Idle Lane, a tavern in the lower part of the city, towards the West Gate. In the large tap-room that formed the whole ground floor, John de Wolfe sat at his favourite table near the fire-pit, with Gwyn and Thomas sitting opposite. Next to him was Nesta, his mistress and landlady of the ale-house. She was a pretty Welsh widow of twenty-eight, with a heart-shaped face and a snub nose, whose auburn-hair peeped out from under her coif, a linen helmet tied under her chin. The coroner and his officer had quart pots of Nesta's best ale in front of them and Thomas had a small cup of cider. The drink failed to cheer any of them, as they were discussing the sheriff's threat to arrest Gwyn.

'He doesn't give a damn about Walter Tyrell or his death,' growled de Wolfe. 'This is just a golden opportunity to get back at me.'

There was a continuing feud between the coroner and sheriff, as John had good reason to suspect Richard of both embezzling from the county taxes and being an active sympathizer with the Prince John faction, still aiming to unseat King Richard from the throne. Though their last rebellion had failed – which was how Gwyn had come by his new sword that had belonged to the traitor Pomeroy – there were still powerful men who supported the younger prince. Richard de Revelle had political ambitions and hoped that by secretly adhering to the rebels, he would eventually reap his reward when John became king.

'He's got no proof, only a couple of lying bastards from St Sidwell who would testify to anything for a handful of pennies!' said the coroner, trying to reassure the Cornishman.

Gwyn was not so sanguine about the situation. 'Tyrell had already got a writ from the sheriff accusing me of assaulting him and demanding compensation for his burned house,' he grunted. 'So when Tyrell turns up dead, de Revelle reckons I had a good reason to get rid of him.'

'But there's no proof, Gwyn,' piped up Thomas, anxious for the welfare of his colleague. Though Gwyn teased him unmercifully, they were the best of friends, the big man always being very protective of the puny ex-priest.

'When did that awful man ever need proof?' said Nesta bitterly. She had seen examples in the past of the Sheriff's vindictiveness.

'What can we do?' shrilled Thomas, almost beside himself with anxiety. 'Would it be best if Gwyn left the city for a while – maybe went down to Cornwall to stay with his relatives?'

De Wolfe shook his head. 'That would be looked on as running away and an admission of guilt. We have to fight this malicious attempt with the truth!'

'Find the swine who really killed Tyrell, that's the only way,' growled Gwyn.

'Exactly! And I'll start this very day,' promised the coroner. 'The problem is that you can't be involved, Gwyn – at least not openly.'

'I'll do what I can, sir,' offered Thomas, desperate to do something to help his big friend. 'I have many contacts amongst the lower ranks of the clergy. They are a gossipy lot and know much of what goes on in the city, as well as in the cathedral Close.'

Nesta, not to be outdone, also promised to sound out her patrons. The Bush was a popular tavern and her strong ale was very effective in loosening the tongues of the scores of drinkers who passed through every day.

With no more ideas to discuss, de Wolfe sent Gwyn back to Milk Lane to be with his ailing family and then took himself up to Rougemont to see if any of the idle chatter in the hall might throw any light on Walter Tyrell's private life.

A little over an hour later, Sergeant Gabriel climbed the steps of the keep, a worried expression on his rugged face. He stood inside the main door for a moment, scanning the busy hall. Clerks bustled about with documents, pushing past groups of townsfolk and country bailiffs awaiting audience with officials. A few off-duty soldiers mingled with merchants and a few priests. Some were eating or drinking at tables, others were in animated conversation or raucous laughter. Gabriel soon spotted John de Wolfe leaning against the bare stone wall near the half-circle of the fire-pit, a quart mug of ale in his hand. He was talking earnestly to a couple of burgesses, hoping to get some information about the dead fuller's business affairs.

The sergeant went across to him and discreetly touched his arm. 'Sir John, I think you had better come down to the undercroft straight away,' he said quietly, with a jerk of his head to emphasize the urgency.

The coroner excused himself from his acquaintances and setting his ale-pot down on a nearby table, followed Gabriel across to the entrance.

'What's going on? Why the undercroft?' This was the damp and gloomy basement of the keep, part of it being used for the castle gaol, the rest for storage.

'The sheriff has had Gwyn arrested! He sent four of my men-at-arms down for him, without even telling me.' Gabriel was outraged at this, as well as being anxious for Gwyn, his closest drinking and gaming friend.

John clattered down the stairs, furious but not altogether surprised at the sudden turn of events. 'The bloody man is determined to get at me over this!' he snarled. 'But I didn't think he'd act so quickly.'

They hurried to the entrance of the undercroft, which was partly below ground level. Ducking under a low arch at the bottom of the few steps, they entered a wide, gloomy vault, the roof supported by pillars. On the left was a stone wall with a rusty metal grille, leading into the prison cells. Outside this was a small group of people, dimly lit by the flickering flames of several pitch torches set in rings on the wall. As well as a few uneasy-looking soldiers standing around Gwyn's towering figure, John also saw the sheriff and his chief clerk. The others included Ralph Morin, the constable of the castle – and Tyrell's widow Christina and his brother Serlo. In the background hovered two men who had been neighbours of Gwyn's in St Sidwell – and there was Stigand, the grossly obese gaoler, looking as if he was hoping for a chance to employ his implements of torture.

De Wolfe strode across to the group and, ignoring the sheriff, spoke to Ralph Morin, a good friend who shared his dislike of Richard de Revelle. 'What in hell's going on, Ralph?' he demanded in a loud voice.

Morin, another very large man with a forked beard

that enhanced his resemblance to a Viking warrior, began to explain, but was cut across by the strident tones of the sheriff.

'I've had him arrested, John! And unless he can produce some very good evidence of his innocence, he's going straight to prison to await trial at my court next week!'

John stepped across to stand close in front of his brother-in-law and glared down furiously from his greater height.

'So, he's guilty until proved innocent, is he? I thought it was supposed to be the other way around!'

De Revelle stepped back hastily, half-afraid that John was going to strike him. Then he swept an arm around to indicate wife and brother. 'These good people came to me after your travesty of an inquest today, to demand proper justice! You did nothing to name or even place suspicion on any perpetrator!'

'If you knew anything about the law, Richard, you'd realize that an inquest is not a trial! That's down to the king's justices when they come to the Eyre of Assize.'

'Nonsense! For centuries, my Shire Court has been sufficient for any type of case. Your new-fangled royal courts are merely a device to extort money!'

De Wolfe gave a mocking laugh. 'Well, you're an expert in that subject, Sheriff! Now what are you doing here with my officer? He's a servant of the king like me, so tread very carefully.'

Serlo Tyrell stepped forward, indignant and truculent. 'That big Cornishman killed my brother and left this woman widowed. Everything points to him, and we want justice!'

'I never killed anyone!' yelled Gwyn, who had so far held his tongue. 'Even though it means speaking ill of the dead, that Walter falsely accused me of letting his poxy cottage burn down. Then he struck me and when I defended myself, he pulled a knife on me!'

'And then you threatened to kill him,' cried the sheriff, in his high pitched voice. 'These two men from St Sidwell will vouch for that.' He pointed at the pair, who shuffled their feet uncomfortably.

'And when and how is he supposed to have done that?' demanded John. The widow entered the fray, with a harsh demand to know where Gwyn was at the time of the murder. 'He could have been anywhere about the streets!' shrilled Christina. 'Ask him where he was.'

'I was down with my family in Milk Lane!' boomed Gwyn, angrily. 'Then I went back to a game of dice in the castle guardroom until I found a bed in one of the barrack huts.'

'That's easy to say, fellow!' snapped de Revelle. 'Can you prove it?'

Exasperated, Gwyn turned to de Wolfe. 'Do I have to answer these damn-fool questions, Crowner? My wife and all my sister's family will vouch for me being there – and half the bloody garrison saw me at Rougemont!'

Before John could answer him, the sheriff snapped out another question, intent on building a web of suspicion around the Cornishman.

'And what time did you leave Milk Lane – and when did you arrive at the castle, eh?'

'How the hell would I know? I don't carry a graduated church candle about with me! The cathedral is the only place that knows the time in this city. It was all before the Matins bell, that's for sure.'

John was getting increasingly angry with his brother-in-law. 'These questions are futile, Richard! As my officer says, who can tell the time except by guesswork? It is either night or day and apart from that, the cathedral bells are the only measure we have. Unless you have some better evidence than this, I suggest we all go home!'

De Revelle smirked and preened himself by throwing one edge of his furred cloak over a shoulder to reveal his fine embroidered tunic.

'At this so-called inquest you held today, you admitted to the jury that the mortal injuries suffered by the victim could have been caused by a sword. Is that not correct, John?'

'Of course, it is possible,' agreed John, suspiciously. 'But they could equally well have been made by a dagger, a large carving knife or even a reaping hook.'

'But your servant there habitually carries a sword,' continued de Revelle suavely. 'In fact, I understand that he has just acquired a new one.' He turned and snapped his fingers at the gaoler, who waddled to a nearby table and brought across Gwyn's weapon, resplendent in its handsome scabbard.

'This is the one, is it not? It was taken from the dwelling in Milk Street when I had him arrested.'

Gwyn stared blankly at the sword, then at the sheriff, who stood with a smugly satisfied expression on his narrow face. 'Yes, that's mine! What of it?'

De Wolfe took a step forward and snatched it from Stigand's hands. He partly withdrew the blade to satisfy himself by the Latin inscription that it was indeed the weapon that he had purchased for his officer.

'So what significance has this, Sheriff?' he demanded. 'Would you like to see my sword as well?' he added sarcastically. 'And those of the hundreds of men in Exeter who carry one?'

'I have no interest in other men's swords, John,' retorted Richard smoothly. 'Only the one belonging to the man who had the best motive and the opportunity to kill Walter Tyrell.'

He stepped across to de Wolfe and withdrew the

blade completely from its sheath. Waving it gently about, he spoke again to the mystified Gwyn. 'This weapon came into your possession only within the last couple of days – and before that, did it not lay for some time with Roger Trudogge, a well-known armourer of this city?'

Gwyn grudgingly grunted his agreement, still unclear as to where all this was leading.

'And no doubt, that good armourer would have cleaned and polished the sword, to increase his chances of selling it?'

Again Gwyn could not deny that that was probable and watched with a furrowed brow as Richard de Revelle pulled out a handkerchief of fine white cambric from the sleeve of his tunic. Stigand had obviously been primed beforehand, as he held out a small leather bucket of moderately clean rain-water. The sheriff dipped his kerchief into it, then squeezed the water from it, so that it remained damp.

'So as that armourer had thoroughly cleaned this blade, anything found upon it must have got there since you took possession?'

De Revelle obviously expected no answer to his question, as he began busily running the folded linen down the full length of the blade, taking particular care to press it along edges of the central rib and into the indentations of the inscriptions. Handing the sword back to Stigand, he opened out the handkerchief and with a flourish, displayed it to the curious onlookers.

With a scream, Christina Tyrell staggered against her brother-in-law, who grabbed her to prevent her falling.

'My husband's blood!' she screeched dramatically, conveniently forgetting that she had gazed unmoved at the far worse sight of his mutilated body during the inquest.

The sheriff triumphantly waved the pink-stained

cloth at de Wolfe. 'Can anyone now doubt that this lethal weapon has been used to slash flesh and draw blood since it was purchased?' he brayed. 'I now charge that man, Gwyn of Polruan, with the murder of Walter Tyrell. Take him away and see that he is brought before me at the Shire Court next week!'

There was confusion in the undercroft for several minutes, as Gwyn struggled against the four soldiers who closed in on him. The widow continued to wail and sob, the dead man's brother began shouting abuse at the suspect and the sheriff hurried away, a satisfied leer on his face.

Only John de Wolfe remained ominously calm, as he picked a small object from the edge of the slot in Gwyn's scabbard and carefully placed it in the pouch on his belt.

'It was a damned set-up, that's what it was!' snarled John, thumping the table with his fist. He was back in the Bush again that afternoon, with Nesta and Thomas, but instead of the usual Gwyn, Sergeant Gabriel was sitting in his place.

'So how did that blood get on the blade, master?' quavered Thomas. 'As the sheriff said, the sword must have been well-cleaned by that armourer, before he offered it for sale.'

De Wolfe fished in the pouch on his belt and pulled out a small wisp of something, which he carefully laid on the boards of the trestle. He placed the edge of his ale-mug on it, to stop it being blown away.

'I picked that from the top edge of the scabbard,' he explained. 'It was stuck by a little blob of dried blood to the slot where the blade enters.'

Nesta peered at it closely. 'It's a tiny feather! From a red chicken, by the looks of it.' John nodded, a grim expression on his face. 'Faked evidence! After Gwyn's sword was snatched from the house in Milk Lane when they arrested him, either de Revelle, or more likely someone acting for him, quickly smeared some blood from a dead fowl on the blade and let it dry.'

Thomas nodded his understanding 'Of course! Why else would the sheriff even think of rubbing the blade with his handkerchief, unless he already knew that he could discover some blood?'

'How can he be allowed to get away with it?' hissed Nesta, livid with anger at this plot against one of her best friends.

De Wolfe shrugged helplessly. 'He represents the king! In Devon, there's no one who can dispute his authority.'

'Can't you appeal to someone over de Revelle's head?' she asked.

'It would take too long, my love!' he replied bitterly. 'It would take a couple of weeks to get a response from the Chief Justiciar in Winchester, even assuming he was there and not in London – or even visiting the king in Normandy.'

The grizzled sergeant nodded. 'The bloody sheriff will have Gwyn convicted and hanged before then, for that's what he wants.'

'Can the bishop do nothing?' persisted Nesta, her face pale with anxiety. 'Surely he wouldn't want an innocent man executed?'

John gave a harsh, cynical laugh. 'Henry Marshal? He's almost as bad as de Revelle. A secret supporter of Prince John's treachery – he wouldn't lift a finger to help.'

Thomas surreptitiously crossed himself at this defamation of the leader of the Church in Devon and Cornwall, though privately he knew it was true. 'Is there nothing we can do?' he wailed. 'We can't let Gwyn go to the gallows next week.'

'He's being kept in the city gaol in the South Gate,' muttered Gabriel. 'The cells in Rougemont are full until the next hanging day.'

The substantial towers that flanked the southern entrance to the city were used to house prisoners remanded by the burgess's court of the city, as well as for some sent there by the sheriff's County Court. It was a foul, cramped dungeon and like most gaols, many of the inmates in there died from disease or being killed by other prisoners, before they ever came to trial.

'The only hope is to find the real killer,' sobbed Nesta, clinging on to John's arm.

'That's almost impossible, given the short time we have,' snarled the coroner.

'So we need more time!' declared the sergeant. 'Which means we've got to get him out of there . . . now listen to me!'

Four heads bent together over the table and began muttering in conspiratorial tones.

The following night, several shadowy figures moved around the city, in addition to the usual drunks and furtive patrons of the numerous brothels.

One who was not out and about was the coroner, who as a royal officer himself, needed to stay well clear of any nefarious activity. To establish his innocence in advance, he stayed in his own hall all evening, much to his wife's surprise, for he usually found an excuse to take his old hound Brutus for a long walk each night, a transparent excuse to go down to the Bush Inn to visit his mistress.

John even raided his wine cupboard and opened a stone jar of his best Loire red, insisting that Matilda sample a few glasses, as they sat by their hearth. This considerate domesticity made his wife somewhat suspicious, but she could hardly complain at his solicitous behaviour, however unusual it might be. Later that evening, when she retired to bed in her solar, John feigned tiredness and insisted on accompanying her, though he drew the line at anything but a rapid descent into sleep.

Meanwhile, out in the darkened city, Thomas de Peyne was slinking around the back of the Guildhall to reach the constable's hut, at a time when he knew they would be fortifying themselves with bread, cheese and ale before going on their late night rounds. Sympathetic to Gwyn's plight and like most people, contemptuous of the sheriff's corruption, they readily agreed to the clerk's request for them to direct their feet towards the north side of the city for the next hour or so, keeping away from the cathedral area.

The disgraced priest then slipped away towards the Close, the large area around the massive cathedral of St Peter and St Mary. This was mainly a burial ground, flanked by the houses of the canons and various small chapels and churches. It had a series of entrances from other streets, in one of which, Martin's Lane, the coroner lived. Thomas kept well away from there and lurked under an arch leading to Southgate Street. It was too early for the bell to summon the clergy to Matins, so the Close was quiet, with just a few beggars and drunks fast asleep against the burial mounds.

Soon, footsteps approached and the figure of Sergeant Gabriel appeared, a hooded cloak over the leather jerkin that was part of his military garb.

'All's well,' reported Thomas, in a conspiratorial whisper. 'Osric and Theobald have decided to patrol up near the North Gate tonight.' He reached into a pocket inside his shabby cassock, the only remnant of his ecclesiastical past, and handed over a heavy purse. 'The coroner says that this should be sufficient for your purpose.'

Gabriel, with a furtive look up and down the dark alley, slid the purse into his own cloak. 'Wait here, Thomas! We should be back within a few minutes.'

He vanished into the darkness, leaving the little clerk in a state of acute anxiety, his teeth chattering partly from the chill night, but mainly from fear of being discovered. The few minutes promised by Gabriel seemed to lengthen into hours and the prospect of being arrested and cast into a cell himself began to strengthen in his fevered mind. He was just trying to decide if the penalty for gaol-breaking would be hanging or mutilation, when the sergeant materialized again, with Gwyn close behind.

'Thank God and all his angels!' gabbled the clerk, crossing himself convulsively in his relief.

'No time for gabbing now,' snapped Gabriel. 'Let's get him safely put away.'

They hurried across the Close, passing before the great West Front of the cathedral, dimly seen in the starlight. A muddy path between open grave-pits and older mounds took them diagonally across to the opening into Martin's Lane, but instead of passing the coroner's dwelling, Thomas stopped before a heavy door set into the front of a small white-washed church with a plain, narrow tower. Twisting the iron ring, he pushed it open and ushered the others inside.

'Here you are, Gwyn, a safe haven for the next forty days! Even the sheriff won't dare to have you dragged out of here, this is God's sanctuary!'

'How did he take it, John?' asked Nesta the next evening, as they lay together on her mattress in the Bush, where a corner of the loft had been partitioned off as a bedroom for the landlady.

De Wolfe's craggy face split into a rare smile as he recalled the sheriff that morning, almost incandescent with rage at the news of Gwyn's escape into sanctuary.

'He was fit to have a seizure, I thought he might have attacked me!' he chortled. 'It was his pride that was most injured, when he discovered that his cunning plot had been thwarted.'

'Did you confront him about the chicken blood?' she demanded, indignantly.

'I did indeed! Of course he denied it and said I had no proof that it was chicken blood. I said he had no proof it was human, so it was a stalemate, but he knows that I know the truth.'

'What about the gaoler at South Gate?' asked Nesta. 'He must be in dire trouble over this.'

'The sheriff was all for locking him into his own cells and throwing away the key!' grinned de Wolfe. 'Thankfully Gabriel got Gwyn to punch his face a few times and then tie him up. The man didn't mind, as he's three marks the richer for it! We let four others escape from Gwyn's cell at the same time, just to avoid making it look too obvious. It's not as if bribing gaolers is uncommon, it happens all the time.'

'But de Revelle must know that you were behind it?'

'Of course he does! But he can't prove it, whereas his own sister can testify that I was never out of her sight all that evening.'

The auburn-haired Welsh woman cuddled up to him under the sheepskin that covered them, but she looked worried. 'But isn't this just delaying the outcome?' she fretted. 'What happens to Gwyn at the end of the forty days?'

Though she knew something about sanctuary, her lover had just explained it more fully. Gwyn could stay in St Martin's church for that period, safe from arrest, but unless he confessed his crime to the coroner in a set form of words and agreed to 'abjure the realm', he would be locked in and starved to death when the forty days was up. 'Abjuring the realm' meant leaving England for ever, on pain of death if he ever returned.

'We have to clear this matter up long before the time runs out,' replied John, serious once again. 'Discover who really slew Walter Tyrell and expose de Revelle's trickery.'

Nesta suddenly sat up, the candlelight revealing her nakedness until she modestly clutched the coverlet to her bosom. 'I did hear something today, John,' she said earnestly. 'A weaver from Tiverton was in here this afternoon. He's a regular customer, calls in for a meal and ale every time he comes to Exeter to buy wool. Everyone was gossiping about Tyrell's murder and I asked if he knew him.'

John pulled her back down and covered her with the fleece, waiting with interest for the rest of her story, his bare arm about her shoulders.

'We got talking about it and I led him on as well as I could.'

'You brazen hussy! Am I to be jealous?' he jested.

'Be serious, John! He said that it was well-known that Walter's brother, this Serlo, has for a long time been trying to buy out his brother's share in the mills, so that he can become sole owner. But Walter refuses and there has been bad feeling between them.'

The coroner considered this, even though it did not prevent him from massaging a shapely breast while he did so.

'Every bit of information helps,' he murmured. 'Though would anyone kill for something like that?'

'There's more,' said Nesta. 'While we were talking, Henry Ockford, the carter, said that there was gossip about Serlo and his sister-in-law.'

'That Christina?' grunted John. 'I'd not be surprised. She seemed hardly grief-stricken at the sight of her husband's bloody body, even though she put on a great act when de Revelle showed his stained kerchief. As for Serlo, he couldn't keep his hands off her at the inquest.'

Nesta rolled towards him and put her arms around his neck. 'I know someone else who can't keep his hands off a lady!'

Further discussion about the problem was postponed for some time.

'It's the Bush's best ale – and Nesta made the pasties herself,' said Thomas anxiously, as he watched Gwyn wolf down the basketful of food that he had brought into the little church. He came faithfully twice a day to keep the big man fed and to offer him some company.

'Your wife is well and so far there are no signs that she has miscarried,' he added comfortingly. 'She says she will visit you as soon as she is able – and bring the lads with her, for hopefully, they should soon be on the mend.'

Gwyn looked up from where he sat on one of the stone benches that ran around the walls. 'How long am I going to be stuck in here, then?' he asked, between mouthfuls of mutton pasty. 'Two days already seems like two months!'

'The Crowner is doing his best, but he needs to discover the real killer.'

The Cornishman nodded. 'I know – and I'm grateful to you all! I only wish I could be out of this place to help you.'

He glowered around the bare chapel with its earthern floor and simple altar that carried only a brass cross and two wooden candlesticks.

'It's better than the gaol at South Gate, but only just,' he growled, but then cursed himself for his ingratitude and apologized to the little clerk. 'Forgive me, Thomas, I'm in low spirits today. Ever since I got that damned sword, everything seems to have gone wrong.'

The former priest nodded his understanding. 'Perhaps it carries the taint of its former owner, the treacherous Henry. And who knows what shameful deeds it performed before that?'

They went on to talk of the escape, the bribed gaoler pretending to be overpowered by the five men in one cell, when he undid the crude lock to pass in their stale bread and tainted water. 'I may have hit him a bit harder than I needed, especially as he was a Cornishman like me, but it had to look realistic, for his sake!' Gwyn said with a grin, as he finished the last of the food and ale.

'Sir John says he'll come in to see you as soon as he can,' said Thomas, putting the remains back into Nesta's basket. 'He doesn't want to make it too obvious, as the sheriff is rightly convinced that the crowner organized the whole affair.'

Gwyn settled back on to the stone ledge, the only seating provided for the elderly and infirm of the congregation. It also had to serve as his bed, softened with a blanket provided by the kind landlady of the Bush.

'The parish priest here seems quite content to let me stay here,' he commented. 'Not like that fat bastard down at St Olave's, when he had that real murderer sheltering in his church.'

'He doesn't have any choice,' observed Thomas. 'Sanctuary is a merciful privilege given by God, not the clergy. But we chose St Martin's for you as Father Edwin is one of the very few Saxon priests in Exeter. He's a bit of rebel and no lover of the Norman aristocracy, which includes the sheriff!'

'Good for him!' muttered Gwyn. 'But I wish he'd put padding on this ledge – my arse will be covered in blisters after forty nights of this!'

* * *

John de Wolfe decided to start his investigation by following up the rather tenuous motives suggested by Nesta's tavern gossip. If the two Tyrell brothers had any dispute, then the obvious place to begin was the fulling mill.

Next morning he took himself off down to the West Gate and strode out on to the large area of marshy ground along the river that was known as Exe Island. Cut through by ditches and reens, it flooded when there was heavy rain up on distant Exmoor, but was an ideal place for the mills, of which there were at least a dozen. They needed copious quantities of water for washing and processing the raw wool, which was the main foundation of Exeter's – and indeed, England's – wealth. The Tyrells had two of the mills side by side, rather ramshackle wooden buildings with short canals bringing water directly in from the river. There was a ragged collection of huts around them, mostly for storage of the fleeces and the finished wool.

De Wolfe enquired for Serlo Tyrell, but was told he was away buying raw material at Buckfast Abbey, the large Cistercian monastery fifteen miles way, which had the largest flocks of sheep in Devon. Instead, he was directed to a shed where he found a harassed clerk poring over a confused mass of parchment rolls. The man looked up in irritation at being disturbed, but when he recognized the King's Coroner, he jumped up and bowed his head obsequiously.

'How can I be of assistance, sir?' he gabbled. 'This is a terrible business.'

John whimsically assumed he meant the death of his employer, not the state of the fulling industry. 'I want some information, which may help in discovering who killed your master.'

The man's eyebrows went up in surprise. 'I thought this was already known, sir!' Then he appeared to recollect that the assumed culprit was this knight's own squire and managed to look embarrassed.

The clerk, who looked about John's own age of forty, was a pasty-faced, overweight man, with thin, fair hair cropped short at the sides and back. He had rather full, pink lips, which covered uneven and badly discoloured teeth. A nondescript brown tunic had splashes of ink on the front and his fingers showed the same trademark of a scribe.

'I am Martin Knotte, sir, chief clerk to the Tyrell mills. What can I tell you?' Without any real justification, the coroner had taken an instant dislike to the man after only half a minute in his company. There was something distasteful about his fawning manner and his moist, mobile mouth. Aware that this snap judgement was quite unfair, John pressed on with his questions.

'You were clerk to both Walter and Serlo Tyrell?'

'I had the honour to serve them both, Crowner. There is a second clerk at the other mill, but he is merely a junior who works under my direction.' He said this with a disdainful air, like a bishop referring to a choir-boy.

'The two brothers were partners, I understand?'

'Yes, but Walter had the bigger share, as he was older and inherited from their father when Serlo was little more than a boy.'

De Wolfe decided to get to the nub of the matter without delay. 'Did they get along harmoniously, or was there any friction between them?

Martin looked slightly affronted. 'I am a steward, sir, my only concern is the smooth running of the accounting and the other chores of running a busy mill.'

The coroner was in no mood for fencing with clerks. 'Come now! I am enquiring into a murder. I have no time for the niceties of polite behaviour. Chief clerks always know more of what goes on than anyone else.' His stern tone and perhaps the slight flattery about the omnipotence of trusted servants, loosened the clerk's tongue.

'Well, between you and me, sir, Master Serlo has chafed somewhat at always being the follower behind Walter's leadership. He has had many notions of improving the working methods and expanding the business, but his brother always over-ruled him.'

'With what consequences?' demanded John.

The clerk rather dramatically looked over each shoulder before answering in the empty hut. 'Serlo has repeatedly offered to buy out Walter's share, suggesting that the older man could retire – or at least use the time and money to expand his other interests, such as buying and renting out dwelling-houses. I think Serlo badly wanted to rise amongst the city burgesses and even had ambitions to become a portreeve.' He shook his head sadly. 'Master Walter should have taken the offer, for now it's too late.'

'Did their dispute become acrimonious – or even violent?

Martin shrugged dismissively. 'Some harsh words were spoken, but nothing more.'

John had the impression that he was considerably understating the truth here. He cleared his throat, one of the mannerisms he used to cover awkward moments. 'And what of Serlo's relations with his brother's wife?'

Again Martin's pale eyebrows climbed up his forehead in surprise. 'Mistress Tyrell? I don't know what you can mean.'

John sighed at the tedious fidelity of the clerk. 'I'm not blind, nor are the citizens of Exeter! Serlo Tyrell, an unmarried man, seems overly fond of his sister-in-law.'

Martin's eyes again cautiously roved the empty room, before he answered in a quite unnecessary whisper. 'It is true that he was devoted to Mistress Christina, but I'm sure there was no impropriety between them. Since the death, he has been most supportive and if they eventually tie the bond, then I'd not be surprised – and most happy about it.'

De Wolfe was irritated by the clerk's pedantic manner, but further questions produced nothing of substance. When he left, he felt that the man's grudging admissions meant that the city gossips were almost certainly correct. Serlo had coveted his brother's business and his status, as well as his handsome wife. He now had all three in his grasp, but had it been a sufficient motive to have hacked through Walter's neck?

Not only did the sheriff continue to harangue de Wolfe about the escape of Gwyn from the gaol, but John's wife joined in the condemnation.

'It is glaringly obvious that you connived at it, husband!' she grated yet again, this time as they sat at dinner. 'No doubt you used our money to bribe that gaoler.'

De Wolfe waited while he picked a fish-bone from his teeth, as it was a Friday and they had the usual salt haddock instead of meat. 'I was nowhere near the South Gate that night, Matilda – as you well know,' he said calmly, knowing that it would irritate her all the more.

'My brother says you organized the whole shameful affair,' she snapped, her square face scowling across the table.

'Just as he organized the far more shameful deception that put my officer there in the first place!' countered John. 'So let's just say that God evened up the score by letting those five men escape, one of whom happened to be Gwyn.'

Matilda angrily thrust back her chair, the legs scraping noisily on the flagstones. 'How dare you blaspheme, taking the name of God in defence of that Cornish savage!' she ranted. 'You've already desecrated St Martin's by housing him there! I'm going to St Olave's to pray for your soul, for it seems in dire need of salvation.' With that, she lifted up the hem of her heavy brocade kirtle and stalked out of the hall, yelling for her timid French maid to come and help her dress for her devotions.

John took his time finishing his dinner, then sat at his hearth with a pot of cider, looking into the fire while he fondled the head of his old dog. The flaming logs reminded him of the destruction of Gwyn's cottage, which had started this sorry chain of events. Though his officer claimed that his recent ill-fortune was due to the acquisition of his new sword, the fire had occurred before that, as had the sickness of his sons.

He churned the matter around in his head, but saw no way of pushing ahead with his suspicions of Serlo Tyrell. He intended confronting him as soon as he returned from Buckfast, though the man was hardly likely to admit his guilt, short of extracting a confession by torture. For a moment, John contemplated Christina as a possible suspect, given her apparent lack of genuine emotion at the sight of her husband's corpse and the patently false hysteria at the sight of the sheriff's stained handkerchief. But though he did not subscribe to the common notion that frail women could not inflict such serious wounds – and Mistress Tyrell was by no means frail – he doubted that she would risk a hanging just to exchange one brother for another.

He heard the street door slam behind Matilda as she

stormed off to pray for his soul at St Olave's, the maid Lucille pattering apprehensively behind her. As he rose from his chair, their cook-maid bustled in to clear the debris of the meal and John put an affectionate hand on her bottom as she leaned over the table. She removed it rather reluctantly and turned to him with a reproving smile.

'That's enough of that, Sir Crowner! Keep that for the ale-house in Idle Lane!'

Mary knew all about his having a mistress, as did most of Exeter, and John suspected she was a little jealous, even though it had been she who had kept him at arm's length these past few months.

Facing him with empty ale jars in her hand, she became more serious. 'This murder that's got poor Gwyn into such trouble – I was talking to a girl I know when I was at the fish stall this morning. She lives in Waterbeer Street and told me something about this Walter Tyrell.'

John's attention was gripped at once. Just as Nesta sometimes picked up useful information from her patrons at the tavern, so Mary passed on gossip from the house-servants that formed an effective grapevine across the city. He waited for more, though Mary looked slightly embarrassed.

'To be frank, she's a whore who works in one of the stews there – but a pleasant woman, with two babes to support,' she said defensively. 'Anyway, she said that the dead man was a regular customer. Not one of hers, but he frequently visited a girl called Bernice. It seems he was always very furtive about going there, muffled in a hooded cloak and using a back alley instead of the street. In fact, the alley where he was found dead, for it's only a few dozen paces from the brothel.'

Mary had no more details to offer, but as John thoughtfully made his way up towards his chamber in the castle, he wondered if the information might be put to any use. Did it strengthen the case against Serlo or perhaps even Christina? If Walter had to resort to harlots, when he had a young, attractive wife at home, did this point to greater marital disharmony than his chief clerk admitted? Could his wife or his brother – or both of them in concert – have followed him to this house of ill-repute and killed two birds with one stone? Removing an unfaithful husband who stood in the way of their own passion and at the same time, gaining the rest of a flourishing business?

His garret at the top of the gatehouse was empty. Thomas was nowhere to be seen and the window-sill where Gwyn always sat was poignantly bare.

John sat at his table and reluctantly picked up a parchment covered with simple words and phrases in Latin, as he was painfully learning to read and write, being coached by both Thomas and a vicar from the cathedral.

His mind kept wandering from the manuscript and after a while, he was glad to hear footsteps on the stairs as a welcome diversion. It was Thomas de Peyne, breathless and agitated.

'Crowner, I have heard disturbing news at the cathedral!' He leaned on the table to gabble at his master. 'A deacon I know told me that this morning, the sheriff arrived seeking an audience with the bishop, but when he learnt that His Grace was in Coventry, he fell into a temper, then sought out the Precentor instead. They had their heads together for some time, calling in two other canons into the Chapter House.'

When Thomas named them, de Wolfe recognized a pair of the sheriff's cronies, Prince John sympathizers like Thomas de Boterellis, the Precentor – and indeed, like Bishop Marshal himself.

'Do you know what it was all about?' he demanded.

'This deacon tried to listen at the door, for he is very nosey,' said Thomas virtuously. 'But a proctor chased him away so the only words he managed to hear were about "breaking sanctuary"!'

The coroner shot to his feet, tipping over his bench with crash. 'The bastard! Surely he wouldn't dare?' he snarled. 'Thomas, you are a churchman, surely it is inviolable?'

The clerk, a fount of knowledge on all things religious and ecclesiastical, explained that though the Church jealously protected its right to sanctuary – especially since the murder of Thomas Becket – it accepted that the secular powers sometimes broke it. 'There is even a scale of penalties for violation of sanctuary,' he explained. 'The fines for dragging a man from a cathedral are far greater than from a mere parish church or a chapel.'

De Wolfe had no wish to see this put to the test and grabbed his cloak as he made for the door. 'Thomas, get down to St Martin's as fast as your legs will carry you and warn Gwyn! Bar the door if you can and only open it to me.'

He hurried across the inner ward and burst in to de Revelle's chamber, only to find it empty, apart from a clerk sorting tax rolls.

'Where is he, Edwin?' he demanded.

'An hour ago, he went in a great state of excitement to find the castle constable, Crowner,' said the clerk. 'He never came back.'

'Damn it to hell,' muttered de Wolfe. 'Perhaps I'm already too late!'

As he turned to hurry from the room, his eye caught sight of Gwyn's new sword leaning against the doorpost. On an impulse, he snatched it up and hung it from his own belt, as when inside the city walls, he rarely carried his own weapon. He clattered down the steps, intending to get to St Martin's as soon as possible, but stopped when he saw Ralph Morin, the burly constable who was in charge of the garrison at Rougemont. Together with Sergeant Gabriel, he was lining up a dozen men-at-arms in the inner ward, but the lethargy in their movements suggested a certain reluctance.

'What's going on, Ralph?' he demanded as he strode up to them.

The constable took his elbow and steered him away from the soldiers. 'Thank God you're here, I was coming to look for you. That thrice-damned sheriff has ordered me to drag your officer from the church. I did all I could to resist, but an order is an order. He's the king's representative here and I am under his control.'

Unlike most castles, which belonged to barons and lords, Exeter had always been kept entirely under royal administration and the constable was his servant. De Wolfe, though angry and apprehensive, laid a hand on Morin's broad shoulder. 'I understand, Ralph. You have to do your duty, however evil it is.'

By now, Gabriel had joined them, livid with fury. In a low voice, vibrant with emotion, he said 'It's madness! First I contrive his escape, now I've got to go and drag him out again! But the bloody sheriff will have us all hanged if we refuse.'

'What about the desecration of sanctuary?' hissed the coroner.

Ralph shook his head. 'De Revelle said to forget it, he'll take responsibility and gladly pay any fine. He claimed that the bishop would gloss over any religious problem, so there'll be no chance of us being excommunicated.'

His voice was bitter and John realized that only the thought of the gallows prevented him from defying his orders.

'Then just do me one favour, Ralph. Give me time to get down there before you. Understand?'

The constable nodded and pointed to a horse outside a nearby stable. It was already saddled up for a castle messenger to ride off on some errand. 'We are marching down, so if you take that gelding, you'll be there at least ten minutes before us. That's the best I can do, John!'

With a wave of thanks, John swung himself into the saddle and tore off through the gatehouse and down the hill to East Gate Street. To avoid the usual press of people in High Street, he dived into the back alleys opposite and swearing at anyone who got in his way in the narrow lanes, pushed his way through to the side of the little church. Abandoning the horse to graze the sparse grass of the Close, he hammered on the door and yelled for Thomas to open it. He heard a bar being lifted inside and when he virtually fell through the doorway, he found not his clerk, but a tall, fair priest facing him.

'Father Edwin, the sanctuary of your church is about to be desecrated!' he shouted.

The Saxon nodded gravely and now John saw that Thomas and Gwyn stood behind him.

'Your clerk, my brother in God, explained what was happening. It is an outrage, typical of the oppression we have to suffer from these invaders.'

John, who though he had a half-Welsh mother, came from a long line of Norman invaders himself, but this was no time to argue politics.

'We have to get him out and hide him,' he snapped. 'They will be here within minutes, so the only place is my house, just up the lane.'

The parish priest shook his head firmly. 'You are a good man, Sir John. You cannot compromise your position like that, it could ruin you.' He beckoned to Gwyn in a way that seemed to defy any argument and led the way to a small door set in the wall to the right of the altar. Opening it with a large key, he turned to John to bar him entering. 'I suggest that you go straight to your dwelling, Coroner, and play the innocent, for they are bound to seek you out.'

He shepherded Gwyn and Thomas into the tiny sacristy where he kept the Blessed Host and his few service books. He waved John back towards the main door. 'Your clerk will come to you later and let you know how matters stand.'

With that, he followed them in and shut the door. Then John heard the key being turned on the inside.

'The man is a saint,' said Thomas reverentially. 'When I am a bishop, I will appeal to Rome for Father Edwin's sanctification!'

It was evening and he was sitting in the Bush with Nesta and de Wolfe recounting to her the exciting events of this stressful day.

'The sacristy had an outer door leading into a small yard,' he explained.

'Here there was a bier used for taking cadavers to the cathedral for burial, a kind of long chest on small wheels, with handles on each end. The lid opened on hinges and the priest made Gwyn get inside.'

In spite of the seriousness of the situation, Nesta could not suppress a giggle. 'I'll wager he didn't like that one bit!'

'The poor fellow had to almost double up to fit himself in, cursing all the time under his breath,' agreed Thomas.

He explained that the Saxon priest had given him an old Benedictine habit to wear, then told him to push the bier from behind, while he himself walked in front, pulling on the other handles. They trundled the clumsy device through the lanes, both chanting Latin prayers as they stared dismally at the ground. Folk in the street removed their caps or crossed themselves as they passed by with their 'corpse', until they doubled back towards the far end of Canon's Row. Here they stopped near the foot of the city wall where there were gardens and some rough ground. In the shelter of some bushes, the lid was opened and Gwyn clambered out, looking even more dishevelled than usual. Quickly, the Saxon took him to a small arch in a stone hut built against the fifteen-foot wall and hurried him inside.

'The city water conduits!' exclaimed Nesta, at this point in Thomas's story. 'The ducts come through the wall there, so I've been told.'

John nodded, having had a murdered corpse in there quite recently. 'The water comes from the springs at St Sidwell – let's hope that Gwyn doesn't catch the jaundice from it, like his sons.'

'He can't stay there long, poor man!' said Nesta in some concern. 'A big fellow like him can hardly stand upright in those low passages. What's to be done about it?'

De Wolfe explained that he had already bribed a carter to smuggle Gwyn out of the city next morning, under a load of finished cloth being taken down to the port of Topsham, five miles down the river.

'But he need only go halfway, as he can seek board and lodging at St James's Priory, where they know him from our previous visits. Even if the damned sheriff gets to discover where he is, he would have to desecrate sanctuary all over again.'

The one-eyed potman limped across to refill their mugs as Nesta asked the coroner how Richard de Revelle had taken this latest setback to his scheming.

'He had his usual tantrum, shouting and screaming at me after Ralph Morin had told him that the bird had flown!' said John with satisfaction. 'I had insisted that Ralph and Gabriel search my house as soon as they had given up looking for Gwyn in the church. They were only too delighted to report to the sheriff that I had been asleep by my fireside and that there was no sign of Gwyn. Thank God that Matilda was on her knees in St Olave's while all this was going on!'

The Welsh woman still looked worried. 'But the sheriff must surely know that, once again, you organized Gwyn's disappearance?'

'He can think what he likes, but he can't prove it – and everyone from the castle constable down to the most junior soldier is being as stupid and obstructive as they can in helping him find Gwyn.'

De Wolfe leaned across the table towards his clerk. 'Thomas, have you wormed anything yet from your cathedral spies?'

The unfrocked priest now lived on sufferance in the servant's quarters of one of the canon's houses in the Close, sleeping on a straw mattress in a passageway. However, lowly as his accommodation was, it was ideally placed for him to hear all the gossip of the cathedral and its many inhabitants, but so far, he had gleaned nothing about any scandal involving the Tyrell family.

'Then I must confront Serlo and Christina directly,' growled John. 'I will shake their tree and see if anything falls from it.'

'What about this harlot in Waterbeer Street?' asked Nesta. 'Those girls always have a man protecting them and taking the lion's share of the money they earn. Maybe he would know something, if the killing was almost on his doorstep?'

'An excellent idea, madam! I'll do that tomorrow, without fail.' John squeezed her thigh under the table. 'I've not seen the inside of a brothel for a long time!' he added mischievously.

*　　*　　*

Next morning, de Wolfe sent Thomas de Peyne down to St James's Priory to check that Gwyn had arrived safely and to hand over some money to the prior for his food and lodging. As soon as he had seen the little clerk jogging off on his pony, which he insisted on riding side-saddle like a woman, de Wolfe made his way to a substantial house near the East Gate.

The young maid who answered the door conducted him to an ante-room off the large hall, where Christina sat near a small fire-pit, a pewter cup of wine in her hand. She was still dressed in a grey kirtle, her husband's funeral having taken place only the day before. However, her widow's weeds were now lightened by a gold cord wound twice around her slim waist, its large tassels hanging down almost to the floor. She wore no veil or wimple around her head and throat, her fair hair being coiled in plaits over each ear and confined in gold-net crespines. Christina Tyrell looked more like a woman expecting her lover than a mourning widow and she seemed annoyed by the appearance of the county coroner.

'Have you come to tell me that they have recaptured that rogue who murdered my husband?' The glare she gave him as she spoke was not a good start to their conversation.

'That man had nothing to do with it, as you well know,' replied John bluntly. 'I am fully aware of the deceit that was arranged between you and the sheriff over that blood-stained sword.'

The woman flushed and protested, but her eyes dropped, unable to meet the steely gaze of the coroner. 'The fellow is guilty, so what does it matter?' she muttered.

'I have a better candidate for the killing, mistress,' he boomed. 'Or perhaps even two! What about you or your lover Serlo? Both of you had reasons for wanting Walter dead.'

Christina lifted her eyes to look defiantly at de Wolfe, a flush of anger flooding her face. 'What nonsense is this? Are you mad?' she shouted.

'Your husband frequented a whorehouse in the city – is that the habit of a devoted spouse? Did you want rid of him because of that – were you a woman spurned? It is well known that you hanker after his brother, a younger man.'

'This is nonsense – you cannot speak to me like this!' she babbled.

John slammed one fist into the other palm. 'I am investigating a murder, madam. I can ask what I want!' he roared.

Her response was dramatic, as well as unexpected. She bent to the circle of stones around the fire-pit and snatched up a heavy iron poker. Raising it over her head, she lunged at de Wolfe with a screech of fury and swung it at him. Startled, he backed away and lifted an arm to protect himself, receiving a stinging blow just above his wrist. With a bellowed curse, he retreated backwards towards the door, where the little maid crouched in terror at her mistress's sudden fury.

'Get out, damn you!' howled Christina, lifting the poker for another blow. 'Get out, you foul-mouthed, evil man!'

As he could hardly draw his dagger on a woman, John decided to evacuate and survive to fight another day. 'You'll regret this, madam!' he shouted. 'I'll be back when you've come to your senses.'

He slid through the door and slammed it behind him, making his way rapidly through the hall to the street. Thankfully the virago did not pursue him and he stopped a few yards away to recover his ruffled dignity. He would cheerfully fight a dozen of Saladin's warriors, but an angry widow with a fire-iron was too much of a challenge for him.

Determined never to let anyone else ever become aware of the ignominious defeat he had suffered, the coroner marched away and went through the city down to Exe Island and the fulling mills.

Half-afraid that his quarry had already left to visit the doughty Christina, he went straight to the clerk's hut to see if Serlo Tyrell was still there. He was gratified to find him leaning against a table, listening to a string of figures that Martin Knotte was reading out to him from a parchment. As with the vast majority of the population, Serlo was illiterate and, like most merchants, depended on someone in the lower religious orders to handle all accounts and correspondence.

The fuller looked up in surprise, which turned to irritation when he saw de Wolfe. 'I've told you all I know, Crowner,' he snapped. 'Why are you persisting with this, when everyone knows who the culprit is?'

De Wolfe looked pointedly at the clerk. 'It would be better if I spoke to you in private, for your own sake.'

'I have no secrets from Martin, you can say what you like. But make it quick, I have other things to do.' The fuller accompanied his words with a scowl.

'Very well – but I have just come from the house of Christina,' John announced. He saw a flicker of apprehension pass over Serlo's face, before he jerked his head at his clerk. 'Perhaps you had better leave us, Martin, if this is to be a personal matter,' he muttered.

When the man had left, the coroner made the same verbal assault as he had on Christina. 'I am well aware of your connivance at the crude deception the sheriff tried with the chicken's blood,' he grated. 'I also know about your liaison with your sister-in-law.'

Serlo paled, but his mouth set into an obstinate expression. 'I deny both your impertinent allegations. The sheriff shall hear of this!'

'He'll hear of it from my own lips, as soon as I can find him!' snarled John. 'Don't play the innocent with me, I know from Christina that you are lovers!' This was stretching the truth somewhat, but he was past caring, with Gwyn in such danger. 'Furthermore, I suspect that both you and she might be directly involved in Walter's death. You stand to gain the whole fulling business now that your mistress is available as a wife. And is she not revenged upon him, for preferring a whore in Waterbeer Street to herself?'

There was no iron poker available in the office, but Serlo looked as if he would have used one if it had been to hand. His pallor turned to red rage and a quivering finger was pointed at de Wolfe's face as he began a stinging tirade of denial and outrage at the coroner's accusations.

As with Christina, John's faint hopes of his frontal attack causing a breakdown and a confession came to nothing. Although the two men shouted at each other for several more minutes, the coroner knew that he had no more ammunition to throw at Serlo Tyrell and, once again, he was forced to beat a fruitless retreat. Outside the hut, he found Martin Knotte, who although now a few yards from the door, had obviously been listening to the heated exchanges inside.

'I'll walk with you to the gate, Sir John,' he said obsequiously and pattered alongside towards the opening in the fence around the mills.

'I was mainly Master Walter's clerk' he said carefully. 'So I know quite a lot about his affairs, both business and private.'

De Wolfe stopped in his tracks and stared hard down at Martin's smooth face. 'What are you trying to tell me?' he demanded.

'I could hardly help hear a little of what was said in there,' he said, gesturing back towards his office. 'As a good citizen, I thought I should confirm that Walter used to frequent the city streets late at night,' he coughed delicately. 'In fact, he used to visit a whore-house very near where he was found dead. I regret to say that his marriage was not a happy one.'

'I knew all this, fellow,' said John suspiciously. 'Why should you be telling me now?'

'Master Walter often carried large sums of money, when he was either buying or selling. The night he died, I know that he had gone to the New Inn to meet a master-weaver to receive payment for a consignment of best wool. Yet that money was never accounted for in my records and both Mistress Christina and Serlo say they have never seen it.'

'There was no purse on his body when it was found,' agreed de Wolfe. 'How much should it have contained?'

'Four pounds, according to my invoicing – a great sum of money to go astray.'

'Could this harlot have taken it from him? Yet he was found dead outside, he would not have let her rob him in the brothel.'

Martin Knotte shrugged. 'Might she not have warned some accomplice that he was carrying such a sum?' he suggested.

'I had considered that before, but I did not know then how much coin he was carrying,' admitted John. 'I must have some words with this strumpet.'

They had reached the gateway and after Martin had smirked a farewell, John strode off in the direction of the West Gate, deep in thought.

Once back inside the city, he decided to follow up these hints that maybe Walter Tyrell's fondness for whoring had some connection with his death. He made his way to Waterbeer Street and, careless of who might see him knocking on the door of a house of ill-repute, was admitted by a toothless old crone who looked as if she herself might have been a harlot around the time of Old King Henry's coronation!

She stared at him in consternation, unsure if the county coroner had come on business or pleasure. He soon cleared up her doubts by demanding to know if there was a girl here named Bernice, his harsh tone indicating that his interest in her was purely professional.

The dingy building had several small chambers downstairs and the upper floor was also divided into rooms that were little more than cubicles. The hag climbed laboriously up a flight of wooden steps and pushed aside one of the hanging sheets of thick leather that served as doors.

'Bernice, here's a gentleman to see you,' cackled the old woman and stood aside to admit de Wolfe, who waved her away before he entered. The dismal cell contained a stool, a straw mattress on the floor and a surprisingly healthy-looking young woman of about eighteen. She was squatting on the stool, biting into a hunk of bread, a large piece of cheese in the other hand. Bernice immediately put the food on the floor, sprang up and smiled ingratiatingly at the visitor, assuming that he was an unexpected client.

'I am the coroner, girl!' said John severely, though he had already taken in the fact that the girl was quite pretty, different from the usual sad drabs that worked in these stews. 'Sit down, lass . . . I need to talk to you about Walter Tyrell.'

A succession of emotions passed across the young woman's face, surprise sliding into fear, then settling into wariness. 'I know nothing about him, sir,' she said stubbornly, in a thick rural accent. 'He was just a man who came here.'

'But he always asked for you, didn't he?'

'He did, sir. That's because I'm cleaner and prettier

than the others,' she added, with a simple honesty that contained no conceit.

'Did he have to pay more for you, then?' asked the coroner.

'Indeed, sir. He always seemed to have plenty of pennies.'

Bernice had a naive directness that John found both touching and rather attractive. He wondered sadly what she would be like after five or ten years in this place. 'And to whom did he pay those pennies?' he asked. 'Was it you or the old woman downstairs?'

The girl shook her head, her brown curls bouncing. 'Neither, sir. He always came late on certain evenings and my man was always here to take the money.'

'Your man? What man is that?'

'Elias Palmer, my protector. He runs three of the girls in this house.'

John nodded his understanding. The premises were used by several pimps and their girls, paying a rent to the owner of the house, who could be anyone, even one of the city burgesses. In some towns, there were brothels owned by senior churchmen. However, this was not getting him anywhere in respect of his investigation.

'What about the night he was killed nearby? Anything different about that night? Was he alone?'

'He was always alone, sir. He never talked to me much, he was too busy doing other things.' She smiled up at de Wolfe innocently.

'Did you see him paying your man? Did he have a purse on his belt?'

A cloud seemed to pass over the girl's face and her manner changed. 'He did have a purse, sir. He always did.'

De Wolfe's instincts were aroused. There was something here. 'Come girl, tell me exactly. Was this Elias in the room here with you then?'

She shook her head, looking decidedly evasive now. 'He never came in, in case the gentleman was still having his pleasure. He always waited at the bottom of the stairs for his money.'

'This night, did he follow Walter Tyrell out into the street?'

Bernice's open nature seemed to return, as she felt on safer ground. 'No sir, he came back up to me as he always did, to give me the two pennies I had earned.' There was a ring of truth about this, but John still smelt a rat.

'Bernice, you are not telling me everything!' he barked, bending down towards her so that his intimidating dark face was pushed almost into hers.

The girl suddenly burst into tears. 'I told Elias that Walter had a very large purse that night. I even saw the glint of a gold bezant, when he opened it to give me an extra penny for myself.'

A feeling of triumph began to steal through John's soul. Here was something worth pursuing. 'So what did Elias do then?' he demanded.

Bernice shrugged, two tears coursing down her pleasant face. 'Nothing, sir. Just went downstairs again.'

De Wolfe straightened up and on an impulse, stroked the top of the distressed girl's head. 'Calm yourself, girl. I'm going now. But where can I find this Elias Palmer?'

The round face came up again, the smile back in place. 'Old Maud might know, sir. He's always around somewhere.'

Downstairs, he found the woman sitting on an upturned bucket in the unkempt backyard. At his demand, she waddled back into the passageway and yelled for Elias outside the first door on the left. Impatiently, de Wolfe thrust aside the leather curtain and saw a man lying face down on the bed, his breeches around his ankles.

As he jumped up in surprise, grabbing for his nether garments, there was a squawk from beneath him and a girl rapidly hoisted a tattered blanket over her head.

'Who the hell are you, damn it?' demanded the man furiously, as he pulled his breeches up below his short tunic and fumbled with his belt.

'Sampling your own goods, eh?' replied John sarcastically. 'I'm the coroner and I want a word with you. Come out into the yard when you're decent.'

A moment later, Elias Palmer appeared reluctantly through the back door. He was a dandified fellow of middle height, with a shock of light brown hair. His otherwise unremarkable face was disfigured by a livid birthmark that covered the whole of one cheek and part of his temple.

'What do you want from me, Crowner?' he mumbled. 'There's no law against running a few girls.'

John was not sure if there was or not, but it was of no interest to him. 'What did you do with the money, Elias?' he snapped, poking his head forward like a vulture examining its next meal.

'What money? I don't know what you're talking about?' stammered the whoremonger, but his whole attitude shouted that he did indeed know.

'Walter Tyrell, that's what I'm talking about!' yelled de Wolfe. 'Bernice told you he had a fat purse with gold in it, didn't she?'

'What if she did?' faltered Elias. 'There's no harm in gossip.'

'But there's harm in murder, Elias!' snarled the coroner. 'You followed him out to that side alley, killed him and stole his purse. Admit it now, for you're going to swing for it, one way or the other.'

Elias looked wildly about him, stammering denials. At the back door, the faces of old Maud, Bernice and the other girl peered out in fearful fascination. With a sudden lunge, Elias turned and made for the fence that ran around the small yard. With de Wolfe pounding after him, he got to the rickety gate to fumble with the rusty catch. John remembered that he had Gwyn's sword hanging from his baldric and with a swish, he drew it from the scabbard. There was a flash of sunlight reflected from its blade as he swung it high and brought it down on the top bar of the gate, an inch from Elias's feverish fingers. The steel sliced clean through the wood and stuck quivering in the thicker central bar, pinning the loose hem of the man's tunic to the gate.

Almost gibbering with fear, Elias dropped to the ground, his tunic ripping, as he held his hands up in supplication to the coroner.

'I didn't kill him, sir, I swear. I just took the purse from his dead body.'

John hauled him to his feet and jabbed him none too gently in the back with the point of the sword.

'You can tell that to the king's justices at the next Eyre of Assize,' he promised grimly.

St James's Priory was a small religious house on the bank of the river, between Exeter and Topsham. The prior and four monks were Cluniacs, their mother house being St Martin's in Paris and they led a quiet existence, tending their vegetable plots and fish-traps on the Exe.

When Thomas had visited Gwyn, he had found him well-fed and comfortable, but fretting at his incarceration, unable to visit his wife and children. On the afternoon following his visit to the brothel, de Wolfe went down to see his henchman. He took care to ensure that none of the sheriff's spies was following him, as he knew that de Revelle was still trying to discover where John's officer was hidden.

'How long am I going to be stuck here?' demanded the Cornishman. 'Thomas has been very good, bringing me news of my family, but if I stay here much longer, I'll turn into a bloody monk myself!'

John brought him up to date on events, especially his arrest of Elias Palmer, who was now confined in Rougemont, where the cells had been emptied by this week's hangings. The pimp, while steadfastly denying the murder, had confessed to taking the purse from Walter's belt and, in fact, led John to a chest in his own room in the brothel where he produced the bag, still filled with coin.

'But the damned sheriff still won't accept that he killed Tyrell, the obstinate swine,' fumed John. 'He still believes that I have spirited you away somewhere and says that he'll wait until doomsday to bring you before his court.'

'Does he admit that he worked that swindle over the chicken blood on my sword?'

'Not at all! Even though I told him that Christina had admitted knowing about it – which is stretching the truth a little.'

'That poxy sword!' muttered Gwyn. 'It's got me into trouble again, damn it.'

John pulled aside his riding cloak to show the ornate sheath dangling from his baldric, the diagonal strap over his shoulder that took the weight of the weapon. 'I've brought it down for you, in case there's any trouble if de Revelle does discover where you are.'

'Thank you, Crowner,' said Gwyn, rather diffidently. 'But that thing has brought me nothing but ill-fortune. Grateful as I am for your gift, I think I'd like to see it exchanged for a less grand weapon, as I'm convinced there's something about it that brings bad luck.'

Gwyn's pure Celtic blood gave him a strongly superstitious nature and John had learned that it was futile to argue with him. He agreed to return it to Roger Trudogge and negotiate for a less ornate blade.

Feeling frustrated with his lack of progress in closing this affair, de Wolfe rode back to Exeter, pondering his next moves in trying to lift the cloud of suspicion that still hung over Gwyn. Every so often, a worm of doubt wriggled in his mind, whispering that the big man might really have killed the fuller, but each time John crushed the notion, knowing in his heart that though Gwyn might swing at someone in a raging temper, there was no way that he would lay in wait for them in a dark alley.

The problem was that the sheriff resolutely refused to give up this golden opportunity to hurt his brother-in-law, in revenge for John's earlier exposure of him as a potential traitor and rebel. Only Matilda's intercession had saved Richard from the ignominy of dismissal and possible arrest.

'How in God's name can I convince everyone that this thieving whoremonger is the real culprit?' he muttered under his breath, as he rode Odin through the same South Gate where his officer had been briefly imprisoned. He thought of putting Elias to the Ordeal, a form of torture involving hot irons or boiling water, but that was intended to try the issue of guilt or innocence, not to extract a confession. Maybe he could submit him to a 'pressing', usually reserved for suspects who refused to answer any questions, being 'mute of malice'. The unfortunate victim was manacled to the ground and had iron weights placed on his chest, the number being increased until he either confessed or died. However, a coroner could not order this without the agreement of the sheriff, which was hardly likely to be granted.

De Wolfe reached Martin's Lane and delivered his horse to the stables opposite his house, then walked the rest of the way up to the castle. He had thought to go straight to see Roger Trudogge and negotiate some kind of exchange for Gwyn's sword, but then decided to see if any new deaths or other mayhem had been reported in his absence. He found Thomas at work as usual on his parchments, as there was much copying to be done to provide duplicates for various courts and the royal archives. The clerk looked up as he entered and enquired after Gwyn, then went on to deliver a nugget of information from the cathedral Close.

'You know, Crowner, that I sleep on a pallet in a passageway of the house of one of the canons. Well, early this morning, as people were stirring to go to Prime, I chanced to hear two of the canon's vicars talking in a room nearby, that had only a curtain for a door.'

John grunted, as he was well aware that Thomas was the most inquisitive person west of Winchester and that 'chancing to hear' probably meant that he had had his ear pressed to the door-curtain.

'One of them was asking the other's advice about repeated confessions he had been hearing from a particular supplicant,' the clerk continued. 'Though he could not repeat the content, even to a fellow priest, he felt it was so serious that he would have to consult their canon, the archdeacon or even the bishop about whether he should break the sanctity of the confessional and divulge something to the secular authorities.'

John frowned at his clerk, puzzled as to why he was being told this, as it seemed a matter for the ecclesiastical community. Usually, such dilemmas concerned flagrant breaches of morals as well as the law, such as sexual transgressions like incest or the ravishing of women or even children.

'But what's this to do with the coroner, Thomas?' he asked gruffly.

The clerk's bright little eyes glinted as he delivered his punch-line. 'The man they were talking about was Martin Knotte!' he whispered conspiratorially.

The coroner hurried down through the city, his wolf-skin cloak flying out behind him in the breeze like a large bat as he loped along, his dark head thrust out before him. Thomas pattered along behind him, unsure of what all this was leading to, apart from the fact that his master was going to have strong words with the chief clerk at the fulling mills.

For his part, de Wolfe turned over Thomas's news in his mind as he pushed his way through the crowded streets to reach the West Gate. What was all this about – or was it a complete irrelevancy? Perhaps the clerk's confession was merely about being unfaithful to his wife, but that would hardly be grounds for the vicar's grave concern.

Could it be that Martin Knotte had learned something damning about Serlo or even Christina? Had he discovered that one of them had in fact dispatched Walter Tyrell? And did loyalty to his employer conflict with his conscience and his public duty?

'Only one bloody way to find out!' he growled under his breath, as he strode along. 'Shake it out of the fat bastard!' De Wolfe always favoured the direct approach to problems.

At the mill on the river, he went straight to the clerk's hut, where he left Thomas outside, fearing that a witness might distract his quarry from John's intended verbal assault. Inside, he found Martin sitting at his table with a quill in his hand, poised over a parchment. The man looked ill, his podgy face almost a waxy colour.

He jumped to his feet and courteously pulled up a

stool for the coroner on the other side of his bench. As John sat down, the big sword jabbed against the wooden floor and became unhooked from his belt, not being designed for warriors who sat indoors. With a cluck of irritation, he pulled it from under his cloak and rested it against the table in front of him, before glaring at the man who had resumed his seat opposite.

'Now then, what's the trouble, Knotte?' he demanded brusquely. 'Never mind *how* I know, but it has come to my ears that you have information that is distressing you. Is it something that I or even the sheriff should know about, eh?'

If it had been possible for the clerk to grow any paler, he would have done so. Stutteringly, he denied any problems, but his demeanour patently gave the lie to his words. De Wolfe kept at him, rasping and demanding that he divulge anything that law officers should know about, but Martin Knotte remained adamant in his tremulous denials.

'Those priests have broken their trust,' he complained bitterly. 'How else could you know of this?'

'Ha! So there is something!' snarled de Wolfe, triumphantly. 'You admit it now?'

Knotte shook his head stubbornly. 'It is a personal, private matter, Crowner. It does not concern you, and you should not persecute me like this!'

John stood up, leaning on the table and glowering down at the seated clerk. 'Does it concern Serlo, your master?' he shouted. 'Or perhaps the widow Christina?'

Martin shook his head violently, 'Why should it? It has nothing to do with them.'

'Are you just being faithful to them?' barked John. 'Misplaced loyalty will not save your neck if it conceals knowledge you may have against the King's Peace!'

Again the ashen-faced man fended off all the coroner's efforts to prise information from him, subsiding into a stubborn denial of any knowledge of wrong-doing by his employer.

Eventually, de Wolfe lost patience and jumped to his feet to wag a stern finger at Martin. 'Then I must go and tackle Serlo himself, to drag the truth from him. It will go badly for you if I discover that you have been concealing anything from me!'

He stalked out of the hut and swept up Thomas outside, hurrying him around the corner of the nearest mill-shed in his search for the master-fuller. If he had not left Martin in such a temper, he would have remembered to ask the man about Serlo's whereabouts, but now he had to seek him himself. As a workman passed, bent under the weight of a large bale of raw wool, John glared at him and demanded to know where his master was to be found.

'Try the lower mill, sir,' replied the man. 'I saw him there an hour ago.' They went across the yard to another large, but ramshackle wooden building and Thomas pointed to a small shed attached to one end. 'That looks like the hut of the other clerk. He may be in there.'

But Serlo was not there, neither was he in the fulling mill, where a score of men and boys, some of them children, were labouring at tanks and troughs of water. They were washing fleeces, some treading them rhythmically with their feet to remove the dirt and grease, throwing in handfuls of fine clay to assist the process.

Above the incessant splashing and chatter, Thomas managed to question several men, but came back to de Wolfe shaking his head. 'He has gone again, no one knows where,' he reported as they walked out of the watery hell that was the workplace of so many of Exeter's citizens.

'Damn the man, he's never around when I want him!' growled the coroner.

'He's unlikely to have fled the country now that he'll soon own all this if he weds Widow Christina,' observed Thomas, waving an arm around them.

'Let's go, then, I've had enough for today,' grunted de Wolfe. Then he stopped walking and slapped his left hip, feeling an empty space. 'Damnation, I've left Gwyn's sword in the clerk's hut. I wanted to take it back to the armourer on the way home.'

They changed direction and went the few hundred paces back to the upper mill. At the hut, John pushed at the door and found it immovable.

'Strange, it must be jammed,' he muttered, putting his shoulder to the door with little effect.

'There's no keyhole, so it must be barred on the inside,' said the observant Thomas.

Now suspicious, John hammered on the boards with his fist and yelled for Martin Knotte to open it. There was no response and he kicked at the door, this time feeling it creak and bend. A few more hefty blows with his foot splintered several of the thin planks, sufficient for him to put his arm through and push the bar up out of its brackets.

As it flew open, he charged in, shouting angrily. 'You can't get away with it by avoiding me, fellow!' he yelled.

Then he stopped dead, Thomas peering round him at a gruesome sight. Martin Knotte knelt in the corner of the room, as if in prayer. His right shoulder was supported by the wall, keeping his body upright, though he was stone dead. He was impaled on Gwyn's sword, the point embedded in the lower part of his chest, the pommel jammed into the angle of the walls and floor. Blood lay in a wide, spreading pool around him and dribbled obscenely from the corner of his mouth.

'Great Christ, what does this mean?' rasped de Wolfe hoarsely, as his clerk began crossing himself rapidly and murmuring Latin prayers for the dead.

The coroner strode across to the corpse, to make sure that he was past any aid, then pulled the body over on to its side, so that he could withdraw the sword.

'Is this another murder, master?' asked Thomas in a horrified whisper.

'Falling on a sword in a locked room?' he snapped. 'I don't think so, Thomas! The man has committed *felo de se*! But why, for God's sake?'

As he removed the six inches of steel from Knotte's chest, the more squeamish Thomas turned away and as he did so, his eyes fell on a sheet of parchment left on the end of the table. While the coroner was straightening out the limbs of the corpse, his clerk began reading the document, the ink of which was hardly dry.

He held it out towards de Wolfe. 'I think I had better read this to you, Crowner!' he said tremulously.

By noon the following day, Gwyn was back in his usual place in the Bush Inn, sitting opposite John de Wolfe at his table near the fire-pit. Thomas de Peyne was next to him, the pair beaming at the reunion, as was Nesta when she slipped on to the bench alongside her lover.

'I've got five minutes before I need to check that stupid new cook-maid hasn't overcooked the mutton,' she said. 'So tell me what happened today.'

'I escaped from that damned priory today!' guffawed Gwyn. 'Their ale wasn't too bad, but they live on bloody fish! I'd have grown fins if I'd stayed there any longer.'

'But why were you able to come out, that's the point?' persisted the auburn-haired landlady.

De Wolfe broke in, to begin telling her the story of his suspicions of the whore's pimp, then of Serlo and Christina, all of which were confounded by Martin Knotte's suicide.

'I had it all wrong, twice over,' he admitted. 'But there was never any reason even to consider that fat clerk down at the mills.' He stopped to take a long pull at his quart of Nesta's fine ale. 'At least, not until Thomas read out that message that Martin Knotte had penned just before he spitted himself on Gwyn's sword.'

'Not my sword any longer, Crowner!' grunted the Cornishman. 'Thank God you've already taken it back to Roger Trudogge. The bloody thing had bad fortune written all over it, not some Latin message!'

Ignoring his officer's interruption, John continued with his tale. 'Serlo and Christina, whatever their secret passions, had nothing to do with Walter's death, glad though they might now be that it's turned out this way.'

'But what about that horrible fellow from the whore-house?' demanded Nesta. 'You said that he had Walter's purse full of money!'

'That slimy bastard told the truth for once, that he had taken it from the corpse. When the harlot Bernice told him how much coin she had glimpsed on Walter's belt, he ran after him, presumably to assault and rob him in the alley. But someone had already done the job for him and all he had to do was snatch the purse and run.'

'He'll hang for the theft anyway, even if he didn't kill Walter,' observed Gwyn with some satisfaction.

'But what did Martin Knotte's message say?' asked Nesta, impatiently.

De Wolfe gestured at Thomas. 'Let him tell you, he was the only one who could read it!'

The little clerk wriggled self-consciously, but was quite pleased to be asked. 'It was a confession of his partiality to the sin of Sodom,' he began portentously.

'You mean, he liked buggering boys?' growled the down-to-earth Gwyn. 'Then at least that sword did a bit of good, in getting rid of him!'

'It seems that he had long suffered from this aber-ration, but had managed to conceal it from everyone, until the night of Walter's murder,' continued Thomas. 'Being a married man, he had to use that hut in the fulling mills for his activities and early that evening, Walter walked in unexpectedly.'

'Caught him *in flagrante delicto* with a lad from Bretayne,' explained John, Bretayne being the slum area down near the west wall of the city.

'His master was outraged and promised to expose him next day to his wife and the cathedral proctors.'

'Why them?' asked Nesta. 'Surely such a crime should go to the sheriff?'

Thomas shook his head. 'As a clerk, he was in lower religious orders and could claim 'benefit of clergy', he explained. 'That would remove judgment on his misdeeds from the secular to the ecclesiastical authorities.'

'Though after the bishop's Consistory Court found him guilty, they might well hand him over to the sheriff to be hanged,' added John, with some satisfaction.

'The note ended with a confession that he had panicked and lain in wait for Walter to come out of the brothel. As his clerk, he knew he was going to the New Inn that night to collect payment for wool, so he followed him and the first chance he had to slay him was in that alley off Waterbeer Street.' Thomas paused to make the sign of the cross at the memory. 'He had taken a large knife that was used in the mill for cutting the ropes binding wool bales. He used it to slash at Walter's neck, then ran away.'

'Yes, but that was days ago,' objected Nesta. 'Why wait until last night to kill himself?'

'His conscience eventually drove him to it,' explained the clerk. 'He knew that Gwyn was being falsely accused by the sheriff and was in grave danger of being hanged. Then the Crowner's persistence in trying lay the blame on his master Serlo and Christina was the last straw. If he didn't own up, someone was going to suffer. Even though Martin Knotte was an evil pervert, he still had some sense of honour.'

There was a thoughtful silence, broken by a loud belch from Gwyn. 'What did that other bastard, Richard de Revelle, say when you took him the parchment?' he asked.

'Huffed and puffed, refused to believe it, saying it was a forgery!' answered John, grinning lopsidedly at the memory of the sheriff's discomfiture. 'It took a view of Martin's corpse, the shattered door and the bloody sword before he grudgingly admitted that it must be true.'

'A bloody sword indeed!' said Gwyn with feeling. 'I wonder what will become of it now?'

John de Wolfe drained the last of his quart. 'Roger Trudogge said that he might already have sold it again,' he said. 'It seems that some knight took a fancy to it before we bought it and wanted the armourer to let him know if it came up for sale again. He wants a good weapon to take on this new Crusade we hear about, the one that's leaving from Venice.'

'I wish him luck with it!' grunted Gwyn. 'He'll need it.'

ACT TWO

Venice, 1262

I stare across over the moonlit water at the two little humps of islands that house the churches of S Cristoforo and S Michele. These are my primary targets, where I can rest and plan my escape properly. The tide is low in the lagoon, but it will soon come rushing back – I will have to hurry. I slide down on to the muddy, weed-skirted margins, and squelch my way out to the water's edge, where I begin wading. Halfway across, I turn for one more look at La Serenissima. Venice is now no more than a long, low line of dark buildings stretching far to my left and right. I wonder if this will be my last view of my home. I refuse to contemplate the thought for too long, not least because leaving Venice for good also means leaving sweet and sexy Caterina. And that I do not want.

The sword is strapped across my back, safe in its sheath from the depredations of the salt water. I prod ahead of myself with a long staff, feeling my way through the mud. Eventually, waist-deep in water, I can't see where I am putting my feet. Only the staff tells me if the next step is safe or not, that I am not stepping into a hole, or into soft, clinging mud. I am sweating despite the cold water, and suddenly the sword slips, lodging awkwardly under my left arm. I stumble, and panic for a moment, recalling this very thing happening in a dream. I lose my grip on the staff, and plunge into an abyss. The cold, muddy waters of the lagoon close over my mouth, choking me. I go down under the surface, the mud churning up as I thrash around. I can taste the fetid water as it invades my mouth – the cloying taste of rotting flesh and cemetery earth. I try to call out for Caterina but the mud in my mouth prevents me from doing so, muffling my cries for help. Then my blindly groping hand finds the staff again. It has jammed upright, and I manage to right myself.

I pause for a while to regain my breath, spitting out salt water and stinking filth. It has been a close call. The softest mud patches can suck a fully-grown man down and down until he simply disappears off the face of God's Earth. Angry at the sword for once again putting me in mortal danger, I rip the binding free that holds it to my body, and feel its considerable weight in the grip of my right hand. This goddamn sword has been the source of all my troubles, including an accusation of murder. Now is the time to be rid of it, and then maybe my luck will change for the better. I steady myself, and yank on the hilt. The sword comes out slickly smooth from its sheath, and I heft it in the night air. The moon reflects coldly on its polished surface, only slightly scarred by my own misuse at the very tip. The light causes the inscription to seem to sparkle mockingly in my eyes. I don't need to read it – the legend is as firmly engraved on my heart as it is on that perfect blade.

'*Qui falsitate vivit, animam occidit. Falsus in ore, caret honore.*'

I growl at such a pious sentiment. What harm does a little lying do to the soul? And as for honour – give me profit any day. I swing the blade in a glittering arc, and stand for a moment with the sword held up to the moon by my outstretched arm. If I swing it once more and let go, it will sail away to disappear for good in the mud of the lagoon. Out of harm's way. Thinking back to how the sword came into my possession, I nevertheless begin the arching swing . . .

The Year of Our Lord Twelve Hundred and Sixty Two started out as a good one for yours truly, Nicolo Zuliani. Everything I touched turned to gold. It culminated with a *colleganza* I set up at the beginning of the year. That's a sort of short-term, high-risk, high-return business venture that appeals to us Venetians. At the time, I was essentially potless, after spending all my previous trading profits. So I was ready to take the risk – with other people's money – on a big gamble. My reputation was good, even if some thought I was a chancer. To many, that was a good thing to be. So, I soon convinced a bunch of silversmiths who traded along the Merceria that I had already leased a 250 ton galley, with which I would transport cotton from Syria for the South German cloth trade. I even offered to show them over the ship in question – the *Provvidenza*. All they needed to do was supply the funds for the cotton, and I would guarantee them a nice little profit for their investment. I didn't mention the little difficulties of high seas, savage rocky shores, and pirates. Well, you don't want to put off investors when you've tapped into their greed, do you? They were on the hook, so I just needed to reel them in. Once I had secured the funds from them for the cotton, all I had to do was find the wherewithal to lease the *Provvidenza*.

Naturally, I had lied to them. I didn't have any share in the ship when I showed it to them. But I had watched the routines of the captain and his crew for four days, until I was certain they all went for lunch around the middle of the day. A lunch sufficiently liquid to ensure they did not return for at least three hours. I even greased the way, as it were, by slipping one of the crew a few coins by way of thanking him for showing me privately over the ship the previous day. You have to speculate to accumulate, and if things turned out the way I hoped, those few coins would be all I would put into the trading enterprise.

The gaggle of silversmiths arrived at the quay close by San Zaccaria Church promptly at noon as requested. I could see them already sniffing profit in the air. Unless it was the smell of the load of fish that was being unshipped next to the *Provvidenza* that teased their nostrils. Whatever it was, I greeted them like some Eastern potentate, eager to show off his magnificent palace.

'Greetings, Master Saraceni, Master Luprio . . .' I shook each man's hand in turn, careful to recall their names properly. I wanted them to feel like we were a bunch of intimate friends embarking on some adventure together. Confidence is what it's all about, after all. The problem was the little, squinty-eyed man who always seemed to bring up the rear. Why could I never remember his name? I squeezed his hand, and stared back genially at his wall-eyed, suspicious stare as I racked my brain. Then of a sudden it came, like a cold shower sweeping across the piazza. 'And last but not least, welcome Master Sebenico.'

He merely grunted, and slid his cold palm out of mine, which had begun to sweat. I knew I would have to watch Maestro Sebenico. From his name, I would guess he was descended from some Dalmatian pirate, and was probably as slippery as an eel. For now, I addressed the assembled throng, extolling the virtues of the galley on whose deck we stood.

'Look at the suppleness of those sheets.' I waved my hand up to the sails, and the spider's web of ropes that ran up to the mast. I wasn't sure which were sheets, but I did recall some of the spiel of the sailor whose lunch I had funded. I employed it as best I could. 'And those cleats are the sturdiest I have ever seen.' Fortunately, my attentive audience were sufficiently overawed not to question my nautical know-how, and contented themselves with looking sage, and nodding their heads. Even Master Sebenico seemed not to wish to betray his ignorance. Maybe he thought his pirate ancestors would turn in their watery graves if he did. 'Let's go for'ard, and examine the hold.'

And before you ask, yes, I did go in the right direction.

That had all been days ago, and as soon as I had got their money in the bag, I had worked on the Widow Vercelli, and Old Man di Betto to supply the funding for the galley. The widow was easily flattered by my flirtatious approaches, though she was old enough to be my granny, and ugly enough to be my pet dog. But a kiss on the hand and she was a cert. As was Pietro di Betto. The old man yearned for the good old days, when he had sailed in trading galleys himself. But now he was too sick to travel, and a little addled in the mind. In truth, I almost didn't take his money, out of sympathy for his affliction. But he insisted, didn't he? And I could not refuse him this last little pleasure in his life, could I? Besides, I wasn't cheating him, or any of them, out of their money. All being well, we would all profit from the enterprise. It's just that I was skating on thin ice, as it was usual for the merchant to put up one third of the funds. I was risking none. The trouble was, even after the widow and the simpleton coughed up, I was still short by a few thousand. So I decided to confide in Caterina.

After a particularly exhausting night of pleasure, she seemed pensive, almost impatient with my attempts at light-heartedness. Normally Caterina Dolfin looked flushed and healthy after a tumble in my bed, but this morning she was pale and wan – sickly even. I tried to laugh it off.

'What's the matter? Can't you take the pace any more? Maybe you should ease up on the wine, my dear Caterina.'

She always tried to match me goblet for goblet, but I was too practised at drinking to be beaten by a mere woman. Even if that woman was Caterina Dolfin, scion of one of the *case vecchie* – the aristocracy of Venice. If her father had known she was romping with a mere Zuliani, a merchant and a penniless one at that, he would have had me whipped out of La Serenissima at best. At worst, murdered in a dark alley and my body dumped in the lagoon. Still, I could not resist the excitement and allure of our assignations. Caterina Dolfin was a beauty, dark-haired and brown-eyed, with a rare figure that shone through the heavy folds of her richly embroidered bliaut over-gown. So, once again I had lured her secretly into my bed, and come the morning, I was caressing her voluptuous naked breasts, as I taunted her about her drinking. But this particular dawn she appeared to have something else on her mind, and she responded distractedly.

'Oh, leave over, Nicolo.'

This made me suddenly wary. She only used my full given name, instead of calling me Nick, when she was annoyed. I tried on my simpering look as she carried on.

'You should buy something more palatable than that cheap Rhenish you are so fond of when I dine with you. Maybe that's what disagreed with me. Unless it was the fish. God knows what they feed on in the lagoon.'

I guffawed. 'I don't need to be God to know what is washed from the Serene Republic's sewers and on to the feeding grounds where the lazier fishermen ply their trade.'

Caterina's eyes narrowed, and she held a petite hand to her mouth at the thought. She began to look even greener than before, her eyes almost pleading. I wondered again if she was expecting me to propose marriage, and I almost did at that point. But though I longed for Caterina, I thought of my own parents' stormy marriage. So I just couldn't bring myself to encompass such a commitment right then, and the moment was lost. Instead, I sounded her out on my small embarrassment with *colleganza* funds. She snorted in disdain.

'If you think I can lay my hands on any of my father's money, you must be mad. He didn't get rich by ignoring the pennies.' She rolled over on to her stomach, presenting her arched back and rounded, bare buttocks to my adoring gaze. 'You should try Pasquale, he's mad enough to risk money on you.'

I tore my eyes from her divine arse. 'Pasquale? Fish-face Valier?'

In truth, I had not considered Valier – he of the bulging eyes, and receding chin – but the more I thought about it, the more I liked the idea. Pasquale liked to mix with the same drinking crowd I did. And although you couldn't say we were friends, we had exchanged a few drolleries over some good wine. Moreover, like Caterina, he was also of the *case vecchie*, which meant he was loaded. And gullible enough to be taken in by my flattery. I would woo him like I had the Widow Vercelli. Just as long as he didn't hope to end up in my bed like the widow had. Hoped that is – my bed I reserve solely for the beautiful Cat. With that thought bringing me back to the present, I ran my fingers down her sensuously curved spine, and over her remarkable arse. And then further on.

If I had been able to foresee the future, I would not have left the question of marriage so unfinished. But then, I had no idea that time was running out for me. That I would only see her one more time, as murder came between us. Back then, I had reckoned there was all the time in the world to settle down. And for the time being, I was content to enjoy myself like any man should. I didn't really want to admit to myself that I was avoiding marriage because I feared ruining it all like my father had done. That was a thought I could not entertain, even while sober.

'Did you hear that there is talk of an election? And Doge Renier Zeno still firmly ensconced with no intention of resigning.'

Pasquale Valier was outraged that any such idea should be contemplated. He drank deep of the good Gascon wine I had supplied him with, spending some more of my precious few coins in a desperate attempt to raise the few thousand I still needed for my *colleganza*. His fishy eyes bulged even further at the thought of tradition being so usurped. These old families hung on desperately to the ways that had served them well. Myself, I thought the ducal election was rigged from the start in favour of the old families. Since when had a Zuliani had a chance to get voted in? Still, I needed to keep Valier sweet, if I was to tap into his money supply.

'Outrageous,' I murmured.

I had been more than a little surprised that he had accepted my invitation so easily. My lodgings were not the most salubrious of accommodation, being close to canal level, and consequently damp and rather smelly. Maybe it was the fact that they backed on to the fabulous Ca' da Mosta, and that I used the palace to describe how to reach my own more humble abode. The Ca' looked out majestically on to the Grand Canal. My quarters squinted blearily on to no more than a dingy alley of mud that you wouldn't dignify with the word canal. I prayed the interior would convey more a sense of modest simplicity to Valier than the reality. That of shabby poverty.

I had no need to worry. Once in his cups, Valier was blithely ignorant of the damp walls, and down-at-heel furniture. All I had to do was to keep refilling his tankard. And listen to him banging on about politics, which interested me little except when it affected business. Since last year, when the Greeks had retaken Constantinople, Venice's influence in that region had been blighted by our old enemy, Genoa. The doge's old title of Lord of a Quarter and Half a Quarter of the Roman Empire had suddenly become increasingly hollow-sounding. It had been won sixty years ago, when Doge Dandolo – the old, blind wheeler-dealer himself – had conned the leaders of the Fourth Crusade into conquering Constantinople instead of aiming straight for Outremer. They had owed the Republic a lot of money, and could do little else, mind you. With a puppet installed on the throne in Byzantium, Dandolo had picked up vast chunks of the newly made Latin Empire, and that lordly title. But now it was gone again, and apparently some blamed the present doge for the inconvenience. Including the erstwhile governor of Constantinople, Domenico Lazzari. Valier continued to blether on about it.

'A properly elected doge is for life, or until he decides to step down himself. How can anyone suggest he should be forced out?' He poured another potful of good Gascon red down his throat, and clutched my shoulder. 'What do you think, Nicolo, old chap? You're an honest fellow. What do you think we should do?'

Sweating a little at the thought he might run through

my slender supply of wine before I had parted him
from his money, I stared sombrely into his bleary eyes.
I found myself using his own drawly accent back at him.

'It's an outrage, Pasquale, old chum. That's what it
is. It makes a fellow want to make his money and run
before the whole fabric of society falls apart.'

He nodded eagerly, then a puzzled look slowly crept
over his blotchy face.

'Make his money . . . and run?'

I could see on his drink-sodden face the sly look of
one who had been hooked. I fed him the line before
reeling him in.

'It so happens I have a proposition to put to you. It
can't fail . . .'

Later that night, a strange thing happened. I had just
got rid of Pasquale Valier by the street door, when I
heard a furtive tapping from the other side of the
house. It took a moment for me to realize there was
someone at the water door. I too had imbibed a fair
amount of the good Gascon, though surreptitiously I
had cut it with cheap Rhenish to make it go further.
Even so, I was a little unsteady on my feet, and nearly
fell in the muddy canal when I opened the door a
splinter to see who was calling so late at night. I had
half a thought it was sweet Cat come to romp the night
away. My heart yearned for that, but my thick head and
tired mind almost prayed it was not.

As I reeled on the step down into the turbid waters
at my door, a firm, but slender hand took my arm.
Whoever it was steadied me, almost at the expense of
his own stability, as he was standing in a small boat that
rocked under him. But he righted himself and me, and
gave a low bow. It was difficult to see his face, as he
was muffled in a hooded cloak, that was draped across
most of his features. All I saw was a pair of brown eyes

staring at me with creases at their corners that betokened a smile beneath the folds of the drapery.

'What do you want, good sir?'

I spoke a little merrily, my tone of voice still in Valier mode, plummy and drawled.

The man refrained from speaking, but his eyes sparkled even more. He drew a long bundle from under the cloak, and with difficulty, as though it was too weighty for him, held it out to me in both hands. Noticing in passing that the hands were gloved, I took the burden from him. In truth, the parcel was heavy, but not so heavy that a fully-grown man could not have handled it. I assumed the deliverer of my gift was perhaps elderly or ill as to find it so difficult to lift. I thanked him for his services, but still got no reply. He simply nodded his head, and turned away, lifting his punt pole into place. I watched for a while until the mysterious figure disappeared into the mists, then hefted his gift in my hand. It had a weightiness to it that promised value, and I eagerly unwrapped the cloth that bound it up.

What was first revealed at one end was a thick, plain disc of steel, and below it a lime wood handle wrapped about with wire. It was a sword, and an old one at that. The cross had been fashioned to look like dogs' heads, but the blade itself was encased in a plain wooden sheath. From its length, I guessed the blade to be around thirty inches long. I pulled the blade a little way out the sheath to reveal a small shield stamped on the lower end. It bore the name 'de la Pomeroy' etched in silver, but it meant nothing to me. As the last of the binding slid off, a piece of parchment fell to the floor. I stooped to pick it up. The writing was in a neat hand.

'My bold entrepreneur – I don't want your venture to fall at the first hurdle. Take this old weapon, and sell it for whatever you can get. My family had it from some Crusader called Ranulf de Cerne, who passed through many years ago. It was left in payment of a debt. But take care, the sword comes with a legend – things happen to its owner, it seems. So sell it swiftly, and return safely.'

The message was finished off with no signature, but a strange scrawl that I could not at first decipher. Then I turned the parchment sideways, and the scrawl resolved itself into a neat little feline shape with a curly tail. It had to be a message from my own Cat – Caterina Dolfin – I was convinced of it. So much so, that I even fancied I heard her laughter carrying over the waters of the canal outside my door. I slid the blade from its sheath, and looked on the inscription for the first time. All talk of honour and soul did not concern me, however. What I was convinced of, was that I would not sell this sword for anything. Especially as I had already got the funds I needed for my *colleganza* from Pasquale Valier.

One month later, I was standing on the quayside of the Giudecca Canal with the sword at my waist, money in my purse, and a bushy, red beard on my chin. It had grown while I was roughing it on the journey to and from Syria, and now I fancied it added to my appeal with the women. With my fine head of red hair, tanned features and green eyes, I knew I couldn't fail. The *Provvidenza* lay proudly at its moorings before me, a little more battered, its mainsail somewhat more ragged. But nothing that some money and the tough, thick pitch of the ship-builders in the Arsenal complex couldn't cure. I had already sold the cotton on to a fair-haired German trader called Bradason, and all I needed to do was pay my investors their margin. Which

would leave a tidy sum for me. I was longing to see
Cat, but decided I should replace my stained and
tattered clothes first. Like *Provvidenza*, I needed a good
overhaul, and it would do no harm to take my costs
out of the *colleganza*'s profits. They were big enough to
absorb it.

I found a good tailor in the Merceria, and bought
an undertunic of red, and a sclavine of blue. Finally I
belted the sword round my waist. Caterina Dolfin would
not be able to resist me, and I swaggered off along the
Spaderia – suitably enough the street of sword-makers
– then made for the Rialto crossing. Passing the Rio
dei Bareteri, I noticed a workshop with headgear
displayed, and was taken by a sugar-loaf cap in green
that I reckoned would sit well on my flowing red locks.
I bought it, and turning the brim up, I set it at a jaunty
angle on my head. Palazzo Dolfin was on the other side
of the Grand Canal, and I made for the bridge of boats
called the Quartarolo that spanned it at the Rialto.
Before I could reach it and pay the toll, however, I was
stopped by a braying cry.

'Zuliani! Is that you? I was told you were back.'

I groaned. It was Pasquale Valier, and he would be
wanting the return on his investment. I had hoped it
would hang at my waist just a little longer, before I had
to disburse it. It felt good to have a heavy purse, even
if most of the money belonged to others. I need not
have worried, though. Valier seemed more concerned
about having a good time than getting his dues.

'I was on my way to meet Jacopo and a few others
to celebrate my good fortune. What a stroke of luck to
bump into you, Zuliani. You must join us.'

He had to be talking about Jacopo Selvo, who though
a scion of one of the old families, was an entertaining
drinking companion. I had caroused away many a night
in his company. I reckoned my ardour for Caterina

could be postponed a little while. Especially if it gave me the opportunity to boast about my exploits over a drink or two to a few young aristos with more money than sense. We started out at some low dive on the northern quay close to the Arsenal, meeting up with two other friends of Valier, Vitale Orseolo, and Marino Michiel. The tavern was more often frequented by tarry ship-builders, than members of the *case vecchie*. But Valier reckoned they would break open the best Apulian wine, if they saw the weight of my purse. He was right – the wine tasted good, and it flowed freely at the sight of my money. We ended up carousing the night away, defying the curfew bell, and lightening my purse more than somewhat.

From there I think we went straight to the Ca' d'Orseolo, though my brain was too befuddled to be sure, where young Vitale Orseolo cracked a cask of Malvasia. I hadn't forgotten sweet Caterina, I promise you. But Pasquale and Jacopo kept leading me astray with more wine. With dawn approaching, and a tankard of sweet Malvasia in my unsteady hand, I tried to break up the party.

'I must go to Palazzo Dolfin now. I promised Caterina I would shower her with riches on my return.'

Jacopo Selvo giggled, and hung his arm over my shoulder. He slopped red wine over my new mantle, staining it, but it didn't seem to matter. Then he snorted the odour of ripe Apulian into my face.

'Later, Zuliani, later. You know, a woman gets riper the longer you keep her hanging on. Leave her till later. In fact, you would do well to leave her hanging like a ripe pheasant for a few days. Then she will really be ready to . . . you know . . . to . . .'

He made a fist over his groin, jerking it up and down, and guffawed in my face. I should have stuck my fist in his florid chops for being so coarse about Cat, but for some reason what he said amused me. I giggled, and grabbed the wine bottle, pouring it straight down my throat.

'Have a care, Jacopo Selvo. You speak of the woman I love.'

I hauled the shiny sword from the sheath at my waist, waving it in the air in mock combat. I nearly sliced Orseolo's head off by accident, and he dropped to the ground in a dead faint. The others crowded around, admiring the blade as it sparkled in the candlelight. Valier was the most impressed, his eyes feasting on the perfection.

'That is a mighty blade, Zuliani. And an old one. It must have been drowned in blood in its time. How did you come by it?'

I feigned indifference to its quality.

'This old thing. I had it from . . . an admirer.'

I leaned on the sword like some old Crusader, but spoiled the effect by falling over in a heap. The blade nicked my arm, and added another stain to my new clothes. It was not long after that the three others fell into a drunken stupor, leaving only Valier and myself to finish the Malvasia. We slumped side by side on Orseolo's couch, and I reluctantly began to count out Valier's share of my loot. His eyes glittered, while at the same time he bemoaned the hard times that made it so difficult to make money.

'And since you left on your trip, Zuliani, Domenico Lazzari has returned redoubling his complaints about Doge Zeno. He has moaned so much that the doge has been persuaded to stand down. They say that Girolamo Fanesi has thrown his hat into the ring, and expects to win. I mean to say, really! He's not even a proper Venetian. And all because of this Byzantine fiasco.'

I was a little slow on the uptake.

'What Byzantine . . . ? Oh, the loss of Constantinople, and the title of Lord of Half-a-quart and a Quart-and-a-half of Roman wine . . .'

Pasquale sniggered at the old joke, and bashed my arm with his puny fist.

'Be serious for a moment, Nicolo. You know, I was thinking that if you could sort of influence who was in the Group of Forty-One, you could virtually guarantee who the next doge was. And prevent Fanesi winning.'

Now, you should know that the method of electing a new doge is involved in the extreme. By a series of lots, the *Maggior Consiglio* – the Great Council – vote for four of their number. This four from the great and good then nominate forty-one of the council members, each of whom requires at least three nominations, and not more than one from each family. Oh, and don't forget that to get on the Great Council itself in the first place, you have to be nominated by two representatives from each of the six *sestieri*, or districts, that make up Venice. So, to get to vote a doge into office, you have to . . . well, I don't want to bore you. Let's just say it's complicated. Just take it from me that the system goes on and on. For several rounds. Until forty-one names are thus randomly selected. And it is they who elect the doge. So I don't know why I agreed with Valier.

'I suppose so. Yes and, if you could influence the vote so that a particular name came up, you could make an awful lot of money into the bargain.'

This was my contribution to the drunken exchange. I cared not, and still don't, which member of the Venetian *case vecchie* – the old aristocracy – was elected doge. My family has been around for as long as any of them. It has even been said that one of our ancestors helped drive the *pali* – the wooden piles – into the sandbanks on top of which the city was built three hundred and fifty years ago. But the Zulianis always made their money by dint of their own labour, and that was enough to keep us out of the inner circle. No, I didn't care if a Tiepolo, a Morosini, or a Zeno won the election. I just liked the idea of making a killing on the result for one Zuliani. Me.

'But there is no way of influencing such a complex system,' moaned Valier. 'And I now have a purse bursting with coins to wager.'

Valier was old aristocracy himself, which is why, along with his *colleganza* profits, he had so much money to waste. And why he hadn't the brains to see an opportunity when it leaped at him. The aristocracy are all inbred, after all.

I grinned. 'There is a way, I am sure of it. Even if it comes with a little bribery.'

Valier's little, pointy rat-face looked blank at first – but then it always did. Finally, his features squashed up in what I think was supposed to resemble shock.

'It won't work! You wouldn't dare!'

I spat in my fist, and held out a steady hand for him to clasp, and seal the wager. See, I wasn't half as drunk as poor Pasquale Valier was. In fact, I had seen the opportunity to get all that *colleganza* profit back from him as soon as he had started talking. Besides, I liked a challenge, and the drink had made me reckless.

'Give me that pile of coins that's burning a hole in your purse, and I'll show you what's possible.'

'OK. But it's my money against that beautiful sword.'

I almost didn't do the deal when he said that. The sword was from Cat, after all. But being a Zuliani, I only hesitated for a second. We shook on it.

I woke to the booming of the Marangona bell in the Campanile. It calls the tradesmen to work, and tolls the curfew in the evening. Just now, it resonated round my tender skull, which throbbed at every clang. I squeezed open my eyes on a scene of devastation. A pile of empty vessels gave witness to the scale of the binge that Valier and I had indulged in, along with Selvo, Michiel and Orseolo. Those last three were still lying in a tangled heap at one end of the long tapestried room on the upper floor of the Ca' d'Orseolo. They were dead to the world. I got up and staggered round the room. I noticed one particularly fine drape had a long cut right through Salome bearing the head of John the Baptist on a tray. I thought now at least honours were even, and the maid had had her head separated from her body too, if only in a woven image. I fingered the extensive slash, and remembered something about waving my fine sword above my head, and threatening the life of anyone who stood between me and Caterina Dolfin. Quite obviously, Salome had done so. I nervously twitched the tapestry together, but it was no use. When I let go, the damaged portion gaped open once again.

Still somewhat disorientated, I went about looking for Pasquale Valier. Had I not made some wager with him in the early hours? My befuddled brain pondered the problem as I brushed down my clothes. My tunic was creased, and smelled of stale sweat. And my mantle had a muddy boot mark on it to add to the wine and blood stains. I searched for my new sugar-loaf cap, and found it gripped in Jacopo Selvo's hand. He had obviously been using it to wipe the stains off the floor where he had vomited. I sniffed it, then crammed it on my head anyway, flipping up the brim. It didn't seem quite as jaunty as it had yesterday.

Valier was nowhere to be seen, and neither was my sword, I realized. I panicked. How could I meet Caterina without her gift at my waist? I scrabbled under the long dining table, searching for it, and then under the couch where Valier and I had made our pact. And then I remembered our wager. I was to rig the doge's election so that Fanesi failed, and one particular name would come up. Any name, so long as we could bet on it. At the time, I had been so confident I could do it. Now, in the cold light of day, I hadn't the faintest idea how I would arrange such a thing. And I still couldn't find my sword.

Palazzo Dolfin was one of the newer buildings along the Grand Canal. It's grand arcade was of red *altinelle* bricks edged in hard white Istrian stone. The same white stone had been used for the flight of steps down to the water. The whole affair was reflected gloriously in the canal as I approached, until the image broke up with the chop of my ferry boat's prow. I pulled nervously at my wine-stained clothes, and tried to set the cap squarely on my head to give the impression of a prosperous and serious suitor. My money purse still hung at my waist, though it had been seriously depleted since yesterday. The ferryman bumped his boat against the lower steps, and I passed him a small coin as I stepped on to their pristine whiteness. As he poled away, I noticed for the first time that the palace's doors were closed. Frowning, I hammered on the forbidding surface to be met only with silence. This was not how my suit for Caterina's hand was intended to be. I knocked again, noting how the sound echoed hollowly behind the door.

Then suddenly a shutter screeched open above my head somewhere, and a coarse, female voice called out in a low Venetian dialect.

'Watcha want?'

I walked back down the sparkling white steps, and craned my neck upwards. From one of the upper levels of the palace, a fat, red face poked out. The woman repeated her abrupt demand, and I was hard put to contain my temper.

'I want to speak to the master of the house, woman. Now come down and let me in.'

I was sounding more like Pasquale Valier every day. The servant woman, for her part, mocked my snooty tones.

'Ooh, yer do, do yer. Well yer can't. They've all gorn to Padua on account of the fever.'

The fever? Was Caterina ill, then?

'What I mean is, to avoid the fever. Don't know when they'll be back.'

With that, she withdrew her head, and abruptly slammed the shutter. I had not heard of a fever being rampant, but then many scares ran through the city. We Venetians did live on swampy mud-flats, after all. With Caterina away for an unspecified time, I would have to be patient in my suit. In fact, I felt some relief at not having to face Cat's father straight away. Maybe marriage was not in my destiny. Besides, her absence would certainly give me some time to work out this voting scam. I didn't have much time, as the election was only a few weeks away. I waved for a passing ferry boat to stop, and immediately began thinking about how to ensure one particular name was selected.

In the end it proved stupefyingly simple. I don't know why I didn't see it straight away, but I didn't. I must have been moon-struck for love of Cat. So I wasted days locked away in my musty, dark quarters. I huddled in one corner, seated at a scarred table with parchment and quill. The waters of the lagoon rose – as they do from time to time – and seeped across my floor. I watched the lapping approach of the fetid waters, noting only that this time they did not quite engulf the tidal mark left by the previous *aqua alta*. I only left my room once to distribute the profits on my *colleganza* to all the investors. Some of them were not best pleased with the thin margin I gave them. But then I had had to pay off my own debts first, and I also seemed to have lost a considerable amount during that first day of carousing. The silversmith Sebenico was particularly tart, screwing his sharp nose up at the meagre coins I gave him.

'What do you call this, Zuliani? I could have made more out of my investment if I had loaned it through the Jews on Spinalunga.'

I mumbled something about unforeseen overheads, and pirates off the Dalmatian coast, and hurried away. Thank goodness the Widow Vercelli, and Old Man di Betti were only too glad to see any sort of return on their money, and too dim to realize they could have had more. Back in my dank cell, I wrapped all my clothes around me, and pondered the little matter of the election fraud.

Getting on for a hundred years ago, the system had been changed from one where the Great Council nominated eleven electors, to a more foolproof method. It was decided to select four of the great and good, who would themselves choose forty names. I began to toy with the idea of bribing the four original nominees. That would be a damn sight cheaper than bribing forty. Oh, except it was now forty-one. Some genius had overlooked the fact that an even number of electors could bring about a tie. Which had happened about forty years ago, forcing the addition of one more elector. The forty-one commissioners operated in a sort of secret conclave, like cardinals electing a pope. Each would come up with a name on a slip of paper. Duplicate names were discarded, until a single slip for each nominee was created. These slips were placed in a vessel, and one name drawn out. A vote was then taken on that name, and if it got twenty-five votes, then that man was the next doge.

So my first idea was to suborn the four, who could then nominate forty-one people inclined to come up with the right name. But, thinking about it, I knew that wouldn't work, and I certainly wouldn't have bet my shirt on them coming up with the right name. No, there was too much chance of a slip-up. Similarly, bribing the forty-one would prove an impossible task. Even if I could get to them when they were locked away, some of those old families are incorruptible, believe it or not. No, I finally came to the conclusion that the trick had to be turned with the mechanics of the voting system. If I could ensure one particular slip of paper came out the voting urn, then I was nearly home and dry. Though this was a contradiction in terms in relation to my own domestic arrangements. The water of the lagoon had nearly reached my toes under the table. I lifted up my chilly feet, and plonked them on the bench opposite where I sat.

But then, to ensure one slip in particular came out, I had to ensure it went in to begin with. And I was back again to bribery. I felt I was in a maze that kept taking me back to the centre instead of out to the rim and freedom. With my brains nearly boiling, and my feet near freezing, I gave up. I needed to talk to someone, and longed for it to be Cat. But in lieu of my beautiful girl, I would have to make do with my old drinking companions. Grabbing my sugar-loaf hat, and cramming it on my head, I decided to make for the anonymous tavern close to the Arsenal, where the drinking session that had landed me with this problem had begun. I squelched through the damp streets as the rain began to fall, taking care not to fall into a canal. The high tides sometimes made it difficult to tell the difference between a watery *rio*, and a paved *calle.* And it was not rare for an unwary Venetian to blithely step into a canal thinking the water was merely a damp sheen on a paved surface. In the nameless tavern, I found only Marino Michiel, his pasty, round face made paler by the weather. I sat down beside him, and ordered the Apulian wine that we had been drinking the last time. When it came, even that seemed to have succumbed to the *aqua alta*. It had clearly been watered.

'Where are the others?' I enquired of the sullen Michiel. He waved his gloved hand in a vague gesture of uncertainty.

'Don't know for sure. All I do know is that Valier has gone to Padua.'

My ears pricked up at the mention of the place where my Cat languished.

'Oh, is he fleeing the fever too?'

Michiel looked puzzled. 'Fever? Is there talk of a fever? I have heard nothing.'

Alarm bells should have rung at that point, but I was too engrossed in my problem with slips of paper to take in what Michiel was saying. Instead I spoke of the up-coming election.

'And its all done in secret with a few big names, as if we, the people, don't have a say. Time was when an *arengo* was called – a meeting of all the people. Now it's just a formality.'

I was forgetting Marino Michiel was old aristocracy, and to him the idea of consulting the people was tantamount to permitting mob rule. He protested that the system was fair.

'But it's all well controlled, so that one man can't push a name through against the will of the others,' he whined. 'They are even trying a new system this time to ensure there's no hanky-panky.'

My heart lurched, and nearly fought its way out of

my throat. Did Michiel know what I was up to? I hoped Valier hadn't let anything slip to his pals.

'What's that?' I croaked.

'Oh, when they have got the final set of slips in the voting urn, they are not going to have one of their own draw one out. Just in case they cheat. It seems they are going to pick a child at random from the street, and he – the *ballotino* – will draw the name.'

Perfect.

Two days later, I still couldn't stop grinning from ear to ear. At the time, I had even bought the bewildered Michiel a drink. He was quite unaware that he had given me the best news I could have expected. Only if I had been told of Caterina Dolfin's immediate return to Venice would I have been more cheerful. Unfortunately, there was no news on that front. In fact, my tentative enquiries revealed nothing – the doings of the Dolfin clan had been shrouded in mystery. Some people repeated the servant's story of them fleeing rumours of a plague, and yet others spoke of the death of a wealthy uncle in Verona. A few hinted darkly at a family shame that had caused the Dolfins' retreat from Venice. I believed none of it, only worrying that perhaps Caterina was being kept from me. Or worse, that she herself had chosen to avoid me.

But all that was of passing concern. I had been buoyed up by the new twist to the selection process for the doge. It had played directly into my hands. Now my task involved nothing more complex than training some urchin – preferably one who was already adept at the art of picking purses – in a little sleight-of-hand. And I knew just who could put me on to such a delinquent.

I put the word about, but had to wait until night for my search to bear fruit. Master thieves did not like the full glare of daylight, and Alimpato was a master among masters. It was he who had taught me much of my card-sharping techniques. A skill that had stood me in good stead when I had been short of cash in my early youth. Young noblemen seemed eager to pour coins into my purse for the sake of a game of cards or dice. Of course, even those dimwits realized after a while that my luck held a little too long to be true, and finally I had temporarily retreated, resorting to a tour of the main-land for a while. There were dupes aplenty in Fusina, Dolo, and Stra. But I yearned for Venice, and when I reckoned my reputation was forgotten, I returned. To a life of honest trading – if that's not a contradiction in terms. However, I still practised with my hands every day, and my manual dexterity was as good as it ever was. You never know when you might need to help Lady Luck along a little. Like now. I was proposing to pass on some of my skills to a young cut-purse, but needed a likely candidate.

Sitting in my damp room as darkness fell, I was im-patient for Alimpato to put in an appearance. Time was running out for me. Then I heard a scratching at the door, and leapt towards it, flinging it open. At first, I thought there was no one there – that I had merely heard the sound of a rat gnawing at the rotting timbers. But then I realized there was a darker shadow inside the shadow of the archway opposite. I smiled, and stepped back into my room, leaving the outer door ajar. A few moments later, the shadow entered my dingy room, and sat across from me at my table.

'Alimpato, you old devil!'

The man pulled the hood of his voluminous cloak back, revealing a cadaverous face beneath a tangled skein of thin, greying hair. Alimpato smiled, revealing a set of blackened, rotten teeth. He more resembled a crippled beggar than what he really was – a prince among thieves. I pushed a flagon of Rhenish across to him, and a cheap pewter goblet. No use putting temptation in his way. Despite our friendship, he would have buried a more valuable vessel inside his roomy cloak.

'Nicolo Zuliani, as I live and breathe. Still earning your bread honestly?'

I never heard a man put so much invective into the word 'honest' as Alimpato. When he uttered it, the word was redolent of shame, stupidity, and absurdity. I laughed and shrugged my shoulders.

'In so far as anyone can.'

'Then why did you put out the word you wanted to see me?'

He filled his goblet, and swigged deeply, wiping his mouth with the back of his hand. I noticed the fingers were just as supple and slender as they had been when last he had shown me how to switch a set of dice.

'It is in the way of a little matter that I need to . . . influence, shall I say. I have a wager on it.'

He nodded, knowing that I would not tell him the details. And that I knew he would not even dream of asking. The less you knew in his world, the easier it was to avoid being implicated, if questioned. I prayed fervently that I would not be discovered, as I could then expect a short stay in the ducal prison, followed by a long death.

'I need a good cut-purse, who can learn quickly how to palm and substitute . . . a small item.'

He nodded, and rose from the table, turning the goblet in his hand speculatively. He sighed, and put it down, then made for the door.

'Wait!' I called out after him. 'Aren't you going to help me?'

He turned in the open doorway, and stared at me.

'Of course. Walk across the Piazza tomorrow

morning on the first stroke of the Marangona bell.
Have a heavy purse on your belt.'

He pulled the hood over his face, returning his
features to the darkness, and disappeared into the
night.

The following morning, still not sure what to expect,
I stood in front of the Basilica of St Mark. I waited for
the ninth hour, when the great Marangona bell in the
Campanile tolled, and started to walk across the old
pavement of herring-bone brick laid by Doge
Sebastiano Ziani a hundred years ago. I promenaded
along, alert for any action, walking towards the quay,
where stood the two antique columns brought back
from the East by an ancestor of Michiel's. When I
reached the columns, nothing had happened, and I
felt very disappointed. Alimpato had let me down.
Then an urchin appeared from round one of the
pillars, a huge grin splitting his grubby face.

'Missing something, mister?'

My hand instinctively dropped to my waist, as I realized the weight of my purse was no longer there.
Instead there were just a couple of sliced-through
cords. The urchin brought his right hand from behind
his back, and waved my purse in the air. I didn't move
to retrieve it however, merely clapping my hands in
appreciation of his feat. The lad, who looked no more
than eight years old, bowed low, then hesitated.

'Don't you want it back, mister? Master Alimpato said
you would.'

'Keep it,' I said generously. The purse strings were
cut anyway. I would let the boy find out that the weightiness of the purse was due to several large nail heads
at his own convenience. 'But you can come with me.'

He looked rather unsure at first, not certain what
my motives were. So I softened my tones, and suggested

we go and find something to eat. By the look of the puny chest that showed through his tattered clothes, I could guess he was half starved. He joined me at my side, and we walked back across the square, like two gentlemen promenading.

'My name's . . .'

I stopped him with a finger to my lips.

'No names. Just tell me where you come from.'

'Malamocca.'

It was a small settlement on the finger of land that protected the lagoon from the Adriatic.

'Then that shall be your name. Come, Malamocco, let's fill our bellies.'

'But what do I call you?'

I thought for a moment.

'Barratieri will do.'

'"Card-sharp"?'

I nodded.

It took an amazing amount of food to fill Malamocco's scrawny belly. That first day I ended up paying for a feast which started with vegetables, then moved on to a lightly cooked dish of flounders, then a stew of wild boar, and to round it off some fresh fruit brought in from the mainland. And if I had not protested that my purse was empty, he would have begun again. His torpid nature after all that ensured we did not begin work till the following day. But then I found him an excellent study. Within hours, he was switching cards with a dexterity almost as good as mine. After three days of relentless effort, I could have put him out on the street, and guaranteed he would win every card or dice game he took part in. That part of the scam was ready. I only debated with myself if I needed to bribe the person in the group of forty-one charged with selecting the *ballotino*. The problem was I had no way of knowing in advance who that would be. I would have to find a fool-proof way of ensuring Malamocco was the only possible choice when it came down to the moment. In the mean-time, I was paying good money to keep my little sly-fingered investment fed and out of trouble.

The day before the voting process would begin, I was walking across the Piazza in front of the Basilica, when a familiar, braying voice called out my name. I stopped in my tracks, and turned to confront Pasquale Valier, newly returned, apparently, from Padua.

'Valier. Where have you been? And where is my sword?'

'Your sword? Oh, don't worry, it's safe enough. I have left it in your quarters.' He grinned inanely. 'I told you the night I left for Padua, why I borrowed it. Don't you recall? I said I would improve it's appearance for when I won it off you. But that is unimportant just now. Let me introduce you to a friend of mine.'

It was only then that I realized Valier was accompan-ied by a small, but wiry fellow some years older than both of us. Despite his small frame, and close-cropped hair, I would have said from the lines on his face that he was over forty. And, from the sour and down-turned shape of his mouth, had experienced disappointment in his life. His sclavine had an ornate, almost Eastern-style edging to it, though it now looked shabby, and ill-kept. I was intrigued, and took his proferred hand.

Valier was certainly awed by his presence, for he spoke in respectful tones. 'This is Domenico Lazzari.'

I almost yelped in horror at the revelation, and dropped his hand like it was a hot *altinelle* brick. Don't get me wrong. I did not disapprove of Lazzari, or what he had done. After all, he was one of the newly rich, just as I aspired to be. He had dragged himself up the ladder, and irritated the old aristocracy in the process. I admired that. But when he lost his coveted post of *podesta* – governor – of Constantinople, to be reduced to a mere *bailo*, he had suffered from a severe case of sour grapes. To so criticize the doge, as he did, took either guts or blind stupidity. And for me to be seen in his company the day before I rigged the election of the new doge was not good news.

Valier should have realized that. Here we all were, standing in the middle of the most public square in Venice, shaking hands and to all intents and purposes agreeing on the overthrow of Renier Zeno. I could be in deep trouble – as deep as that which Lazzari already floundered in. And Valier would not be excluded, as he had wagered on Zeno losing the election this time. What was he thinking of?

I pulled him roughly to one side, and whispered hoarsely. 'What the hell do you think you're doing? This man is poison at the moment. And besides, I thought you disapproved of him forcing the doge into an election.'

Valier pulled away irritably from my grip, while the object of my concern looked on in amusement. He waved away my reference to his former attitude to Lazzari. Clearly the man was now in Valier's favour.

'It's OK. I've told him nothing about your . . . er . . . scheme. But he does know about our betting on a particular name coming out of the hat. He has money he wants to wager. On Fanesi winning. We can't lose. Your reputation is on a high now – make use of it.'

He pushed me towards Lazzari, and like a fool, I could not resist the lure of money. So it was that I allowed myself to be seen accepting a very large and weighty purse from Domenico Lazzari. Then he and Valier went their separate ways, and I rushed home to see what Pasquale had done to my sword. It was only when he was gone that I remembered he had come back from Padua. He might have had some news of Caterina, and I might have been able to learn if I was still in favour or out. I would have to ask him when next we met. After I had won my bet.

The blade lay sheathed, and looking pretty much as when last I had seen it. Only this time it was lying on my scratched and humble table, not Orseolo's ornately carved couch where Valier and I had made our wager. On the surface, there appeared to be no changes to it. The cross of the hilt was still shaped in the form of two dogs' heads, mouths agape. The hilt itself still bore its leather casing, wrapped around with wire – all worn but none the worse for that. It felt comforting to grip the hilt knowing that many an experienced hand had sweated on it and shaped its lumps and bumps. Even the disc of the pommel was untrammelled. I would have killed Valier, if he had ruined its simple honesty. I closed my palm over the hilt. The sword almost felt as if it jumped into my hand, it was so easy to hold. I slid the blade out of its sheath, and at last saw Valier's embellishment along the length of the polished blade. The inscription was in Latin, and in imitation of the original text inscribed on the other side.

qui est hilaris dator, hunc amat salvator. omnis avarus, nulli est carus.

'Hmm. "The Saviour loves a cheerful giver; a miser's dear to no one." Very apt, Pasquale.'

I don't know if he intended it as a joke on my way with money or not. But seeing as I was going to keep the sword after I won our wager, the joke was on him, and the quotation would serve as an ironic motto for me. Tomorrow was the day the vote would be taken, and I hurried off to make a deal with a certain stall-holder I had seen close to the main square.

The next morning, in the church of San Gregorio, I found myself praying fervently for the success of the scheme. Or rather praying that it would not fail hopelessly. All my money, and that bagful of Valier's, was riding on the election of a certain Pietro Orseolo. But already I felt something indefinable had gone wrong, and matters hung on a knife-edge. Valier had handed over his money at the end of our drinking session. But, a week on, I had discovered that he had hedged his bets by wagering even more on Zeno retaining his position. And Valier didn't often pass up a sure thing.

It had gone well to start with. I had loitered round the main doors of St Marks where the representative of the Forty-One had gone to pray. Malamocco, suitably garbed in decent clothes – at my expense – hovered nearby, ostensibly playing some innocent game with sticks. The Piazza was unusually void of other children, chiefly because I had bribed a stallholder who vended sweetmeats made of honey, dates, raisins and liquorice to cry that he was giving away samples to whoever passed his stall. Once Malamocco had passed the word among his young contemporaries, the Piazza had emptied of any competitors for the attentions of the man who would soon emerge from the Basilica. His instructions were to stop the first boy he met, and take him to the Doge's Palace.

When the man, whom I recognized as Vitale Michiel, father to Marino, came out into the sunlight, he squinted in the bright rays, and cast his eyes around. He might have been a little puzzled at the apparent absence of children. But no matter, Malamocco, right on cue, wandered artlessly past him. Fulfilling his instructions to the letter, Michiel hailed the child, and taking him by the shoulder, guided him in a fatherly manner towards the Palace. I breathed a sigh of relief – the first hurdle had been successfully crossed. Now it was all down to Malamocco's dexterity, and my training.

I followed the pair at a distance, and watched them disappear into the fortress-like structure of the Doge's Palace. Then I waited. And waited. When the Marangona struck twelve bells at noon, I began to sweat, fearing that something had gone wrong. After another hour had passed without a result, I was sure the scam had failed. For another hour I wandered Venice, until I found myself again at the church of San Gregorio. There, I sat in the cool interior praying. Under my breath, I cursed my ill luck, and the day I had talked myself into this conspiracy. I had a thousand questions. Why had Pasquale Valier passed up on the opportunity of a lifetime? Had he just hedged his bets, or was there a deeper side to his change of mind? I realized this latest act of mine was proving to be not that of a chancy rogue, but of a gullible simpleton. It had been plain boastfulness to even talk of rigging the future election for Venice's doge. Why hadn't I stuck to good, honest, sharp business deals. Look at me now – I was even resorting to prayer.

'Lord, help me now. Only You know that I am doing it for the best of intentions. The *case vecchie* will never allow new blood into the ruling parties. And only You know how much Venice needs it. But if I am discovered, they will never forgive me for what I have done.'

Even as I spoke, I knew that God was unlikely to respond to the pleasing lies with which I usually beguiled my investors. So, when the response to my prayer came, it came not from God, but from a shadowy figure who had slipped into the ornate wooden pew behind me. From the odour of his bad breath, I knew it was the thief Alimpato. I half turned, but his hoarse voice stopped me.

'No, don't turn round. I don't want to draw attention to us. Just tell me what you needed the boy for.'

'As *ballotino*,' I tried to explain in words of one

syllable, not sure if the thief knew or cared much about politics. 'Whoever is running the doge's election, comes out of the Basilica, and selects the first boy in the street he comes across. And it's that kid who pulls out a name from the voting jar. Into the jar the Forty-One have put a shortlist for doge. It was easy to guess the most likely names that would go on that list. So all I had to do was ensure one particular name from that shortlist was drawn. That name was the one I wagered all on. The boy had a slip of paper with that name on, and I taught him to palm the slip of paper, and appear to draw it from the jar. Easy.'

'Hmmm. Not so easy, it would seem. Last I heard, the boy was being escorted to the prison, and the whole matter was being hushed up.'

I went cold, and a sick feeling spread in my guts. I felt afraid not only for myself, but mainly for poor Malamocco. No one ever emerged alive from the doge's prison.

'What happened?'

'It's difficult to tell. As I said, they are keeping the whole thing quiet. But someone must have ratted on you. I have heard that after the paper was drawn, they opened the jar, and still found the same number of slips inside.'

I marvelled at Alimpato's intimate knowledge of the goings-on of a so-called secret meeting deep in the bowels of the Doge's Palace. But maybe that is why he is as successful as he is. And I might have wished for some of his insider information myself. I begged him to tell me what had gone wrong. His next words were chilling.

'Zuliani. You have been betrayed, and they know everything. But it is worse than that. Domenico Lazzari has been found murdered, and you are in the frame for it.'

Lazzari? What had I to do with his death, or his death with the rigged election? My brain could barely contain the flood of events.

'They say Lazzari was part of the scam, Zuliani, and that you silenced him when the truth came out. Just to save your own skin.' There was a rustling in the seat behind me, as if Alimpato was eager to put a very great distance between himself and me. And I couldn't blame him. But first, he had a final warning. 'It matters little now what has gone before. All is lost, and the *Signori* are on your trail. I suggest you get out while you still can. I know I am.'

So the flim-flam was blown apart like a powder barrel in the Arsenal shipyard, and the *Signori di Notte*, or 'Gentlemen of the Night', were hunting in broad daylight. I twisted round in my pew, but all I saw was the back of the cloaked shape of Alimpato disappearing down the central aisle, taking his own advice. I crossed myself in one last effort to get God on my side, and dashed out of the church into the bright sunlight of a clear Venetian afternoon. Hesitating for a moment in the church's doorway, I considered my options.

My best hope of escape lay towards the marshy wastes to the north of the island republic. But I was trapped on the southern side of the Grand Canal, at the bottom of the reversed S-shaped loop of that wide, watery thoroughfare. The only foot crossing was the Rialto pontoon bridge in the middle of the loop. But that was too far away, and too risky to cross – the *Signori di Notte* police force would have men posted on it. Fortunately, there were also many random points at which the canal could be crossed. On ferry-boats.

I ran along the quay to the tip of the southern island, the Punta della Dogana. But even as I did so, I heard a cry from behind me.

'Nicolo Zuliani – the game's up.'

Glancing over my shoulder, I saw that the man who had called out was dark-browed, solemn and heavily bearded. It was Lorenzo Gradenigo. I knew him from childhood, and he had been a bully then. He strode towards me, as I searched for a way out. Almost upon me, he pointed at my dishevelled mantle with a stubby finger.

'Look, the blood stain is still on you. Murderer.'

I remembered my drunken antics with the Dolfin sword, and how I had nicked myself. But this was not the time to protest that it was an old stain, and my own blood besides. I stuck my fist hard in Gradenigo's face, and drew some fresh blood with which to stain my clothes. As he reeled back, clutching his squashed features, I dodged round him. Not far ahead, I saw the drab, dark uniforms of half a dozen *Signori* coming in pursuit, swords drawn and flashing in the sunlight.

'The game's not over yet,' I muttered through gritted teeth, as I ran down the quay. There was no time to negotiate with any of the waiting boatmen. Their keen sense of a bargain would have ensured several minutes of debate before a price for crossing the canal could have been agreed on. And those were minutes I could not now spare. I was facing the imminent likelihood of capture and incarceration in the doge's prison, from where I was unlikely ever to emerge. Except in a coffin.

Suddenly, I saw a large, flat barge being expertly steered out of the mouth of the Giudecca canal to my right.

'Just in time, my friend.'

I put on a spurt as the boat wallowed past the end of the wooden quay along which I and my pursuers were running. Its prow pointed across the Bacino di San Marco towards the landing in front of the Doge's Palace itself. Without pausing for thought, I sprinted to the end of the quay, and launched myself into space with a yell. 'I hope you're carrying something soft.'

I sailed through the air, and landed right in front of the startled boatman. It was indeed a soft landing. The barge was a rubbish carrier filled with the rotting remains of the leavings of rich men's tables. And there were many rich men in Venice. I was sitting up to my waist in stinking vegetables and rotting fish bones.

Despite my predicament, I laughed uproariously at the frustration of my pursuers, who stood shaking their fists on the quayside. But even as I watched, Gradenigo split his crew into two groups. Some ran off along the quay in a desperate but doomed attempt to cut me off on foot, while the rest hurried down the steps to the water's edge to hire a boat. I knew they would find someone ready to ferry them – every Venetian from the highest to the lowest has his price. Even for the hated *Signori di Notte*. But I had a start on them, and that was all I needed.

'What's to stop me just paddling in circles till they catch us up, maestro?'

The oarsman's tone was wheedling and cunning, and the barge wallowed ominously. I saw that the boat containing my pursuers was already cutting through the waters of the basin at each stroke of the single oar, and sighed histrionically. I pulled my purse from my waist, and jingled the contents.

'Name your price.'

The oarsman grinned, revealing a mouth devoid of anything but rotting stubs of teeth. I could smell his breath even above the stench of the offal on which I sprawled.

'You must be desperate, not to bargain. Give me the lot.'

He held his hand out for my purse. Hesitating only for a moment, I dropped it into the grasping fist. In a flash it was stowed safely in the folds of the man's filthy rags, and the refuse collector returned to plying his own oar with a will. As the landing at San Marco approached, I got ready to leap off, and disappear right under the doge's nose into the narrow alleys beyond the Palace. Not least because my rescuer would be outraged to discover, when he opened the strings of my purse, that he had been caught out like Malamocco had by a few pennies and several rusty nail heads. After all, I had wagered all my money on the election.

The escape provided me with a moment of elation, and I dared to return briefly to my rooms in order to retrieve the sword. Especially as it looked as though I would need it now. I reckoned I could find some respite by lying low in my uncle's palazzo for a while. Uncle Matteo was on the Dalmatian coast on business, so I would have the place to myself. The modest house backed on to the family church of San Zulian, and was as safe a place as I could find for the time being. But even as I drew breath, I knew I would have to go eventually. All the Zuliani family properties would be searched sooner or later. I began to wonder if exile wasn't so bad an option, after all. The alternative – torture, and death in the doge's dungeon – was unthinkable. The only problem was having to give up hopes of Caterina. It was for that reason alone that I went against my own better judgement.

I decided on trying to prove my innocence – at least of the murder of Domenico Lazzari. I thought that maybe, if I could achieve that, I could talk myself out of the accusation of vote-rigging. It was a long shot, but I had gambled on longer odds at dice and won. Though usually I gave blind chance a little helping hand in such circumstances. Now, as I couldn't manufacture my own evidence, I would have to rely on uncovering the plain truth, uneasy as I found such a concept. Especially as my first action was to try and contact the thief Alimpato again. Despite my predicament, I laughed at the thought of my acting like a public prosecutor from the Council of Forty-one. The only problem was that I would have to operate in secret, and largely at night if I was not to get arrested myself, and brought before the *Quarantia*.

Fortunately, Venice is a doubly convoluted labyrinth, well designed for skulduggery and sneaking around in the dark. There is first the maze of streets, or *calle*, some of which cut under buildings. And interwoven with that is a second maze of canals, or *rio*. At various points you can step across from one to the other, bewildering anyone who is trying to follow you, especially if they are strangers, or only know their own district. I am perforce familiar with the whole of Venice and its underworld. Card-sharping often required hasty exits and obfuscated escape routes.

Like many houses in Venice, my uncle's has a back door that opened into an alley barely as wide as a body. You never know when you might need to avoid your debtors. Now, even if the front of the house and the water entrance were under observation, no one would see me come and go. After dark, I slipped through this door, and down the narrow alley which also backed on to the church of San Zulian. With my sword belted to my waist, the passage was a tight fit. But it soon gave out on to a wider *calle* that ran down parallel to the Merceria towards a tiny *rio*. On the water at this junction bobbed a small flat boat with its pole jammed in the Venetian mud. It was my uncle's boat. I jumped into it, and used the pole to manoeuvre it northwards towards a T-junction. There I turned east, and poled to an elbow where I followed the southern arm of the *rio*. As the boat snaked between the buildings on either side, the water plashed against their walls. But no one was made aware of my presence, as all the houses and workshops looked the other way out to the street. On the *rio* side, they were blind. I poled cautiously along, until I came across a building to my right which was heavily fortified. I was at the back of the Doge's Palace, and incorporated in its lowest levels were the prison cells. My expectation was to find Malamocco languishing in one of these.

Despite his avowed intention to go to ground, Alimpato had not been too difficult to find. Especially when he knew I wanted to find out the location of the boy. It appeared Malamocco was still being held in the Doge's Palace, while it was decided if a swift or a slow death was warranted in his case. I was grateful that the doge was still in a quandary over such a matter. It gave me time to effect a rescue. Alimpato suggested I was mad, when I had proposed it.

'I knew you were a gambler. But not one to go against such long odds, Nick.'

Apart from Cat, Alimpato was the only person who used the English version of my name. The fact that previously only my mother had been the one to use it, and then only privately beyond my father's earshot, tells you how precious it is to me. She was born in Salisbury in England, and said she never regretted marrying my father, despite the pain and suffering he caused her. Still, she is free of all that now, God rest her soul. I smiled sadly, and patted Alimpato on his skinny back.

'Such long odds, *and* such a little reward.' I sketched Malamocco's height with my hand, barely raising my palm above my waist. 'Such a small package, and yet such a big appetite.'

Alimpato laughed, knowing that I could do nothing else but take the risk. It was my fault that the boy's short life would soon be ended otherwise. He would have expected nothing less of me. At least he gave me a fighting chance with a sort of plan.

'I can speak to the gaoler – he is my cousin's brother by marriage – and he will arrange for the boy to be in one of the *rio*-side cells. They are below water level, and are damp, stinking and full of rats, so are usually kept for the doge's worst enemies. But for the boy it can be little worse than where he lived before his imprisonment. After that, it is down to you Nick.'

Which is why I was now slowly pulling myself and my boat along the stone walls of the doge's prison, urgently calling into the barred windows that stood barely above water level.

'Malamocco, are you there?'

At the first two windows, my call only elicited a rustling that may have been rats, or the shifting of the starved body of some long-incarcerated prisoner. At the third window I received a reply.

'Who's there?' came the timorous reply. It was a boy's voice, but one that from fear and hunger no longer sounded like that of the cocky Malamocco I had trained in sleight-of-hand.

'It's me – the card-sharp. I'm going to get you out.'

His eager face appeared at the bars, a little paler and a lot gaunter than when I had seen it last. But the gleam in his eyes told me the cockiness was not completely lost. I pushed my boat pole in the mud to secure the little barge in place, and drew my sword. The boy recoiled from the bars in horror.

'Barratieri! What are you going to do? Cut me into little pieces so I can pass through the bars?'

'Don't be silly, or I will go away again.'

I pulled on a pair of stout leather gloves and held the sword in both hands by the sharp-edged blade, my right hand close to its tip. I apologized for the misuse I was going to make of such a fine weapon.

'Forgive me, sword-maker, whoever you were, for mistreating your blade so,'

Then I began to dig at the crumbly stonework round one of the bars. The boat bobbed with my exertions, and because of that the effort proved more awkward and more difficult than I had hoped. But eventually the hole in the stone grew to a shallow groove, and then a deep furrow. Malamocco pushed at the bar, as I pulled, and with a groan that I feared may alert someone, it came free. The gap thus created was big enough for Malamocco to squeeze through. I just gave thanks that he had not put on more weight while eating at my expense. I sheathed the sword, swearing I would have the tip re-sharpened, and helped the boy down into the bottom of the flat barge. Where he lay shivering until we were back at my uncle's house, and relative safety.

A few hours later, I was beginning to wish I had not rescued him. Once he had regained his spirits, he had only stopped talking long enough to stuff most of the contents of my uncle's larder down his throat. Most of what he said was unlikely tales of his own bravado.

'And do you know, Barratieri, I told them nothing. I insisted I did not know anyone called Lazzari, or Zuliani. As indeed I don't, do I, Barratieri?'

At this point he either had his tongue firmly in his cheek, or he was still chewing on my uncle's best smoked ham. I swiped at his tow-head, and he laughed. I knew his incarceration would have been terrifying, and allowed him his little show of braggadocio.

He babbled on. 'Any more than you know a boy called Polo, eh? But what I did learn was the name of the man who denounced this Zuliani fellow to the *Signori de Notte*.'

My ears pricked up. If I was to start on the hunt for who killed Lazzari, I could best begin with the name of the person who had landed me in the shit. I half-expected the boy to say Pasquale Valier's name. But he didn't.

'They thought I couldn't hear. But once, when I was being questioned, I heard them whispering to each other. They spoke of a man called Sebenico.'

I could almost have stepped into Sebenico's silver-smithing workshop on the Merceria from my uncle's front door. But that would have given him the opportunity to see me coming. So that night, I once again slipped out of the back door, and down to the boat moored on the local narrow *rio*. This time I steered the boat in the opposite direction to the previous night. This took me under the Merceria, and round the rear of some of the workshops and living quarters on that very street, including those of Sebenico. At one point a street crossed the water, near a *sottoportego*, or archway, running under the buildings. I quietly moored my boat at this subterranean passage, and stepped on to dry land. Above me and to the left side were the workshop and domestic quarters of Sebenico the silversmith. My denouncer. I still wasn't sure if he himself was Lazzari's killer. I knew only that Sebenico had been the most displeased with his return on the Syrian *colleganza*. Which must have been why he did what he did.

With so much valuable silver on his premises, I knew the doors would be stout and well-barred. But sometimes, the wood that formed the ceiling of a *sottoportego* was thin and rotten from damp. I climbed on to some barrels that had been discarded in the passage, and put my hand to the wooden beams above my head. Over me would be a corridor, or even a room in Sebenico's apartments – I had no way of knowing. I listened for a while, but could hear nothing. It was a risk, but one worth taking.

Once more, I unsheathed my sword, and set it to another task for which it had not been designed. The creator of such a pure sword must now be turning in his grave at my abuse of his blade. I pushed the tip that I had scratched on the doge's prison window arch in between two planks of wood, just where the length of timber ended, and twisted. I was fearful that the blade would snap with such abuse, but instead the wood creaked and one of the short lengths of timber gave way. Sliding the sword back in its sheath, I heaved upwards, pushing the plank out of the way. Sometimes I act without too much forethought, and this was one of those occasions. Having gained access to Sebenico's home, I was not too certain as to my next move. I need not have worried.

No sooner had I pushed away the floorboard, than a startled face, illuminated by a tallow lamp, stared down at me. It was wall-eyed Sebenico himself, roused by my none-too-quiet breaking and entering. Well, I suppose it wasn't really entering, because I didn't get that far. All I did was grab the surprised silversmith by the loose folds of his nightgown, and pull him down head-first into the hole at his feet. Suspended virtually upside-down above my head, he was in no position to resist my swift and brutal interrogation.

'Zuliani!' he gasped, as his inverted features turned a bright shade of red. 'I shall call the *Signori*, if you don't release me immediately.'

'I think you have done that already once before, Sebenico. As I am already on the run, I have nothing more to fear from that quarter. Squeal as much as you like, I shall be gone before they even know I have been here.'

I could hear his feet banging on the boards above my head, but my grasp was firm, and his struggles only served to make him more red-faced and dizzy.

'So tell me, good sir, how you came to denounce me, and what you know about the death of Domenico Lazzari. Tell me now, or I might be tempted to draw my sword, and use your head for target practice.'

His mouth gaped in horror, and saliva dribbled from its corners, as he grappled with the realization I knew what he had done. I could almost see the fervid calculations going on in his head, as he calculated how much he had to divulge. I yanked again on his gown, and he squawked as his shoulders wedged firm in the jagged hole in his floor.

'Ahhh! Let me go. Yes, yes, I denounced you for the murder of Lazzari. But that was not my idea. I merely wanted to find some misdemeanour to land you with. To make things hot for you, after you swindled us over the *collegama*. We both did. But then he said we should stick you with a far more serious matter, and said as how you were already up to no good with Lazzari. So the *Quarantia* would believe it, if you were blamed for his death. He said as how it was likely you were responsible for it anyway, even if it could never be proved. So I would only be helping the truth along. I had heard nothing of Lazzari's murder before he told me, I swear it.'

'He, he? Who are you talking about?'

'Old di Betto's son, Lorenzo. It was his idea. All of it, I swear it was.'

I left Sebenico hanging upside-down in his own *sottoportego*, with the front of his nightgown stuffed in his mouth for good measure. It would not take him long to get free, but long enough for me to return to the barge, and pole myself into the night. But as I crossed under the Merceria, I heard the familiar cry of the *Signori de Notte*, baying in the darkness. Sebenico, it seemed, had been quicker than I had anticipated. I stopped the boat directly under the crude wooden bridge that spanned the *rio*, and crouched in the gloom. The sound of one man's hurried footsteps echoed above my head, quickly joined by those of several others.

At first I thought that the *Signori* had merely converged on the bridge in their search for me. My heart pounded in my chest, and my fist tightened over the hilt of Caterina's sword. Then I heard a strangely strangled cry, and a scuffling of feet. I kept as silent as I could for fear of discovery. The scuffle was oddly quiet, with only a grunt or two to suggest there was a fight for life going on above me at all. I had always imagined a fight to the death would have been more noisy, more dramatic. But when the end came, it came with nothing more than a curiously feeble gurgle.

As I was pressing with both my hands and shoulders on the underside of the bridge, in order to prevent my boat from drifting out from cover, my face was close to the edge of the timbers. Suddenly, a swarthy face appeared right before my eyes, but upside down like Sebenico's had been. I gulped, thinking I had been discovered. But even as I looked back at him, the man's eyes were emptying of life. Streams of blood poured from his nose and mouth and over his forehead. It mingled with his long, black curly hair, and dripped down on to the water's surface, spreading out in pink circles. He gurgled once, and was dead. As his head swung lifelessly backwards and forwards, his face was so close that I could make out an old scar on his lower jaw, and a gold ring in his ear. Then it disappeared once more back above the bridge's lip. The *Signori* were removing the evidence.

I listened for their footsteps fading into the distance, before I risked a glance over the edge of the bridge. All I could make out was a gang of men, dragging what appeared to be a large sack behind them. Even that vision soon converged with the shadows and the silence. It was as if nothing had happened, as if I had dreamed it. But I was sure I had made out the bulky shape of Lorenzo Gradenigo in their midst. My hands were trembling as I poled the boat back to its moorings, realizing the stranger's fate could well have been my own, if I had been caught by Gradenigo.

However, it was another Lorenzo – Old Man di Betto's son – who I needed to track down the next time that darkness allowed me to roam abroad. But first I had to get through the day, cooped up with a restless Malamocco for company.

'Barratieri. Show us the dovetail shuffle again.'

I sighed, and took the boy through some of my classic card-sharp moves, starting with the dealer grip, and moving on to the dovetail shuffle – where you can keep track of a single card, as it's no shuffle at all – and the classic force. Malamocco tried it himself, and laughed at his own dexterity. He was good, almost better than I was, and I mentally noted not to play any gambling games with him in the future. If either of us had a future, that is.

'Who did you say the silversmith ratted on?'

I was getting into a gloomy trough of despondency again, so the boy's question served to sharpen my wits somewhat.

'I didn't. His name is di Betto. Lorenzo di Betto. I conned some money out of his father, and though he got it back with interest, it was not half of what the son had expected. I suppose this is his way of getting his own back on me. Landing me in the sh . . .'

'Lorenzo di Betto?' The boy was now excited, and scattered the cards over the table.

'Hey, that's no way to fool your mark! Never show him the deck broken up. He might see the trick.'

'What? Oh that doesn't matter, now. That name –
it's the name of the witness. The one who said he saw
Lazzari being killed. I should have told you before.'

'How do you know?'

'Master Alimpato came round last night, while you
were out. He told me he had got his hands on the
witness statement taken by the *Quarantia*. Read it and
all.'

Now why did that not surprise me. I reckon Alimpato
has a better spy system than the doge himself. So, he
was able to read the doge's private correspondence. I
railed at Malamocco's inability to pass on a simple
message.

'Why didn't you tell me this before?'

'Because when you got back you went straight for
the bottle,' he grumbled sulkily. 'And then you told
me you didn't want to be interrupted.'

He was right. I had been scared by the sight of what
the *Signori de Notte* could do when they were let loose.
But if Malamocco was going to be a sidekick of mine,
he needed to know when to ignore an order.

'So did Alimpato say what was in the papers?'

'He said this di Betto bloke swears he could not be
sure of the identity of the man who killed Lazzari, as
it was dark. But he says he had red hair. And he
described the sword in great detail. It was an old sword,
he said, with a distinctive cross – dogs' heads that
looked as though they were baying. And it had some
sort of inscription on the blade. He swore that he could
see that as the blade was swung high in the moonlight.
Before it did for Lazzari.'

I could see Malamocco's eyes landing on my
sheathed sword that lay at the other end of the table,
taking in the down-turned dogs' heads with their
mouths wide open. Like mad dogs baying at the moon.
He looked back at me with admiration in his eyes.

'Did you really do it? Cor, I bet a sword like that would take a man's head off. Was there lots of blood?'

I grabbed him by the scruff of the neck, and shook him.

'Get it into your thick head, boy. I didn't do it. I didn't harm a hair on Domenico Lazzari's head.'

Mentioning hair made me think again of the stranger who I had seen give up his life last night. The blood running down his oily hair, and dripping into the canal. His life's blood washing away into the lagoon. And I wondered exactly how Lazzari had met his end. Maybe di Betto had seen him die, maybe not. Either way it looked like I needed to find him. Malamocco straightened his rumpled clothes, which were still the respectable ones I had clothed him in when he played the innocent *ballotino*.

'OK. OK. Keep your hair on.' He began to gather in the scattered cards. 'I just wanted to know what it's like. To kill a man.'

'It's evil, and it makes you feel sick. Even in war. So let's hope you never have to do it.' I tried to lighten the mood. 'Far better to take them for all they've got, and leave them alive to pluck another time. Come on, show me you can do the dovetail shuffle properly.'

Later, I left Malamocco practising, and made for Old Man di Betto's house. I had a rendezvous with his son, who it seems had persuaded Sebenico to denounce me, and had claimed to have witnessed the murder. My route involved crossing the Grand Canal, and as I didn't want to risk being seen crossing by boat after curfew, I decided to venture out in the late afternoon on foot. I was in disguise however, having long ago laid my hands on the brown garb of a Franciscan friar. It had come in useful to escape irate gamblers out for my blood on more than one occasion. I had chosen it rather than the black of the Dominicans because it suited my complexion better. Besides, the Dominicans were building their church out in the marshy expanse on the eastern side of Venice. Not a very salubrious neighbourhood, and I had thought it unpropitious at the time. That choice helped me now, as the Franciscans' pile of Frari was close to where the di Bettos lived. So it would be natural for a Franciscan to be making for that neck of the woods.

Crossing the floating bridge at the Rialto was a bit chancy, but as luck would have it, some merchant was arguing the toss about the toll he should be paying to cross. As he was being stiffed by the guardian of the bridge, I pulled my hood down and hurried across, making the sign of the cross for good measure. He even let me cross without charge, probably aiming to get double out of the unfortunate merchant. On the other side, I avoided the main streets, and detoured through some vegetable gardens, and a nasty muddy *campo* where several pigs were rooting for fodder. Not all was beauty and elegant architecture in Venice, even now.

Finally, after wiping the pig-shit off my boots on a couple of wooden piles jutting out from the side of a *rio*, I made it to where Old Man di Betto's house stood. It was opposite the church of San Pantalon, inside which there seemed to be an unusual amount of activity. It was already dusk, and the light of scores of candles cast a yellow glow on to the beaten earth of the small square before the church doors. More strangely, the street door to di Betto's house stood wide open. Venice isn't such a safe place that you can leave your doors open, and expect your property to still be in place when you return. The unusual circumstances made me instantly cautious, and I just poked my head round the door. A female servant stood weeping at the foot of a spiral staircase. I pulled back, but she had spotted me already.

'Oh, father. Have you come for the funeral ceremony? It's in San Pantalon across the way. Your presence will be such a comfort to the master. Though he hardly knows what's going on, actually . . .'

I laid my hand on the woman's shoulder in what I hoped was a fatherly gesture, and expressed my sorrow at old di Betto's death. Silently, I cursed my ill-luck. With the old man's death so recent, it would make my inquisition of his son all the more difficult. The servant prattled on about the tragedy.

'Yes, father, it is so cruel when a son precedes his parent to Heaven.'

'A son . . . ?'

'Yes, father. Who would have thought little Lorenzo would die so soon?'

I quickly made the sign of the cross over the servant woman, and hurried across the street, and into the interior of San Pantalon. The groups of candles cast deep shadows in the arcades and recesses of the church, throwing the little huddle of people sitting below the altar into stark contrast. Before them, on trestles, lay a coffin, its interior open to view. I felt an urge to run across the tiled floor to see who was inside, but restrained myself enough to keep my pace down to an urgent trot. But soon I gathered pace, and a few heads were lifted in surprise, as I finally passed the mourners at a gallop to come to an abrupt stop at the coffin. I grasped the sides, and peered in at the sightless face that lay within.

'Damnation.'

It wasn't the old man. It was the son, Lorenzo di Betto. The man who had accused me of murder. It was the worst of all situations for me. His witness statement couldn't be retracted now, and I had missed my chance to get the truth out of him.

'Father? Why did you say he was damned?'

It was the quavering voice of Old Man di Betto. The poor bastard was confused at the best of times, so now was not the time to cast doubt on the integrity of his only son. I dipped my head down so he would not recognize me, and kept my voice low and spoke with a heavy Paduan accent.

'I was damning the man who did this to your son. He was murdered, I presume?'

A heavy-set man with thinning white hair separated himself from the group, and grasping my arm, took me to one side. Lorenzo's father remained standing by the coffin, his mouth hanging open. Saliva dripped down the front of his mantle, and incomprehension stood in his eyes.

The heavy-set man spoke. 'I am Carlo di Betto, Lorenzo's uncle. Come, it would be better if my older brother does not hear us.'

We walked side by side back down the nave of the church. In contrast to my arrival, the pace was now stately and solemn. After all, I had nowhere to go now. Carlo di Betto took a deep breath, and then explained what had happened, insofar as anyone could fathom.

'It seems Lorenzo received a message two days ago that caused him a great deal of agitation. But he would tell no one what the content of it was. Nor can we now find the message anywhere. It must, however, have requested a rendezvous, because at some point that evening, Lorenzo left the house alone. We can only assume he didn't ever come back, because his bed lay untouched the following morning. Then around midday yesterday, his body was brought to my brother's door on a pallet. He had been strangled, and stabbed with a dagger. Whoever did this to him surely wanted to be sure he was dead.'

'And does anyone know who did it?'

The man laughed bitterly. 'That is obvious. If

Lorenzo had not happened to witness the murder of Domenico Lazzari, he would still be alive today. And if my brother had not wasted his money on a stupid *colleganza*, Lorenzo might still be with us. No, father, it is obvious as the nose on your face who did it.'

I instinctively buried my face further in the folds of my hood, guessing what was coming next.

'The man who killed my nephew was the man who swindled Lorenzo's father. The same man who connived with, and then fell out with, Lazzari and murdered him. Nicolo Zuliani.'

Di Betto turned back to go inside the church, leaving me standing on the steps leading back down into the square. The door to di Betto's house still yawned blankly open, and I could sense only darkness and sorrow inside. I felt the same emptiness in my heart. My final lead had been snuffed out like a votive candle.

At a loss as to what to do next, I hovered by the church doors, keeping to the shadows in case someone recognized me. It was lucky I did, because who should emerge from San Pantalon but a very familiar figure. Fish-faced Pasquale Valier. I couldn't imagine that he was acquainted with Lorenzo di Betto, or anyone else in that family of merchants, so I was instantly curious as to why he was there. And it may have been the moonlight, shining down cold and silvery on the scene, but I could swear his face looked very pale and washed-out. There was also something furtive about his movements. Though I could hardly comment, lurking secretively as I was in the shadow of the church's portico in the garb of a Franciscan.

As he scuttled past me, he muttered a plea for benediction. I bowed low to be sure he didn't recognize me, and made the sign of the cross. I watched him cross the square, and go over the *rio*, before realizing he was going in the wrong direction for his father's palazzo. On the spur of the moment, I decided to follow him. I had no other plan up my capacious Franciscan sleeve.

As we both passed the building site that was the Frari, he looked anxiously over his shoulder. So I turned left towards the steps of the half-finished building, and through the archway. Pausing for a few moments, I then abruptly turned back on myself. I peered round a rough-hewn column just in time to see Valier make for the imposing street doors of one of the fine palazzos whose water frontages lined the Grand Canal. Deciding my disguise was a hindrance now, I discarded the robe on a pile of stones, but still hung back in the shadows. I tried to figure out on whose door he was knocking, and it was quite a shock when I realized.

More used to seeing the palazzo from the canal side, it was only when the door was opened, and I heard a familiar broad accent, that I saw he was gaining admittance to Palazzo Dolfin. A million questions buzzed around my fevered brain. Had Caterina and her family returned unbeknownst to me? Had they ever been away? If neither, what business would Valier have with the lone servant left behind to look after the house?

I stood on the other side of the small square, and watched the passage of the servant and Valier as they ascended the staircase inside the palazzo. The shutters were still closed but, being old and worn, the candle-light spilled through each set of slats as they passed. The light finally stopped outside an upper room where the shutters stood open, though the room was in darkness. The servant's light now illuminated a figure that had been standing looking out of the window. The silhouette resembled the shape of a woman, but one with a belly big with child. This had me puzzled for a moment, for I knew of no member of the Dolfin family who might be about to give birth. Then the figure turned her face towards the candlelight, and the people who had just entered her room. It was Caterina's face. As I stood watching in confusion, she took a step towards Valier, and embraced him.

I had been tossing and turning in my bed for hours, when the next thing I knew Caterina Dolfin was leaning over me, stroking my brow.

'Caterina! How did you get here?'

She didn't reply, and I saw it was a changed Caterina. Her finely chiselled features were now slack and heavy, her cheeks distended, her hair hung down in lank ropes, and worst of all, as she rose from me, I could see that she was as distended as a ripe melon. Huge with child. I moaned and called out her name, reaching for her.

'Caterina!'

But when I touched her grotesque belly, I could feel it pulsating underneath my palm. Her lips parted in a black-toothed grin then, with the coarsest of leers, she lifted her skirts. Her legs parted, and out from her belly marched a column of little replicas of Pasquale Valier, each with a little knife in its hand. They scrambled up my prostrate form as I tried to rise, killing me with pin-pricks. My leaden limbs would not respond to my commands, and I was unable to swat them off. They climbed over my face, and I couldn't breathe. I was being smothered by an army of Valiers issuing from Caterina's loins. I tried to call out but my frozen vocal cords refused to come out with more than a high-pitched squeal. It was a merciful release when death and darkness came.

I woke up to find myself fleeing from something unknown. But the faster I tried to run, the slower I went. I was wading through the mud of the great lagoon. And the clinging silt sucked at my legs making each step an inhuman effort. I was sinking deeper and deeper into mud as the sound of my pursuers rang out across the open expanse. Voices carried easily in the way they do at sea, the hunters sounding closer than they really were. I struggled, and yanked my legs out of the sucking mud, staggering on at last. I didn't dare look back in case the *Signori* really were as close as they sounded. Then, when I did finally chance a look over my shoulder, I stumbled, and measured my length in the mud and rising waters. I floundered, and some unseen impediment – an ancient log, or fisherman's rope – pinched my leg and held me fast.

I woke up. Tangled in something heavy and clinging. I panicked, called out, and tried to pull free. My thrashing only made my entanglement the worse, and soon I was exhausted, flopping weakly like some beached flatfish on the shore. Only I was not on the shore, but drowning in the middle of a muddy lagoon with the waters rising. My movements were getting slower and slower as some unspeakable pursuer gained ground with every step. Until finally I could feel hot, devilish breath on my neck. I didn't dare look back, for I knew if I did, the demon would grasp me. I heard his voice.

'Barratieri! It's me, Malamocco. Wake up, you're having a nightmare.'

I struggled to wake up, and realized I was wrapped in a hopeless tangle of bed-linen. The boy was sitting on my back, breathing down my neck, and trying to waken me.

'Get off me, you little monster,' I growled. 'And go and get me some wine to drink. My mouth is like a Saracen's armpit.'

'No wonder. You drank as if the end of the world had come last night. I doubt there is any wine left in your uncle's cellar.'

I held my head, which felt as though someone had exploded that new gunpowder stuff inside it.

'It has. The end of the world, that is. My world anyway.'

I recalled the affectionate way that Caterina – the bitch – had stepped into Pasquale Valier's embrace. It showed the child she bore was certainly his. Which meant she had been whoring with him while she had been with me. And I could now see what had happened to get me into the fix I was in. I had been right royally set up.

My thinking went this way. The murderer had been identified by the unique sword he had used. Who had given me that sword? Caterina Dolfin. Who knew I had that sword? Only Caterina and my drinking companions on that fateful night of the wager, amongst whom was Pasquale Valier. Who got me mixed up in the vote-rigging scam? Pasquale Valier. Who introduced me to Domenico Lazzari in the most public place possible? Pasquale Valier again. Who was rutting with Fish-face Valier? Caterina Dolfin. That was the fact that hurt most. Don't get me wrong – I couldn't have cared less if she was whoring with Valier; what hurt was that I had been outwitted and out-scammed by a woman. What's that? You don't believe me? At the time I didn't care.

Defeated, I took the pitcher Malamocco offered me, and drank deeply before realizing what he had given me.

'Yeeeugh. It's water. Are you trying to poison me?'

The boy grinned as I spat it out. 'No. Just trying to sober you up. Besides it's the best rainwater collected off the roof. Fresh as . . . fresh as . . .'

'Fresh as your sweaty crotch, you urchin. You would do better to use this . . .' I threw the pitcher, and the rest of its contents, at Malamocco. '. . . to wash yourself in.'

He dodged, and the pitcher shattered on the stone floor, splashing water over his bare feet. He yelled in horror, and sat down on the floor, wiping his feet on the shabby sleeve of the mantle I had provided for him. But he had made his point. I had wasted precious time in getting drunk last night, and sleeping most of today away also. What I should have been getting on with was finding Valier. And if I couldn't have the truth from him, I would at least have vengeance.

The trouble was, Pasquale Valier was nowhere to be found. Close to curfew, and in the shadows of dusk, I had sneaked around most of his usual haunts. Where I couldn't show my face for fear of being identified, I sent Malamocco to enquire on my behalf. No one had seen Valier for almost three days. His brief excursion to Lorenzo di Betto's funeral must have been the only occasion he had shown his face in public in all that time. Although I had been putting it off, I knew I would eventually have to try at the Palazzo Dolfin.

Having dragged my feet as long as I could, I finally stood in the same doorway from where I had seen Caterina in Valier's embrace. This time, the window she had been looking out of was firmly shuttered, and the house showed even fewer signs of life than before. I sensed Malamocco fidgeting at my side, but still I couldn't stir myself. Finally he spoke.

'Shall I knock?'

'No, boy. There is no point – there's no one there I want to talk to.'

We slipped away into the darkness, and went where I should have gone to start with – Valier's family home. If he was hiding anywhere, it had to be behind the back of his father. The problem was, how was I going to flush him out? The squat palazzo had the appearance of a fortified castle, quite unlike the red-brick elegance of the Palazzo Dolfin. It stood on the corner of the Grand Canal and one of the *rios* running off it. Thus on two sides it was virtually moated, and the water entrance looked as forbidding as the gateway to the Arsenal. It was only the fact that lights burned behind the shutters of the upper windows that confirmed for me that someone was in residence.

Malamocco sighed. 'Jeez. Something's really spooked this Valier, eh?'

'Spooked? What sort of talk is that?'

Malamocco snorted, and carefully explained what it meant in the gutter language he shared with his fellow beggars and thieves. It was almost like a foreign tongue. I liked the sound of it, and decided I would have to learn some of it too.

'Yes, he has been . . . spooked. So we must winkle him out somehow.'

'Leave it to me, boss. Wait here.'

So saying, the boy disappeared round the corner of the building at top speed. Curious, I didn't wait, but followed. When I turned the corner, he was nowhere to be seen. Until I felt something pattering down on my head from above. I looked up, and there was the rear end of Malamocco wriggling into an open upper window that I had hardly noticed on our reconnoitre of the place. I wanted to shout after him to take care, but I didn't want to rouse the occupants of the house to his presence either.

Malamocco, on the other hand, obviously did. I was suddenly aware of a crash of furniture and a great cry of indignation, followed by the thump of running feet. Two pairs, one lighter-footed than the other. The front door burst open, and the small figure of Malamocco appeared, a purse clutched in his hand. He was hotly pursued by a red-faced Pasquale Valier whose purse he had clearly lifted right from under his nose. As the boy shot past me, I whipped my sword from its sheath, and used it to trip the unwary Valier. He sprawled at my feet, staring fearfully at the tip of the sword blade poking at his gut.

His cries were piteous as he grovelled in the dust, near pissing himself. 'Oh, no. Please. Don't kill me, don't kill me.'

Then he looked up, and saw who it was wielding the sword. 'Zuliani! What are you doing here?'

He cringed down on the beaten earth. If I hadn't been so angry and jealous, I would have felt sorry for him. Something, or someone, had scared him stiff. As Malamocco would say, he was well and truly spooked. I pulled him up by his arm, and pushed him inside before he could protest any more. Malamocco followed me in, slamming the door behind him. He smirked, and dropped the purse into the astonished Valier's palm.

'Don't think I couldn't lift it without you knowing, pal. Ask Barratieri here. I done it to him.'

'Barra . . . ? Card-sharp?'

'Never mind that, Pasquale. I'm not here to murder you, much as everyone seems to think otherwise.' I slid the sword back in its sheath. 'Just to talk.'

If anything, Valier looked even sicker at the idea of talking to me than he had at the imminence of death. An elderly servant scuttled into the hallway from the rear of the house, enquiring if his master was all right.

'Yes, yes, Pietro. Make yourself useful, and bring some wine.'

The servant hurried away, returning with a pitcher full of good red Malvasia. He poured two goblets, studiously avoiding Malamocco's outstretched hand. Valier seemed to be recovering his equanimity a little, but when he lifted the goblet of wine to his lips, I could see that his hand still trembled. Even though I felt like skewering him on the end of my sword, I wanted to know why he had done what he had done to get me accused of murder. And to find out if he knew who was actually guilty of the deed. He was my last chance of proving my innocence. The trouble was, Valier was less scared of me than someone else, it seemed.

When I asked why he had set me up, he shook all over, setting the goblet of wine down on the table before he spilled it. 'Don't ask, Nicolo. Please don't get me involved. I just did what I was asked.'

'And what was that? Who asked you?'

'They approached me through my father. He would do anything to stay in with those in power. He asked me to find someone a bit . . . well, dodgy . . . and wager that he couldn't rig the election for doge. I thought of you immediately.'

I didn't know whether to be flattered or outraged, but told him to go on.

'That's all, really. Well, I was to introduce you to Lazzari also. That was part of it. I just thought they wanted to embroil Lazzari in a disreputable deal that would spoil his reputation. I didn't know he would end up dead.'

His eyes widened, staring at the sword that hung at my waist still. 'Did you kill him?'

'You know I didn't.'

He frowned, and that puzzled me. If he and Caterina had set me up by giving me the sword that was then identified as the murder weapon, why was he asking me if I was the murderer? Surely he knew I wasn't.

'You and Caterina set me up. Who was it really killed Lazzari?'

'Caterina? The Dolfin girl? Have you not spoken to her? She sent for me yesterday to find out where you were. Though why she should want to ask me, I have no idea. Anyway, I said I couldn't help, as you had gone to ground after the murder. Probably had already fled Venice.' He frowned. 'What has she got to do with the fix? I don't follow. And as for who killed Lazzari, I think it was the same man killed di Betto.'

As he spoke, Valier went ghostly pale, and stared over his shoulder, as though scared someone might be eaves-dropping. He leaned forward, and clutched at the sleeve of my mantle.

'Forget I said that, Zuliani, and get away. Just go.'

I grabbed his wrist, and twisted it hard. 'Why should I? Who killed di Betto? Did you witness it? You did, didn't you?'

Valier jerked away from me, and vomited the wine in a thin, red spurt over the floor. He groaned, and wiped his mouth.

'Yes, yes. OK, I wanted to be sure it was you killed Lazzari. Idle curiosity, really. Besides, the murder weapon would have been mine, if you had lost the wager. It would have been really something to have owned the sword that killed Domenico Lazzari. I wanted di Betto to tell me what he had seen. So I went to St Pantalon, and observed the family in prayer. When one of the congregation pointed out Lorenzo di Betto to me, I knew I had seen him before. At the sword-smith's who engraved the inscription on your blade. He had been there when I picked up the sword. As I observed him in the church, he was passed a message. It seemed to agitate him, and he ran from the church. I followed him out of . . .'

'Idle curiosity,' I proferred, and he nodded.

'God, I wish I hadn't.'

Valier paused, wiped his mouth again, and reached for his wine goblet. Malamocco filled it for him, and he drank deeply. 'If only I hadn't seen what I did, I wouldn't be scared to set foot outside the door.'

It seems that Valier followed Lorenzo di Betto into

the gathering dusk of a Venetian evening. Mist was beginning to roll in from the lagoon, seeking its way like sensuously pliable fingers down the maze of canals. Di Betto's route was circuitous, but eventually came out at a dead end on the southern side of the Grand Canal opposite the Chiesa degli Scalzi. Here Valier thought he would be defeated in his pursuit of di Betto, for a ferryman holding a lantern stood waiting in a small boat. Di Betto got aboard, and was ferried across the broad waters of the canal. On the far bank, a tall, swarthy man appeared out of the shadow of the church. He strode forward, and despite di Betto appearing to be reluctant to step ashore, the man grabbed his arm and pulled him up on to the bank. Valier watched by the light of the lantern as the person di Betto was meeting apparently punched him in the chest. It was only when he pulled his fist back that Valier realized the man had stabbed him.

The ferryman turned his head, ignoring di Betto's cries of alarm, and poled rapidly away into the mist. So it was that Valier stood helplessly on the wrong bank as Lorenzo di Betto, already bleeding to death, had a cord pulled tight around his throat to finish him off. He could only watch as the life ebbed out of the unfortunate di Betto. Foolishly, Valier then cried out, and the assassin looked up, peering coldly across the stretch of water.

'My life was only saved by the fact the ferryman had left,' muttered Valier, a shudder running through his entire body. He reached for the goblet again. I was beginning to feel very uneasy.

'You say you saw di Betto's attacker clearly by the light of the ferryman's lantern. Describe him for me.'

Valier stared into the far distance as he spoke, conjuring up the terrifying features again. 'He had long, black curly hair, and dark skin like a Dalmatian

177

pirate. I think there was some mark on his face, near his jaw. Like a scar or something. And he had a gold ring in his ear. I saw it sparkle in the light from the lamp.'

I sighed deeply. 'I don't think you need to worry about encountering your assassin friend again. As long as he told no one about you seeing him kill di Betto – and I think his pride in his work probably meant he didn't – you are off the hook. He is no longer alive to hound you down.'

I explained to the wide-eyed Valier how I had been trapped under a bridge when the man he described had been murdered by a band of men I knew were the *Signori de Notte*. I left Valier to drown in his goblet, weak with relief that his life had been given back to him. But I was not so lucky. This was not sounding good to me. And I slunk back through the maze of streets, the fingers of mist curling round my soul, chilling it to the marrow. Malamocco followed in silence, and I think he had come to the same conclusion that I had.

It had been a set-up just as I had surmised. But it wasn't Valier and Caterina who had engineered it. And poor Lorenzo di Betto had been no more than a pawn that had been sacrificed in a much murkier power play. He had been persuaded, maybe with the lure of preferment for his family, to bear false witness against me. And then silenced by the same assassin who had no doubt killed Domenico Lazzari in the first place. Next, the assassin himself had been despatched to close the loop. Except there was still a loose end – apart from myself – and that was Lorenzo Gradenigo.

It was an easy matter to draw out Gradenigo – all I had to do was send a message anonymously disclosing my whereabouts. Malamocco said I was mad, and maybe I was. But I had to know why this disaster had happened to me just when things had been looking up. So I sent the message, and prepared myself to face the *Signori di Notte*. I persuaded Malamocco that he had no place in this final confrontation, sending him away with a purse fuller than he might have ever hoped to steal. I have to admit I was a little disappointed when he didn't put up a fight. But I had also given him a document I wanted him to deliver to the offices of the *Quarantia* judges, stressing its urgency and importance.

After he had left, I had the house to myself for a while, and felt strangely calm. I put on my best clothes, bought with the proceeds of my *colleganza*, and only a little stained. Then set the sugar-loaf hat jauntily on my head, with the brim turned up. The Dolfin sword was comfortingly heavy at my waist. It may have got me into all this trouble, but I trusted it still to do its job.

When the hammering came at my uncle's door, I took my position at the top of the stairs, and called down. 'The door is unbarred, Gradenigo.'

The big, burly figure of the chief of the *Signori* barrelled through the door, slamming each leaf back against the wall. He looked up, and his red lips curled into a sneer amidst the thick bush of his dense, black beard. I was pleased to see that his nose was still misaligned after our last encounter.

'Well, well. I might have known you would be prepared for me, Zuliani. Are you going to come peaceably?'

'And die with a dagger in my back like the Dalmatian assassin?'

Gradenigo's piggy eyes screwed up even smaller than usual, as he assessed how much I knew of his business. I decided to play a few cards.

'Yes, I know all about him, and about di Betto too. How he perjured himself to put the fix in on me. And died for it afterwards. Was my rigging of the election so important that these men had to die?'

Gradenigo had been sidling towards the bottom of the staircase, as I held my ground. However my last statement stopped him in his tracks. His lips curled again, and a deep rumble emanated from the depths of his chest. Disconcertingly, he was laughing.

'Do you really think you are that important, Zuliani? Don't kid yourself. You were just a tool, easily used up and discarded. You were there to enmesh Lazzari in a scandal, and so explain away his murder. Neither you, nor di Betto, nor the assassin mattered one jot.'

My heart sank. It was what I had feared all along. And while I might have flattered myself by imagining all the intrigue was aimed at my demise, deep down I had guessed it was all about Domenico Lazzari. He had made enemies in high places. Particularly with the man who fancied himself as the next doge – Girolamo Fanesi. So the intrigue all came back to Fanesi, and I had no chance of proving my innocence against such a high-level conspiracy. And that was why I had sent Malamocco to the judges with a document faked to make it look like it had been Fanesi who had bribed me to get his name pulled out of the electoral jar courtesy of the tricksy Malamocco. He would deny it of course, but mud sticks – especially Venetian mud – and he would never be doge now. It was the best revenge I could expect out of a hopeless situation..

Gradenigo was beginning to ascend the stairs, and I finally backed off, having got him to confirm what I had guessed. I was about to sneak down the secret rear stairs, when a slender hand grabbed my arm, and pulled me into my uncle's bed-chamber. At first I thought it was Caterina, and wondered how she had got there. And how I was going to get her out of this fix. But then I saw it was the boy, Malamocco.

'You idiot! What are you doing here?'

'Saving your hide, Barratieri.' Hearing the sound of heavy boots coming up the marble staircase, Malamocco slipped the wooden bolt across the bedroom door, and leaned against it. I grabbed his shoulders, and shook him.

'You didn't think I was planning to die nobly and unnecessarily, do you? Where's the profit in that? I had my escape route all worked out, and you've gone and spoiled it, you brat. Now what am I going to do?'

His face went pale as a nun's wimple, as his eyes roamed the trap he had created for us both. 'You could jump out the window into the canal.'

I leaped over to the window, and looked out.

'Are you mad? It's more mud than water.'

'Then it'll be a soft landing. Especially if you land headfirst. Anyway, I had to come back.'

'Eh? Why?'

'Because the lady told me to.'

'What lady?'

'The one who's been trying to speak to you, and was waiting in the *calle* when I left here.'

'Caterina?'

'That's her. She says . . .' he hesitated, obviously embarrassed by the sentimental nature of the message he had been asked to deliver, 'she says she will wait for you, and will look after your child.'

The truth hit me like a mailed fist in my stomach. I groaned at my stupidity, at my crass lack of sensitivity, at my suspicious nature, and finally at my bad luck.

'I think we should . . .'

Before I could reply, the door burst partway inwards, straining the wooden bar and throwing Malamocco to the floor. The metal end of a pike had been thrust through the gap. Had it wounded the boy? Was that blood on his mantle? Impetuously, I drew my blade, and without thinking, lunged towards the gap between the double doors.

'Boss! No!'

Malamocco's cry was in vain as I blindly thrust my sword through the gap. There was a cry of pain from the other side, and the pike end was withdrawn. The gap closed, almost holding my sword fast between the leaves of the door. I yanked it back, the blade smeared with blood.

'Let's go,' yelled an uninjured Malamocco.

I pushed the boy on to the window sill, and he dropped into the darkness of the canal below. I clambered up myself, and looked down. It was a long way, and I am scared of heights. I heard the door bursting open behind me. I jumped.

'Oooooooooo . . .'

The landing was uncomfortable but soft. Malamocco's urgent gestures drew me towards the opposite bank. I told him I was OK, and that he should save himself now. That we would do better to split up. Reluctantly, he took my advice, and slunk off into the dark and back to his own world. I heard the angry voices of the men on the balcony. One, that I recognized as the bearded Gradenigo, gave a cry of frustration that chilled me to the heart.

'Murdering bastard. You killed him. You won't escape.'

I waded along the canal until I was out of sight, dragging my boots out of the sticky mud with ever more exhausted steps. After a while I saw a tiny quay that allowed me to clamber out of the icy waters, and continue my escape on dry land. I was surprised at my own exhaustion, and could barely drag myself over the wooden pilings on to the stone quay. I knew exactly where I was – east of the Grand Canal, and south of SS Apostoli church, and just a few hundred yards from the quay on the north side of Venice that looked towards the scattering of islands around Murano and freedom.

I trudged along the narrow alleys, leaving a trail of murky footprints behind me. I had eluded those chasing me, and my tracks now didn't matter. The day had not turned out as I had expected, but at least I had stuck it to Fanesi, and escaped with my life. One day I would come back for the sweet, foxy Caterina Dolfin. I should now say, the matronly Caterina, and our child. It was best I was not around as he grew up. After all, I was not only a conspirator against the state, but now a murderer for real, it seemed. What had Ranulf de Cerne's sword made me do?

The sword's weight is carrying it in a perfect arc. I am ready to release it. Then I have second thoughts. A sword is just a weapon, so how can I blame this one for what has happened to me? Some like to imbue a blade with a personality – consider even that its maker's own life is somehow hammered and moulded into it. Or that its owners have shaped its destiny by virtue of the way their own lives have played out. But take it from me, it's just a lump of metal without a life of its own. And yet a very pretty lump of metal with an intrinsic value to the right person.

Standing waist-deep in water, and covered in the stinking mud of Venice's lagoon, I should not have been able to see the positive side of things. But I am a Venetian, after all. Well, half Venetian and half stubborn Englishman. A combination that guarantees I see the possibilities of every situation. Here I am – destitute, half-drowned and being hunted for murder – throwing my only asset into the sea. Well, that is if you don't count my considerable talent at making money. But then, only money makes money, and I realize I can

sell the sword for a goodly sum. There are plenty of
Crusaders and Templars passing through this region
on the way to Castle Pilgrim to fight Baybars and his
Mameluk army. Most of them have more money than
common sense, and I can market the sword as a
'veteran' of the Fourth Crusade. Why throw away
money?

The weight of the blade is still carrying it to the apex
of its arc, as these feverish thoughts run through my
brain. I strive to prevent the silver-wired hilt from slipping through my fingers. But my hands are numbed
by the cold waters of the lagoon, and it slides free. I
yell in frustration as the big disc of the pommel skids
over my palm, and I try to clamp down on it with my
other hand. I almost have it, but finally, it slips through,
and the sword sails free. But, thank God, I have slowed
its momentum, and I watch it land with a splash only
a few yards ahead of me. I flounder through the turbid
waters, plunging my hands blindly into them, and begin
to grovel in the bubbling, stinking mud . . .

bistorical note

Historians will know that no such election took place
in 1262, and that Renier Zeno was doge until 1268.
But then no one in authority would have liked it known
that the voting system could be so easily suborned, and
no record of such an abortive election would have been
kept. Suffice it to say that the voting system was made
extraordinarily complex in 1268, though the system of
choosing a child randomly to act as *ballotino* was used.

ACT THREE

At least four people might have seen the body and hadn't admitted to it before Hob the Miller caught a glimpse of it from the corner of his eye that Monday morning.

He was strolling along beside his tired old packhorse, sacks of flour tied to the beast ready to be delivered to his lord's little castle at Nymet Tracy. It was a journey he must have completed many scores of times since he took over the running of the mill from his father. At least once a fortnight he came this way. Otherwise he'd take the road north to Bow for his provisions.

This lane, the leaves overhead dappling the nettles and thick grass with shadows, was as familiar to him as the mill itself. He knew all the ruts and potholes, the thin undergrowth where a man who had drunk too much could relieve himself; the denser brambles, which at this time of year were lethal, with thorns that would shred a fellow's hosen, but which would soon be sought by all the families when the thick, juicy berries were ready to be picked.

The boot lay beneath one of the dense thickets of bramble.

God's pain, but it was tempting to leave the fellow, just as the others had; there were plenty of footprints all about here to bear witness to the fact. It was not unusual for the man who discovered a dead body to walk away. The first finder would have to pay a surety, and no one wanted to be fined for no reason.

He knelt by the body. It wasn't as if he had been carefully concealed. Probably some traveller who had been knocked on the head by a footpad and hurriedly dragged from the path. It was common enough. As Hob halted and poked with his staff in the bushes, a cloud of flies rose, and Hob tasted acid in his throat. The murder wasn't very recent, from the smell. It hadn't happened today. In this heat . . .

Hob was conscientious. If a man committed murder, everyone was in danger. Better that good people should learn who was responsible and bring him to justice. So Hob squatted, nose wrinkled against the foul odour, a short, heavy-set man in his mid-thirties, with pale brown hair protruding from under his hood. He had eyes of grey/blue that held chips of ice as they darted about the ground seeking clues to the killer's identity.

'Who did this to 'un, eh?' he muttered. There were savage slashes which had ripped through the man's cotehardie. Some wounds had toothmarks: wild dogs or maybe a fox or two had come to gnaw at him. The man's head was covered by a cowl, and Hob, grimacing, took his staff and lifted the front.

In this, the seventeenth year of King Edward II, or as the priests would say, in the thirteen hundred and twenty fourth year of Our Lord, men were well enough used to the sight of death, and Hob could see this poor fellow had tried to defend himself. There was a great blow to his head, which must surely have killed him if all the stabs hadn't. Even his hands were badly cut, his right hand was cut almost in two, as though a sword had fallen between his middle fingers. Hob looked more closely at the distorted features, then he pushed the cowl back farther, peered closer, and swore.

He had a choice: he could hurry on and ignore it, as others had, or declare it. Grunting, he stood a while, then took his horse and continued on to the castle.

Others had pretended not to see this fellow; Hob pulled a sour face. Damn his arse, he was a Christian, and he wouldn't leave a man's corpse to rot in the wilds, no matter how high the fine. No, he'd tell Sir William, and ask for the coroner to be called.

In his small castle, Sir William was unhappy to hear that his miller craved a few minutes of his time.

'What? Why? Can't you see I am busy?' he demanded testily of his steward.

'He is very insistent, Sir William.'

'Fetch the fool in. I daresay he's found another fault with my damned wheel, or the shaft, or more cogs have broken. Why can't he mend the thing himself instead of troubling me?'

Even in a small manor like this there were always too many distractions for he who craved solitude. Sir William tapped his foot as he waited, profoundly irritated. A man should be granted peace when he had so many concerns. All he sought was an opportunity to leave this place and seek the quiet of the cloister, where he might reflect and beg God's forgiveness for his sins, yet the petty trials and difficulties of the poorer folk in his demesne were constantly intruding. He had a letter to write to the Abbot of Tavistock, an important letter, now that his main concern in life was gone at last.

'You should be more generous, husband,' his wife chided gently.

Sir William bit back the rejoinder. She could not comprehend the troubles he endured. He had heard her describe him as 'petulant', as though he was some sort of froward child. If he had been more forceful, she would have felt his belt before now, but that was not his way. No, he had been under her spell from the moment he first saw her, all those years ago. Perhaps, if he had never met her, God would not now punish him like this. Yet soon his misery would be done.

She continued soothingly: 'He is a sensible man, and his mill earns a good profit each year. I am sure that if he needs to speak to you, it is for an important reason.'

He forbore to point out that the most important thing to any man should be the protection of his immortal soul. Turning from her and returning to his seat, he reminded himself that this frail woman couldn't be expected to comprehend.

She had no concept of guilt for a crime as vast as that which rested on his shoulders. Christ Jesus! the guilt would *never* leave him! he thought with a shudder.

The door opened. Sir William turned to scowl at Hob. 'Well?'

'Sir, I've found a man's body on the way here.'

Sir William curled his lip. 'Tell the steward and have him call the coroner.'

'I thought you should know: it's Walter Coule, sir. Sir John's reeve.'

Hob later recalled that meeting, and when he did, all he could remember was Sir William's appalled expression.

'Don't worry, lady.'

Mistress Alice felt her heart lurch at the sly voice behind her, and her hand rose to her breast as the after-shock of thundering blood raced along her veins. 'You fool,' she hissed. 'Roger, you nearly sent me to my grave!'

'I think it would take more than a little surprise to do that to you, lady – don't you?'

Roger de Tracy, her brother-in-law, unfolded himself from the corner where he had been lounging. Tall, he always gave the impression of bending slightly, as though there was not the room built that was tall enough for his great height. He loomed over her by at least six inches.

He was good-looking; many of the local women would have been keen to take him to their beds. Slim of waist, with the broad shoulders of a warrior, he wore his clothing with style. The latest, tight fashions might have been designed for him. The red sleeves of his gipon showing his well-muscled arms, while the crimson cotehardie set off his powerful torso.

But Roger was restless and wild. She was never entirely comfortable with him . . . probably it was foolish, but she had an intuition that he desired her. He always had. And now it was there in his eyes: no matter how urbane and sophisticated he appeared, his eyes were all over her.

'Why should I worry?' she demanded as her heart began to return to its normal pace.

'No need to retreat, lady. I was simply attempting to soothe your fears,' he said smoothly. 'Your husband wouldn't have murdered him. Why, just because he's . . . what? bitter towards Coule's master, that doesn't mean he'd kill Coule. His master's slights aren't Coule's fault, are they? Of course, some men might wish to see Coule dead. I would have no pity for him myself, if I were master of this manor. But I am not, of course.'

'No. You aren't,' she said acidly.

'Nay.' His eyes were on her for a moment, and she saw that they had lost any feeling for that instant, as though just then he was contemplating her not as a sister, but as a foe. It was a look that made her wish to draw away from him.

'I must return.'

'You don't believe me?' he smiled then, and it gave a horrible aspect to his features as he lifted his eyebrows in mock innocence. 'Why Alice – surely you don't believe your husband capable of murder?'

'Get away from me!' she spat, and as she span on her heel, she saw that farther down the corridor Denis, her husband's man of law, was standing and glowering at Roger.

'Until later, madam,' Roger said, and pushed past her with a chuckle.

There were two coroners who lived in the north of the county and held inquests, and a third who lived in the east, but when there was a death here in the hundred of North Tawton, it was often easier to contact Sir Richard de Welles, the coroner of the Lifton hundred, because he lived closer to hand and was less encumbered with the sudden deaths of the populations of Exeter and the larger market towns.

Hob knew of him, and when the demand came the next day for him to attend the inquest, he was merely glad that the affair would soon be over. If he had to pay a fine for finding a body, better that he should learn sooner rather than later how much it would be. And he was nervous enough already. He wanted the whole matter over and done with as soon as it may be.

Sir Richard was a tall man with an almost perfectly round face and a thick bush of beard that covered his upper breast like a gorget. His flesh was the colour of tanned hide, his eyes brown and shrewd, his voice like a bull's bellow, as though incapable of quiet speech. He stood before the juries as the men mumbled their way through the unfamiliar words he recited, and raised his eyebrows and rolled his eyes as they stumbled.

'God's blood, where did you find this lot? Eh? All

are here, I suppose. We may as well open proceedings. ALL THOSE WHO HAVE ANY KNOWLEDGE OF THIS MAN'S DEATH, COME FORTH!'

The hoarse roar silenced the crowd, but there was a comfort in his authority. The jurors knew they must investigate and see whether or not anyone could come to a conclusion about the death. Who wished him dead; who killed him; what weapon was used . . . there were many questions to be answered, and Sir Richard was experienced in his job.

Hob was first to be called. 'I found him, sir.'

'He was here?' Sir Richard demanded. 'Good Christ, man! Answer!'

'I don't think he's been moved,' Hob nodded, glancing at the corpse. He could feel a light sweat forming on his back at the sight.

'I congratulate the vill on protecting the corpse so well,' the coroner said sarcastically. 'Although who'd be likely to approach *that*! Come! Let's have the body brought into the open.'

Unwilling men barged through the low vegetation, dragging the noisome figure out on his back.

Lady Alice had to turn away. The cotehardie's breast was black with dried blood, and even from this distance, some twenty yards away, she could smell the rotten flesh. It was enough to make her gag. It was hard to believe that only a short time ago this was a hale, living man.

'Roll him over, then,' the coroner said testily. 'Do you expect us to guess at his damned injuries?'

The two pulled and heaved the heavy body over.

'I'd guess this was no accident, then,' Sir Richard said.

'Time, I think, to strip him,' the coroner continued, clapping his hands together happily. 'Any chance of a jug of wine, Sir William? I'm parched here.'

The procedure continued. Naked, the body was turned over and over before the juries from neighbouring vills while the coroner intoned his conclusions and his clerk scribbled down his findings. The number of wounds was counted, and the length and depth of each gauged, not that the coroner was over-happy about poking in some of the stab wounds: they were already filled with maggots.

'Well, I find this man was set upon and slain by someone unknown. The weapon was long-bladed, and stabbed right through him on three occasions – all from in front of him. There were more wounds on his hands, where he tried to defend himself. One great slash at his head. It's likely the weapon was a heavy bladed sword with weight behind it. A weapon like that would cost not less than six shillings, so I'll guess that to be a fair fine. Now, can anyone prove he was English?'

'I can vouch for him,' said one man from the vill, and then a shorter man at the back of the group of witnesses stepped forward.

'So can I. He was my reeve.'

'You are?'

'Sir John de Curterne.'

'I see you, sir. I accept his Englishry. When did you last see him?'

'On Friday last. When he left my hall to go to Sir William's castle at Nymet Tracy. I have not seen him since.'

'You did not report his disappearance?'

'He had been going on pilgrimage to Canterbury to visit the shrine of St Thomas a Becket,' Sir John said, and he stared as he spoke at Sir William, who studiously avoided meeting his eye.

Sir Baldwin de Furnshill, keeper of the king's peace for Crediton, was staying with his wife at her small manor of Liddinstone when the man arrived from Nymet Tracy.

'I don't understand,' he said when the rider had given his message, panting slightly from his hasty journey in the hot, dusty weather.

'Perhaps if you had given him time to pause and rest, his meaning would be more comprehensible?' his wife Jeanne chided him and turned to the fellow. 'You look tired; please, sit and drink some wine or ale. Have you eaten?'

'My lady, I'm very grateful. Yes, I should be most grateful for refreshment.'

'You are the brother of Sir William de Tracy?' Baldwin said. 'Yet he did not wish to send for my help?'

'I fear . . . this is a matter too close to his heart. He means well, but . . .'

'You say the reeve was murdered?' This was from the other man in the room, a tall, ruddy-complexioned man with calm grey eyes who had been introduced as the Bailiff, Simon Puttock, a friend of Sir Baldwin. He stood leaning against the wall near the door.

Roger gratefully took the heavy pewter goblet from Sir Baldwin's wife and drained half in one long draught. Soon the wine was coursing through his body, and a delicious tingling began in his belly, rippling through his frame.

'Last Friday this man Coule, our neighbour's reeve, came to the hall to speak with my brother. He was left in the hall while my sister-in-law fetched my brother, but when he arrived, Coule had already left. Thinking little of it, Sir William cursed the man, and went about his business. And then the body of this reeve was found. My brother thought immediately of his sword. It had been kept in a locked chest in the hall, but when he looked it was gone. Stolen.'

'It's no doubt a matter of annoyance to have an heirloom stolen, but what of it? If the man Coule had it, would he not defend himself with it?' said Sir Baldwin.

'His master is a powerful man; Sir John de Curterne. We are not on terms of friendship. He would like to have our sword, I expect, because it is a fine thing and he covets fine things. And by killing off his reeve, he would put suspicion for the murder onto us.'

'You have just explained a perfect motive for killing the man yourself – or for your brother to do so. There is a feud between your families: why should I not believe that you took this sword when you heard Coule was in your castle, killed him, and hid the sword to make it appear that it was stolen, later dragging his body to the country and throwing the sword away?'

'He visited our hall often enough. Why should I kill him this time? No, Sir Baldwin. I think that Curterne has stolen our sword, and sought to put the blame for his man's death on us. Why else would he not declare his man missing?'

'He did not?' Baldwin asked, interested despite himself.

'No. He said Coule had asked to be released for a pilgrimage to Canterbury.'

Baldwin absorbed that, then: 'Why should a master have his servant murdered?'

'Ah!' Roger grinned as a servant refilled his goblet. 'His reeve was the most fractious and difficult man for many miles. He did get the harvest in, but only at the expense of many arguments and much strife. I think Sir John is delighted to be rid of him.'

'And this sword was taken, too. Was there anything about it to identify it?'

Roger allowed a fleeting doubt to pass over his brow.

'It's more than just a sword, Sir Baldwin. It's the *Tracy* sword.'

Sir Baldwin smiled. 'Ah?'

'Which means you've no idea what it is, doesn't it?' said Simon Puttock with a chuckle. 'Well, I have no shame about confessing ignorance. I've no idea what you're talking about, so please tell us the significance of this sword.'

'It is the sword of my fathers and grandfathers in direct line all the way back to the invasion of the country under the glorious William of Normandy,' Roger de Tracy said eagerly. 'It's invaluable!'

Baldwin looked at Simon and shrugged. 'It's worth some shillings, I don't doubt.'

'And it's been stolen. That means you, as keeper, have a duty to seek out the thief.'

Baldwin's expression stilled. He disliked being ordered, and he had only recently returned to his quiet manor after a troubling series of Gaol Delivery trials. Simon hurriedly cleared his own throat. 'Did you call out the hue and cry?'

'It was too late. As soon as we realized it was gone, we searched for it in the castle itself, leaving no box unopened. I did that myself. But it's clearly gone.'

'How long ago?' Baldwin growled.

'I personally saw it on that Friday morning.'

'That is almost a week ago! It's Thursday now.'

'You thought you might come and demand help now?' Simon said disbelievingly.

'You must, sir! It is our inheritance!'

'There is no law to say I must,' Baldwin grated. 'You come here and tell me what I must and must not do? You should have asked me to help sooner, if you wished for my aid.'

Roger looked at him and Lady Jeanne was sure she saw desperation in his eyes. 'A man has been killed, and I fear that Sir John seeks to see us condemned for his murder. I beg you, any help you can give, please give it.'

Denis de Topcliffe was used to the gloomy atmosphere in the castle at Nymet Tracy, but it was rare indeed that he heard Madam Alice weeping. She was too strong and proud.

It was a dreadful sound. The deep sobbing of a mature woman wrenched at a man's heart like no other noise, and he wanted to go to her, but as he put his hand to the door handle, he told himself how stupid that would be.

He was only a servant: he was paid to advise and assist Sir William, mainly in his continuing litigation over lands and his disputes with neighbours. That was all. He certainly had no responsibility to soothe a distressed woman; that was a task for her husband. Not that the fool would. He was so bound up in his fear and desperation over the stolen sword that he had no idea what his wife was feeling. It was as though they were already divorced.

It was some years since Denis had first come here, back in the days when Sir Humphrey was still the master of the castle, and his older son was yet a squire. He and Roger had got on better in those far-off days before that cursed sword arrived and reminded Sir William of the actions of his appalling ancestor. What on earth had persuaded Sir Humphrey to name William after the Sir William de Tracy who had committed the murder? It was enough to turn any poor devil's head.

In William's case it had made him appreciate the true depths of his family's disgrace. Recently even catching sight of the sword would make Sir William shudder. Denis had seen him. It was as though there was a malevolent spirit about the thing that would tear at William's soul whenever he came near.

Not only his soul, from the way Madam Alice was crying.

Again his hand went to the door, and he hesitated for a moment, but then he raised the latch.

'My lady, I'm sorry, I thought that the hall was empty.'

Alice had jerked away from the table where she had been sitting with her head bent. Now she swept away the tears with a hurried rub of her hand, her back to him. She sniffed and took a deep breath, then turned to face him with a brittle smile on her face. 'Ah, Denis. Did you want me or my husband?'

'Neither, lady. I sought my penner – I put it down somewhere about here, I think. Have you seen it?'

She shook her head shortly. 'Not here, no.'

He grunted. 'Ah, there it is on the table. And how are you this fine morning?'

She smiled, but her face was blotched, her eyes damp. 'I am well, I thank you. The weather makes all seem good, doesn't it?'

He nodded, and pointedly looked away so that his attention would not cause her shame or embarrassment. 'Sir William is still upset? He has not spoken to me today.'

'Upset? No, not today. He is gleeful!' She looked at him wildly. 'Now the sword is gone, he says he will go to the convent – and that I must to a nunnery as a dutiful wife! My God! What about me? He never thinks to ask me what *I* want!'

The next day Baldwin and Simon ambled their way along the lanes towards the hundred of North Tawton accompanied by Roger de Tracy.

'Come, then, Baldwin. What made you decide to come all this way?' Simon whispered.

'It was an intriguing conundrum: I can see no earthly reason why they should demand my assistance now,' Baldwin confessed. He wore a puzzled expression at the memory of the conversation with the brother of Sir William de Tracy. 'If they were keen to find some felon who had stolen their property, I should have expected them to come to me as soon as they knew the thing was taken. But they waited a week. And now, when the coroner's already been there and buried the body, they come and ask for help. What help can I be? If the sword could be found, surely the coroner himself would have found it. Yet now, when all is done, they ask me to go along and seek their sword for them. It makes little sense.'

'Some swords can be valuable,' Simon said.

'I am a knight,' his friend snorted. 'I know the value of good metalwork. But why did they wait so long?'

'Perhaps as he said, they just didn't notice it was missing?'

'Aye. That's a possibility. And then they called me because they could think of nothing else.'

'They must have heard marvellous reports of your abilities,' Simon said lightly.

'Perhaps. And asking me to waste my time is acceptable to a poorly rural knight like this Sir William.'

'Ah, I shouldn't be too hard. Not all rural knights are thick as a peasant with cow muck between his ears,' Simon said happily, and ducked quickly under the gloved fist that flew at his jaw.

'Next time you won't duck quickly enough,' Baldwin growled, 'to be missed by this example of a rural knight.'

'I shiver in my boots.'

Baldwin chuckled, then called ahead to their guide. 'Master de Tracy, what led you to come to me?'

Roger had clearly anticipated that question. 'It is an

important sword. Our man of law was most keen to have no stone left unturned in seeking it. He demanded that I come to you to find it. Denis has heard great things of your skills at uncovering the truth. Of course we had thought to enlist the help of Sir Richard de Welles, but you know some coroners can be so preoccupied with money that their thoughts can become blurred. We thought that the coroner from Lifton would be more free of such motives, but it became clear that he had his own interests in pursuing our sword.'

'What would they be?'

'It is ancient. Many men would covet a weapon with such a history.'

Baldwin muttered something under his breath.

'Sir?' Roger asked, blankly.

'My companion was marking what you said,' Simon said with a grin. Better that Roger didn't hear Baldwin's sour 'Fools, the lot of them.'

Roger nodded uncertainly, unsure how to take these two men. The last thing he wanted was to have the sword found again in a hurry, but he wasn't sure that Denis's faith in this Keeper was well-founded.

Baldwin looked bright enough, but more likely was used to brute force rather than intellect. He was a rangy fellow who looked as though he'd been in plenty of battles. His frame was as broad as any fighter's, and there was a scar that reached down his cheek almost from his eyebrow to his chin that hinted at a dangerous past; but this friend of his, the bailiff, seemed altogether too light-hearted, as though he could not treat any matter with any seriousness. 'It's a very important affair to us,' he said, looking at the bailiff.

'I'm sure it is,' Simon said affably. 'So! This man who was killed: Walter Coule. He was reeve to Sir John de Curterne, you said?'

'Yes. Sir John is our neighbour. We used to be friends with him when we were all younger. In those days, he was the third son, but the family suffered a number of set-backs. The eldest fell from his horse and drowned in the river, the second was crushed by an ox in their stable, and Sir John took the manor in his turn.'

Baldwin nodded and crossed himself. For a parent to lose a child was appalling, and he feared always that his own precious Richalda might fall prey to an accident. No one could prevent deaths, but it did not make the loss any easier for the parents. Sir John's family had been unfortunate, but crushings by large beasts were common, as were drownings, whether in rivers or wells.

'And Coule's body was found on whose land?' Simon asked.

'On ours. But that means nothing. He could have been dragged there.'

Baldwin grunted at that. It was all too natural that a body might be moved. A murderer would remove a body so that any evidence which may exist would be divorced from the corpse. Then again, the vill in which a murder took place would be fined: often innocent villagers would move a body so that they would not be punished for the breaking of the King's Peace. If evidence about a murder was lost because the actual location of the murder was never found, it made the investigation that much more difficult.

'You said this Coule was unpopular?' Baldwin demanded after a moment's reflection.

'Many had reason to dislike him. He was grasping; he took as much as he could from the peasants on the estate, and they detested him. It made for a lot of trouble. If he exacted more than he should, the peasants complained bitterly, and only last year they took up sticks and attacked the poor devils sent to collect the grains and dues he had demanded from them. Sir John had to arm his men and suppress his own peasants!'

Baldwin studied his laughing face with an expression that could have been carved from moorstone. 'Open revolt?'

'Near enough. It amused us.'

'So I see. Where were you on the Friday Coule died?'

'Me?' Roger blinked with surprise. 'I was out hunting with my raches. I have several pairs of them as well as greyhounds.'

'You were not in the castle?'

'No!'

'I see. Tell me: what is the cause of your enmity with this knight?'

'It's nothing. Not now.'

'Humour me.'

Roger appeared to hestitate. 'Many years ago our lands were in the control of the king. Our old manor of Bradninch escheated to the king.'

'Bradninch was forfeit to the crown?' Simon said with surprise. When a lord died without issue, his land reverted or 'escheated' to the king, his lord. But since there was an heir here telling Simon about the story, the land must have been taken for some other reason; perhaps because of a serious offence: treason. 'That must have been a long time ago.'

'Over a hundred years . . . perhaps a hundred and fifty. In any case, the king gave it to a Curterne, and it was lost to us. It's not in the forefront of our minds, but it means we can enjoy the discomfiture of the Curternes when something goes wrong for them.'

'Your family recovered its fortunes?'

'After a while. After a fashion.' Roger became quiet then, musing, before saying, 'As I say, it doesn't upset us now. It was a very long time ago.'

'So to return to Coule – you say that almost any of the peasants could have had reason to wish him dead?'

'The folk on Curterne's lands, yes. Curterne owns territory all over the county, but it's at Down St Mary where he really has trouble. That's where Coule was in charge.'

'I know of it,' Baldwin said.

Simon knew the area. When he and Baldwin had first met, they had ridden out that way in pursuit of trail-bastons who had slaughtered a party of travellers. Down St Mary was a pleasant vill in rolling hills north and east of Bow, while Nymet Tracy was south. Bow had been created sixty years before as a new town so that the Tracys could take advantage of the income that a market and fair could bring, and they had set aside land on a busy road. They would sell blocks to merchants to come and build houses, and so far as Simon was aware, the market was thriving. It would bring in a goodly sum to the master who owned the place.

'So you and your family own the market at Bow?' Simon said. 'I doubt whether there's any need for you to be jealous of losing Bradninch, then.'

'You think so?' Roger snapped. 'Do you know how much money they make at Bradninch market every week?'

Simon smiled. For all Roger's protestations that the affair was far in the past, it clearly still rankled. 'Don't you make enough at Bow? It has always looked busy enough.'

'Perhaps that is so,' Roger agreed and stared at the ground. 'But when you are a second son like me, all you see is what you've missed out on. If that had been our land still, I could have gone there to look to my older brother's interests. As it is . . . another has the advantage. And my family is deprived of our natural inheritance.'

'Does your brother feel as upset as you?' Baldwin enquired.

'Sir William used to be, years ago, but not now,' Roger's tone became cold and a little distant.

'He has a castle, I suppose,' Simon said, unable to stop himself rubbing salt into the wound.

'And money, yes, but that's not it. My brother is extremely pious. You know, if our roles were reversed, I think that he would be delighted.'

'If he were younger, you mean?' Baldwin pressed.

'Yes. If he were the idle one, and I were the knight with the demesne, he would be perfectly content. He would go to a convent and retire from the world without a second thought. The life would suit him. He has always had a hankering for prayer. The idea of being able to abase himself at the cross every day would appeal to him immensely.'

'I see,' Baldwin said, but in his mind's eye he saw a man gripped with fury in the knowledge that his property had been taken, gripping one of the few remaining family treasures of any value in both hands and using it to hack at a thief.

No matter how religious a man was, being robbed could deprive even a monk of the inclination to turn the other cheek.

Alice de Tracy heard the hooves approaching and felt her heart begin to thud painfully. She lived in perpetual dread of the future now, and those hoofbeats sounded like the drums of doom.

Waving irritably at the maid brushing her hair, she rose from the stool and stood indecisively, unwilling to go straight to the window. Instead she snapped at the maid to leave, and only when the door had closed, the wooden latch dropping into its slot, did she hurry to the window.

The yard was in its usual state of busyness. Henry the under-groom was grooming Sir William's great horse while it tried to nip and kick at him; stable-boys were fetching fresh hay and sweeping out the old straw; the steward was shouting at the brewery, demanding to know what had happened to the gallon of strong ale he'd ordered earlier, and all in all the place was a mess. It was into this commotion that the riders came, led by Roger.

Her lips compressed into a thin line. She knew that it was Denis's idea to fetch someone, but she would have hoped for another messenger to have been sent. Roger had demanded the right to go, and the very presumptuousness of his action made her feel a cold dread. He could have soured the keeper and his companion against her and her husband. It was the sort of thing Roger would do.

The two with him were used to authority. One, the elder of the two from his greying hair, appeared to be a knight, and not one of those modern, primping coxcombs, but a fighting man. He had the breadth of shoulder, the muscled arms, and the air of command. If she had to guess, he was the keeper.

When she looked at the other, she saw a younger man, perhaps only ten years senior to her own two-and-twenty years. Still, from the way he cocked his leg over his mount's neck and slid quickly to the ground, standing with the arrogance born of confidence, she wondered fleetingly whether her estimation might have been wrong. But then she lost interest in the two men as she caught sight of Roger, staring up at her with a vindictive smile on his face.

It chilled her blood.

The castle was only small, obviously built early in the days after the pacification of the country. William of

Normandy had given tracts of lands like this to all his most loyal vassals and mercenaries after the invasion, the only stipulation being that the recipients of his largesse should build their own strongholds to keep the peasants under control.

A low motte had been built, and at the top stood a stone keep. Over the years the original single tower had been expanded, and now there was a thatched hall at its foot, stables, a brewery, storehouses, and even a small blacksmith's, all enclosed within a sturdy wall of grey moorstone. When their horses had been led away to be fed and watered, Roger led them up a staircase to a doorway on the first floor of the hall. There he stood aside to let the guests enter.

'Madame de Tracy, I am pleased to meet you,' Baldwin said as he entered the hall.

'You know me?'

'I have heard of your beauty, madam – and your brother-in-law said you were here,' he admitted with a smile.

She smiled, and Baldwin was pleased to see that the appearance of nervousness and fear left her as she did so. Dimples appeared in both cheeks, and her blue eyes seemed to light with an inner glow. 'You are generous, friend.'

'My name is Sir Baldwin de Furnshill, and I am the Keeper of the King's Peace. This is my companion, Bailiff Simon Puttock, the Keeper of the Port of Dartmouth under the Abbot of Tavistock.'

Standing back as Simon bowed, Baldwin saw her fear begin to return even though her dimples remained.

'You must be exhausted after your long journey,' she said.

'Exhausted? I should think we are!' Roger said as he marched into the hall tugging at his riding gloves, slapping them against his thigh to clear the dust of the road from them. The dirt rose from his cotehardie and hosen as a fine mist, and he waved it away.

'Command wine, then, brother,' she said, and there was tartness in her tone, Baldwin noted.

'Ale for me,' Simon asked. 'And a little bread and meat?'

When the bottler had brought them food and jugs of drink, Simon and Baldwin sat at the table.

'Tell me, lady, where is your husband? I thought he would be here to meet us on our arrival,' Baldwin said.

'He wanted to be here to see you,' she said in a rush. 'He was desperate to hear what help you might be able to give him in this affair.'

'He has been called away, apparently,' Roger said comfortably, leaning back in his chair with a large mazer of wine in his hand. He took a deep draught and continued, 'A matter of the arrangements for the market up at Bow.'

'There must be many things to do in preparation for a market the size of Bow's,' Baldwin said easily.

'He meant no insult to you, I do assure you,' Alice said, and in her eyes there was a fleeting hatred as she glanced at Roger. 'But the bailiff of the market is ill and may not recover, so my husband wished to assure himself that all was in hand.'

'I understand perfectly,' Baldwin said. 'I have been involved in the organization of Crediton fair on occasion, and there is always much to do. When you are not so used to a life of responsibility, it is easy to underestimate the effort required,' he added.

Roger was still for a moment. 'Was that a calculated insult?'

Baldwin had taken a mouthful of meat, and he chewed quietly while contemplating the man. 'I am sure that if I wished to insult you, I should succeed. Just as, if you were to try to insult me, I should take notice.'

'Lady Alice,' Simon interrupted quickly, 'where was this sword kept? It seems curious to me that someone could walk in here and take a weapon with the heritage of this one.'

'You have heard its story?' she said, and her gaze returned to her brother-in-law.

Baldwin raised his brows. There was more to this than Roger had said. 'It is old – we know that. If there is more we should know, perhaps you could tell us?'

'No. It is not my part. My husband should do that,' she responded. 'But to answer your question, Bailiff, it was there, in the chest by the wall.'

This was an older hall, and there was no chimney. Instead there was a large blackened hearth in the middle of the floor, and the rafters and inner thatch spoke of the number of fires that had roared in here. Beyond the fire was a strong chest of wood bound with iron, and a massive lock in the lid.

'It was locked in there?' Baldwin asked with frank surprise.

'I fear not. If it had been locked, it would be inside still. No, I had asked my husband to open it for me to fetch a necklace and it was not locked again. He blames me for the theft.'

'Coule was not seen alive after visiting here? You believe he died that same day?'

'Yes. I fear so,' she said quietly.

'The man who stole it was neither liked nor trusted by you, yet he was allowed in here alone?'

It was Roger who answered. 'Walter Coule came ostensibly to discuss a matter before the courts: some of his merchants have been demanding freedom from tolls at our fair, and we see no reason to accommodate them. He came here and was allowed into the hall, but when my brother returned, Coule was gone. As was the sword.'

'I was in here and received him,' Alice said bitterly. 'I went to fetch Sir William myself. It was my own mistake. I was a fool to leave him alone in here!'

'You are sure it was gone then?'

She nodded. 'Denis saw that the chest was unlocked that afternoon. He relocked it and gave the key to my husband that day. It was only when the body was found that we opened it again.'

'What happened when your husband realized Coule was gone?' Baldwin enquired.

'William was angry, of course, but none of us thought more of it, other than it showed how boorish and unthoughtful Coule could be.'

'Really,' Baldwin said. 'There were how many witnesses to Coule leaving the castle?'

'The ostler, grooms, perhaps the steward . . . any number.'

'None saw him carrying the sword?'

'No. But few would have recognized the sword. It was not out on display all the time.'

'He could have had it wrapped in his cloak or concealed some other way,' Roger said eagerly.

'Of course,' Simon said, smiling understandingly at the woman. She was plainly upset, blaming herself for the theft. Her husband would not have been happy to learn that she had left the man in the hall alone. Especially since she had herself caused the chest to be opened, he reminded himself, and his face hardened. Perhaps Coule's arrival was more than a coincidence. Could this woman have planned it?

Baldwin said nothing. He looked at Roger, then let his eyes move toward Alice. She, he noticed, had begun to flush, her throat reddening. He considered. 'We heard this Coule was often here. Would you usually leave him unguarded?'

Alice lifted her chin slightly. 'I do not expect every

visitor who accepts our hospitality to rob us, if that is what you mean. But yes, Coule would come here once each month or so to speak with my husband on matters that affected our manors. My husband and Sir John do not get on well. Their mutual affairs are conducted by others. We tended to have my husband's man of law, Denis de Topcliffe, speak with Coule.'

Simon had another question which troubled him. 'Roger told us that Coule was an unpopular man with his peasants. How did your folk respond to him?'

Alice took up her mazer and swallowed hurriedly. 'I don't think that they were troubled by him. Not like his own people at Down St Mary. If he had tried to bully our people, I am sure my husband would have seen to his being punished.'

'Which he did, I assume,' Baldwin said.

'I don't understand?'

'Coule came here and stole from you. Surely your husband went to demand the sword's return from Sir John?'

'We didn't realize it was gone until the inquest,' she said defensively. 'Otherwise I am sure my husband would have spoken with Sir John when the disappearance was noticed.'

'Through an intermediary,' Baldwin noted drily.

Simon continued, 'Does your husband never talk to your neighbour?'

'Sir John de Curterne? No.'

Roger said, 'I told you: we are not friends with him.'

'The lands you lost?'

She nodded. 'It was a blow to the family, I think. But it was a long, long time ago. I am sure that my husband holds no ill-feeling about it. He used to be a good friend of the Curterne family. It was only after . . . since I knew my husband that the two manors have been at loggerheads.'

Roger sniggered at that, and the unpleasant sound stuck in Baldwin's ears. 'You say "since I knew my husband" – do you mean that in some way it was because of your marriage that the two men fell out?'

'Perhaps – I was to have married Sir John's brother. We had been betrothed for some months when he died.'

'His older brother?' Baldwin pressed.

'Yes. Godfrey was his name. He fell from his horse into the river and drowned. He was only fourteen. Before then, the two families had been close, I have heard. But not since his death. And then a few years later his poor brother Ralph also died when an ox fell on him.'

'Sir John has not wished to remain on friendly terms since then?' Baldwin asked sharply, his eyes going to Roger.

'If you seek to raise old troubles, let me ease your mind,' Roger responded easily. 'It was Sir William who would have nothing more to do with them, rather than the other way about. Poor Godfrey died of an accident. It's common enough. But afterwards, I think my brother was a little embarrassed when he persuaded Lady Alice's parents to let him wed her. Perhaps he felt that Sir John would have expected her to marry him in his brother's place.'

'He was,' Lady Alice said, her eyes downcast. 'Sir Baldwin, you have to appreciate that my husband is extremely pious. He felt almost guilty to have taken me, his best friend's woman, but he loved me.'

'Pious?'

'There is no man more so,' she said.

Bow was a little town set on the side of a hill with a broad road running through the middle. Baldwin and Simon approached it from the south, riding two fresh mounts loaned to them by Lady Alice, guided by the dour lawyer Denis.

Their way was sheltered by great elms and oaks on either side, and there was a large forest at one point, where the road narrowed alarmingly.

'Do you know where this man Coule was found?' Baldwin asked as they rode.

'It was just up here.' Denis turned in his saddle, a hand on the cantle, a leg crooked over the withers to talk more easily to them, a man well used to riding. 'Hob found him a short way along this lane there.'

They were trailing down a hillside that fell away to marshy land at the bottom. He was indicating a green lane leading westwards.

'What else lies down there?' Baldwin asked.

'Only the mill where Hob lives. He was first finder.'

'What sort of a man is he?' Simon asked.

'Hob? Reliable. Bright. He's lived there all his life, I hear.'

Baldwin narrowed his eyes. 'Good. Now, let us have a quick look at Coule's resting place. Show us where he was found.'

Shrugging unconcernedly, their guide twitched his reins and led the way down the track. Soon they could hear only the swish of grass against the horses' legs, the gentle padding of hooves against soft earth.

Simon took a deep, contented breath. He had missed riding like this since he'd been given his new post in Dartmouth, and the opportunity to enjoy the sunny weather on a good horse was not one he could turn down. Besides, he loved these little trails that criss-crossed the county. Here the road was little used. He could see that from the way that the grass had grown, trampled only a little. A pair of ruts at either side showed where cart wheels were likely to go when a cart came down this way, but as he knew all too well, it was a rare event. Mostly people were forced to use pack-horses on the twisting, steep hills of Devon.

They had just turned a bend in the lane when Denis stopped.

'Just here, I think. This is where the inquest was held,' he pointed to some bushes.

Baldwin, as usual, was keen to drop from his mount and investigate the scene. To Simon's eye there was little attractive about a place like this: it was nothing more than a scene of destruction and death – but at least for once there was no body. The inquest was over, so the body would have been buried.

Here, he told himself, there was no corpse to study, and with that cheery thought came relief. He sprang down from his horse and wandered over to join Baldwin.

'What of it, Baldwin?'

'Stand back, you're blocking the light!'

Simon smiled and leaned against a tree nearby. There was a twig on the ground at his feet, and he picked it up contemplatively. Taking out his knife, he began to whittle at it, conscious of their guide staring at them both. Simon looked up at him. 'He likes to get his hands messy when there's a dead body,' he said helpfully.

Denis looked at Baldwin warily, as though suddenly aware that he was in the presence of a lunatic.

As he watched, Baldwin grasped brambles, pulling them away so he might study the ground more closely. At times, he peered at the stems as though accusing them. At last, he stood and walked about the area, his features scowling darkly at the ground, at the trees, in among the bushes, under piles of rotting leaves.

'There is little to be said about this place,' he said as he went to rejoin Simon. 'It has been so severely beaten down by the inquest. The coroner must have demanded all the juries from the area, from the look of it.'

'He did, sir.'

'They have trampled any evidence into the mire,' Baldwin grumbled. 'What on earth you and I can be expected to learn, I do not know.'

Simon let his stick fall and subjected the land to a brief survey. 'What did the coroner conclude?'

'That Coule had been killed by some unknown footpad. He was stabbed in the breast, knocked on the head, and his hands slashed. Nobody knew who could have done this.'

'Clearly a violent attack, then. And perhaps committed by someone who was known to him,' Baldwin said.

'Why say that?'

'Wounds in the front. A stranger would try to close with his prey from behind. Only a friend or associate would get up close enough to attack from in front. Tell me, did you see Coule that day?'

'Me?' Denis squeaked. 'Why me? It was me suggested you should be asked to come and hold an inquest into the theft!'

'Madam Alice said you live in the castle. I merely wondered.'

'I saw her when Coule arrived. She fled the hall to seek Sir William.'

'And you were there later to lock up the chest.'

'I saw the key in the lid's lock. I turned it, that's all.'

'Where was Sir William?'

'He was in the garden behind the castle, talking with his steward and bailiff. That was where madam Alice found him.'

'His brother?' Simon asked.

'He said he was hunting.'

'What does that mean?'

Denis sneered. 'He is always looking for another ale or wine or wench from the vill to slake his lusts. He often goes out and doesn't return for a day. Usually he's up at the inn at Bow, although sometimes he rides out as far as Spreyton. He wasn't at the castle itself.'

'Did you ride out?'

'No! I was working on matters for Sir William in my chamber. I am no murderer!'

Baldwin nodded. 'I think it's clear enough why the man died here. He was chased from the main road, hurried to here, where he was killed at bay.'

'Why would the man want him here?' Simon wondered.

'The nearest house would be the miller's,' Denis said helpfully. 'Perhaps he sought safety there?'

'Perhaps. How did madam Alice react to Coule turning up at the castle?'

'She was surprised, I think. Who could have expected him to arrive unannounced?'

'Who indeed?' Baldwin said.

'I was in my chamber, and later I heard the master ask where the man was, and that was that.'

'No hue and cry?' Simon asked.

'No one thought he had stolen anything, let alone the sword. He was the family's enemy, but he was often at the castle.'

'What of the miller?' Simon asked. 'Millers often have disputes with others when folk reckon the miller's charging too much. Is there bad feeling generally about this miller? Or was there any between Coule and the miller themselves?'

'Them? No. Not that I've heard. Hob is a good man. Not the sort to upset people. He's fair in his business.'

'Did Hob and Coule get on well?' Simon asked, squinting back along the track they had taken. 'Could Hob have killed him and stolen the sword?'

'What would a miller do with a sword?'

There was no answer. Simon looked westwards. 'This path goes to the mill? Where then?'

'It turns north up to Bow.'

'Where did this Coule live?'

'Up near Clannaborough Cross'

'Which is where, roughly?'

Denis sighed. 'It's over the boundaries of my lord's lands. I don't know.'

'Perhaps you should guess, then,' Simon suggested nastily.

'North east, I suppose.'

'So when he came down here, Coule was not heading even remotely in the right direction,' Simon noted.

'Why come this way, then?' Baldwin wondered. 'I think we ought to ask this helpful miller.'

Hob was at his vegetables when he heard the horses approaching, and he stood up, leaning on his shovel. It was rare that a man would come this way to visit him. His mill was popular when there was grain to be milled, but now, in the early summer, there was little custom.

A good thing, too. While the river was full and the waters rushed past the mill's wheel, he could often find himself overwhelmed. Luckily that tended to be after the harvest, and when the grain was dried well enough. Now, though, was the time when he tended to look to the cogs and see to it that his machine was in excellent condition for when the people brought in their valuable sacks. And made sure that his own garden was growing well.

'Masters,' he called as the three men appeared, and eyed them cautiously. A man was wise to be wary.

Baldwin snapped. 'You are Hob the miller? I am the Keeper of the King's Peace. My friend here is bailiff to Abbot Champeaux.'

As he explained that he wanted to ask about the man Hob had found, Hob nodded resignedly. 'Aye, master. I'll answer any questions you have.'

'Did he often come this way?'

'Coule? No, hardly ever, I'd say. He'd take the direct road. Now and again he would come here when he had need of my mill – their manor's mill broke last year and they had to use ours.'

'We heard that he was at the castle to discuss some matter that was before the courts. It is thought that he died on his way home afterwards. Do you know of any affair that could have brought him this way?'

Hob gave a shy grin at that. 'I'm just a miller, sir. They don't talk to me about things like that.'

Simon nodded, and said, 'Tell us about the day you found the body. Where was it, and did you see anything odd about it?'

Hob sighed, let his hoe fall, and jerked his chin towards the mill. 'You want an ale? It's hot out here doing the garden.'

'That would be good,' Simon said with a smile.

'But sirs, you were supposed to be coming with me to Bow to meet my lord, Sir William,' Denis objected.

'You may tell him we'll be with him when we're ready,' Baldwin said.

'I can't say that to my master!' Denis protested.

But then, looking at Baldwin's steady eye, he found that in all likelihood, he would prefer even Sir William's wrath to this man's.

'This is the best ale I've tasted in some weeks,' Simon said, smacking his lips.

'You dislike the ale at my home?' Baldwin growled. 'You drank enough of it!'

'It is good, but this, this is nectar!'

Hob smiled and nodded at the compliment. 'I

learned brewing early. When a man spends his life breathing in the dust from the flour, any drink takes on a new importance!'

'So tell me, Hob,' Simon said. 'What is all this about the man who died? We've heard how unpopular he was with the serfs on his estates, and it seems that the de Tracys had cause to dislike him, if the rumours about his stealing the sword are true.'

'Was there any sign of a sword near the body?' Baldwin asked.

Hob spat into the dirt of the floor and studied the puddle gobbet. 'If it was, I wouldn't have touched it!'

Simon and Baldwin exchanged a baffled glance. It was Baldwin who asked mildly, 'Why?'

'Don't you know what that sword was? It was the assassin's weapon.'

Simon smiled with blank confusion. 'You say that Sir William or Roger his brother is a murderer?'

'Not them, no. But it was Sir William de Tracy who was there with the other murderers when they martyred the saint.'

'Good Christ!' Baldwin murmured. 'Of course!'

Simon looked blankly from him to Hob. 'What?'

'De Tracy . . . I had forgotten my history. You have forgotten the martyrdom of St Thomas? At Canterbury?'

'Oh!'

'St Thomas a Becket sought to confound the king, and the king shouted out to demand whether no man would rid him of his troublesome priest, so they say. Three of his knights, seeking his approval, took to horse that same night and crossed the channel at their first opportunity. They rode as swift as death to the cathedral, and there they slayed the archbishop in his own church.'

Simon crossed himself. 'To murder in a church . . . they must have been mad!'

'This is that very sword that Sir William de Tracy used to execute the poor saint. So you'll see why I wouldn't touch it myself,' Hob said. 'I couldn't. It must be cursed.'

'What happened to him?' Simon asked.

Baldwin answered, speaking softly. 'He and the other three rode on many adventures, but their crime would not leave them. The guilt and shame was ever at their minds. They rode from Canterbury to Sussex, and there while they ate, the very table on which they had placed their armour and weapons tipped up and threw the lot onto the floor. As it became clear that they were shunned by all men, the King advised them to ride north to live in Scotland, for the Pope had excommunicated them for their crime, but when they arrived, they found that the king of the Scots wanted them arrested, and the people wished to see them hang. So they rode back mournfully to the king whom they had tried to serve. None would sit with them, nor share a meal with them. Even the dogs refused the scraps from their bowls.

'The king had no jurisdiction, for this was a murder of a clergyman in a church. He had to ask the pope what should be done with the three. The pope urged that the three should fast and live a life of continual penance, and that they should be banished from the country and travel to the Holy Land where they might take up arms against the Saracens. De Tracy became a Knight Templar, I understand.'

Simon understood his quietness suddenly. Sir Baldwin had been one of the Poor Fellow Soldiers of Christ and the Temple of Solomon, a Knight Templar, and had only survived the persecution, torture and slaughter of the suppression of the holy order because he had been out of the Temple in Paris when his comrades were all arrested. Yet there was more: a quizzical, doubtful expression had come into his eyes.

Simon looked at Hob. 'Is that true? Did de Tracy die in the Holy Kingdom?'

'I don't know about that. The sword came back only two years ago, though, Sir. It was Sir Humphrey, Sir William's father, who brought it back. He was there in Acre at the fall of the Kingdom of Jerusalem. I think he found it again while he was abroad – in Acre or on his way there – and brought it back for his family.'

Baldwin frowned pensively. 'He was at the siege?'

'One of the few brave men who travelled there to defend our faith and Christ's birthplace,' Hob agreed.

'You reckon he found it out there?' Simon said. 'How would he know it was his ancestor's sword?'

'There are ways,' Baldwin said, but in his mind's eye, all he saw was that terrible battlefield: the great city of Acre, last stronghold of the crusaders, being reduced steadily by the thundering artillery of the hordes outside. The crash and rumble of masonry collapsing as the great rocks were flung at them by the catapults, then the shrieks as the enemy managed to enter the city, swords dripping with blood, eyes filled with the desire for slaughter. There were many died there.

'Yes, well, maybe there are,' Simon conceded. 'Yet a man would have to be entirely convinced to think a sword found so long after being lost was the correct one, surely?'

'The man who sold it told of its provenance, I suppose,' Hob said vaguely. 'Sir Humphrey, Sir William's sire, must have been assured. He looked on it as a sign that his family's crime was forgotten. God had forgiven them.'

'Sir William was happy to have it returned to him, I suppose?' Simon said, ignoring Baldwin's derisive snort.

'Hardly! He is pious. To be named for the ancestor who executed a poor saint, that was bad enough, but to have the sword brought back as well! I think he felt it was cursed – and that was easy to believe since Sir Humphrey died soon after he returned. He had a fever that burst his heart. Many say that the sword should be destroyed for its crime against St Thomas.'

Simon nodded. He had always been prone to an awareness of atmosphere, the sense of evil, the feeling of a devil's presence – the sort of thing that Baldwin laughingly called 'superstitious rubbish', but which Simon knew was a proof of his sensitivity. There had been times when . . . but Baldwin would only laugh. Still, a sword that ended such an important life would likely be cursed until blessed in church to expiate the crime.

Baldwin had no patience with such feelings. 'Well, if you believe that a sword can take on a man's guilt, that is fine. Perhaps it ought to be destroyed . . . but for now, I think I should like to find this weapon and see whether it was used to murder Coule. We have heard that he was unpopular with the villeins on his estate, but was there any one man who hated him enough to murder him?'

'Perhaps only his own master.'

'This man Sir John de Curterne?' Baldwin snapped. 'Why do you say that?'

'Sir John always wanted placid, untroubled serfs. Coule wanted his peasants cowed.'

'Sir John is enlightened, or he has suffered in the past from mutiny and rebellion?' Baldwin asked.

Hob considered. 'I think a little of both. He's no weakling, but his father used to bully the folk too much and he did have a rebellion. Sir John wants no repeat of that. His trouble is, Coule never feared him. The man was determined to get his own way, and he'd argue with his master in front of the villeins.'

'Any fool who tried that with me would get a taste of the lash himself,' Baldwin growled.

'I think it was close with him. When he disappeared, they thought he'd gone on pilgrimage. Everyone could believe that! He had lots to be forgiven for!'

'He didn't fear losing his position and livelihood?' Simon said.

'I never saw him afraid,' Hob said.

'Sir John is well rid of him,' Simon said. He motioned to the sky. 'It's growing late, Baldwin. If we're to get to the town and then back, we should ride on soon.'

Sir John de Curterne was generally a mild-mannered man, and he smiled indulgently at his young son, Matthew. The two-year-old was steady on his legs, and was beginning to talk as he ran about the hall, grasping at balls, sticks and any and every other bauble that took his fancy. He was a son to be proud of. Sir John felt sure that he would be a brave, bold fellow as he grew. The idea made him grin to himself. He had no desire to force his son into a particular mode of thinking or behaviour.

His own father had tried to do that with him. Sir Edward had been convinced that his eldest son, Godfrey, would be a bold, adventurous man with a good estate behind him. He had seen to the marriage with Alice to take over her manors, for her father was wealthy and had no son. Sir Edward had done all he could to promote Godfrey, seeing to his training with a master of defence, acquiring a cleric to teach him how to read and write, as well as the arts of management of estates. He had done well, and until that dreadful day when Godfrey had drowned, he had been a model young warrior.

And then he died, and before long, when Sir John was still a young fellow, his second brother died when the ox fell on him, and suddenly Sir John was the sole remaining heir and must learn a new life of responsibility and duty.

Now in his early thirties, he was proud that he was not at all like his father. Sir Edward had been more keen to impose his will on all those who lived on his lands, and on upholding the ancient liberties and privileges of the manor. Over time the continual struggle had harmed the family. Too much money was extorted from the vills on his lands, and the peasants grew impatient with the constant demands for more taxes, until at last he had been forced to resort to armed strength to keep them quiet.

Not for Sir John a life of litigation and strife. He preferred to negotiate and agree terms that were acceptable to all. His peasants were generally passive, content with their lot. Complaints were few, and he could count on the peasants working harder, now their profits were taxed more sensibly. He was farming his serfs more effectively than his father ever had. It was a source of pride to him, as was his reputation for coolness in adversity and his ability to remain detached and affable under the worst of provocations.

Today, though, as the man was brought to him, he sat back and felt the anger begin to bite at his heart. It was hard to remain in the same room as this arrogant prickle.

'So, Master Roger. You wished to speak with me?'

'Your tone is so bitter, Sir John. Do I deserve your enmity?'

Sir John eyed him calmly. For a moment or two he did not speak.

It was long before the birth of either of them that the argument over the land had first risen; it had been back in the days of old Sir Hugh de Curterne, who had received the lands from King Richard. All this trouble over Bradninch stemmed from that transaction.

When they had all been lads, none of them had

cared about the affair. They had been boys together, playing as equals: Sir William with Godfrey, Ralph and John with Roger. Then, when Godfrey died, William appeared to withdraw from that world. Everyone had thought it was because he had always been fonder of Godfrey, but John knew different. He had spoken to William not long afterwards, and William had told him that his family was little better than thieves. They had taken his manor of Bradninch from him, and he would do all he could to retrieve it. Now Sir William would never speak to him unless there was absolutely no alternative, as though it was Sir John's fault that Bradninch had been taken from him. The fool!

Yet if he was a fool, this brother of his was a snake, and a snake all the more poisonous for the apparent friendliness. 'What do you want with me?'

'Oh, Sir John, there's no need to be suspicious,' Roger said, holding his hands up in mock hurt. 'I am here to help.'

'Why would you want to help me?'

'Why should I not? You are a close neighbour, after all.'

'Don't piss lies into my ear! Whatever you give freely, you give because you want something in return.'

'In that case, let me be frank,' Roger said. 'I have heard that my brother is considering giving up the secular world. You know he is a keen, pious man? He feels the urge to go into a convent most keenly. Since he has lost our family's most precious possession, shame is likely to hurry that ambition.'

'The sword?' Sir John said. He leaned forward, elbow on his knee, resting his chin on his fist.

'The sword. While he possessed it, it was a source of immense embarrassment, naturally, and now he's lost it, he's keen to hide himself from the world – urgently, before anything comparable can arrive to unsettle him.'

'What's all that got to do with me?'

'The sword has to remain hidden. If it is found, Sir William will stay. If it's gone . . . then he will go too, and I will become master of Nymet Tracy. And I'd be a better neighbour than my brother.'

Sir John leaned back again, his head tilted as he studied his guest quizzically. 'You're a devious little bastard, aren't you? You murder my man, take the sword from him, and now you say you want me to take it from you and hide it? Why? To protect you? After you murdered my man?'

Roger's smile broadened. 'I'll bring it here for you and your family. For all time, as a proof of my friendship. We were comrades once. Why can we not be so again? It is very valuable.'

Sir William was in the market hall, an open building with rough wooden palings to act as a screen from the worst of the weather, when Denis appeared riding slowly down the high street. He rose, walking out to the roadway as Denis drew to a halt.

'They are here?'

Denis nodded. 'They are questioning Hob just now. They wanted to speak to him first, before coming to see you.'

Sir William's jaw clenched as he considered all the work he had to do before he could rest that day, and then he nodded curtly. 'Ride back to the castle and tell my wife I shall be back as soon as I may. I have business to attend to while this precious keeper idles away his time with my miller!'

The man of law nodded, relieved to be escaping with no curse ringing in his ears, and Sir William returned to the market hall to the papers and the pasty-faced, unwell port-reeve. 'Come! Let's finish our business this week, eh?'

It had not been perfect, but perhaps that was too much to expect after the last years of strife. Still, Roger reckoned the meeting with Sir John had been satisfactory, and he rode back at a steady pace. The knight would agree once he had considered Roger's offer, he was sure of that, and when Sir William departed, that would seal the contract. There would be an end to this daft dispute between the two manors, and the lawyers could at last pack up their books: Denis could go back to whichever stone from beneath which he'd crawled before coming here and taking the family's money.

Roger's road did not lead direct to the castle. In preference he would go to Bow and take an ale or two at the inn. There was a new maid there who had caught his eye recently, a delightful filly who looked as though she'd give him a good gallop – and ah! when his damned brother had left the manor, life would be so much more sweet! She would certainly be more interesting than a return to the castle. It had all the charm and warmth of a charnel house recently: better, he may stay the night at the inn. There he could keep the sword safe, too.

He had hoped that Sir John would take the thing as soon as it was offered, but perhaps that was a little too much to hope for. As he said, if he took the thing, he could be accused of murder, and he was not yet happy to trust Roger with that responsibility. However, his eyes were easier at the end of their meeting, and Roger thought that they would be able to enjoy a better relationship when Roger was in charge of the manor. No bad thing, either, for Sir John to know that Roger could be ruthless when necessary. Yes. All in all, a good day's work. He deserved his ale.

William would be happier in a convent. There was no point in his remaining in the world when all he wanted was a hermit-like existence in a monastery. Roger was ensuring that he would achieve the ambition he had craved for so long.

He turned one of the last bends in the road on the way to Bow, and suddenly a cloak was hurled at his horse. His beast leapt into the air, neighing with surprise. Roger gripped hard with his thighs, his fingers curled into talons as he clutched the reins. 'Easy! Easy!' he called, trying to keep the anger from his voice.

The beast was startled, but he couldn't seek the culprit as his horse plunged and reared: his concentration was on his mount. Even as he felt the first slip of steel beneath his ribs, he could not face his danger. His mind was so fixed upon his horse that even as the sword thrust upwards, he was at first convinced that it was a strained muscle.

It was only when the strain became a flowering agony that his eyes opened wide with horror. There was a liquid thundering in his breast as blood was pumped into his lungs, and he was starting to drown even before the sword's point burst through his fashionable tight gipon in front of his anguished eyes. He tried to scream, but as he toppled backwards, his weight slipping him down the blade made slick with his own blood, only a gurgling would come from his throat, and he vomited a gush of blood as he died.

Sir William was in the court of the castle still when the two men arrived.

'You are the keeper who told my man of law to come and tell me to wait?'

'I am Sir Baldwin de Furnshill,' Baldwin said coldly. He was not happy to have ridden up to Bow only to learn that he had missed Sir William. The knight had returned to his castle.

At first sight Baldwin thought the peevish knight would be best suited to a convent, just as Hob had hinted. Sir William had that sallow, unhealthsome complexion that was always so common with monks and clerics who took fasting too seriously.

'I had no spare time to wait. Come inside and have a little wine.'

The hall was empty but for the three. Sir William sat on his chair in the far corner, watching them with a grim expression on his face as they entered.

'Baldwin, have you ever seen a cat staring at an approaching hound?' Simon whispered. 'That man hates us: he knows we could destroy him, but reckons he can scratch our noses first.'

'He most certainly has the look of a man expecting to suffer.'

'Enter, Sir Knight, and take your ease. Your man will find ale and cups at the table. Bring me one, too.'

Baldwin opened his mouth, but the knight was already staring up at the wide empty window space with a distracted air. 'Simon, I apologize. I shall . . .'

Simon showed his teeth. 'An easy error to make: he thinks you provide me with these rich clothes? He must consider you a most parsimonious knight!'

Baldwin sat. 'You did not think to seek my help, I believe?'

'No! I would prefer this whole matter was forgotten. I see little need to expose our foolishness further. That fool of a lawyer of mine suggested you to my brother, and he took it on himself . . . No. I see no need for all this!'

Simon had passed wine to Sir William. Now he took a large cupful for himself and another for Baldwin before sitting at Baldwin's side.

'You! We have affairs to discuss. You can leave us,' Sir William grated.

Simon smiled, and Baldwin eyed the knight coldly. 'This is Bailiff Simon Puttock. He is stannary bailiff to Abbot Champeaux of Tavistock and a king's officer. He is here to assist me.'

'Oh? I am sorry, Bailiff. My apologies.'

Simon, enormously enjoying the knight's discomfiture, smiled. 'It's nothing, sir.'

Sir William shook his head. 'My brother and my wife both felt it would be best for someone who could investigate this theft. I think it's ridiculous. What good can it serve? The thing's gone, and that's all that matters.'

'You don't want it back?'

Sir William looked up, and his face twisted. 'Want it back? I would rather cut off my own hand than touch that thing again! It's evil! *Evil!* I am delighted not to have to look at it. It was a constant reminder of my family's crime.' Sir William gave a short, twisted grin. 'I don't like it. I am grateful that someone has taken it. If I'd thought of it sooner, I'd have paid a man to remove it, and thereby save me from keeping it any longer. With it gone, I can happily give up my position here, leave the castle and find a monastery to my liking, there to live in praise of God and seeking His peace. But now . . .'

'Yes? Now?'

'The thing is gone. I am glad of the fact, because to me it seems God has forgiven me. In taking the thing, He has shown me that I am not to worry about it any more. But my wife does not agree. She thinks one felon escaping the law damages all justice.'

'Perhaps that is not your concern. Leave justice to the judges.'

'True. But if I were to enter a monastery, I would expect Alice also to join a convent. She knows that. It colours her judgement. If the sword is found again, perhaps I should remain here to guard it. If it comes back, God doesn't consider me deserving of the peace life in a monastery would grant me. Ach, I don't know! What should I do? If you find the thing, I will be bound to remain here – if you don't, I shall be better pleased.'

'One issue concerns me,' Simon said. 'How can you be so sure that this was your sword? I heard that it was discovered recently by your father and he brought it back. Had he seen it before?'

'My father was convinced when he bought it. That's enough for me.'

'Where did he find it?'

'A trader in Cyprus with some outlandish name. Zuliani or something, who said it was definitely the sword which Sir William de Tracy had used to murder St Thomas. There was no doubt.'

Baldwin said nothing to that. He had met traders in Cyprus and other bazaars about the world, and if he had met an honest one, the experience had evaded his notice. 'What was your father doing out there?'

'I think he had the urge to follow in Sir William de Tracy's footsteps. He only reached as far as Cyprus, but he was able to visit shrines and pilgrimage sites even so. When he brought it back, he was proud! *Proud!* I wanted nothing to do with it, and when my father died only a short while later, I put it to rest, safely locked in that trunk.'

'Except on that day of all days you left the chest unlocked. You had a good reason to wish the sword to be lost. Who else would have desired it gone?'

Sir William's face darkened and he took a long draught of ale. 'Plainly the thief who walked into my hall and took it,' he spat.

'So you say, but what would he have done with it?' Baldwin asked. 'It is a pretty thing, I daresay, but what use is beauty in a weapon that can never be shown or used? If he had ever drawn that steel, he would have been instantly accused of stealing it. I find this idea that he wandered aimlessly into your hall and stole this valuable and famous sword quite incomprehensible. Unless he had been paid to take it, there is no reason why he should have taken it. Someone else must either have wanted it, or wanted it to be gone. It is fair to say that you wanted it gone, and could have paid this man to remove it. Who else had a similar desire?'

Sir William lifted his head truculently, staring. 'You accuse me of having my own sword stolen?'

His voice was low and little more than a whisper. Seeing how his face had paled, Baldwin nodded slowly. 'Perhaps you should consider telling the truth now, Sir William.'

That evening was quiet in the castle. The servants had felt the mood of their master, and all were reserved and cautious in his presence. Simon and Baldwin sat with the lord and his wife on the dais to eat, while half his household ate in the main hall.

Simon and Baldwin spoke little, which was much to the bailiff's taste. Today he felt that talking would be a foolish occupation. He was happier filling his belly with good meat and wine than chatting with the depressing company about the table. There was a sense almost of despair about the place. Simon was almost sad that Roger was not with them.

Sir William spoke not at all, but sat grimly toying with his food, while his wife chewed at hers with a grim determination, with many a loving look at her man. As she finished, she set her hand on his, affectionately, so Simon thought.

If it was intended to comfort or strengthen him, it

failed. He snatched his hand away, and she looked desolate. 'My love!'

Sir William shook his head, then eyed her slyly and raised his goblet in a toast. 'No, dear. No longer. Gentlemen! Please, raise your glasses to honour us! As soon as I may I shall leave here and all will go to Roger. I shall expect my wife to join a convent to serve Christ as I go to Tavistock to serve God. It is good! Freedom from the world at last!'

'Where is your brother tonight?' Simon asked after he had drained his mazer.

'He rode off earlier. Often he will go into town to mingle with the folk there,' Sir William said with distaste. 'He may deign to return later. If he has any sense, he'll stay there the night: he knows I won't have my gates opened between sunset and dawn without good reason. If he stays in Bow, all well and good. If he behaves in the way I expect, he'd find it hard to mount his horse in any case. I only hope we don't have complaints from another peasant's father about a squalling brat in nine months.'

Later, Simon and Baldwin went to walk about the walls where they could be alone.

Simon muttered, 'I've visited happier tombs.'

'There is a great deal of restrained anguish in this place,' Baldwin said. 'I shall be glad to leave. This is not a happy home. The sword has brought only misery.'

'They were all happier when it was gone.'

'Yes. A curious superstition.'

Simon winced. Baldwin had always been scathing about those who ascribed evil fortune to the devil, and had often derided the bailiff's sensible precautions against the evil eye or the other signs of bad luck. 'If it's truly evil, it's sensible to be glad to be rid of it.'

'Then they might throw it away. The idea that an inanimate slab of metal has the ability or desire to harm people is ridiculous. A man does not discover an urge to kill by proximity with a weapon.'

'A man might kill in a rash fit of rage if he has access to a weapon, though.'

'And if he has no sword or mace, if there is no knife or dagger available, he will reach for a club, a rock or a walking staff. What would you do, remove all tools from a man's hand in case it might be used as a weapon in the future?'

'Of course not!'

'No. It is a facile, ridiculous solution. And no more than the innocent stone snatched up to brain a man, or the entirely unmalicious walking staff, or a kindly fist, no more does that sword represent evil. There is nothing evil in a lump of metal, Simon; only in the mind of the man who wields it. The sword is innocent. The man who gripped it is the murderer. It is he whom we must catch!'

'Is there much possibility of that?'

Baldwin glanced at him, then stared out over the dark land below the walls. 'I hope so, Simon. I hope so. Tomorrow we must ride to Down St Mary and speak to Sir John de Curterne. Perhaps we shall learn more there.'

'Let's hope so,' Simon said, but then he touched Baldwin's sleeve. Down in the court he had seen a pair of figures, and even as Baldwin followed his pointing finger, and the two people stepped silently into the shadows, Simon breathed, 'So what would Madam Alice have to say so urgently to Denis, do you think?'

'I am not sure,' Baldwin said, but his face was troubled.

Sir John de Curterne eyed his visitors with a degree of amusement mixed with suspicion. 'So, let me guess: this is about that damned sword of Sir William's? And you want to ask me whether I wanted to have my own reeve murdered, I suppose?'

Baldwin took the seat proffered. 'No. We know why your man stole the sword.'

'You accuse a dead man?' Sir John's face darkened. 'That is vile: slandering a man who is unable to defend himself. Speak no ill of the dead!'

'He was paid handsomely to steal that sword, Sir John. And then someone else decided to retrieve it.'

'Sir William's brother?'

The shrewdness of the knight's eyes made Baldwin frown quickly. 'Why do you think that?'

'He wishes the sword to be gone, for then his brother might relinquish the world and step inside a convent. There is no secret about this: Sir William has willingly told all he meets that he wishes to be free of the guilt he feels for his name and the sword's crime.'

'Why would Roger wish to take back the sword that can guarantee him a manor of his own, then?'

'Perhaps he reckoned to keep it for himself? I would not be surprised to hear it. It's a valuable weapon. Maybe he chose to take it, keep it safely concealed, and then, once his brother was safely out of the way, he could bring it out and have it for himself again?'

'You think he would be so devious?'

'There is little which would surprise me about that man,' Sir John said coldly. 'He came here yesterday to ask me to help him. He wished me to agree to keep the sword. He offered it to me, so long as I kept it secret until his brother had left the manor.'

'He admitted he had killed your reeve?' Baldwin demanded.

'He said he saw Walter leave the castle with something hidden as he rode back himself. Roger went to the hall, saw the open chest and guessed at Walter's theft. That is what he told me. And he killed Walter because he thought the man had robbed his brother. Only later, he said, did he realize that the disappearance of the sword would serve him quite well, so he hid the body and concealed the sword. It makes sense. It's the way he would act – the damned fool!'

'You said that to him?'

'In my own hall I see no need to conceal my feelings, Sir Knight.'

There was a noise at the tapestry behind him, and Sir John turned. Seeing his son, his face broke into a broad beaming smile, and he reached down to the toddler before he could fall. 'Careful, Matt! Walking at that speed is too dangerous for a boy.'

'It's hard when they're that age,' Baldwin observed.

'You have a son?'

'A daughter. My friend here has a little fellow.'

'Yes,' Simon grinned. 'But he's a fair amount older, and I don't worry about him when he falls.'

'We all fear for our children, though, don't we?' Sir John said, sitting with his boy on his knee. 'We wish them to be safe and happy.'

Simon nodded, and then frowned musingly. 'Is that why Sir Humphrey brought back that sword? Did he think it would ease Sir William's mind?'

Sir John shook his head. 'I don't think he ever believed the thing was the same as the one that killed St Thomas. He merely thought it a pretty thing with a good balance.'

'That would make sense,' Baldwin said. 'I've seen nothing to suggest the sword was the same as the one lost by Tracy's ancestor. Tell me: we have heard that Sir William was a close friend to you and your brothers. Is that true?'

'He was – and Roger. But William was closer to my oldest brother, Godfrey. He drowned many years ago now. After that, Sir William stopped seeing us. I felt . . .'

'What?'

'That he was embarrassed. You see he snatched Lady Alice and married her as soon as it was known that Godfrey was dead. I think he was ashamed of being so quick. But who could blame him? She was, is, beautiful. Any man would be keen to win her.'

Simon stopped making faces to amuse the toddler on his lap, his expression suddenly stilled. 'You mean you think he could have killed to win her?'

Sir John's face retained its smile, but his eyes had no humour in them. 'I have never seen anything to prove that.'

Baldwin was frowning. 'So you consider it possible?'

'Sir William had an alibi. He was with someone else when my brother died.'

'Do you remember who?'

'Alice, his wife.'

Simon was watching Baldwin, and fleetingly he saw an expression of shock on his face. Simon pointed out, 'It is Roger who admits killing Coule. Not Sir William.'

Baldwin nodded. 'Sir John, we have heard you made no enquiries when Coule didn't turn up when he was dead. Why was that?'

'He had said he must go for a short while. He had asked to go on a pilgrimage to Canterbury.'

Baldwin and Simon exchanged a look. Simon said, 'It's just as he said last night, then.'

'Who? What was said last night?' Sir John demanded sharply.

Baldwin eyed him measuringly. 'I should prefer that this remains between us, Sir John. Yesterday Sir William told us that he himself paid your reeve to steal the sword because once the thing was lost, Sir William would feel free. He wanted to be able to go into the convent with an easy heart. He told Coule he wanted the thing taken to Canterbury, there to be given to the church. He wanted the guilt to be expiated in the manner best suited to the crime. He wanted it to be kept there, secure.'

'So he paid my man to enter his hall and take it?' Sir John said wonderingly. His face hardened. 'And then Roger killed him!'

'Sir William told us that every time he touched it, it made his skin crawl,' Simon said.

'He appears very concerned about it,' Baldwin muttered. 'Your brother – when he was found, there were no stab wounds, I assume?'

'Of course not!'

'Were there any wounds on his person?'

'He had a bruise on his head, but that was from where he fell into the water. I think that's why he drowned, because he fell on a stone.'

'I see. So he died and soon afterwards your neighbour became engaged to Alice. Now that Sir William wants to go into a convent, the sword is stolen and the thief was killed by Roger.' He frowned. 'There must be some sense in all this! If it's gone, where is it? Sir William wanted it gone so he could join the convent, and so did his brother, presumably, so he could inherit the manor. But Sir William's wife wanted it kept safe so she was safe from the nunnery, unless I misread her . . .'

'I don't understand,' Sir John said.

'It's a common difficulty for those who try to speak to him,' Simon said understandingly. 'I find it's best not to worry.'

Baldwin frowned. 'Why did Roger want to come here to offer you the sword?'

'He said that it had been moved while he was journeying to fetch you two. Someone had found out where he had hidden it.'

'Gracious God!' Baldwin stood, his face suddenly

pale. 'Simon, we may be too late! We have to find Roger – quickly, man! Sir John, I thank you for your hospitality, but we have to leave immediately!'

Denis was strolling from the hall to his small chamber when he heard the excited chattering from outside. He stopped, wondering, and then made a decision, and walked out to the doorway that gave out on to the court.

In the little space inside the wall, five grooms, a brewer and a smith were talking animatedly with Hob. Denis eyed them with a frown. There was no sign of the Keeper, nor of his master. 'What is this? Why all the noise?'

Hob, flushed and anxious, bowed his head respectfully. 'Master clerk, I found this today by the road.'

Denis felt his mouth gape as Hob unwrapped a filthy piece of old sacking, and brought out the stained and marked sword.

'But how could you have . . . ?' he spluttered.

Sir William had arrived in the court with his wife, and now he stared bleakly at Denis, then at Hob. He motioned with a jerk of his chin towards the sword. 'Where was it?'

'Under a bush near the place where Coule was killed, sir,' Hob said deferentially. He glanced up at Sir William, then Denis and Madam Alice, who stood a little way behind the other two. 'It was well wrapped and covered in leaves, sir.'

Sir William nodded, eyeing the weapon with chill disgust. When he heard the calls from the court, he had been in the process of composing a letter to the abbot of Tavistock, Robert Champeaux, requesting that he might be permitted to join the convent. He had felt, for the first time in many years, as though a weight had been lifted from his back. And now it was back, he would be damned if he would give up that hope. Its shame could never be fully expunged from his family, but the sword itself could be. He knew now what he must do, before any more blood was spilled over it.

'Sir William?' It was his steward. The man was at Hob's side, and he looked with concern at his master. 'Sir, do you want me to send for the Keeper and his Bailiff?'

'Do as you will! Give me that sword,' Sir William snapped, and carried it into the hall.

Baldwin and Simon rode as fast as a Dartmoor farmer with the devil's wish-hounds at their backs. Every so often Simon would throw an anxious look at his friend, but all he could see was a troubled desperation as the knight raked his spurs along his mount's flanks, whipping the reins and staring ahead.

Simon usually enjoyed the thrill of a race along a roadway, the wind crackling and snapping at his cloak, the rush in his ears, the roar and clatter of hooves on the metalled surfaces, but not today. There was something deeply troubling Baldwin, and that thought was uppermost in his mind as they leaned into the corners, ever trying to increase their speed. The lanes narrowed, then widened, and suddenly they were at the Bow road, and could hurtle along, then drop down the hillside into the town itself.

He had assumed that they were aiming for the town's market hall, for no specific reason, but Baldwin reined to a halt at the inn a little farther down the hill. He threw himself from the horse, shoved the reins through a ring in the wall, and waited impatiently for Simon before throwing the door wide and bellowing for the innkeeper.

'Last night – did Roger de Tracy stay here?'

'Him? No.'

Baldwin swore under his breath.

'So that's it? He had the sword all along. He murdered Coule, and now he's bolted because he feels we're too close to him,' Simon said bitterly.

Baldwin gazed at him in surprise. 'Roger? In Good God's name, *no*! I fear he's been killed too!'

It took Baldwin a little time to track down the local watchmen. In the end he took the simple expedient of grabbing the horn from the belt of a passing man and blowing on that. Before long, several men had arrived and were standing watching him with suspicious, surly faces.

'I'm the constable. What's the hue and cry for?'

'I am Keeper of the King's Peace, Sir Baldwin de Furnshill. I am seeking master Roger de Tracy. He didn't return home last night, and he didn't stay at the inn here. I want you to organize a posse and find him. If he's not in the town itself, he may be injured and lying in a ditch somewhere between Sir John de Curterne's house or the castle at Nymet Tracy.'

'That might take days!'

'Then you had best hurry yourself, master constable, hadn't you?' Baldwin said nastily. 'And in the meantime, send a man to the castle to let them know.'

The constable had taken a step back as the knight had leaned towards him, anxious to have upset a man of such power, but now, as he was about to shout for a lad to ride to the castle, there was a rattle of hooves coming down the lane, and Simon recognized one of the grooms from the castle. 'What's he want?'

Baldwin chewed at his lip. 'This is all going ill, I fear.'

'Where was the thing?' Baldwin demanded of Hob.

The miller stood disconsolate at his harsh tone, his head hanging. Simon was sitting near Sir William, while

Alice had a seat a short distance behind them. Baldwin gripped the sword in his right hand, studying the metalwork.

'It was right near the place where Coule's body had lain. I think it was shoved there in a hurry, for it was not well hidden. Just had some leaves and twigs thrown over it.'

'It was wrapped in that?' Baldwin prodded the folds of sacking with the point of the sword. The point was scratched and marked, he saw. It needed a good polish.

'Yes. And shoved under a blackthorn. I only saw it because I caught a glint from it when I rode past.'

'Why was it not seen before?' Simon wondered.

'I don't know. But the blade has blood on it still. Perhaps some creature smelled that, and pulled the cloth aside to see if there was food inside?'

Simon nodded. Hob had lost all his earlier affability, and now stood as though terrified. Well, that was understandable. Many were petrified when questioned in front of their master, and this fellow was a villein. 'And you happened to be wandering this way?'

'Yes, sir.'

'Why?' he asked gently.

'Sir?'

'Why were you wandering over here? You said yesterday that you rarely came this way except when you brought milled flour for the castle. When were you here last?'

'Day before that.'

'And you were asked to return only two days later?' Simon asked smoothly.

Baldwin sucked at his teeth, glanced at Simon, and jerked his head to the door. 'You must take us there and show us exactly where you found the thing. Sir William, do you wish to accompany us?'

Sir William shrugged sulkily and motioned with his hand. 'You go. I've things to do.'

Simon threw him a look as he left the hall. Sir William's eyes were fixed unblinkingly on the sword, and there was in his face an expression of such revulsion and loathing, Simon was shocked for a moment. He stood still, staring, even as Alice rose from her seat and went to her man, her arms going about his stiff shoulders. In her face, Simon saw relief as well as resignation, but when she looked across at him, he was chilled by her expression. It was sly delight.

'Here?' Baldwin demanded.

'Yes, sir,' Hob replied quietly.

They had hurried as quickly as Hob's casual trot allowed. He had no riding horse, and had never learned the skill of horsemanship, so the other two were forced to travel at little more than a gentle amble. By the time they reached the spot, it was well past noon, and the sun was in their eyes as they turned westwards along Hob's lane.

Baldwin glanced about him, then dropped from his horse. 'When do you say you found the thing?'

'It was this morning. I took it to the castle as soon as I found it.'

'Why were you coming along here today?'

Hob's mouth opened, but his dismayed expression told Baldwin enough.

'Hold! Good Miller, don't lie to me! It won't do. You should have invented a reason before going to the castle.'

As he spoke he was moving swiftly about the roadway, glancing this way and that. Soon he found a patch of dried soil, and he bent to study it. Up again, he strode to the bush Hob had indicated. 'It lay just here?'

'Yes, sir.'

'You must have good eyesight. Come here!' He stood behind Hob and gripped his shoulders. 'Where were you standing when you saw it?'

'Master, I . . .'

'This is a few yards from where the body was found. Only a very few. And you suggest to me that the coroner and juries could have missed it? There are footprints all over this place. If the sword had lain there, someone would have stumbled over it.'

'But I saw it!'

Baldwin smiled grimly. 'From where, master Miller? Where were you when you say you saw it?'

There was a silence. Simon dropped from his horse and his face wore a harder expression now as he joined the other two. 'Well?'

Baldwin released the miserable miller, who covered his face with his hands and stood quietly trembling.

'Perhaps if I tell you, then,' Baldwin said. 'There was a visitor to you today, who told you to be cautious, to be very careful, and who gave you that sword. Isn't that right? And told you to bring the thing to the castle and say you found it here. Yes?'

'I can't say, sir! If I say yes, I'll be dead. If I say no, you'll have me arrested. What would you have me do? Condemn myself for opening my mouth?'

'You already have, Miller,' Baldwin said uncompromisingly.

The body was discovered in the late afternoon. One of Sir John's peasants saw crows and magpies squabbling, and set off to learn why. When he reached the woods where they had been, he found the corpse.

'Sir William, I am sorry,' the port reeve said, and his expression told better than his words how true was the sentiment. It was not unknown for a man to lose his reason and attack the bearer of such tidings.

The knight sat in his seat with his right hand clenched on the arm rest. His face betrayed no emotion, other than the tic that pulled at his right eyelid every few moments. At his side his wife rested a hand on his shoulder, and he petulantly pushed it away. 'Leave me! All of you. Now!'

Gleaming on the table, freshly cleaned, the object of his hatred lay pointing at him like an accusation, and he felt it like the finger of God.

This sword was the cause of his shame and despair. It had twisted him, making him no better than the murderer Sir William de Tracy who had stormed into the cathedral at Canterbury all those years before, with this sword drawn, and hacked at the saint there in his own church. Abysmal, cursed action! It had tainted and destroyed him, just as it had others. He had been torn from the path of decency and honour, and his life was ruined.

He could not bear to have that thing pointing at him any longer. Standing, he walked around the table, looking down at it with loathing. The thing shone like a new tool, as though it was innocent of any offence. Yet he knew its nature: evil, like a weapon of the devil. It should be destroyed.

It could be destroyed. It would be destroyed! He took it up, revulsion on his face, and carried it to the door. 'Call the smith to me!'

Baldwin and Simon rode into the court after questioning the miller to find the place quiet.

'Now what has happened?' Baldwin said.

'It's a bit grim and brooding, isn't it?' Simon said glowering about him.

This late in the day the place should have been a mess of men hurrying about finishing the last tasks before nightfall. Grooms and cooks should have been running to their jobs, but tonight all was still, as though the place was deserted.

'Hoi! Groom!' Simon bellowed.

There was no immediate response, but then a tousled head appeared in a doorway near the stables.

'Come on, boy! Get over here,' Simon roared, growing irritable.

The lad was clearly upset at being called, but he trotted over to them and took their reins from them as they dropped to the floor.

'Where is everyone?' Baldwin demanded.

'The steward sent many to the body to protect it.'

'Master Roger?' Baldwin snapped.

'Yes, sir. He was dead. Murdered.'

'How?'

'Run through with a sword, they say, and left in the woods to rot.'

'Which woods? Quickly, boy, where?'

He was shocked by the intensity in Baldwin's voice. 'Up near the town, sir, north and east of Bow, so they say. A groom's been sent to the coroner already.'

Baldwin sighed. 'So I was right, then. Where is your master?'

'Sir William's in the smithy, sir. He's having the forge lit.'

'Nonsense!' Baldwin muttered to himself. 'Come, Simon. Let's stop this foolishness.'

Simon opened his mouth, and then closed it again. With a muted curse against all keepers, and especially mad ones from the wilder parts of Devon, he trailed after Baldwin into the smithy.

It was a small chamber, and not yet hot. The coals had been allowed to cool after the day's work was done, and now a small fire had been lit in the middle: tinder was glowing beneath kindling, while the smith blew carefully on it. A boy stood nearby with a bellows in his hand, ready to begin fanning the flames and adding coals.

'You are in time to see this foul thing destroyed!' Sir William spat.

He stood in the far corner of the smithy, in the dark. All Simon could see of him after the light outside was a gleam every so often from the sword's blade.

Baldwin eyed the fire. 'What are you doing?'

'My master wants the blade destroyed,' the smith said nervously, eyeing his master.

'He will change his mind. You can both leave us,' Baldwin said flatly.

The smith looked at him, then at his master. He motioned to the boy, who scampered off, and then with a second glance at Sir William, the smith nodded and left.

Baldwin went to the forge and scattered the kindling. 'It would achieve nothing, Sir William.'

'My brother is dead.'

'I am sorry about that. I feared as much.'

'He was spitted like a boar on a spear, and left to rot in among the trees,' Sir William said softly.

'It is not the fault of the sword, though,' Baldwin said. 'The sword had nothing to do with it.'

'You think so?'

Sir William strode forward and stood before Baldwin, the sword in his fist. He lifted it, and Simon automatically reached for his own hilt, only hesitating when he saw that Baldwin had not flinched.

'See this, Sir Baldwin? It looks so fine, so pretty! But it's the sword that killed St Thomas. They say Sir William hacked at the saint's head as he lay on the ground and opened his skull, spilling his brains on the ground. I expect that's how the point got so scratched and marked, because it clashed on the stone flags of the floor.'

'A sword is not evil. Only the man who wields it,' Baldwin said mildly.

'Or woman, yes,' Sir William grunted, his voice almost a sob. 'Yes, you are right. It's me. *Me* who is evil, not this! I have tainted all I have touched. I am cursed!'

'You are guilty of murder. You have broken two of God's commandments.'

'I know!' Sir William put his hands to his face, the sword's point almost catching in a beam overhead. 'I could not help it, though.'

'You may destroy this thing if you wish, but it will stop nothing. It will serve no purpose. The guilty person is the one who should pay. Not some lump of metal.'

'I can't!'

'There are three deaths already, including your brother.'

'It's all because she won't go to the convent. She has seduced someone to do her bidding, and he has killed for her,' Sir William said brokenly. 'To kill for her ambition and pride.'

'Her?' Simon asked.

'My wife never wished for an arranged marriage between herself and Godfrey de Curterne. So she told me that she had fallen desperately in love with me. I was a willing tool in her hands, a boy whom she had grown to know as she was introduced to Godfrey's friends. Knowing me, it was easy for her to twist my affections and make me love her.

'And that would have been enough. But then this sword arrived back. And with it, the memory of the murder of St Thomas. My God, but it is an evil tale!'

'Yes,' Baldwin agreed. 'But it's not *your* tale, and it's not the sword's. You knew of the story before the sword appeared, did you not?'

'Yes.'

'And you were intending to go to the monastery?'

Sir William let his hands fall. 'The guilt of killing Godfrey has been eating at me for years. I was his best, his closest, friend and I killed him with a rock. I knocked him into the water, and then held him under while he struggled, so that I may keep his woman for my own. Oh, my God!'

'When the sword reappeared, what then?'

'She saw her chance. She said she didn't want it in the castle, said it reminded her of the murder of St Thomas. I could never forget the thing. Nor the murders. My ancestor's and mine. And then I felt I could not remain while the sword existed. I had a duty to keep it safe. That was what she told me: it was my duty. She showed me how it would be the deepest cowardice to leave the sword behind. I should have destroyed it long ago!'

'All this has nothing to do with the sword,' Baldwin said more harshly. 'It's people who have killed. A man killed Godfrey, a man killed Coule, and a man killed your brother.'

'She has her talons in another man now.'

'Who?'

'Until the news today . . . I know she had already won the heart of Roger . . . I had thought he would kill me. I welcomed it. The end of the guilt; the end of the memories of poor Godfrey's face . . .'

'Where is she?'

'I don't know. Perhaps in the hall.'

'Let us seek her out, Sir William. It is time this whole matter was done.'

'Yes. Yes, it is time.'

Later Baldwin recalled guessing the truth in those moments on the way to the hall, but all Simon was aware of was an emptiness in his heart. Sir William was a broken man, his soul ravaged because of the terrible crime he had committed for this woman; killing his closest friend. His brother had been tempted by her, and now was dead because he sought to win her love. Now, apparently, a third had been polluted by her.

Deceit, treachery, and death. They had trailed her footsteps like shadows, and all who crossed her would suffer.

'Husband! I was worried about you,' she said. She was sitting in the hall, a jug of wine at her hand, and she stood and smiled sweetly at the men.

Baldwin was in front, but he paused before crossing the room. This was to be a difficult interrogation, the more so because her husband was the man with the real jurisdiction here in his own hall.

Sir William, too, slowed as he entered. His pale features were drawn and anguished. 'Madam, you have seen to the murder of your last man.'

'Which man is that?' she asked, her face pale. 'Please, husband, I know you feel unwell. I've seen it in your eyes. It is that fearful sword. Cast it down, and come and rest with me. Let me pour you some . . .'

'Poison? Is that what you have there?' Sir William grated. 'You have no wish for my companionship any longer, do you?'

She stood quietly, a brittle smile on her lips, and then poured a large measure into the mazer beside her, and drank it off in one draught. 'No poison, husband. I have no need of such things.'

'Everything about you is poisonous!'

She shook her head, the picture of humility and hurt pride. 'Husband, dear, all I have ever sought is your advantage. You are mistaken if you think that I am trying to harm you. I love you.'

'Even when you flaunted yourself before Roger? When you ordered Hob to bring the sword back here after you gave it to him? When you asked me to murder my own best friend so I could gain you for myself?'

'Why should I do that?' she asked sadly.

Simon leaned against the table. 'Madam, you wanted to marry into Sir William's family because you were offended to be allied to a man without your approval. Sir Godfrey died for that familiarity. Coule had to die because you knew that once that sword was gone, your husband would take himself to the monastery and insist that you went to a nunnery too. And Roger has died because . . . why? He rejected your advances?'

Her face was white. 'I have killed no one. I have no reason to want Roger dead – what reason could I have for wanting him harmed? It would be ridiculous! I made no advances to him. He kept making advances to me!'

'Perhaps that was why Roger died, then. Because you were seen with him, and your lover could not bear to see you in his arms?'

'That is . . .'

'Enough lies, woman!' Sir William snapped. 'You made Roger kill Coule because you wanted me gone, and now you've brought this thing back since Roger's dead. You think I didn't know? I saw it in his room, but how you had it "discovered" by Hob, I don't know!'

Baldwin suddenly felt his mouth fall wide. 'Stand back, Sir William!' he commanded.

'She must die!'

'One problem with Roger's death is there are so many roads from Down St Mary. How could someone know his route?'

'Who cares?' Sir William blustered.

'His brother might, if his brother had travelled that way with Roger. As you did while you were both young. You alone knew his way.'

'She did too!'

'You think so? She was with Sir John's brother in those days, not you. And when Godfrey died and you stole his wife, you lost all contact with Sir John. You didn't go that way, did you? She never knew your brother's favourite paths to Down St Mary.'

'Enough of this!'

'You found the sword in Roger's room,' Baldwin repeated. 'You killed your brother, because he had killed Coule and thwarted your plan of retirement. It was you, Sir William, not your wife!'

Sir William's face grew ferocious with rage, and he turned to his wife again. The tapestry rippled behind Baldwin, and he shot a look over his shoulder in time to see the blade appear, stepping back to give himself fighting room, drawing his own sword in one fluid movement as Denis ran at Sir William.

Sir William was bearing down on her, the sword still in his hand, lifting it to strike. As Simon watched dumbstruck, Denis swung his sword inexpertly. It was not sharp, and slammed into Sir William's upper neck, slashing a thick wedge of muscle from his skull down to his shoulder, then Denis raised the sword again and brought it down on Sir William's head, breaking open his skull.

There was a fine explosion of blood, and Baldwin heard Madam Alice scream as a spray jetted across her face.

Then Baldwin was on him, and his peacock-blue blade flashed as he lifted it and slammed the pommel hard onto Denis's head a little above his left ear. Denis gasped, and his body stiffened, just for a moment, before collapsing like a poleaxed ox, falling vertically to his knees, his haunches dropping to rest on his ankles, and then toppling slowly to his right to fall over Sir William's still-twitching legs.

*   *   *

'I want a rider to fetch Sir Richard de Welles immediately,' Baldwin said. 'You! Get wine and a bowl of warmed water. Hurry!'

He had resheathed his sword, and now he took charge in the room, striding across the floor to where Madam Alice sat in her chair, her face marked with a streak of crimson.

'Madam, I am sorry for all that has happened,' Baldwin said. 'But I was determined that your husband would confess. I had no idea that Denis was there.'

No, he had had no idea that he was there, but he should have anticipated it, though, as he told himself angrily. 'You will wish to leave this room until the coroner's inquest. There is no need to remain in here with the corpse.'

'I shall . . . shall go to my chamber,' Alice said weakly, and stood, only to slump back in her seat as though drained of all energy.

'Where is this lady's maid?' Baldwin bellowed, and soon a pair of women were helping Alice through the door. She paused once in the doorway, her eyes going to the body on the floor, the messy puddle of blood about his broken skull, and then she coughed, or it may be she sobbed, and was led from the hall.

'CAN YOU ALL HEAR ME?'

Baldwin winced at the dull bellow. In a confined space Sir Richard de Welles was deafening. 'They can hear you, Sir Richard.'

'Very well, I call you all to witness this . . .'

After so many years as Keeper of the King's Peace, Baldwin was perfectly used to the routine of an inquest, and his mind wandered until he was called upon to state what he had seen that afternoon when Sir William died.

'I believe that Sir William intended to kill his wife in front of us.'

251

'Why d'you think that?' the coroner rumbled.

'Sir William was eaten with guilt for a murder which he committed many years ago, in order to win the hand of this beautiful lady. He murdered his own best friend, her betrothed, and that crime has remained with him ever since. Every time he looked at her, she reminded him that he had killed to win her. In the end, he persuaded himself that she was herself responsible, I think. His mind was weakened with shame and guilt.'

'Proof?'

'He confessed to the crime before my friend Bailiff Puttock and myself,' Baldwin said shortly. 'It led him to seek absolution. Recently, his father acquired this sword, which Sir William believed was the sword which his ancestor used to kill St Thomas. It seemed to him to indicate God's displeasure at his murder, as though the return to his family of the weapon that had executed Becket was proof of God's anger. Sending it to Canterbury meant the cathedral could dispose of it as they wished. At the same time He could commit himself to perpetual penance by entering the cloister at Tavistock.'

'All clear enough,' the coroner boomed. 'But then the sword was stolen.'

'Not entirely! He paid Coule to take it to Canterbury. Coule gained permission from his master to go, and all seemed well, except Coule was seen leaving by Roger. Perhaps Roger noticed Coule was hiding something, and decided to overtake him. Coule tried to escape to the nearest house, Hob the miller's, but to no avail, clearly.

'Roger had no idea that Sir William was disposing of it intentionally, so Roger struck down Coule as a felon. But then I think he recognized that if the sword was lost, his brother would leave the manor. All would go to him. So Roger concealed the sword and waited.

'Sir William was devastated. His plans had gone awry, and he saw this as further evidence of God's displeasure. Even his attempt at atonement was thwarted . . . but then he realized that he had no duty of guardianship any longer. He began to plan his retreat from the world.'

'Except the sword reappeared,' the coroner said in a muted thunder.

'Exactly. He found it himself. After the murder of Coule, there was a search for the missing sword, but Roger told me he organized the search himself. Sir William must have suspected him. When Roger came to me, Sir William did not prevent him. While Roger was with me, Sir William found the sword among Roger's belongings. It persuaded him that his brother and wife were plotting to murder him.

'He was a jealous husband, and always feared that she might seduce another as he thought she had him. His wife had no vocation, and disliked the idea of the convent. He knew that. But if she was to escape the convent against his wishes, she must have had a means of removing him. The easiest way to achieve that would be to kill him. But to do that, she would need an accomplice. That was his reasoning.

'Sir William knew the sword was in Roger's room, so he decided to kill Roger. On Roger's body, he found the sword, because Roger had been trying to dispose of it. He brought the sword back and concealed it.'

'He killed his own brother?' Sir Richard growled, his voice setting the plates rattling on the sideboard.

'In his eyes, I suppose, it was self defence. He would have killed his wife; he couldn't leave her alive to plot his death with another – he persuaded himself that she could turn the head of any of his staff, even the lawyer.'

'Quite understandable,' the coroner murmured gallantly.

'And the last piece of proof for him was Hob finding the sword again,' Baldwin said.

Madam Alice shook herself. 'I was stupid! I was sure that Roger had the sword, and I looked in his chamber, and found it in his chest. Roger wanted the manor, and he didn't care what happened to me, so he was happy to conceal it. Or so I thought. I sent Denis with it to tell Hob to say that he'd just found it.'

'But Sir William had put it there in a hurry after killing Roger. He simply put it back where Roger had hidden it before,' Baldwin said. 'So when it turned up, he thought it proved his wife was in league with his dead brother.'

'What do you have to say for yourself?' the coroner demanded, turning to the battered lawyer.

Denis closed his eyes against his headache. The Keeper had probably saved his life the day he'd killed Sir William, but he could perhaps have used a little less force. He felt sick again, and hoped he wouldn't vomit. 'Sir, I could see how Sir William had turned against his wife, and I was worried for her safety.'

'Was it your place to worry about her?'

'I thought so, Coroner. I believe any man has a duty to protect those weaker than himself if set upon by a madman.'

'So you hid yourself from Sir William that day?' Baldwin pressed him.

'Yes. To save her life.'

Baldwin turned to face the coroner again. 'You see? Sir William thought that his wife would keep the sword here. While it remained, he could not leave; he *must* get it to Canterbury. When he found that his own brother had concealed the sword, he was enraged – especially since he thought his wife had plotted to save herself from the convent, so he thought, at the expense of his immortal soul.'

'This lawyer protected her by slaying her husband?'

'Precisely. Denis saved her life. And I saved his by knocking him out so that others wouldn't chase and kill him.'

'That sword is clearly cursed. To kill St Thomas and then these others . . . it says much for the foulness of the blade. I consider Sir William had the right idea. It should be sent without delay to Canterbury to atone for its crimes.'

Baldwin made a gesture of disgust. 'You would accuse the sword? It is a lump of inanimate metal, Coroner!'

'You said it was the weapon that killed . . .'

'Sir William de Tracy killed Becket with his sword; Roger killed Coule with *his*; Roger was killed with Sir William's riding sword; Sir William died from a blow by Denis's. Not one of those deaths was committed with this sword.'

'Saint . . .'

Baldwin irritably cut him off. 'That is the greatest irony. This is *not* the sword that killed St Thomas. That was with Sir William when he joined the Knights Templar as his penance and set sail for the Holy Land. He died on the way. I have seen his grave in Sicily, and in his grave, so I was told by the priest, was the sword that struck down St Thomas, so that when his body rose again on the day of judgement, he would be reminded of his crime. This is not his sword.'

'Then whose is it?' the coroner growled.

'Just below the cross there is a mark,' Baldwin said, picking up the sword and pointing. 'It looks like a shield, and the name "de la Pomeroy", I think.'

Sir Richard bent his head and peered. 'Could be . . . But if it's not the Tracy sword, why is it here?'

'I doubt that Sir Humphrey thought for a moment that it was the genuine de Tracy sword,' Baldwin said. 'I knew Sir Humphrey a little. He was cynical fellow.

I'm sure he liked to say that it could have been the original sword, but he bought it for a more mundane reason.'

'What?'

'Pick it up and handle it,' Baldwin urged. 'It has a feel all of its own. Light, nimble, and balanced. He bought it because it is excellent, I deem.'

The inquest took little time. As the jurors filed from the hall and the clerk scratched at his parchment, Sir Richard picked up the sword to pass back to Madam Alice. 'This is yours, lady.'

She flinched. 'I want nothing to do with that thing! Throw it in the river. Or, better still, carry out my husband's last wish and destroy it. I will not have it in the hall here. I want never to see it again.'

'I understand that Sir John was offered it by Roger,' Baldwin said quietly. 'If you really wish to see the sword disposed of, I can take it to him.'

'Please, just take it away from me. I feel as though I am under a curse all the time that shameful weapon stays here!'

When the sword was given to him, Sir John could only laugh at the fortune that had brought it to him. As soon as he picked it up, he could feel the life in the blade. The way that it moved through the air spoke of the marvellous construction, the careful effort taken over the hilt, the bonding of wood and steel and iron together to create such a piece of workmanship.

'This is ours now, Matthew,' he said as his son teetered at his side, standing without support for a moment.

The boy reached up and touched the pommel, and Sir John laughed, bringing the blade lower so he could feel it, but as he did so, the little boy tottered forward.

His hand slipped forward and ran down the blade: only a short distance, but far enough to open his palm on the sharp blade.

As Sir John threw the sword aside and grabbed urgently at his son, he felt his heart pound uncomfortably, and he cast one suspicious look at the weapon lying innocently on the ground, but then he was calling to the maids to bring him water to wash his son's wound and cloths to bind it.

No, it was only a sword, he told himself. Only a sword.

ACT FOUR

I

Poitiers, France: September 1356

Matthew de Curterne lay under the hedge near Nouaille Wood, praying no one would notice him. He covered his ears with his hands, trying to block out the clash of arms and the screams of wounded men, and closed his eyes so he would not see the ground churned into bloody mud by the combatants' feet. When the Black Prince had called for men to fight the French, Curterne had been proud to rally, retrieving the old sword from under his bed in Down St Mary, and selling his family's silver to purchase armour and a horse. Brave men made their fortunes in war, and Curterne intended to return home wealthy.

But the campaign had been a misery of torrential rain, burning heat, scant supplies and disease. And now the Black Prince was trapped at Poitiers by a French force far stronger than his own. Curterne scrambled away when a pair of desperate skirmishers came too close, and raised his sword to protect himself. When they had gone, he gazed at the weapon's tempered steel blade and its dog-headed cross, hating it for making him think he could be a warrior when he had known all his life that he was nothing of the kind. He had always loathed any kind of conflict, and even the sight of blood made him sick to his stomach. It was the sword's fault, of course. When he was a small child it had cut him badly – he still bore the scar across his palm – but the incident had made him nervous and hesitant with weapons, much to his tutors' dismay and disgust.

He glared at the blade, recalling how he had sensed it almost taunting him for his faint-heartedness when he had pulled it from its dusty hiding place all those months ago. He should have known it would bring him bad luck, and he should have resisted the urge to prove it was wrong about him. He ducked down again when a horse galloped past, its rider's shield raised against a sudden hail of arrows. He fought back bitter tears, frightened to keep the weapon, but even more afraid to toss it away from him and leave himself defenceless. He curled into a tight ball and tried to picture the cool green Devonshire hills, and the peace of home.

Just when he thought all was lost and the entire English army would be slaughtered, the enemy began to retreat, first as a trickle, then as a rout. Curterne crawled out from under the hedge, scarcely believing his luck – he had survived and the English had won against overwhelming odds! His four companions – men who had shared his campfire these last few months – came to join him, torn and bloodied from the encounter. Elias Askyl was first, his handsome face lit with savage joy, and his fair curls limp with sweat and dirt. Then came Philip Lymbury, the oldest, who had declared himself unwell that morning, but who had still fought with a courage Curterne found impossible to comprehend. Behind Lymbury was the sly Geoffrey Dole, his face awash with blood; Curterne felt queasy when he saw the injury that had deprived Dole of most of his nose. And lastly, there was William, plump and always cheerful.

'What a victory!' cried Askyl, elated. 'This day will

be remembered for all eternity, and so will the names of those who fought bravely.'

'While those who skulked under hedges will be lost in ignominy,' said Dole, his voice muffled through the cloth he held to his ravaged face. 'We needed you, Curterne, but you ran away and hid.'

'What were you thinking, man?' demanded Lymbury furiously. 'Your timidity might have seen us all killed.'

'And you with that fine sword, too,' added William. His normally smiling face was cold and unfriendly. 'You disgust me.'

They walked away and Curterne began to sob, feeling shame burning inside him like a wound. He was still weeping an hour later when he heard footsteps behind him. He fumbled for his sword, but the other man reached it first, and there was a sudden pain between his shoulder blades.

'Stabbed in the back,' said a soft voice. It was familiar – one of his companions, perhaps – but Curterne's senses were reeling, and he could not remember the name. 'It is a fitting end for a coward. You have brought shame on this fine weapon, but I have avenged it.'

II

Ickleton, Cambridgeshire: July 1357

The rich agricultural land south of Cambridge was burned yellow by the summer sun. Crops swayed in the afternoon breeze, and a robin trilled in a nearby wood. The horses' hoofs thumped gently on the baked mud of the path, punctuated by the occasional creak of leather and the jingle of metal. Matthew Bartholomew, physician and Fellow of Michaelhouse at the University of Cambridge, closed his eyes, relishing the peace after the frantic bustle associated with the end of term.

'This is a nasty place,' said his travelling companion, Brother Michael, looking around him disparagingly. 'It is all trees, fields and water-meadows, and we have not passed a proper building in hours. I wish Master Langelee had not sent us on this errand. The rent we receive from the manor at Ickleton is not worth this inconvenience, and my time could be better spent on other matters.'

'Yes,' said Bartholomew drowsily; Michael had been saying the same thing since they had started their journey at dawn that morning. Personally, the physician was quite happy to spend a few days away. Not only did it mean a respite from examining corpses – part of his duties at the University entailed inspecting the bodies of scholars who had died unexpectedly or violently – but Cambridge reeked in hot weather, and it was good to exchange the noxious stench of sun-seared sewage for grain-scented air. He began to relax for the first time in weeks. The previous term had been desperately busy, and it was a relief to be free of clamouring students.

'I dislike haring around the country on second-rate nags,' continued the Benedictine irritably, eyeing his horse with rank disapproval. 'It is an outrage to provide a rider of my calibre with an animal like this. Langelee thinks of nothing but saving money these days.'

'He does,' said Bartholomew, resisting the urge to point out that Michael's horse was far better than his own. The monk was fat, and Bartholomew had let him take the stronger of the two palfreys on the grounds that he did not think the other could have carried his large friend for the ten miles to Ickleton and then home again. It would have collapsed.

'Our College owns Valence Manor in the parish of Ickleton,' Michael rambled on. 'And the man who lives there, Sir Philip Lymbury, pays us rent each spring. But this year, we have had nothing – except a letter informing us that he has donated *our* money to Ickleton Priory instead.'

'I know,' said Bartholomew, recalling his colleagues' outrage when the missive had arrived. He was more sanguine about the matter: Michaelhouse possessed the relevant deeds of ownership, and the courts would eventually order Lymbury to pay the outstanding debt. But lawyers were expensive, so instead, Master Langelee had decided to send two of his senior Fellows to find out what Lymbury thought he was doing. Bartholomew and Michael were to collect the outstanding ten marks – either from Lymbury or the priory – and return with it immediately. The money was earmarked to pay for new latrines, and Langelee did not need to stress the urgency of the situation to his two scholars: they had been complaining about the state of the old ones for months.

Michael twisted around in his saddle. 'Are you going to agree with everything I say, or do you actually possess a mind of your own?'

'If I voice an opinion you will argue – but I presided over seventeen student disputations last week and I am tired of debate. Here is the ford across the Cam – barely ankle deep after all this dry weather – and Langelee said our manor lies just beyond that wood.'

Michael led the way along a narrow track lined with ancient trees. 'According to him, this copse is also part of our manor.'

Bartholomew was about to acknowledge him with another monosyllabic answer, when there was a shout, followed by a lot of crashing. Suddenly, a deer burst from the vegetation in front of them, then tore away into the undergrowth to their right. It was a beautiful animal, with a coat of russet red. Moments later, three horsemen hurtled from the trees, and the leading one was obliged to rein in sharply to avoid colliding with Bartholomew.

'Watch out!' The rider was a sturdy man with a slashing scar across his face that rendered him all but nose-less.

Bartholomew wanted to point out that he had not been the one careening wildly across a public highway, but his nag had been frightened by the abrupt commotion, and it started to buck. He was a poor horseman, and trying to control the beast took all his concentration.

'Be careful, Dole!' shouted the second man, directing his own horse in a tight circle to avoid the melee. He wore the half-armour of a knight at ease, and rode as if he had been born in the saddle. He was tall and strong, and his blue eyes and mane of golden curls rendered him extraordinarily handsome. 'Lymbury's peasants do not know how to ride.'

'We are not peasants,' objected Michael, moving forward to take the reins of Bartholomew's horse before the struggling physician could embarrass him further. 'We are scholars from the University at Cambridge.'

'Have you seen a deer?' asked the last of the three, trotting up with a smile. He was plump, genial and dressed in the dark habit of a priest. A domed hat kept the sun from his eyes. 'A red one?'

'No,' said Bartholomew curtly, dismounting as soon as Michael stopped his horse from prancing. He felt a good deal safer once on solid ground.

'It definitely came this way,' said the fat priest. 'I saw it myself.'

'It must be over there,' said Dole, flinging out a hand

to encompass a vast swathe of woodland. He also wore robes that showed he had taken holy orders, although they were tempered by good boots and spurs. 'It does not matter – the stag we caught yesterday will provide us with meat for a few days yet. And it is too hot for chasing around the countryside today. Shall we go home?'

'Already?' asked the second man – the knight. 'We came out to practise our skills with weapons, and all we have done so far is wave our lances at the crows eating Lymbury's corn.'

'I did not enjoy using his sword to spar with you yesterday, William,' said Dole to the chubby priest. 'It may have fine balance and a good grip, but it is overly heavy for my taste.'

'It is an excellent weapon,' countered William. 'It is a pity it was not put to better use last summer. That battle would have been over in half the time had it been wielded by a true warrior and not left in the hands of a coward.'

The good-looking knight turned to the scholars when Dole responded with a tart comment and the two clerics began to bicker. 'We three – and Lymbury – were at the Battle of Poitiers,' he explained.

'So was he,' said Michael, nodding at Bartholomew, who looked anything but soldierly as he gripped his horse's reins with obvious unease. Michael could see the knight did not believe him, so added, 'He fought on foot.'

'Why are you so far from your University?' asked William, raising a plump hand to indicate he had had enough of his quarrel with Dole. Dole looked angry to be cut off mid-sentence. 'Are you lost?'

Michael gave a pained smile. 'No, we have come to visit our manor. These woods belong to us – that is, to Michaelhouse.'

William nodded in a way that suggested he was annoyed with himself. 'You must forgive us, Brother. Of course we know Michaelhouse owns Valence Manor – and that our friend Philip Lymbury pays you rent each year. But we were so engrossed with the hunt that our wits were elsewhere. We shall take you to Lymbury immediately. I am William the Vicar, priest of Ickleton church. My companion here is Sir Elias Askyl, knighted for his courage at Poitiers.'

The handsome knight nodded a polite greeting. 'But I do not think Lymbury is expecting you. He said nothing this morning.'

'You did not write, to tell him you were coming,' said William, frowning his puzzlement. 'I am his clerk, as well as his parish priest, and I read all his correspondence.'

'He wrote to us, though,' said Michael acidly. 'He said he was donating *our* rent to the priory.'

William raised his eyebrows in surprise. 'He told me he was *thinking* about deferring payment, in order to raise enough to establish a chantry for his soul, but he did not say he had actually *done* it. He must have dictated your letter to the nuns' chaplain.' He waved a dismissive hand at his fellow cleric.

'That is me – Geoffrey Dole,' said the scarred man, shooting William a sour look for the unflattering introduction. 'After we fought at Poitiers together, Lymbury arranged for me to be appointed chaplain to Ickleton Priory. *I* did not scribe your letter, though. One of the nuns must have done it.'

'Lymbury gave me *my* Ickleton appointment, too,' said William to Michael. 'He is a man who knows how to treat old companions-at-arms.'

'Here comes Sister Rose,' said Dole, looking behind the scholars. He smiled politely and rather longingly at the woman who emerged from the undergrowth.

Bartholomew turned to see a woman sitting astride a horse with an ease he immediately envied. She wore the habit of a Benedictine nun, but it had been shaped to show off the slender lines of her figure, and she had abandoned the matronly wimple in favour of a gold fret that kept her saffron-coloured plaits in place. Her eyes were black and her skin dusky, and Bartholomew wondered whether her ancestors had hailed from the hot lands of the south. Behind her, draped across the saddle, was a red deer with an arrow through its neck.

'God's teeth!' exclaimed Askyl, regarding the animal in astonishment. 'That is the beast we were chasing; I recognize its markings. Did *you* shoot it?'

'Well, it did not jump on my saddle of its own accord,' said Sister Rose with a coquettish smirk. She suddenly became aware of Michael, and the grin faded somewhat. 'Damn! A Benedictine!'

Bartholomew understood her discomfort, given the way she was dressed – and he could hear a distant bell announcing the office of *nones*; Rose was breaking several of her Order's rules.

Michael's expression was stern. 'My Bishop deposed a prioress of Ickleton five years ago for permitting licentious behaviour among her nuns. Perhaps her successor's morals are no better.'

Rose pouted prettily. 'Sir Philip Lymbury invited me to hunt – to give me an opportunity to exercise his horses and provide fresh meat for my sisters. What is wrong with that? Besides, the party includes Chaplain Dole and William the Vicar, so it is all perfectly respectable.'

Michael's expression said there was a very great deal wrong with that, particularly since he was not convinced that the clerics in question were particularly righteous ones. But before he could speak, there was another thud of hoofs, and two more people appeared. One was a large lady in a tight green kirtle. Her head-dress was in disarray, and she made a hasty attempt to straighten it when she spotted Askyl. The second was an elderly nun on a mule, who looked as though she heartily wished she were somewhere else, and who winced as though riding caused her pain.

'You should have waited,' said the woman in green, regarding Sister Rose angrily. 'It was unkind to ask us to put the deer on your horse, then canter off alone. Tell her, Sir Elias.'

'Very mischievous,' said the knight uncomfortably, not looking at either woman. 'You should probably apologize.'

'I do not think so,' said Sister Rose coolly. She turned to Michael again. 'This is Lady Joan Lymbury, wife to the lord of several local manors, which she thinks makes her better than the rest of us. And my escort, to keep me free from sin on this wicked outing, is Dame Pauline de Gras.'

Pauline looked Michael up and down with sharp black eyes. 'The Bishop is always sending spies to learn why our priory is poor, and you have the portly look of an Ely monk about you. Have you come to paw through our accounts again – *my* accounts, since I am the only one there who can write?'

Bartholomew struggled not to laugh. He had visited Ely Abbey, and had never seen so many well-fed men; Michael had appeared positively slender beside some of the monstrous girths that waddled through its cloisters. Michael regarded her icily, he disliked people commenting on his weight.

'I may inspect them, if I feel it necessary,' he replied stiffly. 'However, the main reason for our visit is to collect the rent from Valence Manor.'

'That may be difficult,' said Pauline defiantly.

'Lymbury gave it to our priory, and *we* are in desperate need.'

'So is Michaelhouse,' said Michael tartly. 'And if you saw our latrines, you would know why.'

'But *we* need the money for food,' argued Pauline. She eyed Michael's paunch meaningfully.

'Ah,' said Dole, '*you* wrote the letter to the scholars, did you, madam? Telling them that Lymbury had given Michaelhouse's rent to—'

'What letter?' demanded Pauline. 'I have scribed no letters – especially ones that bring greedy men here in an attempt to deprive us of something that was freely given. Do you think me a fool?'

'You are in an awkward position,' muttered Bartholomew in an aside to Michael, when Sister Rose and Lady Joan started to quarrel about who had shot the deer, both vying for the attention of the god-like Askyl. 'You have your College on one hand, and a house of your Order on the other. You may find your loyalties conflict. Do you want to return to Cambridge, and leave me to deal with this?'

'You are not sufficiently cunning,' replied Michael in a whisper. 'And sly nuns will take advantage of you. I do not like the look of their companions, either – those dubious clerics or that pretty knight. We should stick together if we want to best them.'

'I want to go home,' announced Dame Pauline, flailing with her heels in an attempt to move the mule. It snickered angrily and continued to eat grass. 'My bones ache from all this bouncing about – just as I told the prioress they would. Is this any way to treat the only literate woman in her convent?'

'Perhaps Lady Joan will give you ten marks from her clothing allowance, Brother,' said Sister Rose, abandoning her row with the lady of the manor, and turning to Michael. She smiled alluringly as she adjusted her low neckline. 'She and Sir Philip are *very* wealthy – they rent Valence Manor from Michaelhouse, but they own other estates, too.'

Joan pulled a face at her as she addressed Michael. 'This nun foisted herself on our hunt, but my real companions are these gentlemen. There are the two priests, and then there is Sir Elias Askyl.'

Even Bartholomew, not always astute when it came to romantic entanglements, could not fail to notice the smouldering glance she shot in the knight's direction. Askyl returned the look with an expression the physician found hard to interpret. Was it pleasure that he had captured the affections of his host's wife, or an indication that the attraction was shared? He found the latter hard to believe: Joan was heavily built and plain-faced. However, he knew there was no accounting for taste.

'Sir Elias is a *very* brave knight,' added Rose, treating Askyl to a simper of her own. Askyl bowed in a way that was flirtatious, and Bartholomew wondered what was going on. He glanced at the two clerics, to see if he could gauge anything from their reactions. William was laughing, but his amusement seemed to derive from the fact that Dole's ravaged face was as black as thunder. Did Chaplain Dole hold a fancy for the nun, and resent the fact that she preferred Askyl? But why should William find pleasure in an old comrade's discomfort?

'Sister Rose has taken the veil,' gloated Joan. 'Therefore, most things are forbidden to her, including very brave knights.'

'I am not a nun yet,' said Rose. 'I may not take my vows – it depends on what else comes along.'

'You have a true sense of vocation, then,' remarked Michael caustically.

'*I* have one,' said old Pauline, still trying to drag her

mule away from its grass. 'And it involves an afternoon doze in a cool dormitory before supper. If I do not get it, I shall be vexed.'

'You are always vexed,' said Rose with a sigh. 'Prioress Christiana was cruel to foist you on me – you have done nothing but whine all day. Go home then, and leave Sir Elias and me to take this carcass to the manor-house. Perhaps Sir Philip will spare you its hooves for a soothing broth.'

'He had better not,' declared Pauline venomously. 'Not when I was promised a haunch. Sir Philip is always forcing me out on these vile jaunts – he likes your company and the prioress will not let you go alone. But she should put a stop to it.'

'Prioress Christiana is afraid of losing Sir Philip's good will,' explained Sister Rose smugly to Michael, trying to annoy the old nun by revealing confidences the priory would probably prefer kept to itself. 'He supplies the priory with eggs, and she dares not risk such a valuable resource. She knows my company pleases him, so she lets me go to him whenever he asks.'

She shot Lady Joan a spiteful glance, to see whether the comment had aggravated her rival, too.

It had. Joan glowered sullenly. 'I tell my husband I dislike hunting with nuns, but he always says the priory needs the fresh meat Sister Rose provides. It is not fair because, more often than not, he does not hunt himself, which leaves *me* in the company of dull monastic ladies.'

'Lord!' muttered Michael to Bartholomew, when the hunting party began to debate whether meat was of any use to women who knelt around praying all day. 'What is going on? Joan is married to Lymbury, but clearly adores Askyl. Sister Rose also admires Askyl, but seems to have some sort of understanding with Lymbury. Not surprisingly, the two women detest each other. I cannot decide which of the pair Askyl prefers, but Chaplain Dole has a definite hankering for Rose.'

'Meanwhile, Dole and William the Vicar are at loggerheads,' added Bartholomew. 'And Dame Pauline seems to hate everyone. We have walked into a war.'

Askyl sighed, indicating he was bored with the discussion, and steered his horse towards home. Bartholomew watched fascinated, as Joan and Rose jostled each other to ride next to him. Joan emerged the victor, because her horse was larger, and Rose was livid when she was forced to drop behind. William and Dole hastened to join her, and the former shot a triumphant glance at the latter when he got there first. Chaplain Dole fingered the dagger in his belt as he watched them go, an expression of dark resentment on his face.

'I had better engage Dole in polite conversation before we witness a murder,' said Michael. 'And you should help Pauline: her mule will still be eating grass tomorrow unless someone steps in.'

Bartholomew led his horse and Pauline's mule along the woodland track, well behind the others. The old nun began a litany of complaints about everything – from her painful hips to the muddy taste of river trout – and he reflected wryly that her conversation was no more edifying than Michael's had been.

Eventually, they emerged from the trees and followed a brook through pretty water-meadows. As they approached the village, Bartholomew saw people hoeing the fields. The labourers stopped work to watch the little cavalcade pass, but none returned the physician's friendly greetings.

The village comprised small crofts scattered along a winding road. A large and unusually beautiful church nestled in the heart of the settlement; Michaelhouse's manor lay to its south-east, and the priory to its west. The land was flat, and most trees had been felled for building or firewood, so Bartholomew could see for a considerable distance. He commented to Pauline that some houses were larger than the others. She told him there were several manors in the parish, some of which were owned by Lymbury, although he preferred to live in the one he rented from Michaelhouse because of its central location and its new tiled roof. She pointed to it – a fine hall set amid a range of thatched outbuildings. A track fringed with young oaks led to its front door, and Askyl, who was in the lead, was just about to turn down it, when a youth stumbled towards them. The boy's face was red, and he was panting so hard he could barely breathe. He wore a fine new tunic, so white it hurt the eyes in the strong sunlight.

'There you are, Father,' he gasped to William. 'I have been looking for you ever since this morning – I must have run miles! Sir Philip says please come straight away. He is composing his new will, and wants you to write it down for him.'

'Lymbury is unwell?' asked Bartholomew, supposing mortal illness might explain the man's unusual attitude towards paying the rent.

William shook his head. 'He is always making wills. I have scribed at least six since Poitiers.'

'My husband always leaves me well provided for, though,' said Joan smugly. '*I* am no poor nun. If he dies, I shall have plenty with which to satisfy a new husband.'

Rose's expression was resentful. 'Except beauty, of course. Still, a man could always have his daily bread from you, and go elsewhere for his meat. But my throat is dry, and I imagine Dame Pauline will appreciate a cup of wine before returning to the priory. We shall avail ourselves of Sir Philip's hospitality, and listen to him dictating his latest will at the same time.'

Pauline glared at her. 'I am tired, and want to go—'

'It is very good wine,' said Rose firmly. She slid off her horse and marched towards the house before the nun could object further. Since Askyl was aiming for the door, too, Joan hurried to catch up with him, and Michael sniggered as all three became jammed in the entrance. William gave them a shove to relieve the blockage, and the entire contingent shot through in a rush, leaving the two scholars standing alone outside. Suddenly, there was a piercing scream. Michael and Bartholomew stared at each other for a moment, then entered the manor at a run – up the spiral stairs to the main hall on the first floor.

Valence Manor's chief room was a handsome solar, which smelled of wood smoke and the honeyed beeswax that had been used to polish its fine oaken floor – someone obviously took a great deal of trouble over it. The hunting party and the red-faced boy had gathered around a grey-haired man who sat in a chair near the hearth. At first, Bartholomew thought the fellow was asleep, but then he saw blood. When he looked at the back of the chair, he saw a sword had been thrust through the wooden panels with such force that it had skewered its victim from behind.

'Stabbed in the back,' breathed William, appalled. 'Lord have mercy on his soul.'

When no one did more than gaze at the corpse, Bartholomew went to inspect it. The sword had sliced through the soft tissues below the ribs, probably bringing instant death. The physician rested his hand on the man's neck, and felt the cool skin beneath his fingers. He also noted the blood was beginning to congeal. The dead man clutched a gold coin in his clawed fingers, which Bartholomew showed to Michael. He expected the others to notice, too, but they were more intent on fixing each other with accusing stares.

Joan, who did not seem particularly distressed by the discovery of her husband stabbed in his own solar, rounded on the flushed youth. 'I hope he did not destroy his previous wills before he started composing the new one.'

'You poor thing,' said Rose, her voice contemptuous. 'I see you are grief-stricken by your loss.'

Joan composed her face into an expression that approximated sorrow. 'I am devastated,' she declared, taking Askyl's arm and clinging to it rather hard. 'So I shall need my husband's friends around me, to console me in my time of need.'

'You need a priest, not a soldier,' said Rose tartly. 'Put Sir Elias down, and let Father William comfort you instead. It would be more seemly.'

'How did he die?' asked Dole, aghast. The pallor of shock made his scar more prominent – a raw, vivid slash across a face that had probably once been comely. Uncharitably, Bartholomew wondered whether Lymbury's death might mean the loss of Dole's post as priory chaplain.

'I think it might have something to do with the sword in his back,' whispered William. He addressed the others more loudly. 'I have seen enough death on the battlefield to know this terrible thing probably happened this morning, when we were out hunting.'

'I mean how did he come to be speared in his own home?' snapped Dole angrily. 'I can see he died by that damned sword.'

'Father William is right: *we* were all off hunting,' said Joan. She turned to the youth and a heavyset man who had come to stand beside him. Their looks and ages suggested they were father and son.

'Are you saying a servant did it?' asked Dole, following the direction of her accusing gaze.

The burly man glowered. 'She had better not be – every last man, woman and child on this estate has been busy in the fields since first light. It is a hectic time of year, and there is hard work to be done.' His disapproving tone indicated what he thought about a frivolous activity like hunting.

'Not *every* last child, Hog,' said Joan, her eyes fixed on the boy. 'James was ordered to remain behind, in case Sir Philip needed anything.'

The lad became alarmed when everyone looked at him. 'But I did not see anyone kill him!' he squeaked. His father rested a comforting hand on his shoulder.

'Actually, I was thinking of you not as a witness, but as a culprit,' elaborated Joan.

Old Dame Pauline gave an irritable sigh. 'Do not spout nonsense, woman! Of course James did not kill your husband. Why would he? His father is Lymbury's bailiff, and with Lymbury dead, Hog may find himself without profitable work. James would be a fool to bite the hand that feeds him.'

James gazed at his father in alarm. 'Is it true? Will we be cast out, to live like vagrants?'

'Sir Philip's death *is* a bitter blow,' admitted Bailiff Hog. His expression was defiant. 'But there are still crops in the fields and sheep on the hills. We shall stay here, and hope his heirs will hire us. However, because we have so much to lose from his death, it means *we* cannot be suspects for his murder.'

'Well someone killed him,' said Sister Rose. 'He obviously did not stab himself in the back.'

Michael addressed the gathering, silencing the mounting accusations and recriminations. 'It is too late fetch the Sheriff from Cambridge today, so we shall send word of what has happened first thing in the morning. But meanwhile, I am the University's Senior Proctor and Bartholomew is my Corpse Examiner. Between us, we have solved many murders. Since this death occurred on College land, we are under an obligation to investigate it. The Sheriff is an old friend, and will appreciate our help.'

'Yes, do explore the matter, Brother,' said Rose maliciously. 'Sir Philip had a wife who is now free to take a younger, more comely husband; friends who argued with him – excepting dear Sir Elias, of course; servants who despised him for sitting indoors when he was needed in the fields; and a prioress who was afraid he might withhold donations of eggs. You have a wealth of suspects to choose from.'

'I feel sorry for Lymbury,' said Bartholomew in a low voice to Michael, when everyone started to shout again. 'No one seems very upset by his death, with the possible exception of Dole.'

'Was his killer a man?' asked Michael. 'It must have taken a lot of power to drive a blade through the back of a chair and then into a body.'

Bartholomew did not think so. 'It was pushed through a gap in the panelling. The killer struck hard, but it was not a demonic kind of strength. Anyone could have done it – including Lady Joan and Sister Rose, who are fit, healthy women.'

'But it was *not* my son,' shouted Hog, his furious voice silencing the others by sheer dint of its volume. 'Not James. Whoever killed Sir Philip will be covered in blood, and you can see for yourselves that there is not a spot on James. You also know he is not a cunning boy – it would never have occurred to him to rid himself of incriminating stains if he had committed this crime. You *know* this, because you know James.'

James hung his head. 'A while after you had all gone hunting, Sir Philip sent me to fetch William the Vicar, because he said he was finally ready to dictate his new will. He was alive when I left, and I did not see anyone else nearby. Every villager is out in the fields, as my father said.'

'I do not think this case will greatly tax your scholarly wits, Brother,' said Lady Joan spitefully. 'This morning, I went to escort Sir Elias to his destrier, and I left *Rose* alone with Philip.'

'Not alone,' corrected Rose. 'Dame Pauline was with us – and it was only a matter of moments anyway, because I did not want to be left behind. Sir Philip asked after my health and I told him I was well. That was the full extent of our conversation.'

'I can vouch for that,' said the old nun bitterly. 'I was hoping she might linger, to reduce the time I was obliged to spend astride that horrible mule – you all know how it pains my hips to ride the thing – but she rushed out far too quickly.'

'And it is irrelevant anyway,' added Rose loftily. 'James saw Sir Philip alive *after* all this had happened and we had gone.'

'That is true,' acknowledged James. He looked frightened. 'But that does not mean *I* killed him.' He appealed to Michael. 'Please, Brother! You have to believe me!'

'Well, my husband was hale and hearty this morning—' began Joan angrily.

'He was not,' contradicted Rose. 'He said he was unwell.'

'He often claimed he was ailing,' said William. 'But it meant nothing – he said he was feverish before Poitiers, but that did not stop him from killing a dozen Frenchmen.'

'He had my trouble,' agreed Pauline. 'Aching joints.

What happened to this claret I was promised? And none of that slop you feed the servants, either. I want the good stuff.'

Hog tapped his son on the shoulder, and James escaped to fetch the wine with some relief. Bartholomew wondered whether he would come back: the manor's residents were eager for a culprit, and it would not be the first time innocent blood was spilled in the rush to secure an explanation.

'Shall we remove the sword?' asked Hog in the silence that followed his boy's departure. 'It is not right to leave the thing where it is.'

'That damned blade,' said Dole unhappily. 'It brought him nothing but trouble. Yes, pull it out, Hog. It distresses me to see it there.'

Bartholomew watched Hog extricate the weapon from Lymbury, then helped him lay the body on the floor. Dole muttered a few prayers before asking William to see about its removal to the church. William, however, was more interested in the sword than in the mortal remains of its owner.

'It is magnificent,' he said, taking one or two practise sweeps. 'Look at the elegant dog-head carvings on the cross and this perfectly balanced blade. It belonged to a fellow called Matthew de Curterne from Down St Mary. Remember how Lymbury found it with his corpse after Poitiers? We drew lots for it, and Lymbury won.'

'You did not return it to Curterne's family?' asked Bartholomew, surprised. It was the usual custom in such a situation.

William shook his head. 'Lymbury sent them a silver chalice instead. A fine weapon like this belongs in the hands of a warrior, and Curterne told us all his kin were farmers.'

'It is old and heavy,' said Dole disagreeably, watching William prance. 'And I did not like the tales Curterne told us about its origins – how it brought bad luck and shame to its owners. I particularly did not like the story about the coroner's man in Exeter, who was hanged for a crime he did not commit.'

'He was not hanged,' said William, his priestly robes swinging as he feinted and parried with an imaginary foe. 'Curterne said the fellow's master secured his freedom through some clever thinking. You know how sharp these coroners can be.'

'And there was that business in Venice,' Dole went on, unconvinced. 'It was hurled into the sea, but contrived to have itself hauled out again. Very sinister. Curterne also told me it has the ability to fly through the air and embed itself in people it does not like.'

'Does it, indeed?' murmured Michael. 'That would be a convenient solution for someone here.'

'It cut his hand when he was a child,' insisted Dole. 'He bore the scar to prove it – he said it came out of nowhere and almost severed his thumb. And he mentioned a servant who tried to steal it from him, who ended up breaking his neck when he tried to escape over the roof.'

'So why did Curterne take it to Poitiers, then?' asked Bartholomew doubtfully. 'It sounds as though he thought it might be cursed in some way.'

'He had no choice,' explained William. 'He had spent all his available money on horse and armour, and had no means to buy a different weapon. But perhaps he exaggerated his concerns, thought it was less likely to be stolen if folk believed it might bring them bad luck.'

'No, he should have left it in Devonshire,' argued Dole. 'He said the first time we met him that there was something odd about it.'

'Those were stories he invented around the camp-fire to entertain us,' said William dismissively. 'I am surprised at you, Dole, unsettled by silly tales with no truth or basis.'

'Then why did Lymbury's luck change the moment he acquired the thing,' demanded Dole, unconvinced. 'A wife unable to give him an heir—'

'It has only been a year,' objected William, laughing. 'Give the poor woman a chance!'

'—sheep killed by mad dogs, fires in his granaries,' Dole went on, cutting across Joan's indignant response. 'And Curterne told me it was called the Sword of Shame, and only a fool would willingly take charge of a weapon with that sort of name.'

'So, why did you draw lots for it after Curterne's death, then?' asked Bartholomew curiously. 'It does not sound as though it is the kind of weapon most men would want to own.'

'Superstition is for the feeble minded,' said William; smiling fondly at the blade. 'I am not afraid of ghosts, and neither was Lymbury. I imagine Dole – and perhaps Askyl – would have sold it, had they won the draw. But I would have kept it. These ridiculous tales are a nonsense, and besides, the inscriptions carved into its blade suggest it is a thing of honour.'

Bartholomew took the sword from him. He was no soldier, but even he could tell it was a fine one. He studied the words etched into the steel: *qui falsitate vivit, animam occidit. Falsus in ore, caret honore.* There was too much blood to read the second inscription, but it seemed to condemn miserly men.

'It warns against telling lies,' translated Michael, rather loosely. 'A man who lives out his days in defiance of the truth will lose his soul, as well as his honour. So, let that be a warning to anyone who might be tempted to mislead my investigation.'

*　　*　　*

'We should start from the beginning if we want to reduce the length of Sister Rose's list of suspects,' said Bartholomew, setting the weapon carefully on a nearby bench. 'When was the decision made for everyone – except Lymbury – to go hunting?'

Lady Joan indicated with an imperious flick of her hand that Hog was to wipe Lymbury's chair clean of blood. Then she sat in it, shuffling and testing it for size. A satisfied smile indicated she found the fit a good one. 'The decision was made last night, by dear Sir Elias. He is an honoured and most welcome guest, so my husband was pleased to oblige him.'

'I dislike being idle,' explained Askyl. He watched William take the weapon from the bench and begin to admire it again. 'A man who haunts the dinner table will find his military edge blunted, and we never know when the Black Prince might need warriors again.'

'My husband sent word to the priory, to invite *Sister* Rose to take part,' Joan went on. 'I did not approve. The likes of *Sister* Rose should be on her knees, confessing her sins. Perhaps she should ask absolution for the crime of murder right now.'

Rose did not dignify the accusation with a response, and, aware that both women were looking at him for a reaction, Askyl kept his face carefully neutral.

'I own some small skill with weapons,' said Rose modestly, shooting Askyl a sultry smile. 'My father was a soldier, and he thought women should know how to defend their virtue.' She ignored Joan's snort of derision. 'Sir Philip was impressed with my talents, and always included me on his hunts – so I could provide meat for my sisters at the priory.'

'I am impressed with your talents, too,' gushed Dole, regarding her admiringly. 'We could have done with you in France.'

She inclined her head, then addressed Michael. 'I

came to Ickleton Priory three years ago, and I am still deciding whether to devote my life to God. My family say they do not mind waiting.'

'That is because you have no dowry,' said Joan immediately. 'So, it does not matter to them what you do. *I*, of course, am a wealthy widow, and so I am *highly* desirable.' She looked hard at Askyl, to make sure he had taken the comment on board.

'Wealth and desirability do not always go together,' remarked Rose cuttingly. 'But we are talking about me, not you. It was Sir Elias who brought the invitation to me last night.'

'I did – but not with any intention of securing your company for myself,' said Askyl, earning a hurt look from Rose and a triumphant grin from Joan. Bartholomew wondered whether money was already winning the battle against beauty. Askyl saw he had caused offence, and hastened to explain. 'I mean I did not intend to entice nuns from their devotions on my behalf.'

'But you did just that,' said old Dame Pauline sulkily. 'And *I* was forced to pay the price. Racing around after deer at my age! It is all wrong, and I shall write to the Bishop about it. Prioress Christiana is not fit to rule our house – she cannot even read. I am the only literate woman there.'

'So you remind us day and night,' sighed Rose, stepping smartly to one side when William made a trial sweep with the sword that came perilously close to her elegantly tailored habit.

'You say you are visiting Lymbury,' said Michael to Askyl. 'How long have you been here?'

'A few weeks,' replied the knight. 'I have no family of my own, so it is good to be among friends – Lymbury, William and Dole. Lymbury has been very generous with his hospitality.'

'You are both priests?' asked Bartholomew of the

chaplain and vicar, wondering whether William had been ordained; an interest in weapons was something he should have forsworn.

Dole nodded. 'We took holy orders when we returned from Poitiers. I did it out of a conviction that I had killed too many Frenchmen – along with the fact that I am unlikely to secure a bride with no nose. War has made me ugly, I fear.'

'That is not true,' said Rose. Dole's eyes blazed with sudden hope. '*Joan* will have no trouble getting a suitor – now her husband has left her a fortune – and *she* is ugly.'

Dole's eager expectation faded abruptly, while hot colour rose in Joan's cheeks.

'We shall see who secures the better husband,' said Joan coldly. 'You regard yourself a beauty, but you are swarthy and you dye your hair. *Mine* is naturally fair.'

'Ladies, please!' snapped Michael, when the altercation looked set to continue for some time. 'A man lies dead, and you should be ashamed of yourselves, quarrelling over hair. Now, Dole: you were telling us why you decided to become a priest.'

Dole nodded again, and looked at Bartholomew. 'If you were at Poitiers, you do not need me to tell you that while it was a glorious victory for England, there was something deeply distasteful about so much killing. I was detailed to help bury the dead afterwards, and it took days. When Lymbury told me it was in his power to appoint me as chaplain to Ickleton's nuns, it seemed right to accept.'

'And you?' asked Michael of William, who was removing Lymbury's blood from the sword with some spit and his sleeve.

'Ickleton needed a vicar, and I needed somewhere to live,' replied William. 'Priests have been in short supply since the plague, and villages are grateful for whoever they can get.'

'That is true,' said Michael. 'But there are some standards, even so.'

'Dole and I both know Latin,' said William, as if he imagined this to be the sole criterion. 'And Lymbury liked me to write out his various wills and manage his domestic accounts in addition to my parish duties. Like most military men, he was illiterate.'

'Lymbury offered you and Dole comfortable posts, but gave nothing to Askyl?' asked Michael, turning to the knight.

Askyl shrugged. He was standing by the hearth, poking the ashes with a stick and careful to stand precisely equidistant from his two female admirers. Bartholomew wondered whether he knew how fine a figure he cut in his half-armour and nonchalant pose.

'I am a knight, not a priest,' said Askyl. 'He asked me to be his bailiff, but I think Hog might have had something to say about that.'

'Yes, I would,' said Hog firmly. 'My family have served his for generations, and I would not have stood by while I was ousted.'

'Nor would I,' said James, who had returned with Dame Pauline's wine. 'It would not have been right. My family has always been loyal to the Lymburys.'

'What will happen now he is dead?' asked Bartholomew. 'Is Joan his sole heir?'

'I shall have to dig out his most recent testament and see,' said William. 'He kept changing his mind, and I cannot recall what he said the last time.'

'It will leave everything to me,' cried Joan, suddenly alarmed. Rose started to laugh.

'I do remember that his friends were remembered, though,' said William, still polishing the sword. He smiled, rather nastily. 'Call it self-interest, if you will, but that little detail stuck in my mind.'

The discussion quickly degenerated into another row, and this time even the two servants joined in. Michael rubbed his temples, letting the furious voices wash over him, while Bartholomew went to sit next to him and wished he was back at Michaelhouse. His restful jaunt was becoming unpleasant.

'We are unlikely to get our ten marks now Lymbury is dead,' said the physician to Michael. 'And if several wills exist, all contradicting each other, we shall have to wait for lawyers to sort them out.'

'That could take months, and we need new latrines now,' grumbled the monk. 'Besides, a man has been murdered, and I doubt *these* people will see justice done – they are too wrapped up in their own concerns. I do not think I have ever encountered so many blazing hatreds under one roof. At least we scholars keep our dislikes decently concealed under a veneer of civility.'

'Then you had better resume your questioning, or you will have another death on your hands. Dole's surliness has finally shaken William's equanimity – and William is holding that sword.'

'The so-called Sword of Shame,' said Michael thoughtfully, watching the vicar grip the hilt. 'Is it valuable, do you think? It looks to me as if William intends to keep it for himself.'

'All good weapons are expensive, and that one is better than most. Perhaps he knows Lymbury left it to him – or perhaps he added a codicil without Lymbury's knowledge, to be sure he inherits it.'

'We know Lymbury could not read, so a dishonest clerk could write whatever he liked and be sure of having it signed and sealed. Is William dishonest, do you think?'

'He is not a very devoted priest – he is not rushing

to take Lymbury's body to his church and pray for it. But dishonest? I suppose that depends on how badly he covets that sword.'

While they had been talking, Dole had opened a chest and retrieved several documents. He regarded them with exasperation. 'Here are his wills, but none is dated, and several are unsigned. Lawyers will be wrangling over these for years.'

'This is *your* fault,' shouted Joan, real tears appearing at last as she glared at William. 'You were his clerk – you should have made sure they were in order.'

William was smug. His flash of temper with Dole had cooled, and the sword lay on the bench, gleaming from its recent polish. 'Those are just drafts. The latest will – signed *and* dated – is in a safe place. Lymbury was fond of his riches, and liked thinking about where to bequeath them.'

'All this is very interesting, but it is not helping us learn what happened to him this morning,' said Michael. 'What time did you all arrive for the hunt?'

'Sir Elias and I were already here, obviously,' said Joan, going to stand at the knight's side, 'since we live in the manor-house. William arrived next, then Dole, and finally Rose and Pauline.'

'It was horribly early,' said Dame Pauline bitterly. 'Before breakfast. It is not good for elderly—'

'Hog and James were here, too,' interrupted Joan. 'They had already saddled the horses, and came inside to eat a bowl of pottage with us before we left.'

'When was this?' asked Michael. 'Just after dawn?'

'Much later,' said Hog icily. 'Dawn has different meanings for men who need to make the most of daylight hours, and I had been in the fields for some time before I came to prepare the horses. James and I ate the pottage while we waited for the nuns to arrive. Then, eventually, after more valuable time was lost in idle chatter, they all trooped outside and mounted up.'

'But not Lymbury?' asked Michael. 'Why not?'

'After the pottage, he decided to forgo the pleasures of the kill and think about his last testament instead,' replied Askyl. 'It was not the first time. As William says, he enjoyed composing them.'

'Did anything happen to make him think he might need one soon?' asked Michael.

'He had aching bones,' supplied Pauline, rubbing her hip. 'Like me. But he was not ill.'

'Was there an argument, then?' Michael raised his hands. 'Forgive me: that was an extremely foolish question, given the present company. What I meant to ask was: was there an argument more bitter than your usual quarrels, which prompted him to alter the terms of his most recent will?'

'We do not know the terms of his most recent will,' said Dole, regarding William coolly. 'Someone will not tell us what they are.'

'They are confidential,' said William. 'But you will all know tomorrow, because I shall read them to you. I refuse to do it today, while the poor man is still warm. It would be disrespectful.'

'Unlike playing with his sword,' muttered Dole.

Michael tried to steer the conversation back to that morning, and was obliged to raise his voice when everyone started to yell at William for his hypocrisy.

'So,' said the Benedictine, once he had silenced everyone by picking up the sword and dropping it to the floor with a metallic clang. William squeaked in horror, while Hog was furious about the damage to the highly polished floorboards. 'You all rode away to hunt.'

'James did not,' said Joan. 'He stayed here to make sure Philip had everything he needed.'

The boy swallowed. 'Sir Philip sat in his chair and stared out of the window. Eventually, he said he had thought long enough, and told me to fetch William the Vicar. I looked in the meadows, then down by the river, but there was no sign of him. Then I met Prioress Christiana, who asked me to carry eggs to the convent for her. But by then I was hungry, so I went home for some bread.'

'You were eating, when you should have been following orders?' asked Joan accusingly.

James blushed and stared at his feet. 'I am sorry, My Lady, but I did not linger at home long. I finished the food, then ran to the upper pastures. But William was not there, either. It was only when the whole hunt was coming back to the manor-house that our paths finally crossed. By then, I had been racing around for hours.'

Bartholomew recalled the boy's flushed face when they had first met, and imagined the Lord of the Manor must have been growing impatient, being forced to wait so long for the priest to arrive.

'Did you go back inside the house at all after Lymbury had sent you to fetch William?' he asked.

James shook his head vehemently. 'No, I did not. He would have been angry to see me without the vicar, and I am not a fool. I just told you *everything* I did.'

Michael raised his eyebrows. 'So, no one can confirm where you were for most of the time?'

'I saw James leave the manor-house,' said Hog. 'We are short-handed from losing men in the French wars, so I was in the top field on my own. But I saw James leave, and I did not see him go inside again until you all arrived back from the hunt. James cannot possibly be the killer.'

'He can – if Lymbury was dead before James left the house,' Michael pointed out.

'Well, he was not,' said James firmly. He raised his

chin defiantly, trying to mask his unease. Bartholomew felt sorry for him – his was an unenviable position. 'He was alive. I did *not* kill him.'

'Of course you did not,' said Hog soothingly. 'You have no reason.'

'Except the possibility of losing a hereditary post to Askyl,' said Michael. He raised his hand when Hog started to object. 'I am not saying James *did* kill Lymbury. I am merely pointing out that he has a motive and he was the last person to see Lymbury alive. And the same goes for you, Hog, as far as motive is concerned. You say you were working alone, so it is possible that *you* slipped into the house after James had left, and killed the man who was thinking of dismissing you.'

'It was wicked of Sir Philip,' said Hog sullenly. 'I have spent my whole life on this manor, and he had no right to threaten my position. But I did not kill him for it.'

'So, the hunt eventually comprised Askyl, William and Dole, accompanied by Rose, Joan and Pauline?' asked Michael thoughtfully. 'James was searching for William, and Hog was in the fields?'

'Yes,' said Askyl. 'So *we* six hunters are innocent of this murder, because *we* were away from the house.'

'You remained together all day?' asked Michael.

'We are not wolves, hunting as a pack,' said William scornfully. 'Of course we did not stay together. Sometimes we were in pairs, sometimes in threes, sometimes alone.'

'The woods are not far from the hall,' Michael pointed out. 'So, any of you could have come back, killed Lymbury and returned to your sport with no one any the wiser.'

The six looked at each other. 'Yes, I suppose so,' admitted Askyl. 'But we did not. Someone would have seen us – one of the peasants in the fields.'

'Not so,' said Hog, a little smugly. 'At William's request, I sent them to the far meadows today – as I informed the hunt as it left. No labourer would have noticed anyone moving between house and woods.'

'I was concerned for the welfare of my flock,' declared William defensively, when accusing eyes swivelled towards him. 'I am their priest. Several of them were ridden down last time, and I did not want it to happen again – I did not direct them to the far meadows for sinister reasons. Besides, if Hog was in the top field, he would have seen the killer leave the woods alone, without the others.'

'There is a hollow,' explained Hog. 'I could not see the manor-house all the time.'

'That is not what you said when we accused James of being the culprit,' pounced Michael. Hog glared at him, but made no reply.

'I was with Dame Pauline,' said Sister Rose with a triumphant smile. 'There is *my* alibi.'

'Except the hour she spent asleep under a tree,' countered Joan spitefully. 'I rode past her, but she did not wake. And there was no sign of you.'

'I was resting my aching bones,' snapped Pauline. 'But I *did* see you – you were alone, too.'

'Ha!' exclaimed Rose. 'And you and your husband argued bitterly last night. Do not deny it – Pauline heard you when she came to collect the priory's eggs.'

'I did,' agreed Pauline. 'And I also heard William berating Sir Philip about the cost of the parchment used to write all these wills.'

'I did recommend prudence,' admitted William stiffly. He addressed Michael. 'I am obliged to pay for the stuff myself, and as a scholar, you do not need me to tell you that it is expensive.'

Pauline continued. 'And Askyl took William's side in the row, which Sir Philip did not like.'

'Lymbury was in the wrong,' stated Askyl dogmatically. 'All men disagree from time to time – it means nothing. Do not tell me you never squabble with your Corpse Examiner.'

Pauline was not finished. She turned to Dole and pointed a finger. 'And I heard *him* antagonizing Sir Philip over that sword. Dole said he should get rid of it, because it brings bad luck.'

Dole shrugged. 'It ended up in his innards. I would say that was bad luck.'

Joan offered Bartholomew and Michael a room in which to sleep that night, but she did so with such bad grace that neither was inclined to accept. They left her fluffing up cushions behind Askyl's head and plying him with pastries. Hog and James helped William carry their master's body to the church, while Dole slunk away on unspecified business of his own.

'We shall stay at the convent,' announced Michael, after checking that their horses had been properly stabled. 'I am a Benedictine, and it is a house of my own Order. They will welcome us.' The tone of his voice indicated there would be trouble if they did not.

'You can ask the prioress for Michaelhouse's ten marks, too,' suggested Bartholomew.

'In the morning,' said Michael. 'She might be less inclined to generous hospitality, if she thinks I am about to make off with her money. Here come Rose and Pauline. They can lead us there.'

'We have a cottage for visiting monastics,' said Rose, hips swaying under her tight habit. She walked more quickly in order to speak to the monk alone, leaving the hobbling Dame Pauline behind. She rested a slender hand on his arm and smiled into his face. 'But, when the weather is cold, we let *special* visitors share the fire in our own dormitory.'

'Is that so?' said Michael, unmoved. 'It sounds improper. Should I tell my Bishop about it?'

Rose pouted, not liking her flirtations disregarded. 'I was only teasing, Brother.'

'You were not,' said Michael. 'You were attempting to use your wiles on me. Why? So I will not look to you as Lymbury's murderer?'

Rose grimaced. 'I forgot you are a scholar, and therefore view everything with cold logic. If you must know, I was hoping you would agree to be discreet about my liking for Sir Elias. Since her predecessor was deposed, the prioress has been fussy about what she calls licentious behaviour, and I do not want her to stop me from going to the manor-house.'

'Why not?' asked Michael. 'Your visits there are clearly leading you along the path to sin.'

Rose gave a heavy sigh. 'Because how shall I ensnare Sir Elias in marriage, if I never see him? I do not want to be a nun – and I refuse to let Joan beat me to the post. If you say nothing about my intentions to the prioress, I will name my first child after you.'

Michael regarded her askance, and when he made no reply, she fell behind to walk with Pauline. Bartholomew heard them muttering, and supposed Rose was trying to make a similar arrangement with her chaperon. From the gleeful expression on the elderly nun's face, the offers were being greeted with rather more enthusiasm than the response elicited from the monk.

The sun was setting in a ball of orange, although Pauline claimed her aching bones told her there would be rain by dawn. People were returning from the fields, spades and hoes over their shoulders. They stared at the strangers, but still declined to trade smiles and comments about the weather.

'They are not very friendly,' remarked Michael.

'Lymbury was always telling them how many Frenchmen he had killed at Poitiers,' explained Pauline. 'And they live in constant fear that the French king will descend on Ickleton to avenge the slaughter. They will be all beams and pleasantries tomorrow, when they hear Lymbury is dead. They are not naturally sullen.'

'So Lymbury was unpopular with his people,' mused Bartholomew, exchanging a significant glance with the monk. Here was yet another motive for the man's murder. 'Was there anything that made him especially disliked?'

Rose shrugged. 'Just his unsettling tales about killing so many men who might have vengeful kin. William the Vicar gave a sermon on "an eye for an eye", you see, which started them thinking. I doubt it was what William intended them to do, but there is no telling what simple folk might believe once a seed has been planted in their minds.'

Bartholomew glanced sharply at her, and wondered whether she might have done a little sowing herself, although he could not imagine what she might have gained from doing so.

'Here we are,' she said, bending to retrieve a black garment from under a bush. When she shook it out and pulled it over her head, she was transformed from a woman in a tight black dress to a nun in a baggy habit. A white veil was donned to hide the gold hair-fret and, with her hands folded in her wide sleeves, she looked the picture of demure modesty. 'Do not forget, Dame Pauline – a jug of wine if you say nothing about my chasing after Sir Elias today.'

'Two jugs,' countered Pauline opportunistically. 'Or my conscience will prick me about the fact that I left you alone for so long.' She grimaced at the slip, and glanced at Michael to see if he had noticed. 'I mean alone with Askyl. And *I* was with Joan. I do not mean either one of us was unaccompanied and in a position to commit murder.'

Michael said nothing, and allowed the two women to usher him through a door and into the convent, Bartholomew trailing behind. While Rose fetched the prioress and Pauline limped to the kitchens for something to eat, the physician looked around him.

The priory was tiny and clearly poor. The main part comprised a wooden chapel and a two-storeyed hall – the upper floor was a dormitory and the lower one served as refectory and chapter house. There was a separate kitchen block and a massive barn for storing grain, all enclosed within a double ditch and a bank. A bell rang for vespers, and the sound of chanting drifted towards them. The smell of newly cut grass and warm soil mingled with the scent of incense. It was a peaceful scene, and rather more what Bartholomew had expected when he had left Cambridge that morning.

It was not long before a woman with a grey face came scurrying across the yard. Worry lines bit deeply into her forehead and cheeks. 'Rose tells me you know the Bishop,' she said unhappily. 'Are you here because I allow her out from time to time? Lymbury often demands her company – or he did, before his friends arrived from France. Now he summons her less frequently. She minds terribly.'

'Lymbury used to spend time alone with Rose?' asked Bartholomew, not sure what the prioress was saying in her gabbling rush of words. 'But now he does not?'

She paled even further. 'Oh, damn my loose tongue! I have just told you something the Bishop should not know, and I do not want to be deposed like my predecessor. Chaplain Dole is always telling me to think before I speak, but it is so very difficult. Do you not find, Brother?'

'Not really,' replied Michael, amused by the question. 'Such a failing would be somewhat inconvenient in a scholar – it would see him savaged in the debating halls.'

'Oh, yes, of course. I am Prioress Christiana. But you have already guessed that, I suppose. Rose tells me you are from Michaelhouse, which probably means you have come to demand the ten marks Lymbury gave me.'

'We shall discuss it tomorrow,' said Michael. 'After a good night's sleep, preferably in a decent bed. And we have been travelling all day, so a little bread and meat would not go amiss, either.'

'You cannot have meat, Brother,' said Christiana, startled. 'It is a fish day.'

'So it is,' said Michael in a voice heavy with resignation. 'I had forgotten.'

The guesthouse was a tiny cottage on the edge of the convent, separated from it by a line of apple trees. Birds trilled sweet and clear as the sun disappeared in a blaze of copper, and there was a contented lowing as cows were milked and settled in their byre. Bartholomew smiled at Prioress Christiana, who was distressed because the door had been left open and a goat had eaten the blankets.

'This is a lovely place,' he said sincerely.

She wrung her hands. 'It is a grave responsibility, and my predecessor's fate is never far from my mind – Dame Pauline sees to that. She is always talking about what happened to Alice Lacy, and how she was sent to the priory at Chatteris in disgrace.'

'Chatteris,' said Michael in a sepulchral voice. 'A dreadful place, set deep in the desolate wilderness of the Fens. I have never been, mind you, but I have heard tales of its bitter weather and the way snakes lurk in its mattresses.'

'Oh, really, Brother,' said Bartholomew, watching the prioress's eyes open wide in shock. 'It was rats in the bedding, not snakes.' He saw he had not helped when Christiana's hands flew to her mouth in horror. Rodents were apparently held in greater terror than reptiles.

'I do my best,' said Christiana in a wail. 'But it is not easy when there are women like Rose and Pauline under my care. The others are good, devout souls, but those two are a trial, and Pauline is always challenging my authority because I cannot read. She objects to managing the accounts, but she also complains when I try to relieve her of the burden. I can do nothing right. And now there is trouble with a powerful Cambridge College and a monk who knows the Bishop. What shall I do?'

'We shall talk tomorrow,' said Bartholomew kindly. 'I am sure we can reach some arrangement that suits us both.'

'Such as you giving us our ten marks,' muttered Michael. He spoke a little more loudly. 'Did you like Lymbury, Mother?'

'Pauline said he was murdered today,' Christiana's eyes filled with compassionate tears. 'He was a difficult man, but generous in his way. He was fond of Rose, and I felt compelled to let her go to him when he asked, because we need the eggs he always let us have. Rose was always happy to oblige.'

Michael's eyebrows rose. 'I am sure she was.'

'But I did fear he wanted her for immoral purposes,' confided Christiana unhappily. 'Especially later, when I learned he only invited Rose to the manor-house at times when Lady Joan was visiting her mother. What would the Bishop say if he found out? But, of course he *will* find out now – you will tell him, because I have just told you. Damn my clacking tongue!'

'We already knew,' said Michael. 'Rose is not discreet. How long has this been going on?'

'For about a year. But it faltered in the spring, when Askyl, Dole and William arrived. I suppose Lymbury was too busy with his friends for romantic dalliances.'

'Did Joan know about her husband and Rose?' asked Bartholomew.

Christiana shrugged. 'She might have done – perhaps she was relieved that he had foisted his attentions on another woman, because she did not love him herself. But I must go and say prayers for his soul, or he may come and haunt us. And he had a nasty sword that he liked to show off. I would not like to meet a ghost wielding such a vicious, sharp blade.'

It was soon too dark to do anything except go to bed – the cottage was not supplied with candles. Bartholomew lay on a mattress near the window, enjoying the cool breeze that wafted in. It was a sultry night, and he felt thunder in the wind – Dame Pauline's predictions had been right. Michael complained about the fleas in the bedding and the meagre supper he had been served. Then he moaned about the open window, claiming that a dangerous miasma might enter during the night and poison him.

'I am not sleepy,' said Bartholomew, waiting for a break in the litany of grumbles. He settled with his hands behind his head, staring up at the stars and thinking about Ptolemy's notion that the universe comprised a series of spheres. 'What do you think of the contention in the *Almagest* that eccentric and epicyclic circles account for the observed variations in the distances of the planets?'

Michael sighed. 'I have no idea what you are talking about, and it sounds vaguely heretical to me. Does God have any place in these spheres?'

'I do not envy you your position,' said Bartholomew, concluding the monk was not in the mood for scholarly debate. 'Rose and Pauline were right when they said their priory is poor, and they are fellow Benedictines. But Michaelhouse is equally desperate and you owe us your loyalty, too.'

Michael sighed a second time. 'That is why I have decided to take you up on your offer and let you decide the issue. I do not want my colleagues at Michaelhouse *or* my brethren at the abbey clamouring favouritism at me, so I am passing the responsibility to you. I wash my hands of the whole affair.'

'Very well – as long as you do not argue with me once I have made up my mind.'

'I shall argue if I feel like it – you may do something foolish. Langelee said we were not to return without his money, and he may not let us back in if you are generous to a handful of penniless nuns.'

Bartholomew laughed. 'You say I am free to make the decision, but in the next breath you tell me what to do. You are abrogating the responsibility, without relinquishing the power.'

Michael chuckled. 'You know me too well. But Michaelhouse has a legal and moral right to this ten marks, so there is really no decision to make. If you offer to let the nuns keep the money, Langelee will hire lawyers. The sisters will lose it eventually – along with fees they will have to pay their own clerk to contest the case. We will all be the poorer if you elect to be generous to this priory.'

Bartholomew was silent for a while, mulling over the situation. As far as Michaelhouse was concerned, the debt remained Lymbury's – or his estate's – and he supposed he could insist it was paid by the manor, and leave the nuns out of it. But it might take months to secure payment if lawyers became involved, and the College needed latrines urgently.

'I do not think you should look into Lymbury's death,

Brother,' he said eventually. 'There are too many suspects – especially now we know he was not popular in the village, either. If he was alone in the manor-house all day, anyone could have crept in and driven that sword through his innards.'

'We shall ask the prioress tomorrow if any villager has fallen especially foul of him. Or perhaps we are wasting our time looking for a human hand in this. What did the sword's previous owner – Curterne – tell Dole? That it can fly through the air and kill whom-soever it likes?'

Bartholomew laughed. 'I am sure it can – particu-larly if lobbed by a person.'

'Well, we should concentrate on the suspects we have already met. There are eight of them: Lymbury's wife, his mistress and his mistress's "chaperon"; his friends William, Dole and Askyl; and his bailiff Hog – and Hog's son James. None can prove where they were to my satis-faction, and all had some sort of quarrel with him.'

'Except Pauline and Rose,' said Bartholomew. 'But that may be because we do not know about an argu-ment. He did not sound pleasant, and no one was particularly upset by his death – except Dole.'

'William is my first choice as the killer.'

Bartholomew tried to look at the monk, but could only see a massive stomach rising like a mountain in the glimmering starlight. 'Why? Because he sent his parishioners to the far meadows, thus making sure no one would see him if he returned to the manor-house to kill his old comrade-in-arms?'

Michael nodded. 'And because he has an obvious liking for that sword, and it is clear he intends to have it for himself. When we see Lymbury's will tomorrow, I shall be very surprised if there is no codicil that does not leave the thing to his parish priest and dear friend.'

'Would a man kill for a sword? Especially if it brings bad luck, as Dole claims?'

'I would not want one, but then I have never been to war. Battles do odd things to men, Matt, as you will know from personal experience. William cannot have much money of his own, or he would not have accepted the lowly post of parish vicar, so a valuable sword might be a very tempting prize.'

'I think Lymbury's wife is a more likely culprit. Lady Joan showed no sign of grief when he died – it was Rose who screamed at the sight of his corpse. Perhaps Joan objected to him taking a mistress.'

'Perhaps,' said Michael. 'And with Lymbury out of the way, she is free to make a play for the handsome Askyl. Before, she was stuck with an ageing husband, while Rose was making it clear *she* was available. Now Joan has a sporting chance of snaring a comely mate.'

'More than a chance, if she inherits the bulk of Lymbury's estate.'

'But is Askyl interested? He simpered at both, but I could not tell if he preferred one to the other.'

'His choice is wealth or beauty, as Rose herself pointed out. I think he will opt for wealth.'

'Rose is only right if Askyl thinks she is beautiful. Personally, I find her rather ordinary.'

Bartholomew was surprised. 'Do you? That will not please her. She goes to a good deal of trouble to make herself attractive.'

'She is wasting her time,' declared Michael harshly. 'She does not have the basis for decent looks – she is too swarthy. And her figure is oddly shaped.'

Bartholomew eased himself up on one elbow and stared in the monk's general direction. 'To be honest, I thought she might be pregnant.'

He heard Michael's blanket rustle. 'Really? I suppose you are trained to notice that sort of thing. I wonder if Lymbury is the father. If so, then surely she would prefer him alive? He cannot pay for the brat's upkeep if he is dead.'

'Assuming he is willing to acknowledge it as his own. He might have rejected it – and her at the same time. It is a very good motive for murder. Perhaps I will change my prime suspect from Joan to Rose – especially since I recall her bragging about her skills with weapons when we were in the woods. It was no hollow boast, either: it was she who shot the deer the men could not catch.'

'The prioress noted a recent cooling in the relationship between Lymbury and Rose,' mused Michael. 'I wonder why. Did Rose decline to gratify the plain lord of the manor once she had set eyes on his handsome friend?'

'Dole admires Rose, too, although he cannot hope to compete with Askyl.'

'I told you, Rose is too swarthy for beauty, so she does not stand a chance with Askyl, either. Lord, Matt! I cannot believe you are encouraging me to discuss women with you. We are in a nunnery for God's sake, and I am a monk!'

'What about Pauline?'

'She is far too old to interest me.'

'I meant what about Pauline as a suspect for murder?' asked Bartholomew impatiently.

'If it was Pauline, she would have moaned about blood on her clothing or the weight of the sword. She is a malcontent and grumbles about everything. And why would she want Lymbury dead?'

'She objected to him forcing her out on hunts as an escort for Rose. Perhaps it was the only way she could think of to end it. She had ample opportunity, because Rose abandoned her in order to chase after Askyl.'

'Meanwhile, Hog and James are also obvious candidates. Lymbury offered Askyl the coveted post of bailiff. Askyl did not say whether he would have accepted, but there is nothing to say he would not. His two friends are happily settled here, and Askyl said he has no family of his own.'

'What will happen to Hog and James now? Will Lady Joan keep them on?'

'Who knows? But an estate needs a bailiff – especially at this time of year – and Hog seems competent. Perhaps Michaelhouse will hire him, until a new tenant comes to replace Lymbury.'

'What about Askyl and Dole? Would either of them have killed their old friend?'

'Yes,' replied Michael without hesitation. 'Dole is complex, and I do not know whether he is telling the truth about his motives for joining the priesthood. And Askyl thinks rather a lot of himself. Perhaps one of them learned *he* had been designated as Lymbury's sole heir, and decided to kill the man before he could change his mind and write another will.'

'We will find out tomorrow, Brother,' said Bartholomew feeling sleep approaching at last. An owl hooted, and somewhere in the distance a vixen yapped. 'William the Vicar will read it to us.'

The glorious sunshine of the past few days had gone by the following morning, and there was drizzle in the air. It dampened the thirsty soil, releasing the scent of wet earth, and thunder rolled in the distance. Wisps of mist lay in strips across the fields and in the woods, and a nightingale sang as the land grew lighter. The priory bell chimed for prime, and the nuns made their way to the chapel in silence. Bartholomew stood in the nave with the lay-folk, listening to Michael's pleasant baritone complement the higher voices of the women.

Breakfast at the priory comprised watered ale, bread and honey, and although it was not exciting fare, there was enough of it to satisfy even Michael's gargantuan appetite. After the tables had been cleared, Prioress Christiana came to talk again. There were dark circles under her eyes, and she looked as though she had not slept.

'I had a wretched night,' she confessed, when Bartholomew asked if she was unwell. 'You are here to take our money; I must find funds to buy masses for Lymbury's soul; Pauline tells me she no longer wants to act as Rose's chaperon; and Rose said this morning that she will leave the priory.'

'Let us take these troubles one at a time,' said Michael kindly, taking her arm and leading her to a bench in a sheltered arbour near the refectory. It was full of flowers, bees and dripping vegetation. Bartholomew sat on a wall-seat opposite them. 'First, let us consider the money Lymbury gave you, which rightfully belongs to Michaelhouse.'

'Ten marks,' whispered Christiana, white-faced. 'A colossal sum! I have already spent most of it on essential supplies for the winter, and I need the rest to repair the dormitory roof. The building will collapse if we do not tackle the problem soon.'

'William the Vicar is going to read Lymbury's will this morning, so we shall know the full extent of his assets,' said Bartholomew. 'If he has ten marks in other goods, we shall claim those instead.'

Christiana brightened. 'That would be a relief! I was beginning to think we might have to part with our relic to pay you, although I am not sure whether it is really authentic. It is a splinter of the True Cross, stained with Christ's blood when—'

'No, thank you,' said Bartholomew hastily, recalling the murder and mayhem that had followed when he had last encountered such an item. 'We do not want any Blood Relics.'

'Your second concern is funding prayers for Lymbury's soul,' said Michael.

Christiana nodded. 'That is why he gave us the ten marks – to pay a chantry priest to pray for him in perpetuity. Unfortunately, I did not learn the reason for the benefaction until after I had spent it on food. It came with written instructions, but I cannot read and Dame Pauline had a headache, so was unavailable for translation. I was dreading confessing the misunderstanding to Lymbury.'

Bartholomew and Michael exchanged a glance. Was this yet another motive for murder?

'His soul will have to be satisfied with your daily prayers and a weekly mass from Dole,' decided Michael. 'Your chaplain may as well do something for the convent he serves, and I shall ask the Bishop to send him an official order. But Lymbury was miserly – ten marks could never cover the cost of eternal prayers.'

Christiana swallowed hard, touched. 'You are very understanding, Brother.'

'Your third problem is Pauline's refusal to chaperon Rose,' said Michael. 'That is disobedience, which runs contrary to the Rule of our Order. You are her superior, so where lies the problem?'

Christiana looked close to tears. 'If I order her about, she refuses to help me with the convent's administration. She is the only sister who can read, so it is important I keep on her good side. She says I am unfit to be prioress, and is always threatening to expose my failings to the Bishop – although he did know about my illiteracy when he appointed me.'

'She will do nothing of the kind,' said Michael. 'And *I* shall tell him you are above reproach, so that will be the end of the matter. Besides, you do not need her, because Dole can act as your scribe.'

'She told me men are not permitted to dabble in the affairs of nuns,' said Christiana miserably. 'She said it is written in the Rule of St Benedict.'

'She made it up to maintain her hold over you. However, if she does not obey your orders in the future, I shall arrange for *her* to be sent to Chatteris. But let us turn to your fourth problem: Rose. Why has she decided to leave? Is it because she is with child?'

Christiana gaped at him. 'How did you guess? She said no one else knows.'

'Who is the father?' asked Bartholomew. 'Lymbury?'

Christiana put her head in her hands. 'She said several men have enjoyed her favours. Her family brought her to us three years ago – they paid two months' keep, but we have had nothing since. I could not bring myself to force her out, but now I wish I had – she has brought shame on my priory.'

'Your charity does you credit,' said Michael. 'And it was wrong of Rose to have abused it. Will you summon her, and order her to answer our questions? Her liaisons may be relevant to unveiling Lymbury's killer.'

Christiana spotted Pauline, who was strolling up and down a cabbage patch with a hoe, although she was making no attempt to use it. The old nun opened her mouth to grumble when she was asked to run an errand, but did as she was told when Michael fixed her with a glare. Eventually, she returned with Rose. The younger woman's saffron hair was tucked decorously under her veil, and her loose robes concealed the tell-tale bulges Bartholomew had noticed the previous day.

'Anything else?' Pauline asked impertinently. 'These weeds will not hoe themselves.'

'Forget the weeds,' said Christiana with sudden spirit. 'Go to the kitchens and scour all the pans.'

'I certainly shall not,' said Pauline, regarding her as though she was insane. 'Cold water is bad for my joints. I shall stay out here, and if the sun comes out, I shall have a doze.'

'Did you say there are *several* vacancies for literate nuns at Chatteris, Brother?' asked Christiana, looking at Michael with wide blue eyes. 'And the Bishop is very keen to fill them?'

Michael nodded soberly. 'But no one wants to go, because of the rats – and its tyrannical prioress. The Bishop is always looking for victims . . . I mean candidates, and I have his ear.'

'You need me here, Mother Prioress,' said Pauline sharply. 'I am your *secretarius*.'

'I am to have another,' said Christiana sweetly. 'So your services are no longer required. However, Chatteris is—'

'I shall be in the kitchens,' said Pauline sullenly, hurling her hoe into the cabbages and moving away with a limp Bartholomew knew was contrived, 'scouring pans.'

Christiana allowed herself a smile of satisfaction, then turned to Rose. 'You said you are with child. When did you first realize you were in this predicament? This morning, when you confided in me?'

'I have known since the beginning of summer. I hoped Sir Elias Askyl might take me as his bride, but he has proven remarkably difficult to pin down. He leers and winks, but politely declines my favours when I catch him alone.'

'Perhaps he prefers Joan,' suggested Michael baldly. 'He leers and winks at her, too, and she is no penniless novice.'

'Perhaps he does,' acknowledged Rose with a resigned scowl. 'Despite the fact that she is ugly and I am beautiful. No one can deny that wealth is powerful asset.'

'If Askyl rejects your offers, then he is not the father of your child,' said Christiana. 'So who is?'

'I told you: I do not know. It might be James – a sweet boy, although inclined to fumble. It might be Chaplain Dole, who is a kinder man than his warrior friends. Hog comforted me one night when Sir Elias failed to arrive for a tryst. Then there are several villagers who are fine fellows . . .'

'Lord!' exclaimed Michael, regarding her with round eyes. 'Perhaps it would be quicker to give us a list of the men who have *not* lain with you.'

'Askyl,' supplied Bartholomew helpfully. 'And you did not mention Lymbury, Sister.'

'Sir Philip thought himself a great lover, but he was not very effective with his weaponry, if you take my meaning.'

'No,' said Michael, puzzled and intrigued. 'I do not.'

'Did Lymbury know about the child?' interrupted Bartholomew, not wanting Rose to go into those sort of details in front of Christiana. The poor woman was already pale with mortification.

Rose shook her head. 'I was going to tell him yesterday – I know he would have looked after us both. But the killer got there first.'

Christiana rubbed her eyes tiredly. 'I should eject you today. You have brought my priory into disrepute with your wanton behaviour. What will the Bishop say, when he hears one of my nuns is pregnant, and half the men in the county might be the father?'

'I am not a nun,' said Rose defiantly. 'And I never intended to become one. I escaped after vespers last night, to tell Sir Elias about my predicament – I thought it might melt his heart. But I could not find him – he was not at the manor-house. Neither was Joan. I hope they were not . . . together.'

'Askyl does wander about a lot,' said Christiana. 'He

307

was supposed to be hunting yesterday, but I saw him at the manor-house, arguing with Lymbury. I could not hear what they were saying, because I was too far away, but Lymbury had that horrible sword and was holding it in a very threatening manner.'

'When did this happen?' asked Michael.

Christiana shook her head. 'It was after everyone had gone hunting, because the house was otherwise deserted. I have a standing offer of free eggs, so I collected them from the hen-coop myself. Later, I came across James, who offered to carry them home for me.'

'James said he had met you,' said Michael. 'And we knew Lymbury had quarrelled with his friends, although we were not told that Askyl's most recent spat was when he claimed to be out hunting.'

'If Sir Elias had told you that, it would have been *asking* for everyone to accuse him of murder,' said Rose, defensive of the man she had a hankering for. 'So who can blame him for not telling you? But what will happen to me? My hopes of escorting him to the altar are fading – although I intend to persist until I know for certain my efforts are in vain – and I can hardly stay here.'

Michael was unsympathetic. 'Your predicament is generally known as the "wages of sin", madam. Perhaps I should ask the Bishop to send *you* to Chatteris.'

She gave a wan smile. 'I might go. It is better than being a vagrant, and there are handsome farmers near Chatteris, who might enjoy my company.'

Christiana grabbed her arm and marched her away, presumably to give her a lecture about morals that would be like water off a duck's back.

Bartholomew watched them go. 'Last night, Rose was my favourite suspect for Lymbury's murder, but I think she was right when she said he would have looked after her and her child. His death has put her in an awkward position, and I am inclined to believe she wishes he were still alive.'

Michael agreed. 'I do not think she is the killer, either. However, the man of her dreams – Askyl – did not tell us he had returned to the manor and argued with Lymbury, which in itself smacks of suspicion. Perhaps he would not make such a good husband after all.'

They turned at the sound of a shout. It was James, crimson-faced and panting furiously yet again.

'I think there is something wrong with him,' said Bartholomew. 'It is not normal for a young man to be red all the time – nor to gasp after a run. He works outside and should be fit.'

'Lady Joan asks if you will go to the hall,' the boy gulped. 'She says William the Vicar is dead.'

For the second time, Bartholomew knelt next to a corpse in Valence Manor. William lay in a pool of gore and had been stabbed in the back. From the size of the wound, Bartholomew suspected the vicar had been killed with the same sword as had Lymbury. A good deal of blood had splattered across the floor, covering such a large area that Bartholomew could only suppose that William had staggered around before succumbing to his injury. When he examined the priest's hands, they were red, but not excessively so.

'I think he grappled with his attacker,' he said to Michael. 'Probably trying to wrest away the weapon that killed him. The blood on his hands was transferred to him by the killer – it did not come directly from his wound, because he would not have been able to reach that high up his back.'

'Are you sure?' asked Michael, thinking it an odd conclusion to have drawn.

'Not really. I would have suggested you looked for

tell-tale stains on your suspects' hands, but the killer will have scrubbed them clean by now.'

'Just as you are about to do,' said Michael. 'Here comes James with the water you ordered.'

James had gone from red to white, and after he had delivered the jug to the physician, he stood close to his father, as though he expected Joan to accuse him of another crime. Joan was sitting next to Askyl, who was weeping softly, while Dole stood near the hearth, kicking the ashes with the toe of his boot. Hog sighed angrily when some scattered across the polished floor.

'Stop that, Father,' he barked. 'It takes a lot of work to keep the wood looking nice. And I have asked you before to remove your spurs when you come in here. The metal makes dents, and I have to file down the planks with a special chisel to remove them.' He waved the tool in a way that made Bartholomew suspect the bailiff would dearly like to plunge it into Dole's chest – or back.

'When did you last see William?' asked Michael, when Dole seemed ready to retort with a sharp comment that would antagonize the bailiff. He did not want to waste time with yet another spat.

Askyl raised a tear-stained face. 'After you went to the nunnery last night, William and I practised our swordplay in the yard. He used Lymbury's blade, and I had my own; Dole watched. Then William went to his house, and Dole and I stayed here, talking. When I woke this morning, I came downstairs to find . . .'

'William is cold and a little stiff,' said Bartholomew to Michael in the silence that followed the knight's faltering explanation. 'He probably did die during the night.'

'I have a house near Ickleton Priory,' said Dole, taking up the tale. 'I went there when I had finished chatting to Askyl, but I live on my own, so no one can vouch for me. And I left Askyl alone, so no one can vouch for him, either. I can only tell you that we do not murder comrades-in-arms. We did not kill Lymbury, and we did not kill William.'

'But you disliked William,' said Michael, regarding him intently. 'You bickered constantly.'

'I did dislike him,' admitted Dole. 'Lymbury should never have made him Ickleton's vicar. He had no vocation as a priest, and the villagers deserve better.'

'You *do* have a vocation?' asked Michael. 'Even though you hanker after Sister Rose, and would marry her in a trice, were she to show any interest in you? You may even be the father of her child.'

Dole regarded him contemptuously. 'I wondered how long it would be before accusations were levelled from that quarter. Yes, I admire Rose, and yes, I would have taken her as my wife, had she not been repelled by my injury. But it was not to be, and I only broke my vows with her once. I guessed she was with child, but the baby is unlikely to be mine. Others serviced her far more often than I.'

'It will not be my husband's, either,' said Joan spitefully. 'As Rose will tell you. Oh yes, I knew what they did when I went to visit my mother. But why do you think we have no children of our own? Everyone blames the woman for being barren in such situations, but Philip was married twice before and had mistresses aplenty. And not one has borne him a brat. That should tell you something.'

But Michael did not think Lymbury's ability to produce heirs was relevant to the murders. He returned to the matter of the vicar. 'William was going to read Lymbury's will today. Where is it?'

A search of William's clothing revealed no documents, so Askyl took Bartholomew and Michael to the priest's house, a small, pretty building on the edge of

Ickleton's oak-shaded churchyard. Askyl started in shock when he approached a cupboard in the wall near the fireplace. 'This is where he kept his valuables, but the lock has been smashed. Someone was here before us.'

'Someone *has* broken the lock,' acknowledged Michael. 'But there is a lot of jewellery here. A normal thief would have stolen that, so I conclude the burglar wanted one thing only: the will.'

'Why would the will be here?' asked Bartholomew. 'Why would Lymbury not keep it himself?'

Askyl rubbed his eyes tiredly. 'William always stored them for him. I think he believed no one would risk his soul by breaking in to a priest's house, and so they would be safer here.'

Bartholomew inspected the damage to the cupboard. 'Actually, the lock has not been smashed – it has been prised out of the door. Whoever did this did not strike blindly, but attacked with precision.'

'How curious,' said Michael, inspecting the marks the physician pointed out. He watched hopefully when Bartholomew leaned down to retrieve something from the floor, then grimaced his disappointment when it was tossed away. Whatever it was had been deemed irrelevant. He turned to the knight, who sat on a bench and made no attempt to wipe away the tears that streamed down his face. 'You were seen arguing with Lymbury yesterday – during the hunt. What about?'

Askyl sighed. 'About that damned sword. You see, I slipped back to the manor-house to escape from Rose and Joan. I happened across Lymbury, who was waiting for James to fetch William – to dictate his latest will. He said he intended to leave that sword to William, and I asked him to rethink.'

'Why?' asked Bartholomew. 'I thought you liked William – you are certainly more distressed by his death than you were about Lymbury's. Why should you object to him inheriting a fine weapon?'

'It brings unhappiness and shame,' explained Askyl unsteadily. 'And it has a wicked history, as Dole told you. I did not want William tainted with it.'

'Most men would be flattered by two women lusting after them,' said Michael, curious as to why the knight should have fled their attentions. 'One is pretty and the other is rich. It is quite a choice.'

'I do not think Rose is pretty, and I am not sure Joan will be rich once the will is read,' said Askyl with a sniff. 'I go through the motions, pretending to be honoured by their attentions, but I wish they would just leave me alone.'

'You prefer William,' said Bartholomew in sudden understanding. 'He is the reason you came to Ickleton. And you permit Rose and Joan to fawn over you in order to conceal your true feelings. Did William reciprocate?'

Askyl was ashen-faced. 'I suppose it does not matter now he is dead. Yes, William and I were close and I did use those two ridiculous women to conceal it. I do not know what I shall do now he is gone.'

'Were you telling the truth when you said William came home alone last night?' asked Bartholomew, once the knight had composed himself again.

Askyl nodded. 'I wanted him to stay with me after what had happened to Lymbury, but Dole was beginning to be suspicious, so we separated. The next time I saw William, he was dead.'

Bartholomew looked around the house thoughtfully, then pointed to a domed hat that lay on the table. 'He was wearing that yesterday, so I think he *did* come here after leaving you. Then he must have discovered someone had broken into his cupboard, and returned to the manor-house. Perhaps he confronted the thief and was killed.'

'I suppose Dole could have done it,' said Askyl, speaking with clear reluctance. 'After he and I had finished talking about . . .'

'About what?' demanded Michael, when the knight trailed off unhappily.

'About a man called Curterne. He was killed at Poitiers – stabbed in the back with his own sword. Dole and I discussed it, because it was the same weapon that killed Lymbury.'

Bartholomew frowned. 'Was Curterne killed by a Frenchman?'

Askyl chewed his bottom lip. 'I do not believe so. Lymbury, William, Dole and I saw him alive after the battle – he spent most of it under a hedge. It was cowardly, but not all men are suited to war.'

'I felt like hiding under a hedge at Poitiers myself,' admitted Bartholomew. 'But I did not do it. It would not have been right to let comrades fight alone.'

'Obviously someone else felt the same way,' said Askyl, 'because I am sure it was an Englishman who killed Curterne – all the enemy had been rounded up by the time he died. After, as William told you yesterday, when we found the sword in his corpse, we drew lots for it. Lymbury won.'

'Did Lymbury kill Curterne, then?'

'Possibly. I did not, and neither did William – William would have kept the sword if he had been the killer, since he really wanted to own it. I believe Curterne's killer was either Lymbury or Dole, although I have no evidence to prove it.'

'But *you* are still my main suspect for killing Lymbury,' said Michael, watching the knight begin to weep again. 'You lied to us about your whereabouts during the salient time, and innocent men do not fabricate.'

Askyl raised his tear-mottled face. 'You expect me to

admit, in front of all those people, that I was hiding from women? With Dole already suspicious of my fondness for William? I did not kill Lymbury, Brother. Why would I?'

'Because by making William a vicar, Lymbury ensured he would have to stay in Ickleton,' suggested Michael. 'It interfered with your relationship.'

'But Lymbury invited me to be his bailiff,' Askyl pointed out. 'I could have stayed, too.'

'Speaking of bailiffs, here is Hog,' said Bartholomew, glancing through the open door.

'James is ill,' said Hog, bursting into the house without invitation. 'You must come at once.'

James was lying on a bench in the manor-house, gasping for breath, his face as scarlet as the setting sun. Bartholomew mixed a potion he prescribed for choleric patients, along with a small dose of poppy syrup to calm him, then wiped the boy's burning skin with water-cooled cloths. Eventually, James's face returned to a more normal colour, and his breathing eased.

'He is young to suffer from a morbid excess of this particular humour,' said Bartholomew. 'Such an ailment is more common in older men.'

'His mother was the same,' said Hog brokenly. 'She died before her time.'

Bartholomew suspected James might, too, although nothing would be served by confiding the fact. He did not want the lad's last days to be tainted by fear.

'Have you learned who killed my husband yet?' asked Joan, fanning James with a cabbage leaf.

Michael shook his head. 'Not yet, but I am coming close.'

'It was William,' said Joan, fanning hard enough to make James flinch. 'Probably because he coveted that damned sword. Philip must have decided to leave it to

Sir Elias instead, so William murdered Philip before he could change his will to that end.'

'Then who killed William?' asked Bartholomew. 'Or do you think there are two murderers in Ickleton?'

Joan's voice was cold. 'If William murdered my husband, then he deserved to die – and I shall reward the brave man who dispatched him.'

Bartholomew regarded her thoughtfully. 'We know a lot about William's last movements. He practised his swordplay with Askyl, then went home. When he arrived, he discovered that someone had broken into the cupboard where he keeps his valuables and Lymbury's will had gone. I doubt he would have gone to bed after that, so he probably returned here.'

Michael nodded. 'He would have wanted to confront the thief and demand the will back.'

'That assumes he knew who the thief was,' said Hog.

'I think he did,' said Bartholomew. 'I certainly do.'

Everyone stared at him. 'How?' asked Hog eventually.

Bartholomew pointed to the floor, where grain had dropped from the bailiff's clothing onto the polished boards. 'You have been working in the fields, and corn has fallen into the folds of your tunic. There was corn in William's house, too, near his cupboard – I picked it up, but discarded it as irrelevant. But it was not. It proves you were in William's house last night, because no one else worked near corn yesterday.'

Hog regarded him uneasily. 'That is not true. The hunt went along some of the fields.'

'But they were on horseback. The grain came from someone walking among it. You.'

Hog was dismissive. 'That is ludicrous.'

'Whoever stole the will broke into William's cupboard with a specific kind of tool,' Bartholomew went on. 'Not a knife, but something with a flat end, like a chisel. You have one, because you brandished it at Dole when he walked on your polished floor in his spurs earlier. You used that chisel to break the lock in William's house – you did it when he was sparring with Askyl and Dole, knowing they were enjoying themselves and that you would have plenty of time.'

Hog's face was white. 'And why would I do that?'

'Does this mean Hog killed William and my husband, too?' demanded Joan, cutting across Bartholomew's reply. It was just as well, because the physician did not know why Hog should have stolen the will.

'No!' cried James from his bench. 'My father is not a killer.'

'No, he is not,' agreed Bartholomew gently. 'He is not even a proper thief – no self-respecting robber would have left all that jewellery untouched.'

Suddenly, the door crashed open, and Prioress Christiana marched in, pushing a subdued Dame Pauline before her. Rose had followed, her eyes bright with interest.

'I have just found *this*,' said Christiana furiously, waving an old, time-yellowed garment that was liberally splattered with blood. 'Dame Pauline was about to burn it.'

'Pauline is the killer?' asked Joan, her jaw dropping in shock.

'Of course not!' screeched Pauline, clearly frightened. 'I am a nun! I do not go around jabbing swords into the backs of men sitting in chairs as they count their money.'

'How do you know Lymbury was counting his money?' pounced Michael. 'Matt found a gold coin in his hand, but only he and I knew about that. Your innocence is looking shaky, madam.'

'Pauline may well have been present when Lymbury died,' said Bartholomew, watching the old woman flail

317

around for an answer. 'But she did not deliver the killing blow. That was James.'

Everyone turned to look at the ailing youth, who closed his eyes tightly, as if he could pretend none of them were there.

'That is a lie,' said Hog in a whisper. 'James is ill. He could not have killed Lymbury.'

'He was not ill yesterday,' said Bartholomew. 'He ran all over the manor looking for William to write the new will. And that is *his* tunic in the prioress's hand. The one he wears now is new, very clean and so white it dazzles in the sunlight – but what servant dons such a garment when there is so much work to be done in the fields? The truth is that James killed Lymbury, and his clothes were befouled with blood. Hog said James was too dim-witted to think of ridding himself of stained garments, but someone else was not.'

'I admit I helped him,' said Pauline in a wheedling voice. 'But only because he is a good boy, and I do not want to see him hang for a moment of silly temper.'

'James is not hot tempered,' said Bartholomew. 'He is soft and malleable. He is upset about the prospect of his father losing his post to Askyl – he loves Hog, and will do anything for him.'

Hog went to kneel next to the boy. 'Is it true?'

James nodded unhappily, his eyes still screwed closed. 'Dame Pauline said killing Lymbury would make your position safe. She gave me the sword and said no one would ever know it was me – she said everyone would think one of his friends had done it, because they are warlike.'

'Lies!' screeched Pauline, starting to move towards him. Bartholomew blocked her path.

'I did it for you,' whispered James to his father. 'Pauline said Lady Joan would inherit all his property, including the right to rent the manor from Michael-house, and all would be well again. You love Ickleton, and I do not want your heart broken by leaving it.'

Hog rested his hand on his son's forehead, then stood and faced Michael. 'He is rambling. *I* killed Lymbury. And last night, I went to William's house and stole the will. It is in my house – I hid it under the table. James has nothing to do with any of this. It was me.' He faltered, and gazed uncertainly at Pauline. 'Although I still do not understand why you ordered me to steal the will and hide it until later.'

Pauline licked dry lips. 'Do not listen to him, Brother. I did not tell either of them to do anything. Killing Lymbury would not have secured Hog's post, as any fool would know. Michaelhouse is now free to rent the manor to anyone it chooses, and Hog will be dismissed.'

Bartholomew saw James's stricken expression. 'But the boy did not know that. He believed you when you told him murder would save his father from unhappiness. You preyed on his gullibility.'

Pauline's expression was cold and disdainful. 'What do you know about what James thinks? Besides, you heard Hog. He admitted everything. He killed Lymbury. I did nothing – except burn . . .'

'Except burn *James's* tunic,' finished Michael. 'Which you would not have done if *Hog* had killed Lymbury. This murder is just as much your doing as the boy's. You were like a devil, sitting on his shoulder, whispering evil into his ear.'

'And it was all for selfishness,' added Bartholomew. 'You killed Lymbury so you would not have to play chaperon to Rose on any more hunts.'

'I hate riding,' said Pauline in a pitiful whine. 'It jolts my old joints, and I am often in agony for days afterwards. You are right in that I would do virtually anything to avoid riding – but not murder.'

Bartholomew did not believe her. 'You need not have troubled yourself. In a few weeks, she will not be able to go out into the woods anyway. She is pregnant.'

Pauline was more angry than shocked. She turned on Rose. 'You told me your heaviness was down to too much bread. You lied – and that made me take poor decisions. This is *your* fault!'

'Do not shirk responsibility,' said Michael sharply. 'Take her back to the convent, Prioress Christiana. I shall arrange for her transfer to Chatteris within the week.'

With a screech of outrage, Pauline launched herself at the monk. Bartholomew dived to intercept her, but she was faster than he anticipated and he missed. Joan drew the small knife she carried in her belt, and for a moment, Bartholomew thought she intended to stab the old nun as she hurtled past. But Joan hesitated, and suddenly, the dagger was in Pauline's gnarled fingers. Rose was made of sterner stuff, however. Calmly, she stretched out a foot as Pauline powered past, and the old woman went sprawling across the wooden floor, dagger skittering from her fingers.

'She was going to kill you, Brother,' said Hog in horror, hurrying to grab the weapon and return it to Joan. 'She is truly a fiend from Hell.'

'And I saved your life,' said Rose comfortably. 'So, you would not be sending *me* to Chatteris for disobedience, would you, Brother?'

Later that day, Bartholomew and Michael collected their horses and prepared to go home. There were four hours of daylight left, more than enough time to ride to Cambridge before the sun set. In Bartholomew's saddlebag was a chalice Lymbury had removed from a church near Poitiers, which Dole estimated was worth ten marks. Master Langelee could sell it to pay for the latrines, and the manor's debt to Michaelhouse would be discharged. The two scholars lingered, waiting for Joan to bring them a parcel of pastries to eat on the journey home.

'So, it was all Dame Pauline,' said Michael, rubbing his horse's neck. 'She disliked acting as chaperon to Rose and riding was becoming increasingly painful for her, so she decided to murder the lord of the manor so she would not have to do it again.'

'It does not sound very likely, does it?' said Bartholomew. 'A feeble motive for killing.'

'Perhaps to the likes of you and me, but Dame Pauline is a totally selfish creature, who will do anything for her own comfort. She was willing to see James or Hog hang for the crime she instigated – she cares for nothing and no one but herself.'

Bartholomew thought about how she had achieved her objective. 'So, during the hunt, she escaped from Rose – who had bribed her to doze under a tree anyway – and slunk back to the manor-house. There was young James, and there was Lymbury, counting his money. She played on James's fears and his loyalty to his father, by making him believe all would be well if Lymbury was dead. Then she persuaded Hog to steal Lymbury's will. Why did she do that, Brother? Did she hope *she* might be a beneficiary?'

'When I interviewed her, she admitted that she intended to forge a codicil that favoured the priory. She said she is obliged to eat too much bread and not enough meat, and wants better things in her old age. And then she intended to have Prioress Christiana dismissed for incompetence and herself put forward as a suitable replacement. As I said, Matt, she is wholly devoted to herself and her own wants and desires.'

'Did she kill William, too? I suppose she must have

done, so he would not tell anyone what was really in Lymbury's last testament.'

'When we recovered Lymbury's will from Hog's house, we found it was not as controversial as we were led to believe. He left the bulk of his estate to his wife, and gave his friends Dole, William and Askyl forty marks each. It is not a fortune, but it is a respectable declaration of friendship.'

'But if Joan dies childless, then Askyl is to have everything,' elaborated Bartholomew, who had also listened to the reading, 'on the grounds that William and Dole have received lucrative posts and Askyl has not yet had anything. Joan had better hurry up and bear a son, or we may be called to investigate another murder in Ickleton.'

'The priory will get nothing, though. I suppose Lymbury thought the ten marks he gave Christiana was sufficient.'

'But why did he give away money that belonged to Michaelhouse?' asked Bartholomew. 'It does not sound like something an orderly man would do – and Lymbury was orderly.'

'That was Pauline again. She persuaded him to donate the money to the priory immediately, and *she* wrote the letter to Michaelhouse. She denied it when we asked her, but she was not telling the truth.'

Bartholomew snapped his fingers. 'Of course she wrote it! It is obvious now. William was Lymbury's clerk, but he said *he* had scribed no letter to Michaelhouse, and there was no reason for him to lie. And because Lymbury could not read, he had no idea what Pauline had told us.'

'Precisely, Matt. Christiana told me that Pauline sometimes kept the records of Lymbury's dealings with the priory when Dole or William were unavailable. Also, I looked through Pauline's possessions once she was safely incarcerated in Christiana's cellar, and found an early draft – no doubt the one Lymbury had originally dictated to her. What he had actually asked her to write to us was a polite request for a delay until after the harvest, when the debt would be paid in full *with interest*. I think she changed the wording from spite.'

'Or perhaps she intended to keep the interest for herself,' suggested Bartholomew. He glanced at the monk. 'What will you tell the Sheriff about James? Unlike Dame Pauline, he cannot claim benefit of clergy. He will hang – although it seems unfair.'

'You said he will die soon anyway.'

Bartholomew nodded. 'You could tell your Bishop the story, and ask him to advise the Sheriff. He is not very efficient, and it will take him weeks to draw up the proper writs. And by then . . .'

'That is a devious solution, Matt. But it is one that has already occurred to me.'

Bartholomew dismounted. 'I am going to find out what is taking Joan so long. If we do not leave soon, we will be travelling in the dark, and that would be unwise with a silver chalice in our bags. It would be a pity to lose it, after all we have been through.'

He stepped into the solar, but stopped short when he saw Joan lying on Hog's beautifully polished floor. Askyl stood over her, Lymbury's sword clutched in both hands. When he saw the physician coming towards him, Askyl hurled the weapon at the hearth. Part of the hilt snapped off on the unyielding stone, and a carved dog-head from the cross bounced away under a bench. A distant part of Bartholomew's mind thought how William would have deplored the damage.

'What have you done?' he asked. 'Where is Rose?'

'Gone to the kitchens for a cloth to bind the wound,' said Askyl in a low voice. 'She is taking a long time. Dole has gone to fetch his Bible.'

Bartholomew moved forward cautiously. Joan was still alive, but barely. He heard Michael enter the hall behind him.

'I asked Sir Elias to marry me,' Joan whispered when the physician knelt next to her. 'Philip left me a small fortune, and I need a husband. But I wanted no secrets.'

Bartholomew caught one of her fluttering hands and saw blood on her sleeve. It was not her own, because it was dry. '*You* killed William?' he asked, grappling with the implications. 'I said he had struggled with his attacker – and that his killer would be stained with his blood.'

She started to cry. 'I killed William because I believed he had murdered Philip. You and the monk said he had good reason for doing so. But then you deduced that Pauline and James were the culprits. I told Elias about my mistake . . .'

'You told him you murdered the man he loved more than anyone in the world,' said Bartholomew softly. 'And he was not very understanding about it.'

But Joan was dead. There was a clatter of footsteps and Rose appeared, carrying a bowl of water and a bundle of rags.

'You are too late,' said Bartholomew.

'These are not for her,' said Rose shakily. 'They are for Sir Elias. After he struck Joan, he made the mistake of turning his back, and she stabbed him with that little dagger she carries. A soldier should have known better.'

Askyl crashed to the floor, and Bartholomew saw a bloody slit in his leather jerkin. 'I want only one thing now,' the knight gasped, pushing the physician away when he tried to inspect the injury. 'I want to marry Sister Rose.'

Bartholomew gaped at him, and so did Rose. 'Why?'

'Because it is the only way I can avenge myself on

the woman who murdered my dearest friend,' said Askyl hoarsely. 'Here is Dole at last, and he has brought Hog and Prioress Christiana with him. They will be witnesses to the rite he is about to perform.'

When Askyl smiled, his teeth were red, and Bartholomew knew the wound was beyond his medical skills. He shrugged helplessly when Rose raised hopeful eyes.

'You cannot do this,' said Michael, as Dole struggled into his vestments. 'It is a ceremony founded in spite and deceit.'

'It will give Rose a home, and her child a legal name,' argued Askyl softly. 'Joan died childless, and Lymbury's will stipulated that I will inherit under those conditions. And my last testament – which Dole has already written for me – says I will leave all to my wife. Rose will rent this manor from Michaelhouse, with your blessing, and Hog will continue to be her bailiff. What is spiteful and deceitful about that?'

Michael ignored the question. 'You cannot marry Rose here – this is not a church.'

'I shall ask the Bishop for special dispensation later,' said Dole. 'He will not deny a dying man's last request. And you are not an unkind man, Brother – you will not stop us.'

'Hurry, Dole,' whispered Askyl. 'My eyes grow dim.'

The chaplain gabbled through the ceremony at a furious lick, while Askyl's breathing grew more laboured as his lungs filled with blood. Rose cried when it was finished, and kissed his cold hand.

'And now I shall absolve you of your sins,' said Dole in a voice that cracked with emotion. 'But I wish to God none of this had happened.'

'I killed Curterne after Poitiers,' breathed Askyl, almost inaudibly. 'I did not do it because I wanted the sword, but because the sword had made him a coward.

I never intended Lymbury to find it, or for us four to draw lots to keep it. I was going to drop it in the nearest river, but I did not have time . . .'

'You did not have time because *I* suggested we search for Curterne's belongings when his corpse was discovered,' said Dole, self-disgust and bitterness strong in his voice. 'I thought his armour and purse might soften the news of his death for his family. But Lymbury found the sword and declared Curterne's family would have no need of such a weapon. We should never have let him convince us that keeping it was right. It was a shameful thing to have done.'

'Lymbury and William were stabbed in the back,' whispered Askyl with the last of his strength. 'And now the blade has led a knight to slaughter a woman. It is truly a Sword of Shame.'

III

Rose's child was born on a bitter January night. Prioress Christiana came to sit with her, Hog stood ready to run for the midwife should anything go wrong, and Dole whispered prayers for her safe delivery. Later, when the child lost the anonymity of babyhood, Hog liked to think the boy took after him.

The bailiff was content with his life, although he grieved for James, who had died quietly in his sleep just after the harvest had been gathered. Rose never meddled with his running of the estate, and since Michaelhouse always received prompt payments, their distant landlords did not interfere, either. The villagers were happier once the spectre of vengeful Frenchmen had been erased, and saluted strangers who rode through their parish.

Christiana received many piteous letters from Dame Pauline, begging to be allowed back because she was half-starved and constantly cold, but Christiana could not read, and her new secretary, Chaplain Dole, always told her the old nun was happy at Chatteris.

Dole baptized Rose's child Elias Askyl. The boy's mother wanted him to be a warrior, and return home loaded with the spoils of war, but Elias preferred ploughs to weapons, and showed no interest in the broken sword Rose kept hidden in a disused chimney. His son – also Elias, although he preferred the more refined 'Haskell' to Askyl – inherited his father's love of the land, but he paid a smith to repair the sword, although the job was poorly done and the weapon was never the same again. Rose died at a great age bemoaning the fact that she had sired a dynasty of farmers, and the sword was consigned to the chimney again.

Another Elias Haskell found it many years later, when he demolished the old manor house and built himself a larger, grander home. He polished it up and hung it over the fireplace, where it remained until a bitterly cold winter, when a stranger from the Globe Playhouse in Southwark, London arrived cold and weary at Valence Manor.

HISTORICAL NOTE

Michaelhouse was granted the hundred-acre Ickleton estate known as Valence Manor in 1349, and the rent was an important source of income for the College – it funded two fellowships and a chaplain. Joan and Philip Lymbury were lords of Lymburys Manor in the mid-fourteenth century.

Ickleton Priory, a house of Benedictine nuns, was founded in the 1150s. Prioress Alice Lacy was deposed by the Bishop of Ely in 1352, and her successor may have been Christiana Coleman, who was in post by 1361. Other nuns were Pauline de Gras, mentioned in a deed of the 1350s, and Rose Arsyk. William the Vicar was priest of St Mary's Ickleton after 1353, and the nuns' chaplain in 1378 was Geoffrey Dole. An Ickleton villager, who destroyed all the convent's deeds during the Peasants Revolt of 1381, was called James Hog.

The Battle of Poitiers was on 19 September 1356.

ACT FIVE

Ickleton, 1604

It was early afternoon but already the weather was closing in, so I was relieved to see the arrow-shaped spire of the church and a scatter of houses. The snow, which had been falling in a half-hearted fashion, was starting to come down in great wet gouts. I reined my horse in and took stock of the surroundings. What little I could see of the landscape stretched flat and lifeless beyond the confines of the village. Bare trees marked the lines of watercourses, before everything was swallowed up in the snowy haze.

My hired horse shook his head as if in doubt over the whole enterprise. The horse's name was Rounce. Rounce wasn't happy. Well, that made two of us. The extra sense which animals are said to possess probably told him that I wasn't comfortable in his company.

I glanced over my shoulder as if I might have been able to glimpse the city of Cambridge but, of course, it lay several miles behind me. If I turned round straightaway, I'd probably get back by nightfall – or I would have done in the absence of snow. Now the track would be growing obscure and I risked blundering into some fen. There were more ditches, rhines and fens in this part of the world than you could shake a stick at. In any case, I was reluctant to give up my quest.

I'd found the village of Ickleton, identifying it by the

arrow-like spire of the church. An old fellow who was a member of one of the university colleges had been very helpful, even if he turned out to be somewhat deaf so that I'd had to repeat my request several times. He told me that the Maskells were long-time inhabitants of Ickleton, a village to the south of the city. The kind old gent had even traced out the route on a scrap of paper. Finding the house called Valence should be the easy part. And at least I had come this far, although the journey had taken longer than I'd thought and I hadn't foreseen the change in the weather. My horse and I had started off on a cold, crisp morning with the sun burning fair in the sky. Now I was growing anxious about the return. But before I could turn round I had to reach my destination.

If only this damned snow would lift for a moment . . .

And, as if my thoughts had been overheard up above, it did lift when the wind dropped momentarily and the snow paused about its business. To my left was revealed a large house standing in isolation. Trees lined the sides of a track leading towards it. The house looked flat in the whitened air, as if cut from card. Instinctively I knew that this was the place I was looking for, the house called Valence. More cheerful now, I turned Rounce's head in the direction of the house. But the animal's gait altered within a few paces and I realized something was wrong.

I dismounted thankfully – getting off a horse is always a pleasure as far as I'm concerned – and lifted Rounce's front hoof, his left one. Sure enough, a stone was lodged there. I took off my gloves and tried prying it out with my fingers. But my hands were cold and clumsy, and the horse suddenly grew restive. Rather than attempting to get the stone out myself it would be much easier to lead him the short distance to the house I'd just glimpsed and let the stable-hand take care of him. Why, old Rounce might even be fed and watered there, and old Nick Revill receive some refreshment indoors.

While I was down at ground level I saw that I was having trouble with my own left foot. It wasn't so much that my shoes weren't watertight – nothing new there, I'm only a poor player who must wear his shoes to the bone – but that the copper buckle on the left one was loose. The buckle has no value but I like it because it is in the shape of a love-knot. Rather than risk the buckle falling off and getting lost, I detached it altogether and slipped it into the pocket of my doublet.

Taking Rounce by the bridle I paced towards the house. The view down here wasn't as good as it had been up on horseback, and the snow had started to fall again, but from what I was able to see it appeared a ramshackle sort of place. But I was glad to see smoke from a couple of chimneys mixing dirtily with the falling snow. There were people inside. There was warmth.

While I walked towards the gatehouse whose thatched roof poked above the wall, I ran through the reasons for my visit to the Maskell household, rather as if I was accounting for myself like an everyday hawker or pedlar.

Who are you?

Revill's the name, Nicholas Revill. I work at the Globe Playhouse in Southwark. That's in London. (*Pause*) I'm with the King's Men.

The King's Men!

(*Modestly*) That's right, the King's Men.

Sounds impressive.

Now – and not that I'd repeat this to anyone outside the trade or mystery of playing, you understand – it may be that the best thing about being part of the

King's Men was the *sound* of those words rather than their substance.

Soon after the arrival of James (the sixth in his native Scotland but the first of that name ever to rule over us in England), our playing company had been elevated from being mere Chamberlain's Men to being the King's. In truth, James the Scot wasn't very interested in the playhouse, unlike his predecessor, Elizabeth. James's consort, Queen Anne (hailing from Denmark), showed some taste for the theatre but her preference was for masques which, in my view, don't have much to do with real playing. Just about all we'd received as a mark of royal favour were four and half yards of red cloth each to make doublet and breeches for the coronation procession. That, and a couple of guineas for the whole company which scarcely covered the cost of getting our collective beards trimmed for the great day.

Don't be dazzled by titles when it comes to patrons, then, however elevated they are. What we want above all from these gentlemen – or ladies, since we're not particular – is a passionate interest in the theatre. And a deep purse. Or the other way round. As I say, we're not particular.

Which goes a little way towards explaining why I now found myself leading a hobbling horse up a snowy, tree-lined track towards a large, dilapidated house in the country. As you'll have guessed, the time now was the middle of winter. But I'd been visiting Cambridge to discuss the possibility of the King's Men doing a tour the next summer. Summer is the season when playing companies go on the road. It's good to get away from the stench and heat of London, for all that it's the finest city in the world. It's good to bring the gift of our playing to different towns and parishes in the kingdom when people are in holiday mood. And, more practically, the roads aren't so passable the rest of the year.

We'd played Oxford before but never Cambridge. University towns are tricky places. They're stuffed full of people who consider themselves to be clever. These clever people can be sniffy about 'uneducated' players, even if, in my opinion, our principal playwright, William Shakespeare, is cleverer and more witty than a whole college-full of students. In addition, the authorities sometimes take a dim view of players as likely to foment trouble. At least it had been so when we visited Oxford in the year of Queen Elizabeth's death. But I enjoyed a warmer reception in Cambridge, where various civic worthies assured me that they'd be delighted to receive the King's Men the following summer.

So this was my business, entrusted to me by the Burbage brothers, Richard and Cuthbert, and the other shareholders who ran the Globe. Or part of my business. The other was to call on the people who lived in the house now looming through the snow. Like all playing companies, however humble or grand, we are quite happy to stage private performances as well as public ones. I had no idea why the Maskell family wanted us to perform in their house next summer, but the usual reason for a private show is to celebrate a wedding. We've done a few of those in our time, marking forthcoming nuptials with dramas such as *A Midsummer Night's Dream* or *Romeo and Juliet* (though the last one's a bit of an oddity if you're planning on a long and happy union). What the shareholders wanted to know was whether there would be adequate playing space for us in this house. From the outside the place didn't look very promising. I visualized an old-fashioned hall with a low ceiling, full of draughts in winter and stifling airs in summer. Still, as long as it didn't fall down about our ears while we were mouthing our lines, it would do. And even if it did fall down, we'd probably be able to stage something in the grounds.

By now I'd reached the gatehouse. This wasn't much more than a blocky swelling in the wall, with a couple of pinched windows set above an arched, gated entrance. The arch was wide and high enough to drive a cart through, with a postern-like door set into the larger wooden gate. A wisp of smoke fluttered from the gatehouse chimney. With Rounce breathing down my neck, I raised my hand to rap on the little door. To my surprise the door opened before I could bring my fist down. A young fellow with jug ears stuck his head out. He looked at me without surprise. It was almost as if I'd been expected, an impression reinforced by his first words.

'Another one,' he said. He peered more closely at me, while the snow flakes swirled between us. If his first words had been odd enough, his next were totally inexplicable.

'Though I can't say as you've got the nose.'

'Pardon?'

'The nose. You haven't got it.'

'Perhaps it's fallen off in this cold,' I said, resisting the temptation – which was quite a strong one – to reach up and check that my nose was still attached to my face. 'Is this Valence House?'

The jug-eared boy nodded as he continued to inspect my face. Maybe they had people turning up every quarter of an hour, even on a winter's afternoon, to present their noses for inspection. If I hadn't been so taken aback I might have felt that jug-ears was being insolent or playing a joke. With some reluctance, I was about to account for myself when he stepped away from the little door and disappeared. There was the sound of bolts and bars being withdrawn, and the large gate slowly swung open. It gave a view onto a snow-covered courtyard.

I led the hobbling Rounce through the deep archway. A door pierced it on the right-hand side. The door was open. Smells of smoke and cooking crept out and I remembered I'd eaten nothing since breakfast. A man appeared in the doorway. He stretched out his arm and collared the youth, who was standing to one side to let me through. He yanked the boy towards him and cuffed him on the side of the head. The boy yelped like a dog when you tread on its tail.

'That'll learn you to show some respect for your betters, Davey,' said the man. 'I heard every word about noses.'

It was easy to see that the man was the lad's dad. For one thing they had the same protuberant ears. Still angry, he spun Davey round and made to boot him in the rear. Without thinking, I put out a hand to restrain him. The man looked at me but lowered his foot. Rounce grew uneasy and started shifting behind me. I was growing uneasy too. What was this place? A madhouse, a Cambridgeshire bedlam, where people were obsessed with noses?

'Leave him be. The boy meant no harm, I'm sure,' I said, slightly fearful of what the man might do next and wondering how I might make my excuses and leave this place. In fact, if the snow hadn't been coming down more heavily now and if Rounce hadn't been limping, I might have turned tail with my horse and made my way back to Cambridge, mission unaccomplished. If only I had done just that thing, I would have saved myself from a great deal of discomfort – to say nothing of danger.

'Meant no harm? You don't know him,' said the man, watching as his son slunk inside the little gatehouse with a puzzled glance in my direction.

'I don't know him, true, but then I don't know anyone here,' I said.

The man – the porter or lodge-keeper, I suppose – looked slightly askance at this, as if I ought to be familiar with at least some of the inhabitants of Valence House. He didn't ask my business, though.

'My horse needs attention,' I said. 'He has a stone in his hoof.'

'Girl'll take you to the stables.'

He turned his head and bellowed into the interior. A large girl emerged, another of this man's brood, I guessed, although she had a pig-like cast to her countenance with little red eyes and a narrow mouth. The smell of cooking clung to her ample frame. She went up to Rounce, stroked his nose and took the reins from me.

Without a word, she led me and the hobbling horse into the large quadrangle that fronted the house. There were low-lying thatched outbuildings on either side. The impression of neglect hung over the whole place. The gusting snow stung my face and my shoes were leaking.

'What's your name?' I said.

'What's yours instead?'

'Nick Revill. I'm a player.'

'Do you play the fool?'

'I've never played the Fool – never on stage, I mean.'

'They are all fools that come here.'

The conversation was more than I'd bargained for. By this time we'd reached a broken-down outbuilding to one side of the house. The girl gave a shrill whistle and a shambling young man emerged from the dilapidated structure. A hank of pale hair hung over one eye like the forelock on a horse. He grinned vacuously, before saying, 'Why, it's Meg.'

'Horse, Andrew. Take care of him.'

'I'd rather take care of you.'

Meg giggled.

'My horse has a –' I started to say, but the shambling youth took Rounce by the reins and led him inside the stables, looking over his shoulder at the girl. Meg hesitated, then indicated with a wave of a podgy hand that I should go to the main entrance of the house. She followed the stable-hand inside.

I felt at a distinct disadvantage, having been put in my place in different ways by the lodge-keeper and by his boy and his girl, and now by the stable-hand who'd scarcely so much as glanced at me. So much for hoping to impress these people with my provenance as one of the King's Men. If the retainers of the Maskell household were able to treat visitors like this, then what would the actual residents be capable of? And my business here was, or should be, so straightforward. It was merely to establish that the house would provide a suitable playing area for the King's Men next summer. But my most immediate concern now was to get out of the cold.

I walked back to the main door which was sheltered by an ornate porch that looked more recent than the rest of this section of the house. I half expected my approach to have been spied on and the door to be flung open before I could rap on it. But nobody was watching or waiting on the other side. There was a great knocker on the door, but it was swathed in cloth to muffle its sound, the usual sign of sickness in a dwelling. I raised the knocker and let it fall with a dull clack. After a time the door opened to reveal a stoutish, middle-aged man wearing a grey-white cap.

'Come in,' he said.

He spoke wearily. Was he a servant too? He didn't look like one. I went in and he shut the door firmly behind me.

Inside, it wasn't quite as I'd visualized it. A sizeable, old-fashioned chamber, panelled, yes, but with a high ceiling and a gallery at one end, reached by a flight of stairs. From the actor's point of view, and at first glance, it would do well. A large dining table was set to one side of the hall. There was a welcoming fire in a chimney-piece opposite to the front door and a few tapers had been lit to ward off the growing gloom of the afternoon. Another man was standing by the fire, leaning against the carved chimney-piece. There was a woman sitting in a chair nearby. None of them said anything but all three looked at me with curiosity and, I thought, a touch of wariness. Back in London I'd been told that the head of the household was called Roger Maskell – and one of the Globe shareholders added that he had the reputation of being a jovial old fellow. Neither of the two men here fitted that description. For one thing, they didn't have enough years on them.

'Nicholas Revill at your service,' I said, dipping my head slightly and feeling that they needed a lesson in manners. 'I'm the player.'

'Player? The *player*?' said the woman in the chair. She did not speak with recognition but rather with bemusement.

'From the King's Men. Of London.' I put a tiny emphasis on *King's* but to no effect. To look at the expressions on the faces of these three I might as well have dropped down from the moon.

'You're here to see Elias?' said the one who'd opened the door to me. He had moved across to stand by the woman, holding the back of the chair where she sat. Now my eyes were more accustomed to the light indoors, I noticed that what I'd taken for a greyish cap was in fact his natural hair but cut very short and fitting as snugly to his head as a baby's caul. While I was wondering who Elias was – for he certainly couldn't be the Roger Maskell I'd been told of – the individual by the chair said, 'You're here to see the old man?'

'I suppose so,' I said.

As if this was a cue in a play, it was an old man that now entered the room by a side door. He was clutching a stick and shuffling along with an odd sideways gait. Somehow sensing a newcomer, he steered himself in my direction. The others watched as he approached. When he was a few feet away, he halted and peered at me through the spectacles perched on the tip of his long nose. He was very thin and stringy, as if he was already rehearsing himself for death. Presumably this was old Elias. I did my best to smile. I went through the motions of introducing myself all over again although without adding the 'King's Men' bit. In response the old man cupped his hand to his ear and said, 'Revill?' as if I was some strange species of animal.

'You won't get anywhere with him,' said the man standing by the fire. It was the first time he'd spoken. I wasn't sure whether he was addressing me or the old man. The remark would have fitted either of us. The bespectacled individual continued to stare at me, like the boy at the gate. I decided that this wasn't Elias after all. For two pence, I would have turned on my heels and made my way back to Cambridge, leaving my horse behind and going on foot if necessary. But a growing impatience – even anger – at the manner in which I was being treated made me stay. And say what I said next.

'Look, I don't know what you imagine my business to be. But I have been given a task to do on behalf of my company of players and I would like to talk to the head of this household. Then I'll leave you to your own devices. Happily leave you.'

Now it was the woman's turn to intervene. She got up from her seat near the fire. 'I'll take you to Elias,' she said.

As she rose I saw that she was younger than I'd first thought. I followed her to the foot of the stairs that led to the gallery, assuming we were going to go up there. Instead she picked up a taper from a small table and made to turn a corner that led into the depths of the house. I put out a hand to detain her.

'Madam, I . . .' I began.

'Not yet.'

She nodded in the direction of the hall. I looked back. The three men were in the same positions: one leaning against the chimney-piece, the stout individual still clutching the back of the chair even though it was empty, and the old one with the stick and spectacles stooped in the middle of the hall. The stout one said something like 'Give our greetings to Master Grant', but since the remark made no sense to me and I was unsure whether I'd heard him properly, I didn't respond.

The woman and I walked down a passage and came to a kind of lobby where the taper's uncertain light showed a couple of doors.

'Elias is in that room,' she said, gesturing with the hand that held the candle. She spoke in a whisper. I lowered my head in case she was going to say anything else but she remained silent. I remembered the muffled knocker on the door.

'Is he sick?' I said.

'Sick enough,' she said, then added under her breath, 'And like to die, they hope.'

They? She must have meant the three men out in the hall. I grew even more uncomfortable.

'Then there's not much point in seeing him . . .' I said, '. . . if he is so ill . . . I really wouldn't want to disturb him . . . I have come only to convey my share-holders' respects and to enquire if the master of the house has any preference for the play which he would like us to perform here next summer.'

'Play?' she said.

'Yes,' I said. 'Play. The King's Men can do things at the last moment of course. We're very good at last moment things. Though all in all, and taking the rough with the smooth, it's best to know in advance what the patron requires. That way we can ensure we have everything we need before we set off from London.'

I was babbling away like this, in a half whisper and scarcely aware of what I was saying, because I had a growing sense that something was terribly wrong.

'Elias likes plays,' she said after a pause, 'but I do not know of any performance next summer. Indeed I am surprised that he should be thinking so far ahead. A performance in *this* house?'

'Madam,' I said, 'you have me altogether at a disadvantage. I have come here on the understanding that Mr Maskell wants us to stage a drama for himself and his, er, family next summer. Mr Roger Maskell. For a wedding perhaps. A private performance is often desired at a wedding.'

'Maskell?'

'Yes, Maskell.'

She laughed, a low sound, quite an attractive one, but my guts did a little dance to hear it.

'Why, we are all *Haskells* in Valence House. I am a Haskell too. There are no Maskells here though I believe there is a family of that name on the other side of Cambridge. You have taken a wrong turning. You have come to the wrong house, Master Revill.'

Somehow the fact that she'd got my name right after hearing it only once made my blunder even more humiliating. Of little use to complain that I'd been directed here by that helpful fellow from one of the university colleges. Too late I remembered that he'd been somewhat hard of hearing and that I'd had to bellow the name in his ear. He must have misheard me when I asked for the whereabouts of the house and family. Had picked up *Haskell* and not Maskell. Told me they lived in Ickleton, south of Cambridge. Even drew a chart of how to get here, which I followed faithfully. Nobody's fault but my own. I was glad of the near-darkness of this lobby. I went red in the face and started to sweat.

Fool, Revill! Twenty times over, fool!

How my company would laugh if they ever got to hear of this misadventure (which they wouldn't, I determined there and then). I must leave the Haskell home straightaway, ride or walk back to Cambridge through the dark and snow, find the whereabouts of the *Maskell* dwelling and conclude my business there tomorrow.

But my business here was by no means done.

I don't know whether it was the conspiratorial way we'd been keeping our voices down, or the fact that the Haskell woman was quite a lot younger and more attractive than I'd first taken her for, or the general strangeness of the whole situation, but the next thing I found myself saying was: 'What do you mean, they hope he's like to die? Who are they? Who is Elias? Who are *you*?'

These questions were a bit direct, perhaps. But then I'd blundered in so deeply by now that a bit of outright curiosity hardly counted.

'I am Martha Haskell,' she said. 'Elias is my uncle and the head of this house. My father was his younger brother. The men downstairs are part of the family too, distant cousins.'

'They are here because they think your uncle is . . . dying?'

Again she laughed that low, fetching laugh. Was she heartless? I didn't think so, instinctively I didn't think so.

'Elias has always been a mischievous man. My uncle

is not well, there is no doubt about it. But he has played this game before. About three years ago, it was put abroad that he was on his death-bed and the cousins flocked here like so many carrion birds. He wanted to see who came to curry favour and was pleased at the expressions on their faces when he recovered. They brought gifts as tokens – of course they couldn't ask for them to be returned afterwards. Some of them even altered their wills in his favour, hoping to outlive him by many years.'

'Has the gentleman no wife?'

'She is long since dead.'

'No children?'

'No children,' she repeated.

'You mentioned your father just now. What about him?'

'All dead and gone. I am the closest in blood to Elias.'

'Well then . . . ?'

What I meant was that she should surely be the one to inherit this ramshackle estate when Elias Haskell decided to stop his games and die for good. But considering that Martha and I had only met a few minutes earlier and that I'd already shown a deal of curiosity, this might be a step too far even though we were still talking by conspiratorial candlelight.

At once there came a voice from within the chamber which she'd identified as Elias's. The voice was thin and querulous but penetrating.

'You've been whispering out there long enough. I can recognize your tones, Martha, but who's that with you?'

'You'll have to go in and see him now, Nicholas Revill,' she said. 'Explain how you confused your Maskells and your Haskells. He might be amused.'

She didn't sound very hopeful of this last proposition.

But it was the least I could do, for her if not for the individual who lay beyond the door. Besides I was curious to meet this mischievous person who exaggerated his illness in order to tease his would-be heirs. It was the kind of far-fetched thing which might happen in a play.

She put her free hand on my arm and directed me to open the door. I crossed the threshold. The first thing that struck me about the room was the smell, a kind of warm, musty smell, as of a place which has been long occupied and rarely aired. By now my eyes were adjusted to the indoor gloom, even though there was little light inside the chamber.

A fire slumbered under another ornate chimney-piece. The chamber was full of furniture: chests, tables, an old coffer-seat, and other items piled into dark corners. There must have been a window in the facing wall but heavy curtains shut out the winter evening. Everything looked old and fusty. The largest and fustiest item was a great bed with bulbous foot-posts supporting the tester overhead. Under an ornate coverlet was a figure half sitting, half lying, propped against a mound of pillows. A large woman wearing a brown overdress was leaning in a familiar manner against the bed, wrestling with the pillows. I was surprised to see two people in the room, since I hadn't hear any sound of conversation from outside. I halted some way from the bed, the momentary sense of conspiracy which Martha and I had enjoyed now gone.

Elias Haskell waved a stringy arm at the woman, who was kneading his pillows with her powerful hands. 'That's enough, Abigail. I am quite comfortable.'

'Thank you, Abigail,' said Martha.

The woman did not go immediately but delayed to fiddle with some items, a bowl and a few stoppered bottles, which were disposed on a table by the side of the bed. She scowled at me as she passed.

When the servant had left the room, Martha Haskell said, 'Uncle, here is someone come to see you,'

Elias was wearing a white night-cap. His eyes were dark pools in a long-nosed face. All of this was fairly plain to see, for a pair of candles were burning in the recesses at either side of an intricately carved head-board. The whole scene made me think of a shrine or a tomb.

'What have you brought me?' he said.

'Nothing.'

'Nothing will come of nothing.'

'I expect nothing, sir,' I said, 'since I find myself here under . . . false pretences.'

'At least you admit it.'

The voice might have been thin but the mind behind it was sharp. Elias Haskell looked unwell but he did not have the appearance of someone on the verge of death.

'This is Nicholas Revill, uncle,' said Martha. 'He's a player. He took the wrong turning.'

Swiftly she explained the circumstances by which I'd arrived at the Haskell rather than the Maskell house-hold. It made me appear foolish all over again, but I suppose I deserved it at least once more. I looked around the room in my discomfiture and moved nearer to the fireplace. I noticed that a large H, wreathed with fruits and foliage, was the central ornament in the chimney carvings. H for Haskell, presumably. Above the fireplace a great sword was displayed, while on either side of it there hung a tapestry. One tapestry depicted Judith holding up the decapitated head of Holofernes, while the other showed St Christopher carrying the Christ child on his back across the river. I looked towards the bed to see Elias smiling slightly.

'A player, eh?' he said. 'I remember the old London playhouses. I remember the Red Lion.'

'Before my time, sir,' I said, but warming to him on account of his knowledge.

'A player makes a change from the usual visitors.'

His tone was more welcoming than that of the other men in the household. Now I smiled back, in gratitude and to show that I bore him no ill will because he knew of my blunder. I felt more at ease. Someone touched my right knee. For an instant I thought it was Martha and wondered why she was stooping. I looked down. And almost threw myself into the open fire, in fear and surprise. As it was I found myself jammed up against the chimney-piece and holding out my hands to ward off any attack.

Crouched on the floor nearby and looking up at me was a wrinkled child. No, not a child, but a horrible, diminutive old man, with long arms and a bare head and great eyes.

But it was neither a child nor an old man. Rather it was a creature, one of which I had often heard but seen on only a single occasion. The beast wasn't in the menagerie of the Tower, as you might expect, but in the company of a sailor on one of London's wharfs. They'd appeared to be good friends, the sailor and his creature. So, after the first shock had subsided, I instinctively recognized this specimen for what it was.

'You've taken his place by the fire,' said Elias Haskell.

I couldn't reply straightaway, I was still shaken, but I noticed that he was smiling more broadly now. Even Martha seemed amused.

'Grant does not like the fire,' she said, 'because he singed his fur one day. But he thinks that the place in front of the fire is rightfully his. He resents anyone who stands where you're standing.'

Grant? Hadn't the stout man in the hall told me to

convey their greetings to just such an individual? Who would have thought that Master Grant would turn out to be a monkey. I'd wondered at the gatehouse whether I was entering some private bedlam. It had been an idle thought. Now I began to consider whether I really had wandered into a madhouse. Either that or I was dreaming.

'Where does he come from?' I said for the sake of saying something. I continued to eye the monkey while he continued to gaze on me with his large eyes. He was crouched on his hind legs and with his forelegs – or arms, I suppose – scraping the floor. I was afraid that he might take it into his large, furrowed brow to leap up at me and fling his hairy arms around my neck. That was how I'd seen the sailor carrying his monkey on the London wharf, the man striding along, his face all brown and creased, with the beast clinging round his neck like a wizened child. They'd looked alike, the sailor-man and the monkey. I realized now where the musty smell in the room came from. It wasn't so much the sick man in his bed or the unaired state of the chamber. It was this brown creature that crouched underfoot.

'Grant came from Africa,' said Elias. 'He belonged to one of the fellows at a college in Cambridge, though I do not know how *he* came by him. The fellow was called Grant too. When the man died he left me the monkey.'

'In God's name, why?' I said.

'Because I once said to him that the creature had more sense in his head than a whole tribe of humans. Not just more sense but he is better-natured too. Grant the man was glad that I approved of Grant the monkey, while I was glad to take the monkey when his owner died. See what he can do.'

I turned aside to look, relieved that the monkey had

shifted his ground. He was waving his arms above a pair of upturned pots set in a clear space on the rush-and herb-strewn floor. The pots were small, such as you might keep trinkets in. When he was sure I was watching him, he lifted up one of the pots. Nothing there. He lifted the other. Something glinted dully. I craned forward. It looked familiar. It was familiar. My hand flew to my doublet pocket. The copper buckle I'd removed from my shoe in case it was lost in the snow, the buckle in the shape of a love-knot, was gone. Whether it had fallen out or whether this monkey had somehow picked my pocket, I didn't know, or care. I made to retrieve my property. At once, Grant started gibbering angrily and shifting on his haunches.

'It's his game,' said Elias Haskell. 'Let him be.'

I stood back, in a state that wasn't amusement or anger or amazement, but some mixture of all three.

The monkey lumbered round so that he was hunched between me and the two pots. His long arms fiddled with the pots, sliding them around the floor. I knew what he was doing of course. I've seen similar tricks played by the coney-catchers on the London streets. So have you, I expect. Admittedly, the tricks are usually played out with three containers rather than two, but we must give the monkey some leeway. The coney-catcher waits for a country bumpkin to come along. He bets the bumpkin that he won't be able to locate some small item hidden under one of three upturned goblets or coconut shells which are then shifted rapidly around. The bumpkin wins on the first couple of occasions and that encourages him to wager heavily on the third. Surprisingly, that's the time he loses.

I've seen this trick performed on the Southwark streets by all manner of humans but I've never seen it carried out by a monkey. As it happened, the monkey wasn't quite as adept as his human counterparts and I was able to glimpse which pot my buckle was secreted under as he shuffled them about. When he'd finished I pointed to that one. The mischievous beast deliberately lifted the other. Martha laughed. I felt annoyed, with her, with Grant the monkey, with myself. Fearing this might go on all night, I looked in despair at Elias Haskell.

The old man said, 'I know what you're thinking, player. But Grant does not outstay his welcome, unlike human beings. See.'

Elias snapped his thin fingers. The monkey swivelled his head towards the sound and then abandoned his upturned pots. He moved across the room with a queer, lolloping gait, like a man who can't quite decide whether he's going to walk or to crawl. In a dark corner on the far side of the chamber, I now saw, there stood a kind of large cage made out of wooden slats. The monkey called Grant entered the cage and pulled the door to after him. It was like a prisoner returning to his cell. Before he could think better of it, I picked up my copper buckle and put it back in my doublet.

'Have you had any refreshment since you arrived?' said the man in the bed, and then without waiting for a reply, 'I thought not. Those carrion in the hall are too busy watching and waiting to be hospitable. Martha, bring our player-guest a beer.'

The girl had all this while been watching the monkey and his tricks with indulgence. Now, uncomplaining, she left the room. Elias Haskell indicated a covered chest which was positioned near the bed. I sat down on it. No longer caring whether I appeared inquisitive, I cast my eyes over the sick man.

'Well, player, do I look the part?'

'I am not sure what part you mean, Mr Haskell.'

'I heard you and my niece talking outside the door.

She doesn't approve of my little games, as she calls them. I expect she told you I was shamming illness to torment the carrion in the other room.'

By carrion, he meant the three men whom I'd encountered in the hall. It seemed strange that he should refer to his cousins as carrion birds. But I suppose that a man who keeps a monkey as a pet may well regard his fellow men strangely, whether they are kin or not.

'Your niece said nothing about shamming.'

And, indeed, now that I was looking at him more closely there was something hectic about the old man's face. The skin on his high forehead was as wrinkled as parchment or the monkey's brow. His eyes were murky pools but with a glint of mischief – or malice – at the bottom of them.

'Nor am I altogether shamming, Nicholas Revill. Even so my death is not to be as imminent as they hope. I'll send them home with their tails between their legs, like whipped curs!'

From carrion to curs. I suppose I must have looked baffled or taken aback at the force of his words, despite the thin tones in which they were delivered, for he went on: 'You wonder why I bother to torment the carrion. But I don't torment them, player. They torment themselves, the crow and the raven and the vulture. They come flocking here because they fear that they will miss out on all the juicy pickings. They're almost more frightened of each other than they are greedy for themselves. That's my name for them, crow, raven and vulture – it suits their function, you see. Oh, I almost forgot the woodcock. Mustn't forget the woodcock. They are very stupid birds, woodcocks.'

He watched to see how I was taking this information. The light from the candles in the recesses of the headboard glinted off Elias's parchment-skin and now I wondered whether he was actually sicker than he supposed, sicker in mind rather than in body. But he followed this with a remark that showed he was in full possession of his faculties.

'Don't look at me so askance, Nicholas. *You* have your audience as a player just as I have mine. Both audiences must be tantalized.'

'Our audiences are tantalized by arrangement,' I said, stung by the comparison. 'And they don't go home with their tails between their legs. They go home cheerful, or thoughtful – or both.'

'The Haskells are a very old family,' said Elias, ignoring my words. 'It is generally believed that old families must be rich, especially when they've been reduced to the nub. Martha and I are the nub. Crow and vulture and so on, the carrion cousins, certainly believe it is so. Rich, ha!'

There was the sound of the door opening and Martha Haskell returned, bearing a mug of beer which she handed to me. Gratefully I took a draught from the mug. It was the first drink I'd had since setting out from Cambridge that morning.

'Master Revill will have to stay the night, uncle,' said Martha. 'The snow is coming down good and hard now. The road to town would be difficult enough to find by day.'

'Then he shall stay,' said Elias. 'He can be entertained by our guests. I'll be interested to know what he makes of them. Come and talk to me again after supper, Nicholas. Let him have a room on the upper floor of the house, Martha. Go now. I am tired. No doubt I shall have a parade of cousins coming to bid me goodnight.'

Elias fell back on the pillows and shut his eyes. Martha led the way from the chamber, taper in hand. The large servant woman who'd been struggling with the pillows was standing outside.

'My uncle is very tired, Abigail,' said Martha. 'I do not think anyone else should be admitted to see him for the time being.'

The woman was like a sentry. I said as much to Martha when we were out of earshot.

'Abigail is fierce in guarding Elias. We have few servants in this house, in fact only Abigail as housekeeper and one of the Parsons in the kitchen.'

'Parsons?'

'Oh, that is the family in the gate-house.'

We went down another passage and turned a corner.

'You are thinking this is a large house for so few people?' said Martha, reading my mind over her shoulder.

'It's like being in a maze,' I said.

'The Haskells were a great family once, with many limbs and branches. But now only my uncle and I are left. And all our cousins.'

We came to a cramped flight of stairs. We climbed them and arrived at a low door. Martha lifted the latch and it opened with a creak. Inside was a small and stoop-ceilinged room. She held the taper up. There was a plain bed in a corner and a squinty little casement window.

'I will tell the housekeeper to bring some more blankets,' said Martha. She bent down and touched the taper to another candle which was set in a grease-pan on the floor.

'I'm used enough to the cold,' I said.

'Cambridgeshire has its own special cold,' she said. 'The wind and snow come straight from Muscovy, they say.'

'You should see my lodgings in London – feel them rather – for a taste of true cold and damp.'

'You are not a householder, Master Revill?' she said.

'Why no, a lodger still.'

She seemed to be about to ask something further, perhaps whether I was married and had children (the answer was no to both), but instead she said, 'I've never been to London.'

'You ought to visit us. It is a great city.'

'My uncle needs me here. He gets fretful if I am away even for half a day. I have lived here since my father died.'

'You're a very devoted niece.'

'He has his odd ways but he is a good man,' she said. 'You have no bags with you, Master Revill?'

'Do not be so formal but call me Nicholas. I didn't expect to be staying the night, whether with the Maskells or the Haskells. I set out before the snow came down, thinking to get here and back in a day. All I have with me is a letter of introduction from the shareholders. My gear is at an inn in Cambridge.'

'I shall ask Abigail to find you a night-gown also. There is everything hidden in this place if you know where to look.'

'Is that why the cousins are here? Do they believe there is hidden treasure?'

'Probably,' she said. 'I must go attend to the supper arrangements, Nicholas. Come downstairs when it pleases you.'

'Wait,' I said. 'What reason are we to give for my visit here? You're not going to tell the story of my . . . blunder, are you? How I mistook the Haskells for the Maskells.'

It was strange but if she'd said that she was going to repeat my foolishness once more round the supper table, then I think I'd have taken my chances with the snow and the darkness and the fens and the rhines beyond the door. Death before humiliation.

'Don't worry, Nicholas,' she said. 'I shall think up some excuse for your presence. After all, everyone else is here on false pretences.'

And with that she exited the room. I moved a couple of paces to the window (those two paces being about the width of the room) and wiped at one of the panes to peer outside. The glass was thick and distorted the view. As far as I could see we'd come in a circuit in our journey through the house, and I was now peering out of a room somewhere above the front door. The snow was coming down so thickly that it was impossible to discern much but I was looking at the courtyard and the little gate-house by which I'd entered. I hoped that Rounce was being well cared for in the stables, assuming that Meg and the stable-hand Andrew had been able to keep their hands off each other long enough to tend to him. Considering the foolish error I'd made, I had been quite kindly received, at least by Martha and Elias Haskell. It was a strange place, though, this Haskell household. I remembered the words of the podgy Meg in the courtyard: 'They are all fools that come here.'

As I'd said to Martha, I had nothing with me apart from the clothes I stood up in. There wasn't much to detain me in this little room either. So, picking up the grease-pan which held the candle, I made my way back down the stairs and along the passageways which Martha and I had threaded moments earlier. I passed the kitchen. A woman was standing over the table, working a pestle and mortar. I stopped. She glanced up. It was Abigail, the housekeeper. Evidently she had abandoned her sentry-duty outside Elias's door. The light was stronger in the kitchen, a combination of fire and candles, and I could see surprise, even suspicion, on her face before she recognized me.

'You are staying the night, master?'

'It seems so.'

'You need more blankets?'

'I'll manage,' I said. 'Don't trouble yourself.'

She snorted and returned to her work. Over her shoulder I could see a girl struggling with pots and pans.

I walked on and after a couple of false turnings reached the entrance hall where there was a table which had been laid for supper and which was already occupied.

It took me a little time to work it out but eventually I understood that the carrion bird names which Elias had bestowed on his cousins – crow, vulture and so on – were not only linked to the way that they came flocking to the house at the first whisper of his illness. The names were also suggested by the appearance of these men. By the better light around the supper table I had a chance to study my fellow-guests. This was a beaky, big-nosed family – undoubtedly it was the lack of this feature which had caused the disrespectful Davey Parsons at the gate to tell me that I hadn't got the nose – and it made them look bird-like. Elias too was long-nosed and even Martha's was slightly too large for her face.

The three men whom I'd first encountered on my arrival were at table. The old man, with stick and spectacles, was called Valentine. He was stooped with age and mumbled his words and his food together in one spittly stream. Fortunately, he didn't say much but he was sharp enough when he wanted to be. He looked closer to death than Elias Haskell lying in bed at the other end of the house. From some remark, I learned Valentine lived in Cambridge. I doubt that he'd have been able to travel any more than a handful of miles to visit his 'dying' cousin, and marvelled that he'd come as far as he had. He had no occupation – the old are exempt from all that. The stoutish, middle-aged individual with the close-fitting cap of grey hair was

Cuthbert. He was a lawyer hailing from, I think, Peterborough. The third man, the one who'd been standing by the chimney-piece when I arrived, was called Rowland. He was a merchant from Huntingdon. They were Haskells by name, every one of them. This simplified matters, I suppose.

Elias Haskell had mentioned four carrion birds, though. An empty place at the table indicated that someone was still expected. I wondered who this person was. It seemed unlikely that he would arrive now, in the darkness of a winter evening and through the perils of a snow-storm. Meantime I was glad enough of the food, which was plain and wholesome – beef and barley bread, brawn soused in beer, and so on. The service was plain too, at the hands of the other servant I'd glimpsed in the kitchen and who, judging by her narrow mouth, was sister to the porcine girl in the lodge. The guests at the table kept darting wary glances at me, and from one or two remarks dropped by Martha I guessed that she'd spun them some story about Elias's interest in the playhouse to account for my presence in Valence. Perhaps they had jumped to the conclusion that the old man was going to leave his money to a troupe of players.

They made a couple of perfunctory enquiries about the health – or more precisely the sickness – of the man in the neighbour room and I noticed that Martha made Elias out to be rather worse than he had seemed to be. I wasn't sure whether she was doing this on her own initiative or because he had instructed her to give a bad report. I noticed also in the three men a kind of satisfaction, which they scarcely bothered to conceal, that their cousin continued in his apparent decline. They were curious to know what we'd talked about.

'This and that,' I said. 'He showed me Grant the monkey.'

'And did he show you the sword?' said Rowland Haskell.

'That rusty old thing,' said Cuthbert.

'I saw a sword over the chimney-piece,' I said.

'Elias believes it can sprout wings,' said Rowland.

'Pah! Superstition!' said Cuthbert.

'Stranger things have happened,' said old Valentine.

Rowland the merchant turned to me at another point during the meal and said, 'That William Shakespeare is one of your fellows, isn't he?'

'He is a shareholder in the Globe. Sometimes he's a player but mostly he's a writer.'

'I saw his play about the mad Dane who murdered his uncle.'

'That is *Hamlet*,' I said. 'But the Prince was provoked and it was not altogether murder. The uncle had killed his father first.'

'There was a deal of killing anyway,' said Rowland. 'And a lot of silly talk about hawks and handsaws and crabs going backwards.'

'*I* saw one of his plays in London,' said Cuthbert the lawyer, narrowing his eyes as if he were examining me in court. 'I chiefly remember a single line in it. Do you know what it was?'

'No, but you are about to tell me, sir.'

'The line was "The first thing we do, let's kill all the lawyers".'

'Kill all the lawyers,' I repeated.

I must say that, in the present company, I rather relished the words and perhaps I didn't much bother to conceal the fact.

'Good, good,' said Valentine, 'Kill all the lawyers. That would be a start.' The old man's spectacles glinted sightlessly in the candlelight.

'Is that Master Shakespeare's true opinion, do you think, Master Revill?' said Cuthbert. 'That the world

357

would be a better place if we lawyers were all . . . no more?'

This might be quite close to William's opinion – certainly it is the view of plenty of other people in this island of ours – but I said, 'I do not think so, sir. Words only, from a character in a play.'

'I deal in words,' said Cuthbert.

'You're no better than a tanner,' said Valentine to his cousin. 'You deal in skins. In the sheep-skins and calf-skins which you write your double words on.'

'You dislike lawyers, sir?' I said.

'My father was a lawyer, sir,' said Valentine, though he looked too old to have any father apart from Adam.

Cuthbert ignored all this, perhaps putting it down as the bitter ramblings of an old man. Instead he simply grunted and levered another slice of brawn from the dish on the table. Now it was the turn of Rowland the merchant to accuse me and my kind.

'But you can't deny that you players are against authority, can you? That is why audiences are drawn to you. The people who attend your performances are not respectable people.'

'Then you'd have to say that the King and Queen of England are not respectable,' I said. 'King James is our patron while Queen Anne has even performed in a masque.'

'Oh, he is Scottish . . .' said Cuthbert.

'. . . and she is Danish,' said Rowland. 'Foreigners both.'

Cuthbert and Rowland Haskell looked slightly uneasy at this point as if a government agent might be about to sneak out of the wainscot and arrest them for treason. For my part, I would have welcomed one.

'Uncle Elias likes plays,' said Martha. 'He remembers the old playhouses in London.'

What else she would have said to bring a bit of goodwill back to the conversation I don't know because at that moment we were interrupted by a figure who swept into the hall and took her place at the table with a great fuss and bother. The missing guest was no man, as I'd expected, but a formidable-looking woman. I was startled because she bore more than a passing resemblance to our late queen – I mean, the great Elizabeth. This person had the same pinched face and aquiline nose and haughty manner. (And I should know because I was once in personal conversation with Queen Elizabeth for at least a quarter of an hour.) But the nose alone revealed this newcomer to the dining table to be yet another Haskell cousin. Also the way in which the three men reacted with impatience to her presence.

'Why did no one wake me?' she demanded. At the same time, she stabbed with her knife at the beef and brawn and other dishes, using the implement as if it was a weapon rather than an eating tool. When her plate was piled high, she looked round. 'Well? Why did no one wake me?'

'You must have been tired after your journey, cousin Elizabeth,' said Martha.

I almost jumped to hear that this woman was even named for our late queen, but then I suppose many women of the older generation must have been baptized in the sovereign's honour.

'True, I have travelled in the dead of winter and over terrible roads all the way from Saffron Walden to be at the bedside of dear Elias,' she said. 'True, a lady of my age is permitted to be exhausted after such a journey. True, she may be allowed to lie down on her bed for a few minutes to recover from her travels. But it was light when I arrived and now it is dark. I should have been woken. You must speak to your servants, Martha dear, and to that housekeeper in particular.

Naturally the first thing I did when I awoke was to go in quest of poor Elias. But, on reaching his door, I was refused admittance. I was told that he was asleep.'

'He is very ill,' said Martha.

'He would have been pleased to be woken to see his cousin Elizabeth. I have a gift to give him. Yet the woman – what's her name, Abigail is it? – barred me from the door, and said that I must wait until he asked to see me. Who are you?'

This last remark was directed at me. Whether she really hadn't observed a stranger at supper or whether she'd wanted to unburden herself of her complaints first, I don't know. Swiftly I introduced myself, adding for the third or fourth time that day that I was a player with the King's Men.

'So what are you doing here?' said Dame Elizabeth.

'Master Revill is here by appointment. He has brought a letter of introduction from his employers in London,' said Martha. 'You know how much uncle Elias enjoys plays.'

Elizabeth humphed at this as if she couldn't see how anyone might enjoy plays, but she asked no further questions. I was grateful for the deft way in which Martha had dealt with her. She had not lied – I *was* carrying a letter of introduction, after all – but she had left out the fact that I'd come to the wrong house.

The conversation wore on, fuelled by drink. Cuthbert the lawyer boasted of how much money he was making from his cases. Rowland the merchant boasted of how much he was earning from his deals. They were well-to-do, you could see that from the quantity of rings they wore on their fingers. Valentine nodded away at all this, occasionally interjecting some crabbed comment. Dame Elizabeth looked ready to be offended. Towards the end of the meal, the house-keeper called Abigail appeared. She came across to me and whispered, a little too loudly, that the master of the house would like to see me now. This provoked glances between Cuthbert and Rowland, while Dame Elizabeth objected, 'But he hasn't even seen *me* yet!'

'Those are my orders, my lady,' said Abigail.

Reluctantly I got up from the table. The reluctance wasn't altogether put on. I felt as if I was taking part in a play where I knew neither my lines nor how things would unfold. I didn't even know whether I was participating in a comedy or a tragedy or something in between. Nevertheless, I had little choice but to follow Abigail and once more go down the passage to the sick man's chamber.

I knocked and entered. Elias Haskell was lying almost flat on his back, his head propped up on a bolster. I glanced towards the corner which was occupied by Grant the monkey. The door of the wooden cage remained closed, as if he'd shut himself away for the night. Elias motioned for me to sit down once more on the chest near the bed.

'Well, what did you make of them, my carrion birds?'

Elias's voice seemed to have grown weaker. Only his eyes remained lively, with that glint of malice or mischief at the bottom of them.

'They are very much as you described them.'

'That's disappointing. Can't you say anything further?'

'The two, er, younger men are so prosperous by their own account that you wonder they need to come sniffing round someone else's fortune.'

'Fortune, ha! Yet it's true they are well-to-do. Cuthbert in particular thrives as a lawyer with his twists and turns. But it's a wise man, Nicholas, who knows when his plate is full. Some are never satisfied. I can see that *you* are one of those wise men, you would not go grasping when your hands were already full.'

'I'm not so sure,' I said. 'I have never had what you call full hands.'

'Of course not, you're a player.'

This was halfway to being a compliment, perhaps, yet it made me uncomfortable. I changed the subject.

'It seemed to me that the old man – Valentine – might be better occupied in thinking about his own end instead of . . .'

'Instead of dwelling on mine. But the prospect of gold is a great preservative. It makes people think they will live forever.'

'Is there gold here?' I said. The question made me feel that I was playing his game.

'All rumours,' Elias said vaguely. 'My cousins are like chameleons. They can eat the air, it is so full of promises. In return they give me gifts. Their tribute. Over there. Plate from the lawyer, a goblet from the merchant, and a mirror from the old man. He'd have done better to examine his own visage for signs of decay.'

I glanced towards the area of the room which he was indicating. A little mound of objects was heaped there although I could not distinguish one from another. This was the tribute of the heirs, little gifts given in expectation of a greater return.

'Shall I show you my most precious object, player?'

I nodded, almost beyond caring at the next twist in this peculiar evening yet at the same time thinking that here I was sitting inside a sick man's chamber, in the presence of a monkey called Grant, within a ramshackle, snow-bound house in Cambridgeshire. A few hours ago I had never heard of the Haskells. Yet now I had been thrust into the heart of this strange family, and already knew more about them than was perhaps proper or prudent.

'Why not?' I said. 'Let me see your most precious object.'

'Then go and take that sword from its resting place,' said Elias Haskell, nodding in the direction of the chimney-piece.

I walked over to the fire. The sword rested on a couple of iron brackets. This was what had been talked of briefly at supper.

'Lift it up, Nicholas,' said the man in the bed.

It was heavy and cumbersome but there was nothing to prevent anyone taking it. Elias wasn't concerned about thieves, I assumed, otherwise this item would be locked up in a chest if it was really valuable.

I cradled the sword in both arms for fear of dropping it, and also because I was curiously unwilling to wield it like an old-time soldier.

'Lay it on the bed near me,' said Elias.

I did so and, half sitting up, he reached forward to grasp the circular pommel and raise the sword. The blade shook with his effort. The man had strength, old and sick as he was. The sinews stood out and his arm quivered as he lifted the dead weight a couple of feet into the air. The weapon gleamed dully in the candle-light. Despite its age and battered condition, there was still a bluish sheen to the blade. I am not particularly knowledgeable or comfortable with weapons but even I could see that in its own way this was an object of beauty, one forged with a craftsman's care and, more important, a craftsman's love. At the same time it gave me the goose-bumps to see the old man half sitting up in bed and raising aloft this antique weapon.

'It is ancient,' I said.

'Centuries old. They say that it was used against the Normans who first came to this island. It has been with my family alone for more than a hundred years. That is why I call it precious.'

'How did you come by it?'

'It was discovered in that very chimney,' said Elias,

363

obviously unwilling to say more. 'Try it for yourself. Hold it properly.'

I took the sword from his grasp again. The blade was long and straight, tapering only near the point. The cross was like a down-turned mouth. Studying it more closely, I saw that each end had been carved into the shape of a dog's head. Elias waited until I'd had a good look before saying, 'There are strange stories attached to that weapon, shameful ones too. Sometimes it almost seems to have a life of its own. As if it had a mind to think with, or wings to fly through the air with. That's the legend of it. Also that it brings bad fortune.'

'Why do you keep it then?'

'In the hope that it will bring bad fortune to my enemies,' said Elias.

Whether it was the nonsensical words about flying and fortune, or whether it was something within the sword itself (but how could that have been?), it seemed to me that the weapon gave a little start in my hand and I nearly dropped it. I took a firmer grasp on the hilt and banished these foolish thoughts. The sword was weighty. Only an expert would be capable of wielding it to good effect. I wondered how many lives this blade was responsible for finishing. How many fatal slashes and stabbings it had delivered down the years. Many, no doubt, many slashes and stabbings. This was a foolish thought in its way, since it was not the blade but the men who had hefted it that were responsible. Even so, I shivered without knowing why. Perhaps to disguise these feelings I made one or two experimental sweeps through the air, holding the hilt two-handed. I glanced in the direction of the cage in the corner. If Grant the monkey had chosen to reappear at this moment I would have shown him who was master.

The door opened and Martha entered the room. She was carrying a small bowl. She almost dropped it, I thought, perhaps under the impression that I was about to attack her uncle. I lowered the sword-point to the floor and grinned sheepishly. Martha took the bowl across to Elias and cradled his head in her hand so that he might drink from it. After a couple of sips, he said, 'That's enough. I'll finish it later.'

'You must drink it, uncle. It is a soporific,' she said, more to me than to Elias, then turning to him once again, 'You will have a restless night otherwise. And I cannot sleep if I know that you are not sleeping.'

Nevertheless she did not compel him to drink any more but placed the bowl on the floor beside the bed.

'Is cousin Elizabeth here?' he said.

'She tried to see you before supper but Abigail would not admit her,' said Martha.

'Send her to me now.'

'But you are tired, uncle.'

'Now,' he repeated. His voice was unexpectedly firm.

As she turned away with a hurt expression, Elias took her wrist. I was surprised at the speed of the gesture. Also, I could see he was grasping her hard. But his tone was gentle.

'Dear girl,' he said. 'You are always concerned for my welfare . . . unlike those carrion.'

She bent forward and kissed him on the brow. Then she straightened up and, with a nod, indicated that it was time to leave Elias. He told me to replace the sword on the brackets above the chimney-piece. I did so and then returned to the dining hall with Martha. In my brief absence, the diners had drunk deeper. Now it was cousin Elizabeth's turn to be informed that she was required and she bustled her way to Elias's room.

Cousin Cuthbert rounded on me. 'Well, Master Revill, what success did you have with the old man?'

'Did you squeeze anything out of him?' said Rowland.

'Did you creep into his confidence?' said Valentine.

These were such objectionable questions that I didn't dignify them with an answer. From the words being bandied round the table I gathered that they each of them planned to visit Elias once more before turning in for the night, no doubt to try and impress on him their love and devotion to his welfare.

For myself, I was too tired to stay up any longer after the day spent riding from Cambridge and the dispiriting sense that the journey had been futile anyway since I'd come to the wrong house. To be frank, the company at table was not altogether to my taste either. Martha, once again bearing a taper, escorted me to the foot of the narrow stairs that led to the next floor. She seemed more attentive to me than she was to her cousins.

'Goodnight, Nicholas. I hope you sleep well.'

'Perhaps I should have swallowed some of your concoction. Your uncle's, that is. The soporific.'

'Mine?' She looked confused. 'No, Abigail makes them to his specifications.'

The point hardly seemed to matter and, taking the offered taper, I climbed the stairs to my little room. It was only when I was inside that it occurred to me I should have thanked her again for the night's hospitality. I would never have made it back to Cambridge. There was no denying that this was a strange household, though. The little casement window was fogged up but I wiped at it with my sleeve and gazed out. The snow had stopped sometime while we were at supper and it lay, smooth and unmarked, across the courtyard. There was no light from the gatehouse and a dead, blank silence reigned over all.

A night-gown had been thrown across the bed. I suppose I had Abigail to thank for that. It smelled musty. Apart from removing my shoes, I didn't undress or change. It was too cold. I should have insisted on more blankets after all. I lay down on the narrow bed but without snuffing the taper. Having felt sleepy downstairs, I now discovered that, within reach of a bed and without anything else to distract me, my tiredness had departed. Failing a soporific, perhaps I should have drunk more at supper like the other guests. I wondered again exactly what pleasure or satisfaction Elias Haskell could hope to gain from the presence in Valence House of his would-be heirs, when he so despised them. Surely there must be limits to his fondness for mischief. He was a sick man, even if not in quite such a bad state as he pretended to be for the others. What did he expect to gain? A few trinkets, goblets and mirrors and suchlike? Even if, as Martha had claimed, some of those round the table had altered their wills in his favour – as a hypocritical sign of good faith, presumably – what use would that be to a man on the edge of his grave?

Yet, looking at things from the other side, what fortune could any or all of the Haskell cousins hope to come by in this place? Even to my unpractised eye, the house and its outbuildings were in a state of disrepair. Wasn't that evidence of a lack of fortune? Not necessarily of course. Some would say that the less there was on display the more must be hidden away. 'All rumours,' Elias had said, but he hadn't denied them. And he'd also claimed that it was a general belief that old families must be rich, especially when they'd been reduced to the nub. Nevertheless, I didn't quite see it. The cousins were prosperous, even if they weren't wealthy. It must be as the old man had said, that some people were never satisfied, always wishing to pile their plates higher.

And this made me think of my own situation. Nicholas Revill of the King's Men, the finest and grandest company of players in London. But Revill's circumstances were neither fine nor grand. I was still a lodger in other men's houses and without any place to call my own. With hands not full but more or less empty. I retrieved out of my doublet pocket the buckle from my shoe, the one in the shape of a love-knot. I looked at its copper burnish in the taper's feeble light. Somehow all this confirmed me in my impression of myself as a poor player. Perhaps there's something about lying on a bed in a strange house during a silent and snow-filled night which encourages introspection and self-pity. I blew out the taper and settled down to a wakeful few hours.

But I must have slept because I woke with a start. At least I think that I woke, since everything which followed seemed to take place in a kind of dream – or nightmare. There was a noise from outside, a panting sound. As I've said, there was a little window in my room overlooking the courtyard which lay between the main building and the gatehouse. To peer outside, I had only to swing my legs to the floor and crane forward. The panes in the window were rimed over. I rubbed at one of them and the cold burned my finger-tips. I put my eye to the little circle I'd created.

Outside all seemed as before. There was no moon but the stars overhead were blazing fiercely and the snow cast a chill glow of its own in response. The outline of the gatehouse, wearing a new thatch of snow, stood in front of me. Beyond it the skeletal shapes of trees were just visible. Almost immediately my breath fogged up the window again. I wiped at it once more. What was I looking for? I didn't know. Then I heard that strange panting sound again. It came from below. I peered down. The angle was awkward and it was difficult to see clearly because the porch blocked the view. But there was definitely someone down there, a person standing a few paces in front of the main entrance to the house. I could just glimpse the top of a head. I had the impression of height, unusual height. More than that, the figure seemed to cast a kind of elongated shadow on the snow. Then the pane of glass filmed over once more. Shivering, I wiped at it a third time. When I tried to peer down again, the figure had vanished.

It was cold up here, as I crouched at the narrow window, attempting to keep clear a little circle of glass that gave a glimpse of the night. I told myself that whatever was happening outside was no concern of mine. I was only in this house because of an absurd error, though admittedly one of my own devising. I lay back on the bed. No more sounds came up from outdoors but I heard a subdued shrieking from somewhere within the house which caused my hair to prickle. And then I remembered Grant the monkey and breathed deep and promised myself that I would quit this place on the next morning.

I fell into a shallow sleep and dreamed I was escaping somewhere on a horse which was floundering in the snow. A monkey was clinging round my neck. I didn't know what – or who – I was trying to escape. Perhaps it was the monkey. Eventually the horse stumbled and I was pitched headlong into a bank of snow. The monkey released its grip and ran off. I thought I might hide from whatever was pursuing me under the snow-blanket but another voice told me I would be suffocated there.

I woke up aching and unrested. The little chamber was bathed in a lurid light. The memory of suffocating in the snow was still in my head and the room felt airless. This time I opened the casement window. It creaked on unwilling hinges and let in a draught of cold morning air. After the stuffy fears of the night, this was refreshing. The sun was just rising, a tight red ball, beyond the fringe of trees that fenced the house.

The arrow-shaped spire of the church was dyed red. The sun's rays struck the upper storey of the house. My first thought was that, provided there was no more snow, the road from Ickleton back to Cambridge might be passable. With luck I could get away from this strange spot. If I set off straightaway, with the minimum of farewells and assuming Rounce was fit to ride . . .

Without thinking, I gazed down into the snow-filled courtyard. It was still in shadow at ground level and my eyes were full of red dazzle from squinting at the sun. Even so I could make out a darker shadow lying at full length in the snow and almost jumped back from the casement in shock. A second glance confirmed what instinct had already told me. There was a body down there. Whose I did not know.

Pausing only to put on my shoes, I was out of the room and down the narrow back stairs almost before I knew what I was doing. Past the kitchen from which clattering sounds and cooking smells were emanating. I should have stopped there and then to summon help. Got the housekeeper Abigail or the other servant to accompany me. I wish I had now. It would have saved me a deal of trouble later on. Instead, like the fool I was, I half ran down the passage which led to the dining hall. The large chamber was empty. Evidently no one in Valence believed in early rising. The remains of last night's fire smouldered in the great chimney.

At the main door, I halted for an instant. Even now I might have called out for help. There were at least a couple of able-bodied individuals in the house who would respond. I ought to leave it to them. This was none of my business after all. Yet there is an urge in some of us to be first on the scene of a disaster, a foolish urge. I unbolted the main door and tugged it open. By now the sun had risen a fraction higher so that its first rays were slanting right into the courtyard, glaring off the snow. I shaded my eyes and, standing in the porch, gazed outside.

There was a body perhaps a half dozen paces away and lying in a direct line from the front door. I could not identify him, but he was showing me a clean pair of slippered heels, half buried in the snow. The upper part of the body was pitched forward so that the head was face down and almost completely sunk in the snow. His arms were flung out. It was as if he had set out to leave Valence and stumbled in the snow and not troubled to raise himself again. I recalled my suffocating dream.

But this was real and no dream. I made to step forward, away from the shelter of the house. Not that I could do anything to help the poor fellow – for it was certainly a man (and I had a fairly good idea which man it was by now) – since his whole posture showed that he was long past help. His posture, and the blood which spattered the snow in the area of his sunken head. Even at this point, I did not take fright for myself. After all, what had the goings-on in the Haskell household to do with Nicholas Revill? I was merely an accidental player who'd stumbled onto the wrong stage.

I stepped through the snow, which rose above my ankles. I skirted the body until I came level with the man's head. He wasn't wearing a hat nor even a nightcap. Not the kind of weather to go out bare-headed. Not that he would ever care about such matters again, I thought. And felt an unexpected pang and wiped away some water from my eyes. It was Elias Haskell, the old man, the owner of Valence House. His hair, now revealed, was long and white and flecked with blood and snow. There was more blood spilled in the snow beside him although not in great quantity.

My guts did a little turn as my eyes confirmed what instinct had already told me. Even then I didn't have the wit to be properly alarmed. Instead I examined the scene as if it was going to tell me something or other of interest.

I was facing the body. On my left hand was the little gatehouse. A curl of fresh smoke issued from the chimney, showing that the lodge-keeper or one of his brood was up and about. There was a single small window on this side of the gatehouse, looking into the yard, but evidently no one had yet observed Elias's corpse. This was not surprising since the whole yard had been in shadow until moments before. As for the main house, most of the rooms lay in the rear area. In fact the only one, apart from the dining hall, that appeared to have a direct view of the courtyard was the chamber I'd been sleeping in. The outbuildings, their roofs newly covered with snow, looked more dilapidated by the bright light of the morning than they'd appeared in the gloom of the previous afternoon. There was no sound or sight of anyone else. Just the dead man and I.

I wondered how long Elias had been lying out here. I was reluctant to touch the body, which would have long since turned cold anyhow. Presumably it had been he whom I'd heard – and glimpsed – last night, the panting sound some sort of death-rattle. What time had that been? For no good reason, it had seemed during the earlier rather than the later part of the night. Why had he been out here at all, the old man, when his proper place was tight asleep in his bed?

And had he been alone, Elias Haskell?

Why, yes, he must have been alone. Because there was only one set of footprints leading from the porch and they belonged to the slippers which protruded, heels uppermost, from the snow.

Or rather there had been one set of footprints. Now they had been joined by another pair belonging to a

witless player from London. And something else was
nagging at the edge of my mind. Something which
suggested that the dead man might not have been altogether alone when he met his end, footprints or no
footprints. Something to do with an action I'd
performed only moments earlier. What was it?

Yet even then, looking at my own tracks and knowing
that something was amiss, I did not grasp my danger.

What I did grasp instead was an object lying in the
snow at some distance from Elias's outflung left arm.
I hadn't seen it at first because it was half buried in
the snow and because the sight of the dead man was
more pressing. There were no tracks or other marks
around the sword, indicating that it had been thrown
there rather than dropped on the spot. I bent down
and once again gripped the sword which I had originally lifted from the wall-brackets in Elias Haskell's
bedchamber. The sword which was hundreds of years
old and had been discovered up the chimney. The
sword which seemed to possess – how had Elias put it?
– a mind to think with or wings to fly with. And now,
in an easy action considering its weight, the sword
seemed to rise free of the snow in which it was
embedded. The hilt and pommel were cold to the
touch. When I'd handled the thing before it had been
by firelight and candlelight. But even in the dazzling
sun, the blade was dull as if tainted with those bluish
patches and other stains which I didn't care to examine
too closely. I noticed what I hadn't noticed in the
chamber, that an inscription ran the length of the blade
down the centre. Two inscriptions, for there was
another on the reverse. They were in Latin. I made out
the words as best as I could but they did not seem to
be much help or use in this present situation. How had
the sword come to be out here? Had someone taken
it from Elias's room while the old man slept? Was the

blood in the snow the result of wounds caused by the sword?

Well, there was a mystery here but it was nothing to do with me.

I was wrong, of course. It was everything to do with me.

Something else about the sword drew my attention but before I could do anything further a movement in the corner of my eye made me look up. There was a cluster of people standing in the entrance to the house. With that clarity which sometimes comes with great danger, I saw myself as they must be seeing me. Here is an old man lying dead and bloodied in the snow. Has he been unlawfully killed? It seems so. Two sets of footprints, and two only, are linked with the body. One of them belongs to the corpse. The other belongs to an interfering player, who has most definitely stumbled onto the wrong stage. To make matters worse, the player is brandishing a sword which, to all appearances, could be the murder weapon. That he now lets fall the weapon, so that it drops with a dull thud into the packed snow, makes no difference. In fact the panicky gesture only makes him look the more guilty.

I was sitting on the chest in the bedchamber, the third time I'd attended on Elias Haskell in less than twenty-four hours. As before the old man was lying on his great bed with its bulbous foot-posts. The only difference now was that he was dead. When I first saw him, his long face illuminated by the candles which glimmered in the recesses of the head-board, I'd been reminded of a shrine or tomb. Now it was that, almost literally.

But, otherwise, being in Elias's chamber was like being in a cell. I was a prisoner or near enough, confined and unable to make my escape without violence. The heavy curtains remained drawn as a mark of respect but a gap between them admitted a shaft of winter sun which provided enough light. By now it was mid-morning. Lounging near the door – and preventing my exit should I have attempted to make one – was the young, hulking fellow from the stables, the one called Andrew. He smelled of horses. Sometimes I caught his eye, the one that wasn't covered by his forelock of straw-coloured hair. When I did catch his eye he grinned, vacuously. He obviously did not share in the general mourning for Elias Haskell. Whenever I got up from the chest to stretch my legs he stiffened by the door as though as I was going to attack him. He hadn't said a word in the couple of hours or so we'd been penned up together in the dead man's chamber. If I hadn't heard him wooing Meg the previous afternoon – 'I'd rather take care of you' he'd said – I might have wondered whether he could actually speak at all. It hardly mattered anyway, since I didn't feel much like talking.

The members of the household, clustered in the doorway, had witnessed me standing over the corpse of Elias Haskell, sword in hand. They'd observed my footprints in the snow alongside those of the dead man. They had come to the obvious conclusion, which was the very one I would have arrived at, had I been in their shoes. I had killed the old man outside in the snow in the morning just as the sun was rising. I had killed him for reasons best known to myself. And I'd been caught red-handed.

Scarcely had I let fall the sword to the snow-covered ground than the individuals in the doorway began advancing on me in a timorous fashion as if they were approaching a dangerous dog. There was the furious-looking Abigail, the tottering Valentine, the shocked-seeming Martha, the dapper Rowland, the imperious

Elizabeth, the lawyerly Cuthbert. The bad-tempered gatekeeper came from the other side while the hulking lad with the forelock of hair emerged from the stable-block.

I might have made a run for it but something kept me rooted to the spot. Was it fear? Anger? Disbelief? All of these, perhaps, but the main thought in my confused head was: this is absurd! I haven't done anything. I'm not even meant to be in this house. It's all a mistake. A moment or two of explanation will clear matters up. Besides, if I had run, it would have confirmed my guilt in the eyes of the others. Protesting that I'd done nothing, knew nothing, I allowed myself to be led inside. For a time we all stood around in the great hall, while singly or in twos and threes the rest of the household went out to examine the corpse of Elias, some of them several times. Martha Haskell returned with a frozen expression, but the others, such as Cuthbert or Dame Elizabeth, put on long faces like paid mourners. Not wishing to view the body again, I remained where I was, standing by the chimney-piece as far as possible from the entrance. The servants – Abigail and the kitchen-girl and her sister, in company with the shambling stable-hand – came clustering into the hall. I heard speculation about the ill-fated 'flying' sword, and all the time they darted glances at me and I felt their suspicions hardening into certainties.

When the cousins had done with their viewing of the corpse, a short conversation ensued between them. The purpose of this was clear. They had all gone to bid goodnight to Elias after I'd gone to bed the previous evening. They were all eager to assure each other – and possibly to assure me as well – that he'd been alive when they left. Tired, yes, on the verge of sleep, yes, but living and breathing still. As far as I could tell, they had entered the chamber in the following order:

Elizabeth Haskell first, because she had actually been summoned by Elias and hadn't yet seen him on this visit to Valence House; then Cuthbert, followed by Valentine and, after him, Rowland. To hear them talk, everything had been easy and natural between these loving cousins, all of them. Inevitably, some slight suspicion attached to Rowland, as the last of his kin to visit him, but Abigail butted in at this point to say that she had entered the chamber shortly afterwards to ensure that her master had drunk his soporific. And, she stated categorically, he was alive when she'd been there.

All this seemed to point the guilty finger even more clearly at me. I had the sense that the household, whatever their differences, whether visitors or permanent members, was uniting in the face of an outsider. I shifted uncomfortably under their gaze and looked down at my feet. As I've said, I was standing by the chimney-piece which contained the remains of last night's fire. A little heat still emanated from the remains. Because of the turmoil in the house, nobody had cleared them out or laid any fresh logs. The area in front of the fire – bare oak boards rather than the rushes which were strewn around much of the hall – was covered in a thin grey veil of ash. A backdraft must have blown the ash out of the fire. But what was most interesting to me was the image of a footprint, no a pair of footprints, in the dust. I squatted down for a closer look. They were small prints, like a child's. The outline of a long toe was visible. Not only a child's footprint but a barefoot child! There were no children in the house as far as I knew. There was Mr Grant the monkey, however. He had been out of his wooden cage at some point during the night. It was a cold enough morning but, even so, I felt colder within.

After a time, I was shut up in Elias's chamber, with

Andrew in attendance. A little while later, the gate-keeper, assisted by his jug-eared son and Cuthbert and Rowland Haskell, carried in the corpse and deposited it on the bed. It was the natural and inevitable place for the old man to be laid out but perhaps there was some idea of making me confront what I'd done, or what they believed I'd done. I was regarded with hostile looks. Davey was the only exception. The boy gazed at me with frank curiosity. Most likely it was first time that he'd clapped eyes on a supposed murderer.

When they left, I had the opportunity to examine Elias carefully for the first time, although this did not reveal much. There was a severe gash in his forehead, which would probably have been the blow to kill him. It was the kind of wound which should surely have bled heavily, yet there had only been spatterings of blood on the snow outside.

The three of us – Andrew, Elias and I – weren't the only occupants of the chamber, of course. I haven't forgotten about Grant the monkey. But one could have overlooked the fact that he was here, so quiet was he inside his cage in the far corner of the room. It was only by his smell that you'd have known he was still present. When the body of his owner had been brought in he had lumbered across and pawed at the dead man's arm. But he had done nothing else, had uttered no cries or gibbers, had not attempted to climb up on the bed. I sensed that the others were impatient or fearful of the animal and were glad when he slunk back to his cage. For my part I was quite glad of his presence. His silence in the matter of Elias's death seemed more eloquent than the probably hypocritical words of the Haskell cousins.

If not exactly a prisoner, I was no longer a guest. Accompanied by Abigail the housekeeper, Martha brought me some bread and ale and told me that, if the road to Cambridge was clear enough, the coroner or magistrate would be summoned to Ickleton to take charge. She had been weeping for her uncle and cast frequent glances at his corpse. Abigail divided her gaze between me and the dead man, looking with disapproval on both. As a mark of respect for her dead master she had changed into a black overdress. I looked to Martha for some indication that the young woman, at least, did not think me guilty of murder but she gave none. She would scarcely meet my eyes. This, and the fact that it might take a day or more for a magistrate to reach Valence, caused a black cloud to drift over my spirits. I knew that I was innocent, certainly, but to judge by the wary manner which even Martha was showing no one else did. I realized that you can be as innocent as the day is long and yet still be accused and tried and . . .

I'm well aware that this is not exactly a fresh revelation, that the innocent are sometimes accused and . . . all the rest of it. I should know. I've even been imprisoned, on false charges, before now. I know the way the world wags. This time I had the creeping sensation that things might turn out badly. With a hostile coroner or magistrate, or an incompetent one, things might turn out very badly indeed. Particularly as none of the individuals in Valence House, with the exception of Martha and Elias Haskell, had been well disposed towards me in the first place. And now one of the two was dead and the other must suspect me of having a hand in her uncle's demise. As for the rest of the occupants, they either had some rank or they were local. How would a strange player from London be regarded? With suspicion even in the best of circumstances.

If I was going to be saved I would have to save myself. I cudgelled my wits to think of a way out of this predicament. I went over in my mind all the details to do with my discovery of Elias's body. I thought back over the

previous night when I'd been woken by that odd
panting noise. I'd had no more than a glimpse of the
figure standing in the yard but it had surely been Elias.
Why was he outside? He was meant to have taken a
soporific. Presumably he had not drunk it or it had
been ineffective. Yet this was a minor point which didn't
explain his presence in the courtyard on a very cold
night.

I'd assumed he was bed-ridden, but no one had actually said as much. It was evident from the way he'd held
the sword or gripped his niece by the wrist that he still
possessed considerable strength. So he must have risen
from his bed and struggled outside. Yet he had been
wounded in the head, plainly wounded. He could not
have received the injury out of doors, otherwise there
would have been signs of a scuffle, more footprints
besides his. And more blood on the ground perhaps,
although it was likely that the snow had had the effect
of stanching the flow. So did Elias stagger outside,
mortally wounded as he was? Was it possible, that an
old, sick man could move even a few yards with such
an injury? I knew from a good friend of mine who was
also a member of the King's Men and who had seen
service many years ago in the Netherlands war that
wounded men are capable of extraordinary feats in the
heat of battle, even if they fall and die straight afterwards. So it must be that Elias had run out of the house
to escape from someone. But that someone had not
come after him, since there were no other tracks in
the snow (apart from mine).

But somebody else had been down there in the hall.
I knew this because I'd had to unbar the door in order
to get outside. Which meant that a second person had
barred it *after* Elias had left the house in the night.
Had it been Abigail or Martha, making sure the house
was secure and unaware that the body was lying in the

snow, dying or already dead? But I'd heard sounds outside in the early hours of the morning, long after the rest of the household should have retired to bed, all doors and windows secured.

Or – and this seemed the more likely event – had the person who'd had a hand in Elias's death stood by the entrance long enough to make sure the old man was good and dead before closing the door once again and barring it for the night? To leave a body lying on the ground was hardly satisfactory but to have attempted to remove it would have left even more traces in the snow. Perhaps the person, whoever it was, hoped that the death of Elias might be seen as accidental. And, except for the presence of the cursed sword (and a few blood stains), it might have been an accident. Men and women and children have died of cold on the London streets in winter. Why should it be any different in the wilds of Cambridgeshire?

But this looked like an unnatural death. How had it happened? I tried to think it through clearly.

There were some highly unnatural explanations. The sword had a legend attached to it suggesting that it could fly through the air of its own accord. Also, it was said to bring bad fortune in its wake. So maybe the sword had lifted itself clear of its brackets above the fire and attacked Elias. Divine – or demonic – intervention? Pah, superstition! (in Cuthbert's words) would be my rejoinder to that. Another freakish thought which passed through my head was that Elias might have inflicted the wound on himself prior to staggering out of doors. An even more freakish idea was that Grant the monkey might have had a hand in all of this. He had certainly been present in the hall during the early hours of the morning. His footprint was in the ash which had blown out from the dying fire as the door had been opened. It was very likely, therefore, that

Grant had witnessed his master's last moments, or some of them. Of course, this was knowledge that the monkey could not impart. Or perhaps it would be more accurate to say that no one could have interpreted his gibberings.

So much for clear thinking.

No, leaving aside flying swords and the testimony of monkeys, this was murder through a human agency and the finger was pointing towards one N. Revill. Now, it wasn't me, presently moping on a chest in the dead man's chamber. So who was it? Who had a motive to do away with Elias Haskell? The answer to this was obvious, any of his would-be heirs, frustrated by his game-playing, hoping to lay hands on his supposed fortune.

Clear thinking once again.

I rose from the chest where I was sitting, uncomfortably. Andrew shifted from his slouching posture but I paid him no attention. I wandered across to where Grant the monkey was moping in his cage. 'Cage' was really a misnomer since he was free to come and go as he wanted, and there was no catch or hasp on the door. At the moment Grant didn't want to go anywhere. He crouched in the corner, head hanging down, his brow wrinkled in perplexity. It struck me that his grief at Elias's death was probably deeper than that of anybody else in the house apart from Martha. However, he hadn't completely quit his old habits for there was something gleaming on the floor inside the cage. I opened the door and reached for it but the beast let out a great shrieking and I withdrew my hand quickly. Nevertheless I had a fairly good idea what it was. I moved away from Grant and ambled across the room. I moved casually so as not to alarm Andrew, who continued to lounge by the door.

I was looking for signs of struggle or some disturbance in the chamber. There was nothing evident. Some of the furniture might have been shifted slightly but because the room was packed with stuff it was hard to tell. Nor could I see any evidence of blood, although the floorboards were already old and stained, and covered in a haphazard mixture of rushes and herbs, some of which had been freshly laid to dispel the scent of death. I glanced towards the chimney-piece. Above it were the iron brackets in which the sword had lain. A ghost image of the weapon seemed to be imprinted on the wall. It must have hung there for many years. But unlike Elias's body, the sword hadn't been restored to its resting place.

I recalled holding the implement out in the open air and looking at the inscriptions on the blade. They were in Latin and hard to read after so much age and wear and tear. But my Latin is good – my father, a parson, saw to that (with his rod if necessary) – and my eyesight is keen. I hadn't paid much attention when I was outside but I recalled the gist of the words now. One said something about the false speaker forfeiting his honour while the other side of the sword offered a different quotation to do with God loving a cheerful giver and everybody hating a miser. Who was the miser in this case? Elias Haskell, hoarding his tributes and playing games with his heirs? Who were the lessons on the sword for, I wondered. The man wielding the weapon or the unfortunate individual on the receiving end of it? Did they mitigate the act of killing or salve the wound?

Another aspect of the sword occurred to me too. It had been damaged. The end of one of the cross-pieces, depicting a dog's head, had been broken off. Now, this might have been its condition on the previous evening when I'd first examined the blade and hilt in this very chamber but I was almost certain that the cross-piece was whole and undamaged then. If that was the case, the dog-end must have been snapped off during the night. Not surprising, considering that the weapon had seen action before being discovered next to Elias's corpse. But, in that case, what was the missing piece, the dog's-head, doing in the monkey's cage?

At that moment I heard a noise behind me and a hand brushed at my knee. Fortunately I wasn't altogether unprepared and, unlike the last occasion, didn't leap back in shock. Grant was hunched behind me, his arms dangling along the floor, his furrowed brow raised expectantly. I noticed Andrew watching us. When Grant was sure he had my full attention he started to bounce up and down, and to gesture and gibber.

What was he trying to tell me? I was standing near the fire (which was not lit). Perhaps the monkey was outraged that I was stationed in his favourite spot. But, no, it wasn't that. He was trying to tell me something else. I looked behind me. There was the chimney-piece with the great capital H in its centre. There were the tapestries on either side of – ah, I had it! Or I thought I had it. One of the pictures depicted Judith in the act of holding the severed head of Holofernes. A bloody story it is too, when the beautiful widow insinuates her way into the camp of Nebuchadnezzar's general so as to to take him by surprise and deprive him of his noddle. The tapestry showed her grasping the general's head in her left hand. She held it by the hair. The other hand gripped a sword which she held erect. There was fresh blood on the blade. Judith was wearing a red hat, the same shade as the blood. This was undoubtedly what Grant was trying to draw my attention to. Someone had killed his master, old Elias, with a sword like the one depicted in the tapestry. Elias hadn't been decapitated but he had certainly been struck around the head. The only trouble was that

Grant wasn't telling me any more than I already knew. Still, never let anyone say that monkeys are dull-witted or unfeeling creatures.

And then another idea occurred to me. What if . . .

The door opened and Martha Haskell entered the room. This time she looked full at me.

'It is all right, Nicholas.'

'All right? What's all right?'

'You were seen.'

She nodded to Andrew that he should go, and the stable-hand grinned his empty grin and slipped from the room.

'Before you were seen standing by my uncle's body –' she swallowed hard then had control of herself once again – 'you were seen in the courtyard coming out of the house.'

'I don't understand.'

Swiftly she explained. It was my good fortune that the lodge-keeper's boy Davey Parsons, the one with jug ears, had been gazing out of the little window which gave onto the courtyard at the very moment when I'd emerged to examine Elias's body. He had seen me pick up the sword and then discard it as the rest of the household appeared at the door. Davey had gone not to his father, who would most likely have cuffed him about the head or booted him in the rear, but to his sister in the kitchen who had, in turn, reported to her mistress. I could only suppose that Davey was grateful to me for having saved him from a kicking on the previous afternoon. Or perhaps he had a disinterested regard for justice. Whatever the reason, his testimony, haltingly delivered to Martha and then repeated to Cuthbert Haskell and the others was sufficient to exonerate me from blame. Davey had particularly noticed that I'd shed a tear over the cold corpse of Elias Haskell. He had seen it glittering on my cheek. Perhaps he wasn't used to the sight of tears. I did remember wiping an eye which had watered at the sharpness of the winter morning. But it might have been watering for Elias also.

In addition there was another reason why I was being permitted to leave this place of confinement, Martha said. Cooler heads had prevailed. Although my guilt seemed to speak loud and clear when I'd been discovered clutching the sword over the body of the master of the house, a short period of reflection had been enough to convince the Haskell cousins that there could be no strong cause for me to do away with Elias. No cause at all, in fact. I was a stranger to the house, I had no interest in whether the old man lived or died, he was not going to leave me any portion in his will. This, combined with the jug-eared boy's witness, was enough to set me free.

'You should leave here, Nicholas,' said Martha. 'There is no reason for you to stay the arrival of Mr Fortescue.'

'Mr Fortescue?'

'The magistrate from Cambridge.'

'The road is clear then?'

'It is passable now. Parsons in the lodge has been despatched to request his presence. Even if you don't get as far as Cambridge there is an inn on the road. You could put up there. Get on with your business. Leave now. Visit the Maskells.'

'I'd almost forgotten about the Maskells. Forgotten I was in the wrong house.'

'If you don't go now, Nicholas, you may be stranded at Valence House for longer, much longer.'

'You'd like me to go, Martha?'

'This is a family matter.'

'Don't you need me as a witness?'

'You said yourself you know nothing.'

'That was earlier. I know now.'

'Know what?'

'Who it was who murdered your uncle.'

She took a bit of persuasion but I eventually convinced Martha that she should call all the cousins into the hall so that I could explain things to them. I hinted that I had seen something from my window during the night, something which would throw light on the death of Elias and unmask the perpetrator. I was by no means as sure of my ground as I appeared. But I had a good idea or two, and I was depending on that – and my skill as a player – to see me through the next stage.

There was a risk, I knew that. But I felt as though this household owed me something for having falsely imprisoned me in the first place. The finger of guilt had been pointed in my direction, and now I would point it at . . . someone else. Besides, I've always enjoyed that moment when the villain is revealed at the end of the story. It happens at the close of the play of *Hamlet*, for example. And it was, in part, this same *Hamlet* which had given me a notion as to how this strange crime could have been committed.

However long it might have seemed, only a handful of hours had passed while I was shut up in Elias's chamber and it was late morning. Motes of dust danced in the sun-beams that shot through the hall windows and, outside, the snow was turning into slush. On the dining table the sword had been laid out on a fusty blanket, perhaps as evidence for the magistrate to see. Taking care not to touch it, I established that the end of one of the cross-pieces was indeed broken off.

There was a mixture of resentment and curiosity as the Haskell family gathered in the hall at Martha's urging. She told them that I had something to impart about the death of Elias. Even Grant the monkey put in an appearance before being shooed away by the housekeeper Abigail. For my part I was rather sorry to see him go, regarding him as an ally. Meanwhile Cuthbert watched me with his lawyer's gaze while Rowland seemed affronted with the world in general. Old Valentine's glasses glinted in my direction and Elizabeth stuck her nose in the air. Nothing seemed to link them except their noses and a mutual dislike. Martha hovered on the edge of the scene and Abigail provided ale and wine. The sword remained where it was on the table, the spectre at the feast. I think that no one was willing to lay hands on it, as if it carried the taint of guilt, otherwise it might have been removed.

'If you've something to say, Master Revill,' said Cuthbert, mindful of the law, 'then it would be best to save it until the magistrate arrives.'

'I agree,' said Rowland. 'We should wait for the proper authorities.'

'The trail might be cold by then,' I said, and that silenced them for a moment even though I wasn't exactly sure what I was talking about. Nevertheless it was plain from the way they were sitting around the table that they were waiting for me to deliver, to make good on my promise to clear up a mystery. All except one of those present (or that's what I assumed).

So I started.

'I know that Elias Haskell was murdered, and I know how. Each of you went to see him last night and . . .'

'Yes,' said Dame Elizabeth, 'and my dear cousin was alive when *I* left him.'

'He was alive when you all left him,' I said. 'We know that because Abigail here was the very last in his chamber – and her master was on the verge of sleep then.'

Somewhere in the background I was aware of the housekeeper nodding her head vigorously.

'But,' I continued, 'there's nothing and no one to say that one of you didn't return to Elias's chamber later.'

'Why should any of us do that?' said Cuthbert. 'Be careful, Revill. There is a penalty in law for those who make false accusations.'

'I haven't accused anyone yet,' I said, feeling increasingly uncomfortable and doing my best to conceal it. 'But it stands to reason that one of the Haskell cousins has the best of motives for wanting to get rid of old Elias – certainly a better motive than a player who happened to have wandered into Valence House by chance.'

'By chance? I thought you were here by appointment, young man,' said Dame Elizabeth.

'So I was but never mind that. I don't know whether it was exasperation or greed or despair, or a mixture of all three, but one of the people in this room was driven to assail Elias with the sword – the very one that lies before you on the table. Elias was mortally wounded by the blow, perhaps already dead. Then this . . . individual . . . decided that it would be safer if the body was to be found outside, perhaps at some distance from the house.'

'Oh yes, Master Revill,' said Rowland, not bothering to keep the sneer out of his voice. 'And how was that done? Did the dead man walk? There was only one set of footprints outside, remember, and those footprints were only going in one direction. One set of footprints apart from yours. We saw that clearly this morning.'

'That's because Elias was *carried* outside the house. When I looked out of the window last night I saw a tall figure standing in the snow, taller than anyone here. The reason was that old Elias was being lifted on another's shoulders. He was already a tall man, but this way he was a good head higher.'

Carried like St Christopher bore the Christ child across the river. It was that image which Grant the monkey had been trying to draw my attention to in the tapestry depicting a man carrying someone on his shoulders, and not the tapestry showing Judith with the severed head of Holofernes. This was what the monkey had seen as he stood in the hall last night. His master, dead, being shifted out of doors and into the snowy night. The door swung open, causing the ash from the dying fire to blow across the hall like a grey veil, and the monkey left his imprint. And he gibbered. I heard him from my little room upstairs.

'But there was only one set of tracks, going out,' said Valentine. 'Nothing coming back.'

The gentleman might have been old but he had his wits about him.

'Ah, I have worked out how that was done,' I said. '*Hamlet*.'

I had their attention now, even though some of them were regarding me as if I'd lost my wits, rather like Prince Hamlet himself.

'It was you,' I said, nodding in the direction of Rowland Haskell, 'who said at supper that you'd seen Master Shakespeare's play about the mad Dane. You said there was a lot of silly talk in it, talk about hawks and handsaws and crabs going backwards.'

'I remember,' said Rowland, 'but what has this to do with the death of our cousin?'

'Because the person who carried the body out of the house took it only a few yards before depositing it on the ground. That was far enough to achieve the right effect.'

'What effect?' said Martha.

'That Elias had been by himself when he died. That perhaps his death was the result of divine intervention – or demonic intervention I should say.'

I waited for someone to object but none of those seated round the table said a word.

'Then, once the body had been tumbled onto the snowy ground, that same person was careful to retrace their steps – by walking backwards *like a crab* and treading in the imprints already left in the snow. That way it would appear that Elias was alone when he died.'

'And the sword?' said Cuthbert. 'How do you explain that?'

'I believe it was thrown from the doorway after Elias had been left on the ground. I remember thinking it odd that the sword was some distance from the body. Most likely it would have been too difficult for the individual who killed the old man to carry body and sword together. I suspect that he came back inside, and threw the sword from here.'

I gestured over my shoulder towards the door.

'In God's name, why?' said Rowland. I noticed that the sneer had gone from his tones.

'Because of that story about the sword being cursed and flying through the air of its own accord, and so on. I know it sounds unlikely, the kind of thing you might read in a story or fable. But this killing was not planned, I believe. It occurred on the spur of the moment. This was the best the murderer could come up with to give a kind of superstitious gloss to the whole business.'

'Superstition!' said Cuthbert, but not so dismissively as he had on the previous evening.

'Well, you can stop looking in my direction,' said Dame Elizabeth. 'I have the body of a weak and feeble woman, you know, and could certainly not have carried my cousin on my shoulders and then thrown a massy sword out into the night. It's preposterous.'

I wasn't sure whether she was referring to the whole story I'd spun or only to the idea that she might have been the perpetrator. I admired the way in which she'd brought in our late, great Queen Elizabeth, who had described herself as a weak and feeble woman (but one having the stomach of a king) during the Spanish Armada of '88. For all her protestations, though, I reckoned that this Elizabeth might have done it, for Elias was all skin and bone and there is no limit to what a determined woman may accomplish.

Now it was Valentine's turn to pipe up.

'You may leave me out of the reckoning too, Master Revill. Like my dear cousin Elizabeth I am far too old for all this. I have enough trouble lugging my own bones around.'

I was inclined to agree with him. He was quicker-witted than he looked and might be more robust too, but I doubted that that would extend to his cutting down his cousin and carrying him out of doors. So that left just the two of them, the lawyer Cuthbert and the merchant Rowland. It was interesting that no one had yet disputed this version of events, but I had been relying on my account to flush the guilty party from cover. Yet both Cuthbert and Rowland continued to look baffled. The silence lengthened.

There was a sudden crash from beyond the table. Abigail the housekeeper had dropped the jug of ale which she had been holding all this time. The jug shattered. This was no great disaster but a trifling household accident. Yet Abigail flung her hands to her face and rushed from the room, wailing. Nobody spoke. I looked down at the floor where what was left of the drink from the jug was being speedily absorbed by the rushes that were laid there. And I recalled the fresh rushes in Elias's room, put down to dispel the scent of death – but laid even *before* Elias's body had been returned to his chamber, *before* I'd been imprisoned there. Very meticulous the house-keeping in this place.

Unless, of course, the rushes were laid down by

someone who perhaps wished to cover up fresh, bloody marks on the floor. And who was in a better position to put down a new covering of rushes and herbs, and to know where the stores of such things were kept, than the housekeeper of Valence?

Abigail.

Abigail, who had not merely renewed a floor covering but had changed her clothing as well. She was the sole member of the household to appear in a different outfit this morning. I'd taken her black smock for a mark of respect for her late master but suppose that the real reason for the change was that the old oatmeal-coloured smock was stained with blood, Elias's blood? And, if we were looking now for someone who had the sinews to carry the old man outside and then to toss the sword into the snow after him, then Abigail certainly had the strength.

All this flashed through my mind much more quickly than it takes to put it down here. Indeed, my mind was still racing as I took off in pursuit of the housekeeper, followed by Martha and the others. We reached the door of the kitchen. It was shut. Meg's sister was outside, looking confused and fearful. Abigail had ordered her out of the kitchen, and when the girl seemed to hesitate had seized her by the hair and dragged her to the door and pushed her to the far side of it. She'd then bolted it.

We listened at the door but could hear nothing. There was a window, Martha said, which gave onto the yard. We tore through the house and into the yard. The snow had turned slushy and the place where Elias's body had lain was already no more than a vaguely darker shape on the ground. Round the wing of the house, and towards the back quarters where the kitchen was. The casement window was open, Abigail had not thought to secure herself that way.

But then she hadn't needed to. All she wanted was to buy herself a few moments, enough to swallow the concoction that she must have had stored away for just such a terrible pass, to use either on herself or on another. By the time I'd climbed over the sill and entered the kitchen and unbarred the door to admit the others, it was too late.

Or almost too late. The housekeeper was dying but not quite dead. Perhaps she had misjudged the poison dose (which I think was aconite but am not absolutely sure) and so condemned herself to a few hours of life rather than a few minutes. She was carried, in great distress, to her private room which was scarcely larger than a cupboard. She lay on her trestle bed, shaking and sweating and bringing up terrible-smelling bile. The kitchen girl, Meg's sister, attempted to give her an emetic but Abigail gestured her away. It was too late. We took it in turns to keep watch on her, for if she was a murderess she was also a dying woman, and afterwards the story was pieced together from our rags of testimony.

Abigail's dying words were the most potent witness to her guilt that there could have been. Her dying words and her despairing choice of suicide, and one other thing which I'll come to in a moment. But we heard – those of us clustered about her poor, wracked body – we heard that it had been she who had killed Elias with the sword. She hadn't intended to kill him in that way, although she had been a long time killing him another way, by feeding him soporifics mixed with traces of belladonna. He had promised her part of his estate, as he had promised the cousins, and she was trying to hasten his demise. Otherwise he might never have gone, she said, he was a tough old bugger who'd've outlived them all.

But he had grown suspicious of the nightly soporifics and other remedies (which were perhaps the reason for his latest bout of illness) and, after many hints, had openly accused her when she was in his chamber the previous night following the visits of the Haskell cousins. An argument ensued, then a fight when Elias had struggled up from his bed, his bony arms flailing. As the dying Abigail told it, to defend herself, she had seized the sword from its place over the chimney-piece and struck her master a single blow on his forehead. He straightaway expired.

In a panic, she disposed of the body and the sword in the way that I had described (though without ever imagining that it was the housekeeper who'd done it). She wanted to remove the body and sword from the house, from her domain. Perhaps she thought that his death would be seen as a queer form of suicide, perhaps she was trusting to the superstition surrounding the sword to divert the blame from her. Perhaps her thinking was a strange mixture of sense and nonsense. She returned to clean up the bloodstains from the chamber as best she could, laying fresh rushes to obscure the marks. Of course she had had to change into a different over-dress as well because her clothes were stained. She had chosen a mourning black. Widow's weeds.

And indeed from the strangled comments Abigail let fall it was apparent that she had once entertained hopes of marrying Elias Haskell herself but that the old man's interest and favour had transferred to Martha on the death of the girl's father. So the housekeeper had seen her chances of becoming mistress of Valence fade. Resentment had turned to slow-burning anger and the determination to salvage something from the wreckage. She knew her master's habit of toying with his cousins in the matter of promises and bequests, but it did not seem to have occurred to her that he might be doing the same with her.

Whether there was any treasure or anything of real value in the house I did not discover. The next morning, after the death of the housekeeper, I rode away from Valence on Rounce. I was pleased to quit this strange house for good and intended to return to Cambridge before calling on the Maskells, who dwelt *north* of the city. I did, however, make Martha promise that she would visit me, should she ever come to London. She thanked me for my part in solving the mystery of her uncle's death. I asked her what she was going to do with the sword.

'I shall keep it,' she said. 'It was not the sword but Abigail killed him.'

'And you will take care of Grant?' I said.

'I am fond of the monkey. I did not care for him at first but my uncle liked him and I believe he liked my uncle.'

'Yes, I think so,' I said. 'The monkey did him good service at the end.' Martha looked baffled but just then Mr Fortescue arrived at her side with some questions and I took advantage of her distraction to clamber onto my hired mount and ride out of the gatehouse.

In the latter stages of the housekeeper's confession, Mr Fortescue the magistrate had appeared, in time to to hear her final self-incrimination before she expired. Her mode of death was terrible enough but perhaps preferable to the punishment visited on poisoners, whose crime is so heinous that they may be burnt as heretics are burnt. And it was not only her dying words, and her chosen suicide, which gave force to her testimony but also an item that was discovered in a pocket of her black mourning smock. It was the end of the sword's cross-piece, the image of a dog's head. It was generally assumed that she had picked it up when it had been broken off the sword during the tussle between her and Elias, and put it in her pocket. But I knew better. I'd seen this very object in the monkey's cage the previous morning. I recalled the way in which the monkey had clamoured for admission to our session in the hallway and the way in which Abigail had shooed him impatiently off the scene. While that had been going on, I reckoned, Mr Grant had slipped the piece of the sword into her garment, a kind of pick-pocketing in reverse. It was his way of linking the house-keeper to the death of his master.

Nor did the genius of Grant stop there. I couldn't help thinking that perhaps he had been trying to alert me to *both* of the tapestries which hung by the chimney-piece in old Elias's room. Not only the image of St Christopher but also the picture of the murderous Judith, holding her upright sword. Abigail had enacted both parts, killing a man with a single blow from the ancient weapon and then carrying his body out of doors, in the attempt to sow confusion about the cause of Elias's death. Yet Grant had witnessed all this and then done his best to tell me about it, as well as to provide evidence against the wrong-doer. Never let anyone say that monkeys are unfeeling creatures – or dull-witted ones.

EPILOGUE

London, 2005

The silver metallic-finish Porsche Cayenne eases its way down the fast lane of the M11 towards London. Insulated by his laminated privacy glass, and in an air-conditioned, pollen filtered cocoon, auctioneer John Lascelles never even notices the little village of Ickleton on his left. It is now wedged in between the motorway itself, and the access road to the M11 from the A11. He reaches into the refrigerated glove compartment, and pulls out a bottle of water, sipping one-handed from the nozzle. Red wine always leaves him with a dry mouth the following day. And even though the wine's alcoholic effects have safely dispersed from his blood, he still feels parched. It was a good dinner party last night, celebrating with a few select friends the coup he has pulled off. Today, on the other hand, is going to be all business. The Porsche's V6 engine ensures his smooth delivery to the outskirts of London.

Wallis Barker pushes down on the pedals of his heavy, black Raleigh bike, cursing the choking fumes of the congested traffic stalled on Chiswick High Road. A black-bearded tramp dashes into his path causing him to swerve. He pulls on the calliper brakes, and waves a fist at the madman. But the tramp has disappeared into the morass of stationary traffic. Barker momentarily considers catching the Tube at Chiswick Park, but that will entail him chaining his bike up, and risking it not being there when he returns. He decides to continue, and taps the ring-binder sticking out of the wicker basket on the front of his bike. Sure that his new information is still secure, he pedals off towards Kensington, weaving in and out of the traffic.

John Lascelles is always nervous before important auctions, and the one due to start at noon the following day is going to be one of the best. Lascelles can feel it in his water. He paces nervously around the sales room, looking at the items of arms and armour that will fall under the hammer. Each item is carefully displayed on purple velvet, and artfully lit from above. Even though he knows his staff have done a well-nigh perfect job, Lascelles feels fidgety. He stops here and there, once to move a European swept-hilt rapier a millimetre to the left, a second time to turn a sixteenth century mitten gauntlet, that resembles a dead armadillo, so that the light striking it does not dazzle the eager viewer. He does not have to make either adjustment, and is only putting off the moment when he is going to have the joy of feasting his eyes once again on the spectacular centrepiece of tomorrow's auction.

The sword.

Wallis Barker is late. An accident at Hammersmith Broadway involving two cars and a dispute over road space has caused that part of London to grind to a halt. After an infuriating wait of fifteen minutes, he has been compelled to dismount, and push his bike along the pavement, closing his ears to the protests of the pedestrians crowded around him. He has finally got to Kensington twelve minutes after his appointed meeting time with John Lascelles, and still has to chain up his bike to the railings in front of the Victorian building. Hot and not a little bothered, he hurries up the steps of Lascelles Historica Specialist Auction House pulling at the bicycle clips on his ankles as he goes.

Seated at his desk, John Lascelles is tapping his ivory gavel on the immaculate and uncluttered surface. He does not notice how small, round indentations are appearing in the highly polished mahogany. Opposite him, late but apparently unrepentant, slouches the historical researcher who has compiled the story of the sword from fragmentary documents, and family references. Like many of his ilk, Wallis Barker affects the dress of a Victorian eccentric. His tweed jacket is buttoned only at the top, and where it flares open below, his stomach is resplendent in a mustard-coloured velvet waistcoat. A watch chain dangles portentously between the waistcoat pockets. He flicks his deliberately quiffed hair, and curls one side of his long moustache. He drawls as he speaks.

'You want me to tell you the results of my most recent research?'

Lascelles nods impatiently. He cannot stand the man's affectations, and is amused to see that Barker has forgotten to remove a bicycle clip from his left ankle. Incongruously, he sees it as some sort of fetishistic adornment. Chasing this fresh image from his mind, he reminds himself that Barker is good at his job, rooting out provenance for important items. Like the ancient sword the auctioneer is to sell tomorrow.

Barker hooks his thumbs in each waistcoat pocket, and leans back in his chair. For the first time he sees he has not removed one of his bicycle clips, and quickly crosses his right ankle over the offending left one. He delineates again the known details of the sword's ownership by the Devon branch of the de la Pomeroy family. All traced back from the small crest added in medieval times to the bottom of the blade. Barker is particularly pleased how, from fleeting references, and oblique asides in the family's archives, he has traced the sword's passage down through the years.

'Of course, what is most interesting is the hint that the sword is associated with dark deeds, or bad luck. I seem to recall that once . . .'

Lascelles shudders, and raises his elegant hand to stop the historian's flow of words. 'Wallis, please. Nothing about bad luck.'

Barker tips his head to one side in an interrogatory fashion, the wattle under his chin wobbling. Lascelles is put in mind of a pompous bantam cockerel strutting in the farmyard. Suppressing a smile, he is at pains to explain to Barker that any attachment of ill luck to an auction item can drastically affect its potential value.

The historian nods sagely, as if he knew that all along. 'Yes, yes, naturally.'

He returns to safer ground with what he has found out about the sword's recent history. 'When it came to you, I believe you were surprised by its good preservation.'

Lascelles nods, and unconsciously returns to tapping his gavel on his no-longer pristine desktop. 'Yes. Most medieval swords are dug up from the ground, and are fragmentary at best. You've seen this one. It's in excellent condition, considering its age.'

'Indeed. But then it does come from the Barnwell collection.'

'That's right. And we might have ignored it in the circumstances, guessing it to be some sort of Victorian fakery. Sir Gregory Barnwell was one of those seemingly interminable Victorian eccentrics who collected anything and everything, regardless of quality or value. That's why his collection is mostly worthless.' Lascelles fails to see Barker bristling at his assessment of the

Victorian philanthropist, so he presses on. 'But it was soon apparent that the sword is something else entirely. And you say you have some new information?'

Barker licks his lips, and frames the enquiry he has been yearning to put since arriving in Lascelles's office. 'Yes. But first, may I see it again?'

The sword seems to be gleaming even brighter in the light of the spot that illuminates where it lies on its bed of velvet. John Lascelles approaches it reverently, his hands gloved in white cotton. Beside him dances the excited figure of the historian Wallis Barker. For a moment it seems like Barker is tempted to touch the sword with his bare hands.

'Don't!' admonishes Lascelles. And Barker jumps away at the abruptness of his companion's words. He is peeved at Lascelles's possessiveness, and for a moment he is tempted to relate a family tale of how Sir Gregory came to own the sword. But he decides to keep his mouth shut.

By rights, the sword should belong to Trinity College, which owned Valence House in Ickleton. The sword was found hidden in a chimney there, hence its good preservation. But then some debauched nineteenth-century poet rejoicing in the name of Alfred Sturge Bliss, filched it from Trinity College before it was properly recorded, and sold it to Barnwell for a song. The fact that the poet was later found with his skull crushed in the strangest of circumstances was glossed over due to Bliss's irregular lifestyle and imbibing of drugs. So the sword was subsequently untraceable back to its proper owner. A stroke of luck for Barnwell that a modern police service might have found more suspicious than did their Victorian forebears. At least the sword's long residence in the Barnwell collection did much to re-establish its bona-fides.

And that was where Wallis Barker came into the story, tracking it back to the de la Pomeroys. But now, he has linked the sword to an old Conquest tale that led him to identifying the name of the swordsmith. Now, greedily drinking in the vision of the sword lying on its velvet cushion, he tells Lascelles his news.

'The story goes that two brothers, separated at birth or some time later – the details are not accurate of course – ended up on opposite sides at the Battle of Hastings. Their father was the swordsmith, and his name was Bran. One of the brothers is called Deda and the other Swine, and they meet in the heat of the battle. But the curious thing is that one of them – Deda – has their father's sword, and he uses it to kill his own brother before he realizes who his adversary is. Then he falls on his own sword. Or something like that. The last bit may all be romantic embellishment, after all. But it's satisfying, is it not, to imagine the father's sword taking the lives of both brothers.'

He looks at Lascelles, who seems unimpressed by the implications of the story. In fact, he seems to be strangely protective of the sword. He reminds Lascelles of the swordmaker's name, sure that the thought of owning a sword that had been forged a thousand years ago by the hands of a man called Bran will appeal to a certain someone with money.

'If I hadn't have uncovered the probable name of the maker . . .'

Lascelles ignores the man's bleatings, and cannot stop himself from laying his hand on the hilt. Suddenly, he feels electrified. He sees himself grasping the sword, and hefting it like a medieval knight. He swings it in a glittering arc, and separates Wallis Barker's chattering head from his overweight body. The blood spurts from the historian's severed neck in a great arc, splattering the walls of the sale room. Slowly the headless body crumples to the blood-stained carpet.

'. . . it would sell for far less than if . . .' Barker drops his voice to church-like tones. '. . . a certain person was interested.'

Letting go of the sword, Lascelles recovers his senses. He smiles at the smug Wallis Barker, whose head unfortunately is still attached to his body. He looks in wonder at the gleaming blade, afraid to touch it again.

'You're quite right, Wallis. Wealthy bidders are what we will be looking for. And soon, the sword will belong to a new owner. Let's hope the bad luck you talk about does not follow it.'

The night security man is about to close the imposing front doors of the auction house, when a portly, moustachioed figure thrusts his velvet-clad stomach into the gap. He is red-faced, and flustered.

'Ah, thank goodness I caught you in time. I left my files here earlier in the day, when I was speaking to Mr Lascelles. I would leave it till tomorrow, but I need them for the research I'm doing in the BM.'

The guard is not sure he should be letting the man in, but he is familiar with the historian, even though he doesn't know Wallis Barker by name. The man is always coming and going, and he can well believe the oddly-dressed fellow is absent-minded by nature. It doesn't occur to him to question why Barker should be professing to be on his way to the British Museum at ten o'clock at night. The ways of academics are beyond him. He lets Barker in, and idly watches him hurry up the stairs to John Lascelles's office before returning to his perusal of the *Sun*.

At the top of the stairs, Barker glances back to make sure the security man is not looking. Then he turns away from Lascelles's office, and down the back stairs the auctioneer used to take him to the gallery that morning. He has left his file behind, not accidentally but deliberately, in order to have an excuse to return to the auction house. It is not in Lascelles's office, but in the gallery tucked behind the stack of catalogues that describe the contents of tomorrow's sale. Barker has no intention of the sword – his sword – becoming the property of anyone else. He has long realized he cannot hope to bid for it and succeed. So he has decided to steal it. Wallis Barker's great-great-uncle was Alfred Sturge Bliss, disregarded and underrated Victorian poet. And one-time possessor of the sword, until he was murdered over it by Sir Gregory Barnwell. Now Barker proposes to rectify the situation.

He sneaks across the polished wood floor, his only illumination the red emergency lights. They cast an ominously sanguineous glow over the exhibits. He slips as he makes his way across to the de la Pomeroy sword, and in reaching out to save himself, knocks the European swept-hilt rapier off its bed of velvet. Cursing under his breath, he bends down to retrieve it.

John Lascelles is perusing the auction catalogue for the thousandth time. He is itching with excitement, and cannot imagine sleeping tonight. He cannot even bring himself to leave the office, and though it is late, he goes over the words he will utter tomorrow.

'Ladies and gentlemen, we now come to the apex of the auction – the star of the Barnwell collection. An unusually well-preserved medieval sword with a blade bearing two inscriptions, and the crest of the de la Pomeroy family. The blade is approximately thirty inches in length, and shows signs of having been reworked on the tip at a very early date. The cross is fashioned in the image of baying hounds, and has also been repaired a very long time ago. The hilt still has remnants of the original leather and silver thread binding. Its provenance can be established as far back as the thirteenth century, but there are unsubstantiated rumours that it may have been forged around the time of the Norman Conquest. What am I bid for this extraordinary and unique item. Shall I start the bidding at £100,000?'

As his lips drool over the shapely figure, he hears a clatter somewhere in the gallery below. He glances at his watch, noting that it is past ten o'clock already. There should be no one in the building other than Rex, the night security man, who is probably dozing over his copy of the *Sun*, as he usually does. Puzzled, Lascelles rises from his desk, and makes for the old servants' stairs of the Victorian mansion that is his auction house. They take him directly down to the gallery of exhibits.

He stops abruptly in the open doorway, and sees a burly figure standing close to the sword. He appears to have a weapon in his hand. Appalled that something may happen to his prized exhibit, John Lascelles rushes across the gallery floor, grabbing the sixteenth-century mitten gauntlet as he passes. He slips it on his hand, and clubs the burglar over the head with the armoured appendage. An inexplicable rage has taken him over, and he hits the man again and again as he collapses.

Wallis Barker slumps lifeless to the floor, his brains bashed in just like his great-great-uncle's. Blood spurts from the open head wound, splattering over the inscription on the ancient blade. On its bed of purple velvet, and bathed in red light, Bran's sword seems to sing.